tHe LaSt

sEweR BaLL

Also by Steven Schindler

SEWER BALLS

FROM THE BLOCK

FROM HERE TO REALITY

ON THE BLUFFS

tHe LaSt
sEweR BaLL

a novel

by Steven Schindler

The Elevated Press

Los Angeles

This is a work of fiction. Names, characters, places and incidents are the products of the author's imagination or are used fictitiously. Any similarity to events, locales or persons, living or dead, is entirely coincidental.

The Elevated Press

PO Box 65218

Los Angeles CA 90065

www.TheElevatedPress.com

ISBN-13: 978-0-966240809-4

ISBN-10: 0-9662408-9-8

Library of Congress Control Number: 2013930728

The Elevated Press Original Trade Paperback

First Edition June, 2013

Cover Photography: Steven Schindler

Cover Design: Craig Wolf

www.craigwolf.com

Printed in the USA on recycled paper

Acknowledgments

Thanks to Brian McKernan, Jim Schneider, Patty Williams, James Hannon, Jim Tuohy, and Barb Slater for their thoughtful insights and critiques.

Designer and photographer, Craig Wolf

Editor, Jill Bailin

and especially...

To my wife,

Sue

Twenty-five years

Thousands of miles

and still

Going strong

About the Author

Born and raised in the Bronx, Steven Schindler is an award-winning novelist and television writer/producer. After graduating from Hunter College with a degree in Film and Theatre, Schindler soon found himself acting in some of New York's off-off Broadway productions. Bartering a deal at a prominent acting school to videotape classes in exchange for acting lessons, he discovered he enjoyed life more from behind the camera than in front of it. Enrolling in a video documentary class was the first step in a career that has spanned more than twenty years in television as a writer, producer and director in news, sports, reality, documentary, entertainment and magazine programming. Awards include four Chicago Emmy Awards and Best Fiction at the DIY/Indie Book Awards for *From the Block*.

His first two novels, *Sewer Balls* and *From the Block*, were artfully gritty portrayals of the neighborhood characters who hung out on the stoops, playgrounds, rooftops and barstools during the crazy days of the Bronx in the sixties and seventies

From Here To Reality (Simon & Schuster/Pocket Books) received praise from the *NY Post*, Jay Leno, and Roger L. Simon (*The Big Fix, Down and Out in Beverly Hills*)

On the Bluffs is a thrilling love story wrapped in a dysfunctional family mystery that begins in Washington, D.C. and winds up in a rundown mansion on the bluffs of Cape Cod.

The Last Sewer Ball is Schindler's fifth novel.

He is married and currently lives in Los Angeles.

Praise for Steven Schindler's novels

"Sewer Balls" is about growing up in the Bronx, NY, in the sixties, and Schindler writes with a style that reflects the best of Betty Smith's "A Tree Grows in Brooklyn" and Philip Roth's "Portnoy's Complaint." Every kid who grew up in the East knows what sewer balls are: those prized rubber balls that were always going down the corner sewers and retrieved by daring poor kids. Schindler brings the '60s alive with images as clear as if they were photographed; his sentences are deceptively simple but full of euphony. It won't be surprising if someone in the next millennium writes that this was **probably the best novel produced by the small presses in 1999.**---*The Small Press Review*

"From the Block" Winner- Best Fiction 2003 DIY/Indie Book Awards

"From Here to Reality" Required reading! - *New York Post*

"A very funny Hollywood story told with wit and passion by someone who's obviously been there." -Jay Leno

"What's real? What's fake? Who knows anymore? But I do know "From Here to Reality" made me laugh. Great book!" -Roger L. Simon (Author-The Big Fix)

"On the Bluffs"- "Schindler could be the male version of bestselling author Nora Roberts, blending the right amount of romance and suspense... a captivating writing style." - *Glendale News Press*

TO THE READER

I call *The Last Sewer Ball* a "sort of sequel" because, although it picks up where *Sewer Balls* left off, this story can stand on its own.

While we are the result of what came before, we are not bound by our past if we choose not to be. I've often wondered how it's possible that certain people in our lives, people who for a time were closer to us and, perhaps, more influential than our own family, are nowhere to be found. We may not even remember their names- yet there was a time when we were inseparable. Whether we were toddlers or teenagers doesn't matter. You are still you. And they are still who they are, whether they're dead or alive. We affected and influenced each other in lasting ways that, perhaps, we aren't even aware of. But deep down, there's a place that indeed was touched by someone who no longer exists, because they are gone forever.

Or are they?

Steven Schindler

Los Angeles

Spring 2013

tHe LaSt

sEweR BaLL

Chapter One

—Now—

I sat in the church parking lot in an old beater, an '89 Toyota borrowed from my niece, looking at my name tag. In large letters it read *VINNY SCHMIDT,* and underneath in smaller letters, *Sewer Balls.* I folded it in half, creating a crease, tore off the bottom, leaving only my name, and stuck it onto the outside pocket of my just purchased thirty-nine dollar blazer. I wasn't in the mood for shameless self-promotion. I just wanted to meet some old friends. And maybe find a lost one.

It would be the first Presentation Grammar School reunion I attended in my old Bronx neighborhood. Back in Los Angeles, where I lived for a couple of decades until recently, people were amazed on two counts: first, that we called it "grammar school," which to them sounded Victorian, and second, that I actually still knew anyone from so long ago, never mind enough for a full-blown reunion. Needless to say, people were even more shocked when I told them that I still kept in touch with some guys who were with me on the very first rainy September morning that we crammed into a classroom with sixty or so other first graders, and sat stunned at the sight of Sister Joan clad in black from head to toe. Her rosy red chipmunk cheeks were the only indication of her youth and humanity that enabled her to deal with the five dozen male and female offspring of the lower-middle class to downright poor Irish, Italian, Polish, German, and mixed breed Catholics of that northwest Bronx parish officially called Presentation of the Blessed Virgin Mary, but known to everyone simply as Presentation.

In my experience, Catholics in New York City tend to identify more with their parish than they do with any other geographic classification. No matter where you find yourself living, time after time, you find yourself sitting in the same pews, ritually celebrating or mourning the same life events that continue to bring you and your

1

fellow parishioners together since the days when you laid down in the pew sucking your thumb with your head in your mother's lap as you napped. Baptisms, weddings, graduations, and more often than not, funerals still bring together the legions of kids who have since scattered across the suburbs of New York, as well as across the globe.

It is there in that humble Presentation Church where you can hear the rumble of the number one elevated line just a block away every three to five minutes, that we try to, but can't hold back tears of joy and sadness at life's milestones: birth, sacraments, graduations, marriages, and deaths.

An added wrinkle to this reunion was the fact that I'm attending after the modest success of a novel called *Sewer Balls* that I wrote about the parish and the neighborhood. Having the book published while I was living in Los Angeles meant that I wasn't immediately exposed to any reactions the book may have elicited from the denizens of those streets that stretch just above the Harlem River, which separates Manhattan from the Bronx at West 225th Street, just below Yonkers, and in the valley between the hills of Riverdale to the west and the hills approaching Gun Hill Road to the east. Three thousand miles had protected me from any fallout that may have occurred from using the people, places, and events of our collective youth in a book I didn't think would ever get read by anyone except me and a small circle of friends and relatives.

It was only through a bizarre bit of serendipity that *Sewer Balls* became a modest success at all. During a recent writer's strike, late night TV talk show host Sean McGillicuddy, desperate for material, saw the book on a crew member's bench and began doing "dramatic" readings from it purely for the comedic effect of having grown-ups talking like kids from the 1960s. Raging teenage hormones, Catholic school shenanigans, and the street games of Presentation Parish were broadcast across America for just a few minutes on each of two nights. But as the saying goes, any publicity, even ridicule, is good publicity, so the book actually began to sell a little. Even though it had already been out for several years, the sudden spike in sales made enough money for me to buy a Mercedes. (Okay, so it was about enough for a ten-year-old "C" class.)

I'm sure some people at the reunion will think that because I sold a few thousand books, and used to work in television, that I'm doing really well. In fact, it wasn't all that long ago that I was married and gainfully employed as a TV news production executive for a major television network. But I'll be attending this reunion unemployed, divorced and in a borrowed car, visiting from Bronxville where I am camped out at my sister's, sleeping on the pull-out sofa in her basement.

In the weeks since I relocated back to New York I hadn't ventured to the old neighborhood. Especially not to the immediate vicinity of Presentation Church or School. It's Irish poetic justice that the church is just one block away from West 238th Street, where for over a hundred years the half dozen or so bars there, depending on whether or not one has the alcoholism gene, have provided a respite for relaxation-seeking individuals, or sucked the life out of you slowly until you wind up slumped over the bar needing just one more shot, with a liver on the side.

There was a time, in my teenage years, when being able to drink in one of those dark watering holes was a rite probably akin to a Southern California kid getting his first set of wheels. The drinking age in New York at that time was eighteen, so getting served at sixteen (or even fifteen for kids with early surges of testosterone) was commonplace. Having a baby face and hovering around 115 pounds until the age of twenty was probably the only factor that delayed my foray into the weekend binging, brawling, and power-puking that most of my friends got caught up in during the couple of years I was being kicked out for looking too young. Of course, after I turned eighteen, that was a whole 'nother story. I was able to drink heavily with my buddies in order to find girls or lose girls, play sports or watch them, celebrate or mourn, for excitement or out of boredom. It seemed no matter what the situation or occasion, it called for drinking heavily – a tradition that for some of my friends started around fourteen or fifteen and continues right up to this very moment, a block from the

3

Presentation Church and School, in one of those very bars on West 238th Street.

Having moved out of the neighborhood more than twenty years ago, my trips back two or three times a year gave me an outsider's perspective on the decline of the block and those who still sat on the same bar stools as our grandfather, fathers, uncles and big brothers did before us. It also gave me the false perception that "they" were the ones wasting their lives away, and certainly not me! After all, I worked in TV, was happily married and living in sunny Los Angeles. But once my own world started to fall apart, when I was neglecting my wife and young son, denying I had a drinking problem, and finally having to face the pressures of a job designed for young, talented people with ambition, not cynical middle-aged men who know it all, what made me different from the guys hanging onto the stools at the Punch Bowl or J.C. Mac's or the Goal Post? Maybe like the great baseball sage Earl Weaver once said with the title of his memoirs, "It's what you learn after you know it all that counts."

I'd avoided going to 238th Street since I got laid off and divorced, and took up residence on the creaky pull-out sofa in my sister's unfinished basement just ten minutes away in Bronxville. Not only because I didn't want to be tempted to pick up where I left off twenty years ago as an undisciplined, pot smoking, beer guzzling college student who somehow managed to talk his way into pretty girls' panties and a degree magna cum laude. I knew that seeing those balding, graying guys would be a mirror into myself, reflecting an image I wouldn't much care for.

But here I was, pulling into a parking spot in the same schoolyard where I spent every single school day from grades one through eight. The gigantic oak tree was gone – the majestic, sprawling tree that in the early grades was home base for tag or ringolevio, and in later grades provided cover from the nuns for a quick feel of Tina Robustelli's overdeveloped eighth-grade boobs, or for kids smoking Camels and sniffing airplane glue. Amazingly, you could still see and feel where the roots pushed up the blacktop even though the tree was cut down more than twenty years ago. I parked at the end of the lot

4

right on top of where the tree had stood for probably one or two hundred years, and I could hear the sound of loud rock and roll reverberating in the auditorium where the reunion was taking place. Music always bounced and echoed off the marble floor, cinderblock walls and concrete ceiling, even when it was Mrs. Schmelzer, the skinny old lady who taught music to generations of kids, stomping wildly on the pedals of her pump organ during religious and patriotic assemblies.

As cars filled the parking lot, groups of people met in the darkness, generating waves of laughter and joy as they headed for the entrance to the reunion. You could tell it was already picking up steam by the loud music and louder voices that echoed through the entryway directly under the church, which sat dark and silent above the activities as its offspring gathered below.

I turned off the engine and sat in the car, beginning to mentally prepare for the questions I'd be getting: *"Where's your wife?" "How's your kid?" "How's your job?" "Where are you living?" "Are you writing another book?"* I knew I couldn't just answer: *divorced, I don't know, unemployed, my sister's basement,* and *no.* I'd do what everyone else does at reunions: lie. Then I started asking *myself* questions, one in particular: *What am I doing here?* As I stepped out of the car and stumbled slightly on the broken pavement over the roots of a two-hundred-year-old tree that no longer existed, I hoped I'd find the answer to the mystery that's bugged me for a few decades.

Two men were smoking, about twenty feet from the stairs that led down to the auditorium where the reunion was. As the wind blew in my direction, I realized the guys were smoking weed. I took a deep breath and wondered if I'd ever smoke pot again. It had been over thirty years since I realized that taking a drug that made me even lazier than I was already inclined to be wasn't for me.

Not only had I avoided coming to the old neighborhood, I was also avoiding old friends from the neighborhood. Most had realized it was better for their health to move away from the temptation of the street of broken dreams, and were raising families in the suburbs. I hadn't called anyone to say that I was attending the reunion, because I didn't know if I'd be able to walk down the steps into the auditorium once I arrived and took in the waves of memories that would begin to course through my central nervous system… which is just what started happening as I stood there.

I looked up and saw the large stained glass windows, barely illuminated in the locked church above. The one right above me was the one depicting a scene with St. John Vianney. As kids, we assumed that all the saints and holy people portrayed in the huge stained glass windows were of equal stature. There were of course Jesus, Mary and Joseph, each with their own lead and glass tableaus, mostly of reds and blues. Then there was St. Michael slaying some serpents, and a pious St. Theresa in what looked to be a habit similar to the Sisters of Charity who taught at the school and herded us into the pews for special occasions. But St. John Vianney? A little research revealed that he was born during the French revolution, was drafted into the army as a teen, and soon became a deserter. After the government granted amnesty, he signed up to be a priest. He was a miserable student and barely made it through the seminary. The two main evils he railed against from the pulpit once he was ordained were cursing, which oddly enough he was apt to use during his tirades against those same curse words, and dancing. Then after many years of being a popular priest and confessionist he deserted the priesthood, only to be cajoled and pretty much forced back into the cloth. So whoever designed Presentation Church back in 1950 or so must have been divinely inspired to know that in these pews would be kids who were inclined towards bad grades, cowardice, dereliction of duty, cursing and partying. We had our own patron saint.

The two guys who were smoking pot by the stairs walked by me and headed towards the reunion entrance. Molecules of weed hung in the air as they whisked by, giggling and ignoring me. I think I recognized them from day camp, when I was a counselor and they were probably "midgets." Being close to three hundred pounds each, it was hardly an apt category for them now. I had a knack for remembering faces and details, but not names. They screamed "holy shit" after walking through the double doors to the party, and I glanced up at St.

John Vianney, who appeared to be scowling at me. What the hell? I'd paid my seventy-five bucks. I might as well go in.

The double doors were the same original heavy oak doors we struggled to open as kids. I pushed one open and immediately knew the inspiration of the "holy shit." Right in front of me was a life-sized cardboard cutout of Monsignor McNamara, the extremely unpopular pastor of the parish throughout the most of the sixties, seventies, and into the eighties. His cold, aloof and sometimes cruel demeanor didn't endear him to anyone in the parish or school, whether student, parent, or nun. The sight of this surreal full-color representation immediately sent a chill down my spine, and gave me pause to consider whether or not I should continue into the party that was going full-throttle just behind another set of double doors. Was this a joke? Or perhaps a message from the current pastor, Father Landers, a beloved and warm man of the cloth, reminding us all that we can learn from those who went before us, whether the examples they set were good or bad.

I pushed through the doors and I was shocked by the enormity of the crowd. Everyone in the scattered groups of circles had drinks in hand. "Louie Louie" was blasting through the DJ's immense speakers set up on the stage. There was colored crepe paper draped over the fluorescent ceiling fixtures, giving an eerie red and blue glow to everyone's face – not unlike the stained glass in the church. I'd told myself I wasn't going to drink this night, having borrowed my niece's car and all. Apparently I couldn't help myself, though. I immediately headed over to the table loaded with tubs of ice and canned beer and grabbed a cold one. I scanned the throngs of partygoers who all seemed to be in groups of five or six, facing inward, which made it hard to see any faces at all. I downed my beer in a few gulps, dropped it into the garbage can and plunged into the crowd.

It took about three steps to spot three guys from my old gang, Jimmy Joe, BB and Flynn, in a tight circle of guys. Before I could make a witty remark to get their attention, Flynn's arm shot up to point at me, knocking a can of beer out of BB's hand and sending most of the spillage right into my face. Everybody laughed hysterically. Except for me.

7

"Yo, it's Mr. Hollywood!" Flynn yelled. I wiped the beer from my face with my blazer sleeve and was sucked into the group for a flurry of hugs, back slappings, and a stubbly kiss on the cheek or two.

Like it or not, I was back. Flynn didn't know it, but it was something he said to me off the cuff over a decade ago that got me to finally sit down and attempt to put pen to paper and tell the stories about growing up in the neighborhood, resulting in *Sewer Balls*. I'd been visiting from L.A., hanging in the Goal Post, talking the usual small talk, and Flynn said to the small group in his inimitable stuttering speech (triggered when his brain cells reach a certain alcohol saturation point), "Every important m-m-m-memory that I have in my life happened b-b-b-before the age of f-f-fifteen."

The beer-fueled conversations quickly shot to other topics, like the Yankees relief pitchers, how drunk BB was the night before, which girls "gave" and which girls slapped, but Flynn's observation was still bouncing around in my brain. I had read Ray Bradbury's *Zen in the Art of Writing* on the flight from L.A., and his main thesis is that there's a reason you remember things. We forget what we did last year or last month or what we had for breakfast this morning, but certain memories from decades ago sit there, as vivid as the moment they happened. Those are the moments you must explore, not just for writing but for your own life journey. And Flynn's words rang truer even than Ray Bradbury's.

When I wrote *Sewer Balls* I did my best to change the names of the characters who appeared in the threads of happenings that ranged from slapstick comedy to brutal, violent reality.

Of course, it holds true in most of the creative arts that the devil is in the details. And in the book I relied more on the indelible, life-changing people and life-altering events than I did on plot. There was, however, a motivating force behind the entire endeavor, which ultimately I thought fell terribly short. It was a serious attempt on my part to reconcile what exactly happened to a very dear friend of mine. A friend I hadn't seen or heard from since those glory days, but who, like a guiding spirit, pushed my fingers across the computer's keyboard for nearly two years as I attempted to relive the joy and sorrow of our close friendship, and solve the mystery of his disappearance from my life. That was Whitey.

"Did the juice in your BlackBerry dry up? Why didn't you call me, asshole?" BB said, putting me in a headlock and giving me noogies.

"I've been busy," I said, as I tried not to spill his beer while untangling my head from his grasp. "I've got a heavy social calendar."

Small talk with the rest of the gang followed: excruciating details about working with computers at the phone company, intricate travel plans for a daughter's journey to the state figure skating finals, a surprise "happy ending" after a professional massage on a cruise in the Caribbean.

As I managed to scan some of the nearby faces, my brain would crackle with flashbacks: the boy from day camp who dared you to make him cry … a girl I made out with during kiss-o-leario in a vacant tree- and brush-filled lot where an apartment building now stands … the guy who my brother beat the shit out of because he had kicked the shit out of me.

"Hanky Panky" was shaking the translucent chicken-wire-lined casement windows. It took about fifteen minutes to bring our little group up to date on current events, like how the new Bruce album sucked, and the Yankees having a good shot again this year, and *I should hope so, with yearly player salaries approaching the GDP of some third world countries.*

These guys, who I've loosely kept in touch with in the two decades since I moved out of the neighborhood, haven't mentioned *Sewer Balls* since the week it was released. But as I stood there for about an hour, people I didn't even recognize started approaching me. "Aren't you the *Sewer Balls* guy?" "Your book was pretty good, but I should write a book!" "I made my kids read it so they'd know how fucked up we grew up."

Others came up to me, claiming to know all the secrets of *Sewer Balls*: who was really who, what was really what. I would smile and use my pat answer. *The names have been changed to protect the guilty.* I enjoyed it when people I barely knew back in grammar school gave me a wink and a nod and told me they didn't have a problem with that fact that I included them in the book. If they pushed me, I of course told them that all the characters were composites, pieced together from all my best friends and worst enemies. "Some of it's true, some of it's made up, and I'll never reveal the ratio of one to the other," I would say, still smiling.

I was only drinking beer, because I wanted to feel bloated and uncomfortable before I got too drunk, and my plan was working. I avoided the people who gave me the willies back in the day, as if the long-forgotten angst of our relationships would instantly take over if any eye contact was made on the way to the bathroom or just wandering around the party.

After a trip to the men's room, I bumped into an attractive blonde, a little younger than me, but looking unlike any of her contemporaries. She still had what the moms back in high school would say about drop-dead knock-out girls with perky tits and ass: she had a "cute figure." Oh, there were some laugh lines at the eyes and marionette lines from nose to mouth, but nothing sagged or dragged on this petite beauty.

"You're Vinny, right?" she asked, smiling.

Trying not to reveal my drunken horniness, I replied coolly, "I'm not sure. Which Vinny do you mean?"

"*Sewer Balls* Vinny?" she asked, the smile gone and now serious.

"Yes, that's me."

She moved her head slightly in subtle jerks towards the oak double door exit and began to walk. I followed her through the doors up the stairs, and over to the darkened stairs outside the church where the pot smokers had been hiding earlier.

"I need to ask you something about…" She paused and tightened her red lipstick-glossed lips. My eyes had adjusted to the darkness and on her lips there was a glint of reflection from the dimly lit lamppost across the street. The darkness made the lines on her face disappear and it was easy for me, in my beer-soaked state, to imagine I was back in grammar school and about to make out with a cute girl outside the dance. Her boobs were tantalizingly at full attention with more than ample Victoria's Secret technology-enhanced cleavage. "Do you remember me?"

I felt woozy and sat down on the step. She joined me.

"Do I know you?" I asked.

"I was one of Josephine's girls."

A wall of memories came crashing down. Josephine was the counselor at Presentation Day Camp who I mightily lusted after for a summer. Physically, she was a woman among children and the first girl I ever got to first base with. And she had a left hook that Joe Frazier would envy.

"I do remember you. You were a cute tiny little thing. You were one of the sailor hat brigade, right?"

"You remember the sailor hat craze? Oh, my goodness. Did you ever, you know, get serious with Josephine?"

"Do I look like the kiss and tell type?" I joked. She didn't appear to take it as a joke.

"I agree. None of my B. I. business. You might know my ex-husband, Ralph Pugliese."

"Puggy?"

"Yes, Puggy," she said without a hint of a smile.

Puggy was one of those guys every kid ten years older and ten years younger than me knew about. If you were minding your own business on a stoop or a pizza parlor or in the park, and turned around and Puggy was standing there, chances were you soon felt some kind of sharp pain. Maybe it was a boot in the ass, or your underwear pulled up to your Adam's apple or simply a closed fist against your eye socket, but you felt something you'd never forget.

"Puggy's your ex?"

"Yes, and I lived to tell about it."

"Where is Puggy these days?"

"He works for sanitation, still, but last I heard he was living under a bridge by the river."

"How long did the marriage last?"

"Oh, a cup of coffee. Maybe two."

11

"I'm sorry, that's none of my B.I. business either..."

"Don't apologize. Live and learn. Listen, what I really want to know is if you're still in touch with Whitey. He was very close to my family before he went into the service. I heard he's dying of cancer."

A jolt of sobriety straightened my back and raised a few hairs on my neck. The truth of the matter is I had no idea what happened to Whitey. It seems strange that a close friend could drop off the face of the earth so completely, but sometime during the high school years, that's exactly what happened. And frankly, after the few rumors I heard about him over the years, I was surprised to hear he was still alive. And here was this beautiful creature I just happened to bump into with the exact same thing on her mind. Weird.

"He's a vet? Dying of cancer? Really? Where did you hear that?"

"My mother knows someone who knows someone in the town upstate where his mom used to live."

"You were close to him?"

"Yes, he was sort of seeing my sister Meg. I think he enlisted in the army after his mother died. We never heard from him again."

"I've only heard...rumors about him over the years."

"I've heard them all. Let me just say, I know he's a murderer and everything, but he always treated me and my family like gold."

I just nodded my head, and thought to myself, *A murderer?* And I was worried about my cousin getting pissed off that I made her father out to be a cheapskate in the book?

"I never heard that one," I said flatly, not wanting to reveal my shock.

She scooched closer to me on the rough concrete step. I could smell the sweet fragrance of her hair. She took a stick of Juicy Fruit out of her purse and popped it into her mouth. Then she pulled out a pack of Marlboros. She flicked her lighter and for an instant the lines on her face became prominent again. But once the red glow of the cigarette took hold, and the first whiff of cigarette smoke mixed with Juicy Fruit came my way, mixed with the aroma of her recently shampooed hair,

12

my head became dizzy with sensual excitement. She sucked hard on the cigarette and the red glow was so bright, I could see tears welling.

"I quit smoking years ago. I only smoke when I'm tense. I heard some stories. Viet Nam, getting kicked out of the army, murder. I could give a shit," she said, fraught with shaky emotion. "I don't care. Whitey was a sweetheart. A gentleman. I'd really like to see him. One more time..." Her voice trailed off as she placed her head on my shoulder.

I put my arm around her and gently pulled her closer to me, overwhelmed with the sensual intimacy I was now sharing with this nameless stranger. I took a deep breath through my nose just a half inch from her hair, and remembered similar moments my wife and I once shared.

"You probably think I'm a nut, acting like this," she said, looking up at me. "Even though I know a lot of your book is made up, I could see how you loved Whitey."

Now I felt like tearing up. It was true. I did love Whitey, yet when he went away I didn't do anything to reconnect with him. I let him down.

"I don't think you're a nut. Actually, I am trying to find him. Maybe you can help.
You know somebody who knows somebody upstate. That's a start."

"I could make some calls and get on it," she said, straightening up as she snuffed out her cigarette on the church step. She wiped her eyes. "I'll do it. I needed a little motivation, that's all," she said, giving me a soft kiss on the cheek. She stood up.

I joined her again. "Let's go back to the reunion," I said, motioning for her to lead the way. "Before the evening's over, let's make sure we get each other's numbers."

We walked down the stairs and through the double doors, and even though we'd only been gone for fifteen minutes at the most, the room seemed darker, the music louder, and nearly the entire auditorium was crowded with dancers.

"I'm going to see some friends," she said, waving.

13

"Wait! I don't know your name!" I shouted after her. She didn't hear me and continued through the crowd. *I guess "the ex-Mrs. Puggy" will have to do for now,* I thought to myself.

I stepped over to the bar and asked for a beer, and when I turned back around, there was a huge hulking figure standing in front of me. I smiled and excused myself. He wasn't smiling.

"You wrote *Sewer Balls?*" he asked in a manner that told me he wasn't going to be requesting an autograph.

"Yeah," I said nervously, scanning the immediate vicinity for Flynn or BB or anyone else who might provide a lifeline.

"Yeah, well, my wife is Tina Robustelli, smartass!"

"There's no such person as 'Tina'..."

But it was too late. His right arm was raised above his head, with a clenched fist that looked like a honey-baked ham. I lifted my left arm, which he knocked out of the way with a great force, and then I felt an impact on the left side of my face that I thought might make my brain gush out of my ears, mouth and nostrils. The sound of his fist against the side of my face was so loud, it was more like a church bell clanging than skin and bone being smashed ... soon followed by a flash of bright light... then nothing. Darkness. Black silence.

14

Chapter Two

—Then—

I wasn't sure exactly what I was doing or where I was. All I knew was my head felt like the A train had just clattered through it. As my eyes fluttered, the brilliant light they let in was overwhelming and made my head hurt even more. A blurry image began to appear – then it all came back to me.

"Whitey, you fuckin' asshole, I told you to slow down!" I yelled with newfound energy.

"Are you all right? Christ, I thought you were dead! Shit, I was already planning the lies I was gonna tell to avoid going to jail for killing you," Whitey said. With his big head, thick black glasses, pimply face, buck teeth and garlic-pizza breath just inches from my face, he reached down to help me up from the middle of the street. As I sat up and shook the cobwebs from my brain, a car went slowly by and a family of Puerto Ricans stared at us in disbelief. "I didn't think the manhole cover was that high."

"Shit, am I bleeding?" I said, feeling the back of my head, which had slammed onto the street. Now I remember. I was riding backwards on Whitey's high-rise monkey handlebars for a goof, and he tore-ass down the middle of Orloff Avenue, which isn't a bus route, so the surface is even more uneven than most Bronx streets. We were laughing hysterically as Whitey piloted his bike like a maniac. The last thing I remembered was his stupid grinning face transforming from out-of-control laughter to panic, as I went flying ass-over-elbows onto the pavement. I checked out my hand after feeling the tender part of my skull, and found only a trace of blood.

"Good thing you landed on that thick skull of yours, or you really could've gotten hurt," Whitey said, picking up his bike.

"Was I knocked out?"

"Are you kidding? You looked like Sonny Liston after Cassius Clay kicked his ass."

"For how long?"

"I forgot my egg timer, but I'd say under a minute. What was it like? Did you, like, start to see the light at the end of the tunnel? Did you hear the sissy choirboys singing and shit? Damn, my fork is bent!"

"Fuck your fork, my goddamned spine is bent because of you!" I shouted as I meandered over the sidewalk, with Whitey behind me lifting the front end of his pseudo-stingray bike because the front wheel wouldn't turn. Whitey's bike was a homemade stingray, with added-on high-rise monkey handlebars, a banana seat and a spoiler. The bike itself was probably from the early fifties, and a retro-fitted hand-me-down, no doubt.

"Should you go to the doctor or something?" Whitey said, laying his bike on the sidewalk next to the city steps. We could see all the way down the hill to Bailey Avenue where we usually hung out.

"Nah, I think I'm okay," I said. Still smarting and feeling woozy, I rubbed the back of my head and began to pull out little pebbles and dirt from my scalp. "Where'd everybody go?"

When Whitey and I had begun our ride on the highway to hell, Jimmy Joe, BB, Carrie and Donna were hanging out by the steps with us, but now they were nowhere to be seen.

"Probably making out in the lot," Whitey said in disgust. "They missed the whole thing!"

I was going to be pissed at Whitey for saying that, but then I thought to myself he was right. What fun was it doing something totally reckless and crazy if other kids weren't there to witness it? Especially having two girls watch me smash my brain into the street – that could've gotten me some good sympathy points for future use.

Those four were always running off and making out, no matter what the weather or the circumstances. It didn't matter if it was the dead of winter and we were sleigh-riding on the eighteenth hole at the Van Cortlandt golf course; they'd be next to some bushes pulling off their mittens and grabbing at each other under their layers of winter clothes while we were doing stunts, whizzing down the hill on our garbage can lids.

So of course, it being a warm July afternoon, they'd be in the bushes in the empty lot across the street from the city steps, groping each other and swallowing tongues the second me and Whitey were out of their sight.

"Let's go get a soda," I said.

Whitey was kneeling next to his front wheel and tried bending the front fork back into shape. "Okay, and I'll drop my bike off at my building on the way," he said, lifting the front of the bike. We began to walk towards his building down the hill.

"Should we tell them we're leaving?"

"Are you kidding? They could care less," Whitey said, resigned to the fact that both he and I knew we were probably the last two kids in our group that weren't constantly running off and making out with whatever girls were willing to swap spit.

Whitey's building was crappier than my building, which is saying a lot. Both were built probably around 1910, which was when the elevated portion of the IRT extended up into our neighborhood. I saw a picture in a book of the West 238th Street station the year it opened, and it was literally in the middle of a swampy field. And there we were, more than half a century later, the neighborhood thick with decrepit apartment buildings jammed practically on top of each other, except for a few private houses thrown in, and a couple of remaining empty lots filled with thorn bushes, old tires and beer cans.

We walked through an alley on the side of Whitey's building and pulled open a heavy steel door that led into the basement of his building. It was always creepy, going into someone else's apartment building cellar, instead of your own. In your own building, you knew all the nooks and crannies, cubbyholes, storage rooms and possibly the porter or super who lived down there. Any other cellar was fraught with strangeness and danger. So Whitey led the way through the maze of dank, dark halls with walls of crumbling ancient stones oozing stinky green and yellow stuff. There were a few light bulbs dangling above, but none of them were on. There was only whatever ambient light seeped from small windows at the top of the walls, that could bend around the corners.

But those weren't the reasons I felt weird going into Whitey's building. The reason was that only a few months ago, in the courtyard of his building, Whitey and I stood over his brother's dying body after he fell off the roof in a tragic freak accident. It was something we never talk about. Probably because there's nothing to say.

I almost jumped out of my skin when we came upon what I thought was a dead body in a doorway.

"That's the super. He's a drunk," Whitey said matter-of-factly as he walked past, and stopped in front of a crooked wooden door. He reached above the frame for a key and opened the padlock. He opened the door just enough to squeeze the bike through, pushed it to the side, closed the door and locked it again. The super was still asleep when we left.

As we walked down the street, there were kids playing everywhere, as they always were after school, and of course during summer vacation. Little kids, still in grammar school. Little snot-nosed kids chasing balls and each other down the sidewalk, hollering *freeze* or *you're it* or *olly olly oxen free* or some other silly stuff. Whitey and I weren't part of that scene anymore. In a couple of months we'd be attending high school.

We jumped down the three steps into Snookey's, which usually is bustling with high school kids, but the only other teenager in there was Billy Fricker, sitting alone with a magazine on a stool at the counter. Yeah, Billy Fricker was in high school, but neither Whitey or I were excited to see him. He didn't hang out with any of the cool high school kids from the block. He didn't even hang out with the lame high school kids. He didn't hang out with anybody.

Whitey and I sat one stool over from Billy and ordered two cherry lime rickeys.

"What are you reading?" Whitey asked Billy.

Billy's head jerked up. He appeared shocked that someone else was close by.

"Huh?" Billy said nervously.

"What are you reading?" Whitey asked again, pulling a pretzel rod from the round plastic container on the counter between him and Billy.

A slight smile formed as Billy proudly announced, "*Argosy.* You ever read it?"

"We sold it one time in the Cub Scouts, but I never read it," I said, also grabbing a pretzel.

"This isn't for kids, you know," Billy said as he moved one stool over, right next to Whitey. Whitey shot me a look with one eyebrow raised high over the black frame of his glasses.

"You mean, like *Playboy?*" Whitey asked, busily chomping on his pretzel.

Billy Fricker was maybe three or four years older than us, but he dressed like an old man. He didn't wear dungarees or khakis like most teenagers. He wore those dark blue or brown pants with cuffs on the bottom that are thicker than suit material. My dad calls them work pants. His belt is worn, thin leather with extra holes punched at one end and you can see the indentations from when he was much skinnier wearing the same belt. He was wearing a plaid, short sleeve shirt with a regular collar and only the top button opened. In the top pocket there was a pencil and a pad. It seemed like Billy never hung out with the other teenagers, but usually was seen hanging out with the old men in Bill's Deli, or Vito the shoemaker's.

"No! Not like..." he leaned over to us and whispered, "*Playboy.*" He straightened back up. "*Argosy* is an adventure magazine."

"You mean like cowboys and Indians and jungle stuff," Whitey said, with pretzel crumbs falling out of his mouth.

"No, *real* adventure. Like...Bigfoot," Billy said, eager to see our response. "And UFOs."

"That magazine is about Bigfoot and UFOs, and it's for real?" Whitey asked, after swallowing a lump of pretzel.

Billy leaned in even closer. I could smell the Brylcreem he used to plaster down his neatly parted hair, something nobody used anymore. The only people who still greased their hair back were the hitters and greasers who pretended the Beatles never happened. Those guys were mostly out of high school. Not in college, but out of high school, anyway.

19

"This magazine reveals things other magazines are afraid to," Billy said intensely. "I know. I've seen them."

"I've gotten some big foots up my ass, but there ain't no big foots in Van Cortlandt Park," Whitey replied.

"I know that! Bigfoot is in the Pacific Northwest. But I've seen UFOs right from the roof of my building. More than once."

Our cherry lime rickeys arrived and we started to gulp them down.

Billy put his money on the counter and rolled up his *Argosy*. "If you guys want to come up to the roof with me one night and look for UFOs, let me know." As he walked past he bopped me over the head, triggering a blast of pain through my still tender skull. I hid the discomfort from Billy and Whitey, both.

"Hey, Billy, where is everybody? I mean all the high school guys?" I asked, rubbing the top of my head before Billy exited.

"You ever hear of summer jobs?" Billy said, walking out the door.

I reached into my pocket and fished out my lucky Irish penny from 1917, the year of my father's birth; a rock-hard nearly petrified chestnut which I was seasoning for chestnut fights; and fifty-three cents.

Whitey pushed his lips out as far as one could, then twisted his face into all kinds of contortions as he fished around in his pockets for money, even digging into the small auxiliary key pocket of his dungarees. He held up a single quarter. "This is all I've got," he said woefully.

I grabbed the quarter from between his thumb and index finger and counted out the money needed. "You owe me seventeen cents."

"I'll pay you back, I swear," Whitey said earnestly, kissing his two fingers and then tapping his chest over his heart.

We walked back up the hill to where we'd left the horny foursome and they were nowhere to be found. We even searched the woods of the empty lot thinking maybe we'd find them half naked, deep in the throes of puppy love, but nope. We sat on the big wedge-shaped boulder that we used to play on.

"Remember when we were little we used to pretend this was a rocket ship?" I asked, kicking shards of glass from a broken beer bottle. Whitey stood on the rock and pointed across the tree-filled lot. "And we'd put bottles and cans up in the branches and shoot them from here with our sling shots."

"Do you believe in UFOs?"

"Of course! They show them on the news and in newspapers all the time," Whitey said, picking up an empty Rheingold quart bottle. He began to slowly run the bottle's mouth across the smooth part of the rock we were perched on.

"You think Billy Fricker has really seen them?"

"I don't know. Do you?"

"I know he goes up to the roofs at night. But maybe he just wants us to go up there to make his rocket ship visit Uranus," I deadpanned. Whitey started chortling with laughter as he bent forward and shut his eyes.

"What about the summer jobs, though?" I asked seriously.

"One minute," Whitey said in a hushed tone, as he continued to run the bottle across the boulder. Suddenly the very tip of the bottle's neck popped off. "Perfect!" Whitey proclaimed, picking up the dark brown ring of glass that actually looked like a ring. He tried to slip it onto the ring finger of his right hand, but he barely got it over his finger nail. "Shit, last summer when I used a quart bottle of Rheingold, it fit! Look, it barely goes onto my pinky!" he said, sliding it onto his finger. "Always have the cut part facing out. It comes in handy in a fistfight," he said, punching the air.

I did remember Whitey having bottle-neck rings on all fingers last summer. *I'll bet I could still put the rings on each of my fingers, no problem.* Whitey was growing a lot faster than I was. Some people thought he was a junior or senior in high school, and wondered what he was doing hanging out with a pipsqueak grammar school kid like me.

"Where could we get a job?" Whitey said, rubbing the cut-glass side of the ring. "Ouch. I cut myself."

"I don't know, delivering for the dry cleaners, the grocery... Hey, I know! What about day camp?"

21

Whitey's eyes widened and his jaw dropped. "Are we old enough? But wait, it already started."

"I heard you only have to be graduated from grammar school to be a junior counselor. Maybe they still need counselors," I said, rising from the rock and jumping off.

"Father O'Shaughnesy's in charge, right? Let's go to the rectory right now!"

"We're not dressed up or anything. And you have blood on your shirt."

"So what, let's go! Come on!"

I was surprised Whitey was gung ho about the idea. He never even went to Presentation's day camp, and in fact, he made fun of me for going. "All you do is ride the damn old bus, drink sour milk, and go to Miramar Pool in freakin' Inwood. Big deal!" he'd say, and he was pretty much right. The buses were dilapidated, with no air conditioning, and for some reason, wooden crates of small cartons of warm milk were the only refreshments available, causing projectile vomiting at least once a trip, and we almost always went to Miramar once a week. Miramar was one of the last of the public pools around. It was a giant fetid saltwater pool a block from the el, where they made you walk through showers and a disgusting footbath when you went from the locker room to the pool. And since it was a public pool in the city, you can imagine the perverts and freaks hanging out in the lockers.

We stood on the rectory's stoop and looked at each other. I'm certain I must have had the same look of terror on my face as Whitey had on his. The rectory door appeared to have been made from the same heavy wood as the pews in the church. And perhaps even the same wood as the giant, super-realistic life-sized crucifix with the bleeding, dying Jesus that hung on the wall over the altar.

"You ring the bell," I said to Whitey.

"You think it works?" he asked sheepishly.

The bell was an ornate brass key in the middle of the door that apparently you were supposed to turn. Whitey reached out and turned it weakly a quarter turn, barely making a sound.

"Turn it good!"

Whitey contorted his right arm and gave the key a twist with enough strength to open the cap of a fire hydrant, causing a bell blast loud enough to wake a fire house.

We looked at each other, not knowing whether to laugh or run away before somebody answered the door. But it was too late to do either.

The heavy wood door swung open, with a pissed-off Mrs. Carmichael standing there. My entire body tensed up with fear, and I'm sure Whitey's did also. I had forgotten that Mrs. Carmichael worked in the rectory, even though that was her main duty. She was also in charge of the innermost workings of the church itself, maintaining the altar and the sacristy, and subsequently she was the dictator de facto of the altar boys. Sure, the monsignor signed you up and gave you the test where you had to recite all the prayers in Latin, but once you were in, it was Mrs. Carmichael who gave you your assignments, made sure your cassock and white surplice were clean, and gave you bloody hell if you stepped out of line. Stepping out of line could mean many things, from chewing gum and giggling during a funeral, to stealing hosts and bottles of wine. But no matter what the infraction, you didn't want Mrs. Carmichael on your case. She may have been five foot three and ninety pounds, but her sinewy arms and bony hands could leave welts even through a cassock.

"Sure, you're trying to wake the dead by ringing like that," she said in a stern Irish brogue, staring at us through her thick ladies glasses tapered at both ends like Chinese eyes. "State your business or be off with you."

"Um, we'd like to see Father O'Shaughnesy about day camp," I said after a long pause, hoping Whitey would chime in first.

"You can apply with a membership form in the vestibule of the church. No need to bother the Father."

"No, that's to be a *camper*. We want to apply for counselor jobs. Junior counselors."

She looked at me and shook her head. "Weren't you both altar boys?"

"Yes, Mrs. Carmichael," we said in unison.

23

"Come in and sit in the parlor," she said with disgust. "Don't touch a thing," she warned us, knowing full well what damage an unsupervised kid from the parish could do, ex-altar boy or not.

We sat in two plush, but worn, upholstered chairs separated by a dark wood table. Next to a lamp was a framed eight by ten picture of the Blessed Mother, as we called Mary, getting visited by the angel. That was the biggie around here, since this was Presentation of the Blessed Virgin Mary. Kind of like seeing a picture of Henry Ford by a Model T in a Ford dealership.

I thought about the couples who sat in those chairs – couples getting ready for marriage, parents planning a christening, families arranging a funeral.

I looked at Whitey, and he pointed his finger up in the air as if he were about to proclaim an epiphany. As he looked to the ceiling with head cocked to the side he lifted one of his butt cheeks and...

Brrrraaassstttppphhhtttttt

He let out a long, juicy, musical fart. Before I could say word through my laughter, in walked Father O. He stopped dead in his tracks and his nose and upper lip scrunched together first, then his mouth widened as if to say *eeewwww,* although he didn't make a sound. He turned and stepped into the hall just outside the parlor, and said in a loud stage whisper into the office where Mrs. Carmichael was, "Mrs. Carmichael, did Mr. Cooper fix that plumbing problem?"

"Yes, Father," replied Mrs. Carmichael in a *how-many-times-do-I-have-to-tell-you* lilt.

Father O. came back into the room and shook his head as if he was shaking what little hair he had on his head dry.

"Well, what a pleasant surprise! We always hope graduates will return to see us, even if it is only a few weeks after graduation," he said, shaking our hands. He sat down on a simple wooden chair across from us. "Nice to see you, Robert and Vincent. To what do we owe the pleasure of this visit?" Father O. asked, straightening his long black cassock.

Father O. always talked in a fancy way. He didn't sound at all like my father or any of my uncles, or for that matter, any of the grown-ups I knew. He was pretty much bald, but the hair that went around his head wasn't gray at all. He didn't wear glasses all the time, but a pair dangled around his neck on a string. His high-pitched voice reminded me of the cartoon character Underdog. In fact, he resembled the actor who voiced Underdog, Wally Cox. It was hard to say how old Father O. was. You couldn't pin an age on him by his wardrobe, for obvious reasons, and even though he seemed like a gentleman from a generation even before my dad's, he probably was only about thirty.

Whitey looked at me with an expression that told me to answer first.

"We were wondering if there were any job openings at the day camp this summer, Father."

"Now this is serendipitous! Do you know what that means?"

Whitey and I looked at each other like two cavemen in a spelling bee. "Is it something good?" I asked in a peep.

"Yes. Have you heard of serendipity?"

"Is that what they make Dippity-do out of?" Whitey wisecracked.

"Serendipity is when something is fortuitous," Father O. said, waiting for any sign of intelligence. "Do you know what a coincidence is?"

I raised my hand. "Yeah, that's like when your mother spends all day cleaning the house, and then your father shows up when she's all finished. At least that's what my mom says."

"Yes, it's a lucky coincidence. Because it just so happens there are some changes at camp this summer, and due to unforeseen circumstances there may be an opening or two. Mrs. C., can you please bring me two applications for day camp counselor positions? Now why do you wish to become counselors? Robert?"

Whitey looked as though he was just asked to explain photosynthesis or name the main exports of Bolivia. "Um, well, me and Vinny need a job…"

"Vinny and I need a job," Father O. corrected him.

"Oh, you need a job too, Father?" Whitey shot back with that goofy smile that sometimes earned him a history textbook over the head from an irate nun. Thank God, Father O. smiled slightly.

"Just kidding, Father. Vinny and I aren't going away this summer, and we'd, um, like to keep off the streets and have a job doing something... constructive."

Constructive... Nice one, Whitey.

Mrs. Carmichael extended her arm into the room and handed Father O. the applications.

"Very good. And you, Vinny?"

"Yes, Father, I agree with Whitey. We don't want to just hang around all summer and not do anything. It would be a...beneficial experience before entering high school."

"Excellent, boys. Take a few minutes to fill out these applications, and I'll talk to the new camp director to see if there isn't a need for two more junior counselors. Leave the applications with Mrs. Carmichael on the way out." And Father O. was gone in a whisk.

Mrs. Carmichael poked her head into the doorway. "Hurry with that and be on your way!"

"Yes, Mrs. Carmichael," we said in unison.

We finished up the applications, were out the door, bounded down the steps, crossed the street and were into Van Cortlandt Park in a flash.

"Let's go down to the tracks and walk up to the lake. This could be one of the last days we just bum around," I told Whitey as I picked up a nice sized stick that would be good for knocking old cans or chasing away any pervert lurking in the bushes.

The single line of railroad tracks went right through the wooded eleven hundred acre park. It's now a freight line with a train going by only once or twice a day. It made a perfect, direct path to deep into the more inaccessible areas of the park, like the swamps just above the golf course. The railroad company used tons of three- to four-inch rocks as a foundation for the railroad ties that went through terrain that was boggy in places and virtually a swamp in others. Whitey picked up a rock and put it in his pocket. I knew why he did it, so I didn't need to

26

ask. It was always a good idea to have some kind of weapon when walking into the nether lands of the park. We'd been hanging out in Vannie since were old enough to cross the street by ourselves and we'd seen just about everything imaginable: nude bums sitting by campfires in the woods, couples screwing, herds of rats, perverts whacking off, giant dead turtles, piles of porn magazines, even a guy screwing a tree! So having rocks in your pocket and a big stick were par for the course.

"Ooh, look at this!" Whitey said, using his stick to pick up a used condom and wave it around.

"Don't wave that thing so hard....arghhhhh!" I said, ducking as the flying scumbag barely missed my head. "You shithead!" I laughed.

"You were almost a *real* dickhead, dickhead."

We walked north into the park, passing the lake where a few kids were fishing, like we used to when we were in grammar school. In the swampy area just above the lake, there were woods where we knew perverts hung out sometimes.

"Let's see if we can hit Marilyn," Whitey said, picking up a few rocks. He threw them at the tree we named for Marilyn Monroe after we saw a guy screwing it. It became a tradition to throw the rocks at the tree, because that's what we did to the fruitcake who was sticking his dick in it. We didn't hit him, though. He ran too fast.

We continued our trek, going farther up, past the golf course and into the swampiest part of the park. We stopped at a hole in the fence leading to the path that took you right into the reed-filled black-muck swamp.

"Want to go?" I asked, knowing that more than likely it could mean a new adventure, but possibly wet stinky feet, or worse.

"Sure," Whitey said, leading the way.

We left the elevated dryness of the railroad rocks and immediately felt the mud slosh under our sneakers as we passed through the hole in the chain link fence. It only took about thirty seconds for the rank smells of the swamp to become totally obvious: sludge, turtle crap, mucky water and dead fish mixed with oil and gasoline runoff from the nearby Saw Mill River Parkway. The path went through ten-foot-high swamp reeds and it was impossible to see what might lie ahead.

"You think that boat from last summer is still there?"

"That would be great!" Whitey said, poking his stick into a puddle to see how deep it was.

The summer before, we "borrowed" a rowboat from the park's boat house. With great effort that included carrying the boat up the railroad tracks, pulling it through disgustingly smelly swamp waters, and lifting it over a chain link fence, we'd hidden it next to the swamp pond for future adventures.

"Do you remember where we hid it?"

"I think so," Whitey said, pushing his way through the brush. All of a sudden, he stopped dead in his tracks. "Oh, shit!" he whispered.

"Don't fuck with me, asshole," I whispered back.

"It's a bum. He's by the boat. He's eating."

"What should we do?"

"I think it might be... Dunleavy."

I gasped. Dunleavy the bum? That was like Billy Fricker finding Bigfoot in the park. We all knew about Dunleavy, but sightings were rare, and I had never seen him up close. It looked like he was sitting on a bucket right next to the bushes where we'd hidden the rowboat. It was upside down and pretty well camouflaged with branches, dirt and trash. Actually, from this distance of about twenty yards, Dunleavy did look like Bigfoot. His hair was the color of baseball field dirt and his skin was about the same, except there were black blotches and red sores on his face and arms. His clothes had a dark sheen to them, as though brushed with used auto oil. And I was pretty sure that I could smell him, even at that distance.

We crouched lower behind the brush as he stood and up and gingerly walked the few steps to the overturned rowboat. He bent over, lifted one end of it a few inches, reached under, and pulled something out. Back at his seat, he began pulling meat off what looked to be a large bone, using his teeth..

28

"Holy shit, this is like watching a *National Geographic* special on cavemen," Whitey whispered to me.

"Let's get out of here."

"No, I want to check this out," Whitey said. He moved a few steps forward, breaking a branch underfoot.

Dunleavy stopped chewing and looked precisely in our direction. Whitey and I froze.

"If somebody's over there," Dunleavy said in a gravelly, but commanding, voice, "show yourself, or I'll shoot your ass."

This was no time to call anybody's bluff. Even if he looked like a bum who couldn't catch us if his life depended on it, the "shoot your ass" line got our attention. We stood and stepped from the brush out into the open.

He stuck his hand into the waistband of his pants and yelled, "Get your asses over here. Now!"

"What do we do?" I said. I wondered if Whitey could hear me over the sound of my knees knocking.

"Fuck it, let's go," Whitey said, walking calmly towards Dunleavy.

I followed right behind Whitey and began reciting an "act of contrition" to myself. We were about six feet from Dunleavy and the stench was overwhelming. In some bushes about five yards behind him that there was a roll of toilet paper stuck onto a branch.

"What are you doing here?" he asked, sitting on an overturned wooden milk crate.   The lines of his face were filled with dirt, almost like badly done stage makeup trying to age someone. He wasn't old, but it was impossible to put an exact age on him.

"We were looking for our boat. We hid it here last year," Whitey said, without any fear in is voice.

"*Your* boat? Ha!" Dunleavy laughed without smiling. "You mean the boat you little shits robbed from the boat house," he said, revealing a pistol in his grimy hand.

"Well, I guess," Whitey said.

"Please don't shoot us…" I blurted out, my voice cracking, just a few knee-knocks from crying like a girl.

"No, I'm not going to shoot you...*unless*..." Dunleavy said leaning towards us. "Unless you tell somebody you saw me. Then I'll find you and I will fucking shoot your motherfuckin' brains out," he said, waving a revolver. "You ever see one of these?"

Whitey's eyes narrowed and his lips tightened. I could see a vein throb in his neck. "Yeah, my brother had one of those. He was a cop."

Dunleavy stuck the gun back in his pants. "What's your last name, kid?"

"Shelley," Whitey said.

"Your brother...was...Brian?"

Whitey's head lowered. His chin touched his chest and his eyes closed but only for a second. He raised his head proudly and said, "Yes, sir."

"Sorry, kid."

"You knew him?" Whitey said, not looking up.

"I was a cop. I knew him well. Helluva guy. That was a cryin' shame what happened to him. God rest his soul."

Whitey stood at attention, staring at Dunleavy, a blank look on his face. Suddenly he turned and ran faster than I'd ever seen him run, right through the bushes, and he disappeared. I could hear branches breaking and puddles being splashed in the distance.

"You better go find your friend," Dunleavy said, shaking his head.

I jerked my body around, took a giant step, slipped in the mud, and extended my hands in front of me to break my fall. I felt a sharp pang in my left hand where something pierced my palm. I still managed to smack my head onto a rock, and the impact of the blow reverberated to the back of my skull, reminding me of the smash I had earlier on the bike. I couldn't forget it now. I pulled a small sharp piece of wood out of my hand, and instantly recalled when Whitey's brother was killed. Him lying there in a pool of blood, having just fallen six stories from the roof onto a picket fence and smashing into the courtyard of Whitey's building. I remembered the sight of Whitey standing there in shock, unwilling to believe the horror before us. I closed my eyes, not caring that my face was in the mud, my head was pounding, my hand was bleeding, and a bum with a gun was a few yards away.

Chapter Three

---NOW---

I opened my eyes. It was hard to see anything except strangely colored lights, and shadowy figures slowly coming into focus. *Oh, yeah. The reunion. The punch in the face.*

"Are you okay? Can you hear me?" one of the blurred figures asked.

They came into focus: Jimmy Joe, BB and Flynn were leaning over me as I lay on the hard marble floor of the auditorium.

"Yeah, I'm okay," I said, feeling like I'd leaned too far over the subway platform and got slammed by an express train speeding through the station. "What the hell happened?"

"I guess Tina Robustelli's husband didn't like your writing style," Flynn said as he and the others helped me into a waiting folding chair.

"Everybody's a critic," I said, feeling the painful, still pulsating orb of my left eye. "Doesn't that asshole know that there's no such person as Tina Robustelli? She's totally made up!"

I looked at Flynn, who had a knowing smirk plastered across his face. He winked at me. "Yeah, I know, that's your story and you're sticking to it."

I winked back at him.

"And if you hurry, you might be able to catch her hubby in the parking lot and explain it to him," BB said, patting me on the back.

"No thanks. How do I look?"

"Not as bad as he does," BB said. His hand, wrapped in a napkin with red blotches blooming over his knuckles, offered me a can of beer.

I learned that a woman (who shall go unnamed) from our class in grammar school took umbrage that the slutty character in *Sewer Balls* was possibly based on her. I didn't even know this classmate was a whore back then, or I would have paid more attention to her. Tina Robustelli truly was a composite character. The truth was, no one girl I

32

ever knew in grammar school or high school had all Tina's sleazy characteristics. It was pure fantasy.

In the boy's bathroom, I was shocked at how low the urinals and the sinks were. I had to lean over to get a good look in the mirror at my developing shiner. I decided I shouldn't let a little thing like a nearly lethal punch in the face put a damper on the party. Grabbing my beer off the top of the urinal, I headed back out for some more fun.

In the dim lighting, I didn't attract much attention and blended nicely into the crowd. The guys were busy doing goofy white-guy dances.

When I felt a tap on my shoulder, I instinctively threw my right arm up in a defensive posture. It was Mrs. Puggy again.

"I had nothing to do with that."

"With what? Oh, this," I said pointing to my eye. "I didn't even get your name."

"Elizabeth, but everyone calls me Betty Ann."

Living in Los Angeles for around fifteen years, I don't think I ever met one Betty Ann, a real old-fashioned sounding name. Nor do I ever recall anyone telling me they didn't mind if an old friend was a murderer.

We talked more about Whitey. Betty Ann filled in a little bit of the gap in the mystery of Whitey's timeline for the months before he joined the army. I knew he had gone upstate, and I didn't realize he was coming back down to visit Betty Ann's sister. To this day, it amazes me how Whitey seemed to completely fall off the face of the earth. No one even talked about him. It was like the Soviet Union where leaders suddenly disappeared, their names erased from the history books and their images cut out of official photographs.

"Was your sister getting serious with Whitey?" I asked Betty Ann, shouting directly into her ear trying to be heard over "In the Navy." I again got a head-full of the aroma of her thick fragrant hair.

"It was purely platonic. My father had just died, and my mother had cancer at the time," she yelled in my ear. "Whitey was great to each of us. My mother was friends with his mother. She adored him."

33

Betty Ann excused herself to dance with a gray-haired fat guy who I'm pretty sure was one of Puggy's pugnacious cohorts.

My eye really started to hurt and I wasn't sure if staying up all night and drinking with the guys in the bar afterwards was the best thing for me right now. But strangely, the pain was focusing my thoughts on Whitey. Maybe I could piece together some stories of Whitey's mysterious departure. It was a rare opportunity to have this exact group of people start remembering stories, with alcohol loosening up the trapdoors of their minds.

I pushed through the sweaty dancers and tapped Betty Ann on the shoulder. "I heard a bunch of people are going to the Goal Post afterwards."

"I'll try to make it," she said, her smiling eyes flirting with me.

I noticed that the bruiser she was dancing with narrowed his eyes to glare at me, exposing his crooked lower teeth.

"How ya doin', Ray Ray?" I said, using the grammar school name he hated, which when used openly usually led to a bloodied nose or black eye. I smiled and went to look for BB, Jimmy Joe and Flynn.

As I watched the three of them laughing hard, drinks in hand, I didn't see three overweight middle-aged men, one bald, one balding, and one with white hair. I saw three kids who knew more about me than everybody I'd met in twenty years in Los Angeles put together.

It was sardine time at the Goal Post. It appeared that every drinker from the reunion had gotten the word and crammed into the place. And it wasn't just the people with thinning hair and expanding waistlines who were enjoying happy times from long ago. The bar was taking on a role it hadn't seen in years. When most of these folks were young bucks on the prowl for good times, this was the site of many a wild time with wall-to-wall action. The Goal Post was the place to be any night of the week, for the best jukebox, the most buy-backs, the most single chicks, and the most trusted bookies. And even during the coke years, and later, the devastating crack years, the Goal Post never degenerated into a junkie hangout like some of the other bars in the neighborhood did. That was because there were more than a few cops, firemen and court officers downing a cocktail or two after work, who drew the line at shooting up or smoking rocks in the bathroom. Nobody cared what you did outside, but a small group of guys enforced the "no hard drugs in the bar" rule with iron fists. Literally. These days, the bar is what we used to call an old-man bar: a bar busier during the day than at night, with workaday, functioning alcoholics, recreational drinkers, recovered alkeys, and gamblers. The busiest day would be a Sunday during football season when guys bet their rent money on games from the first contests on the East Coast, straight through the last West Coast game on Sunday night football.

As I caught a glimpse of myself through the top shelf of dusty Irish whiskey bottles on the grimy back-bar mirror, I realized it wasn't just the bar that had transformed into *old man* status. Ties and belts were slipping down farther and farther and skirts were riding up women's ass cracks as backs were patted harder, hugs became tighter, and kisses between puppy-love boyfriends and girlfriends went from pecks on the cheek to sloppy make-out sessions that had to be hidden from husbands and wives. Through the haze of tobacco smoke (despite its ban in New York City) and most of the dim light provided by the jukebox and the West Coast horse racing recaps on the several televisions, the harshness of aging wasn't quite so apparent. Okay, so Denise O'Day had gained a good hundred fifty pounds since eighth grade. She still had sparkling green eyes, inch-deep dimples, and tits even more humongous, which still stand at attention thanks to technologically-advanced composite materials that have only been made commercially available in the past few years. It was pretty easy to gauge by the Chanel dresses or Rolex watches which ones had boob-and/or eye-lifts and the expensive Scarsdale hair plugs installed without the help of coupons from the back of the *New York Post*. But nobody seemed to care about the non-factory-installed add-ons. It seemed to me that despite the extras the decades had piled on, the popular girls were still popular, the funny guys still funny, and not much had changed at all.

A rotund man stood before me and bent backwards in amazement, with mouth and eyes stretched beyond limit. If I'd seen this guy on the street, I'd have thought he had to be at least ten years older than me. In a split second, I tried to look beyond the ring of gray hair around his bald dome, the blurry tattoo on his forearm which could be either a diseased heart or the Rolling Stones' lapping tongue logo, and the hairy belly protruding through a gap in his button-down shirt, which probably would not be tucked back in for the rest of the evening.

"You old fuck! How the hell are you?" he laughed as he lunged and hugged me way too tight. "I haven't seen you since you threw a firecracker at me out your window!"

Can it be? Terry Kwykelski? The little kid from my building? I remember how I laughed hysterically after throwing handfuls of pennies out my window onto the roof of the stores below and watched Terry and his other prepubescent partners in crime scurry to gather up the coins. When they got directly under my window I'd either dump water balloons on them or a firecracker. I was probably fifteen and he was six or seven.

"Terry! Wow! How are you?" I said, trying to pry myself from his bear hug. "I think if I did today what I did back then I'd be arrested."

"You and me both! Those were some fun times!" he said, breathing heavily and sweating profusely. He caught his breath, tucked his shirt into his pants, straightened himself upright and like the little kid I remembered him as, asked earnestly, "So what've you been doing?"

It seemed that all evening I had been dancing around this question. I'd even avoided sharing the truth with BB, Jimmy Joe and Flynn, casually sloughing off any serious questions with wiseass retorts as though everything was just peachy. Maybe it was the sight of this man-child in front of me, Terry, who I knew once looked up to me as an older kid, or maybe after six hours of drinking my mix was finally right. But for some reason I thought I'd be straight with him.

"I moved to Los Angeles about twenty years ago..."

Terry smiled and moved in a few inches for more, as he put his hand on my shoulder.

"I was doing great, worked my way up in the television news production side of things to a pretty good position, but with all the work bullshit, I neglected my wife and my kid. I thought my job was my life, started hitting the sauce, and now I've lost everything. I left my ex-wife and my son in L.A., or should I say, just like Felix Unger, I was asked to remove myself from my place of residence. So I moved into my sister's house in Bronxville a few months ago. I'm sleeping on a pull-out in her basement. Back where I started, I guess."

"You fucked up, huh?" Terry said, squeezing my shoulder hard. "That sucks. When I moved out of the neighborhood, I promised myself I wouldn't be like my father."

Terry didn't have to explain. Everybody in the neighborhood knew Terry's old man, especially the people in our building. He'd be under the stairs, in the cellar, on the roof, passed out with some kind of bottle next to him, whiskey, beer, or even cough syrup sometimes.

"I've got five girls," Terry said proudly, pulling out his wallet to show me photos. "Okay, a stupid joke: So this guy in a bar announces, I've got five boys, a whole basketball team. The guy next to him says, so what, I've got nine boys, an entire baseball team. The bartender drops his washrag and says, I've got you both beat. I've got eighteen daughters, an entire golf course." Terry smiled and nodded his head; I laughed out loud. "So what are you doing?" he asked, still smiling.

"I guess I'll just hang out..."

The smile went away. "No, seriously. What are you doing with your life? Can I help you? What do you need? Money? Contacts? I know people in the city in the catering business. There's always work. Good tips. You can get back on your feet and take care of things. What grade's the kid in?"

My laughter at Terry's silly joke had hardly subsided, and I wanted to cry at his thoughtfulness. "He's a senior in high school."

"He needs you, pal. Don't fuck up."

It hit me like a ton of bricks. Here's a guy I haven't seen since he was a few years out of Pampers, and he's giving it to me straight from the heart like he's Dr. Phil or something. And I'm listening like he *is* Dr. Phil.

"Thanks, Terry," was the only sensible thing I could come up with. I pulled him in for a bear hug. Terry pulled out a business card from his wallet.

"Call me if you need anything," he said, wagging his finger as he walked away. I knew he meant it. "By the way, I read your book," he said turning back to me. "I heard Tina Robustelli's here somewhere." He winked as he pushed through the crowd.

"Hey, it's Vinny Knucklehead," Flynn said, picking up one of the several tumblers of brown liquid that were plopped in front of him. "Have a Jack!"

"Beginning old number seven thread," I said, knowing full well that a tumbler of Jack Daniels would lead to another and another. Which it did.

It wasn't long before the entire bar was slowly revolving like one of those tourist restaurants on the tallest hotel in some Midwestern city. I bounced from clique to clique. First it was groups of people whom I recognized. But after my third or fourth tumbler of brown stuff, I was barging into groups of total strangers and laughing hysterically at nothing with people I didn't know or didn't care to know anymore.

Throwing up is bad enough. But throwing up between parked cars at six-thirty in the morning on a Sunday as some seven o'clock churchgoers pass by is about as low as a person can go.

"Get up, you bum, it's almost noon!" Flynn said, placing a cup of tea on the coffee table. "I already showered, shitted, shaved, had breakfast and read the sports section while you were farting up my living room in your sleep."

Flynn was a professional drinker. He knew how to drink himself to the edge of oblivion, get up in the morning and maintain a normal life. Of course, that was the life of a bachelor. He was probably the most naturally gifted athlete in the neighborhood. He could throw a wicked slider in little league, dunk a basketball at five foot nine, and hustle grown-ups at Van Cortlandt golf course when he was fifteen. He started drinking when he was twelve and hasn't stopped yet. He's achieved his full growth of five foot ten, two hundred fifty pounds, but still has the grace of an athlete and hustles yuppies on golf courses from the Keys to Pebble Beach. I'm a month or two older, and unlike me, Flynn is retired and living comfortably with the help of New York taxpayers and a nice pension from twenty-five years as a toll collector.

"I've got a three o'clock tee time in Westchester if you're interested," Flynn said, stirring a glass of something red with a celery stalk.

"Is that a bloody Mary?" I asked, disgusted and revulsed by the sight of alcohol.

"Yeah, you want one?"

"Sure." I pushed off the covers and sat up in my briefs and white t-shirt.

Flynn swiftly returned with a bloody Mary and placed it next to my tea.

"I'll start with the tea."

"You hit the Bronx trifecta last night! A fist fight, making out drunk in public, and throwing up."

I took a tiny sip of tea, and decided the bloody Mary was preferable. "Whoah, I remember the fist fight and throwing up. What's with the making out drunk in public?"

"Don't play that with me," Flynn said, shaking his head as he slowly practiced his swing with an imaginary golf club.

"I'm not shitting you. Who was I making out with?"

"Mrs. Puggy."

"You're jerking my chain."

Flynn kissed two fingers then held them up high over his head. "My lips to God's ears, Betty Ann Pugliese and you were in a corner swapping spit like two eighth graders on the graduation boat ride."

I wasn't sure if my head hurt from my hangover or the shiner. I took a gulp of bloody Mary. "You're not bullshitting me."

Flynn pulled his cell out of his pocket. "Who do you want to call and ask? It's not like you were under the pool table! You were right under the goddamn TV, fer chrisake!"

"And what happened? She left me? I left her?"

"You remember hurling?"

"The experience still lingers," I said, tasting it in my mouth.

"Well, you were about to get into her car when you had the good breeding to pause and deposit your load behind her car. Needless to say she took off without you."

"I guess I didn't get a kiss goodnight?"

Flynn laughed as he put his phone away and continued working on his swing, now with a real golf club. "She's still a hottie. Too bad you fucked that up."

The hot shower felt soothing. I stood backwards under it as the water blasted the back of my head and ran down my back. Although my shiner hurt when the water hit it directly, it didn't look so bad in the mirror as I shaved. I borrowed some clean underwear from Flynn, which didn't fit, but he wore boxers so it didn't matter that much, and the shirt he had outgrown felt pretty alright. I felt even better when I saw he had placed on the kitchen table a toasted English muffin, a fresh mug of tea and another bloody Mary.

"You'd make a lovely wife, Flynn."

"I learned a long time ago, it's a bachelor's life for me."

"I learned that lesson a little late."

Flynn was kind enough not to berate me for fucking up my marriage, job, and life in general. It was as obvious as the black and blue on my face. "Did you know Betty Ann's family was close with Whitey?" I asked Flynn.

"Mrs. Puggy's family and Whitey? Never heard that one. Fuckin' Whitey. Too bad. I heard he's dying or dead."

"I don't know. She wants to help me find Whitey. I think she's got some leads."

"Good luck there. Last I heard, and I'm going back a few years, he was hiding out upstate after he killed somebody or something. Not exactly somebody who you want to go digging up."

After breakfast, Flynn drove me back to the church parking lot where I had left my car from the night before. I threw the plastic grocery bag with last night's clothes onto the front seat and a slip of paper fell out. It was a handwritten note that read "Betty Ann" and had a phone number underneath. I don't remember her writing it, but it was a good sign that it was in her handwriting and not mine. That meant she wrote it voluntarily. I stuck it in my wallet for safekeeping.

Mission accomplished. I wanted to go to the bar afterwards to see if I could come up with any clues as to Whitey's whereabouts, and I succeeded. I did get a punch in the face, but I guess it was worth it. Unless finding Whitey led to something worse.

As I drove up the highway my cell phone starting vibrating in my pants pocket. I struggled to get it out in time, but missed the call. I didn't recognize the number until I parked the car outside my sister's and took Betty Ann's number out of my wallet. It was her.

I decided not to call right away. I didn't want to appear too anxious; playing a little hard to get usually pays off. Suddenly with it still in my hand, the phone vibrated, startling me. I answered it this time.

"Betty Ann?"

"Listen," the harsh female voice harped, "if you think you're gonna use me just so you can get some information on Whitey, you're barking up the wrong tree, mister!" Then silence. She hung up on me.

I folded my flip phone and stuck Betty Ann's number back into my wallet. Fortunately no one was home at my sister's and I felt relaxed as I went down the stairs to my lair. There was a note from my niece on the table: "Call me when you get back I need my car!!!"

I sat on the couch and lowered my head into my hand, and stupidly bumped my injured eye orb, bringing back the pain from the night before. *Maybe I'll just have to find Whitey by myself,* I thought.

41

Chapter Four

--Then--

Branches thwapped me in the face as I cut through the brush. My socks were getting soaked in the black sludge of the swamp, mud seeping into the holes at the bottom of my Converse All Stars. It was difficult to stay on the right path because there really wasn't a path at all. I just ran as fast as I could, away from the bum with the gun, and towards what I thought would be the hole in the fence at the railroad tracks. If there was a puddle to the right, I'd go left, then cut to the right and backtrack through some bushes there and here and *ouch!* Damn thorn bushes! I plunged through the thickets and almost smashed my face into the chain link fence. But no hole! There were vines everywhere and I couldn't walk the length of the fence to find the opening. I would have to somehow find the original way we got in here.

I was deathly afraid that backtracking might take me back to Dunleavy, so I pushed through some bushes even though they were even thicker with thorny vines. It was hard to believe that less than a half mile from this swampy jungle there was a highway, an elevated subway line, and thousands of people crammed into apartment buildings. I stopped dead in my tracks because there was an enormous ancient fallen oak tree right in front of me. My worn sneakers slipped on the bark as I tried to find my footing, but I managed to get up to the top of it and whoa! I peeked over the top and there they were! My eyes immediately focused on two huge wildly undulating tits! A teenage girl was nude, facing me, on top of a nude guy, riding his bucking body like a rodeo cowgirl. I stopped breathing. My fingernails dug deeper into the bark as I steadied myself, hoping I could remain invisible from my perfect perch. Wow! I'd seen my share of topless girls in *Playboy*, and I'd seen almost total nudity in "nature" magazines where they show bush, but erase the nipples, but I never, ever saw anything like that live and in person! She kept going and going! I've heard about 8 millimeter porno films where they show hardcore sex, but I never saw one. This was unbelievable! I couldn't help myself. My dick was as hard as the dead oak, and my eyes went from her bouncing boobs down to her hairy crotch, back up to her tits going so wild they're going every which way, and up to her face... and holy jumpin' shit – it's Tina Robustelli!

I quietly pushed my way backwards through the brush and suddenly a hand grabbed my ass and another put a hand over my mouth. I turned, expecting to see Dunleavy with a knife clenched in his teeth like a pirate, but it was Whitey, with a smile from sideburn to sideburn.

"Did you see that?" he whispered, taking his stinky hand away from my mouth. "They're fucking *fucking!*"

"Man, did you see those tits on Tina? They're even bigger than they were at graduation!" I said breathlessly.

"Want to go back and look again?" Whitey said with mad glee in his eyes.

"I don't think so. We might get caught. Did you catch who she was screwing?"

"Puggy."

"That crazy guy Pugliese? Shit, if he sees us we're dead! Let's get out of here!"

"I ain't scared of that big faggot."

"Yeah, well, going by what I just saw he ain't no faggot, but he sure as hell is big. Let's get out of here."

We scrammed back to the fence and eventually found the hole we were looking for. The railroad tracks were an easy path for us to take back to the neighborhood. Whitey didn't say a word about Dunleavy referring to his brother getting killed and I didn't either. In fact, I don't think I've ever talked to him directly about it, even though there isn't a day that goes by that something doesn't trigger a memory about that day. When it rains and I smell the wet apartment building bricks and concrete sidewalks, I think of us hanging out that day across the street. Whenever I hear a loud noise in the distance, like something large crashing to the ground, I think of the moment when we wondered what that sound possibly could have been. And whenever I see a wooden picket fence I can't but help remember that Whitey's brother fell from the roof onto a picket fence and died in a pool of blood right in front of us. I'm also a stickler for remembering the house keys whenever I go out. I heard it was a freak accident, that he was trying to get in through his window on the top floor, slipped, and fell six stories.

I'm certain Whitey goes through the same flashbacks, only ten times worse. Why should we ever talk about it?   We also hardly ever mention his other older brother, Alfie, who was a brainiac in school and on drugs for a while. Once all that horrible stuff came and went I just figured that we'd go back to being friends like we used to, which we did. But the confrontation with Dunleavy was the first time we both were face to face with dealing with that awful day that changed us forever.

Whitey stepped over a log, reached down and held up a flattened-out dried-up dead squirrel. "Look, it's Rocky the flying squirrel," he said, and he flung it like a Frisbee high into the trees. We watched in awe as it somehow cut right through the tree branches and landed on the green of the golf course, just as a golfer was about to putt into the hole. Needless to say, it ruined his swing and he looked over at us.

"You goddamned hooligans! I know who you are! I'll have you arrested," the old duffer yelled, shaking his putter in the air.

We laughed as we ran down the tracks, knowing there was no way he could catch us.

"Rocky the flying squirrel strikes again," I yelled though my guffaws as we chugged down the tracks.

We exited the park across from the rectory and we saw Mrs. Carmichael sweeping the front stoop.

"I hope we get those jobs," Whitey said solemnly.

"Yeah, that would be a gas!"

"I need the money."

I was stunned when Father O. called that night informing me that I was hired as a junior counselor for the ridiculous sum of fifteen dollars a week. In the seventh grade I made that much in one day delivering for the dry cleaners next to my building. Okay, so it was because I got a ten dollar tip from a guy who everybody says is a drug dealer, but it happened.

"Um, Father, did, er, uh, anyone else…" I nervously asked Father O. on the phone.

"Yes, your friend Robert was also hired. I'm going to call him right after we hang up. One other thing, Vincent…"

"Yes, Father."

"The pay situation is between me and you and no one else. Don't disappoint me."

"No, Father. Thank you."

That was the absolute worst thing Father O. could have said: *Don't disappoint me.* That was the most pressure you could put on a kid. My parents started using that one when I got a little bit older. In third grade, I got a 79 in something and it was circled in red, with a note from Sister Annunciata on the bottom reading *I'm very disappointed in Vincent's lack of effort.* My parents looked at me like it said I was caught pulling my pecker out during high mass. From then on, whenever I'd screw something up where an older child should know better, they'd scrunch up their face, shake their head and reveal how utterly, shamefully, disgustingly, *disappointed* they were. Of course if I did something really stupid, like getting caught throwing firecrackers out the window at six-year-olds, then I'd just get called a little son of a bitch, and get smacked over the head a few times. That was much easier to handle.

The phone rang again, and I picked it up before the first ring was finished.

"Hello?" I said, hoping it was Whitey with good news.

"Is your refrigerator running?" Whitey asked in his phony grown-up voice.

"Yeah."

"Well, you better run and catch it before it gets away! Hey, Father O. called and told me I got the job."

"All right!"

45

"Yeah, for a measly ten bucks a week. Oh, well, it's ten dollars more than I'd have if I didn't take it."

"I'll call for you tomorrow. See ya."

"See ya."

Ten bucks? Holy crap. Should I say something? I better not. But why would he get ten and I get fifteen? I thought to myself.

That was one of the first times in my life that I realized there were forces in the grown-up world that could actually separate best friends. My silence sealed the deal. I knew I wasn't going to say a word to Whitey about getting five bucks more than he was. If I did, then he'd go to Father O. to complain and he would know how Whitey found out. This was my first real look into the dog-eat-dog world of grown-ups.

No matter what I did that entire weekend, all I could think about was day camp starting that Monday. My mom kept us all busy with chores, shopping, and visiting relatives in Brooklyn all day Sunday. Whenever we go to Brooklyn, it means we make a trek to Calvary Cemetery either on the way there or the way home. My father's parents and my mother's parents are all buried there, along with aunts and uncles I never heard of. We drove from gravesite to gravesite in silence and my dad always leading the way, winding through a maze of gray tombstones until he stops in front of one. It usually takes a minute before we even realize whose grave it is. Usually my dad will just say softly, *Aunt May* or *Grandpa Papalardo* or *Uncle Carmine*, and my mom will instantly get teary-eyed and weep softly. It seems strange to see my parents so sad and crying for people I never even knew.

I woke up to a steel gray summer morning. I had no idea what day camp had scheduled for a day like this, but hopefully it wasn't a trip to Jones Beach. My parents were already at work, so I made myself a baloney sandwich, wrapped it in wax paper and stuffed it into an insulated paper bag with a picture of an Eskimo on it, the kind that supermarkets put ice cream cartons in. We had a lot of those nice, thick paper bags and my parents had the bulging bellies to show for it.

46

Once I left my building and walked down the hill, I began to see kids walking with their dark blue day camp sacks, and a strange feeling came over me. There I was, after eight long years of wanting more than anything to get out of grammar school, and I was walking the exact same path at the exact same time to the exact same location. Well, not *exactly* the same. Instead of pulling open the heavy oak door at the school entrance, I bypassed the school and walked through the parking lot to the auditorium located directly under the church. I heard a loud roar as I rounded the corner of the school, and there were three yellow school buses with their engines running and kids streaming out of them. Standing next to steps of the bus were Father O. and a college-aged guy with a Beatle haircut wearing a day camp counselor shirt. He held a yellow wiffle ball bat and as each kid bounded off the bus, he tapped them on the butt with the bat, and counted out loud.

Father O. smiled at me and pointed to the stairway that led to the auditorium, signaling for me to go there. The college guy ignored me. I felt like I was one of the campers as I got in line with them and headed downstairs. It wasn't a typical auditorium with theatre-style seating, but a large room with a cold marble floor and a raised stage at the front end. Of course this was the same auditorium I had been in hundreds of times before. But I had never seen or heard the place in the state it was in this morning.

I remember being paraded through the schoolyard in first grade and into this auditorium for one of the first real shocks of my life. We entered from the rear of the room and there on the stage, students were walking slowly past a long black box surrounded by flowers and crosses. When we finally walked up the five steps onto the stage, I almost shat my pants. In the box was a dead person. And not just any dead person, it was freaking Monsignor Gilmartin! The monsignor who just a few weeks before came into our class and read from the Catechism. And there he was, dead as fish in a bucket in a rowboat, with his monsignor hat on his head! I remember all the kids, eyes bulged out, eyebrows raised and mouths open as we walked past him, from his feet to his head, like we were zombies. Girls were sobbing, more than likely from seeing a corpse, rather than from grieving. The

47

auditorium was filled with the entire school, faculty and all, yet the room was practically totally silent. Unlike now.

I stood in the back of the auditorium and couldn't believe the anarchy in front of me. Boys were chasing each other, screaming and yelling. Girls were sitting in circles playing super-hyped versions of pattycake hand-slapping games. Other boys were sitting in circles playing cards. *"Ouch,"* one kid yelled as another took a pack of cards and smashed his hand with the tightly held deck, something I immediately recognized as a game called "knucks." Another circle of girls had a portable record player and were spinning forty-fives! The song "Rag Doll" was playing too loud and a girl counselor wearing a sailor hat like nearly all the other females in the place told them to turn it down.

Although it was pretty much pandemonium all around, there were six loose groups of kids sitting on the marble floor, three groups of boys on the right side and three groups of girls on the left. The youngest campers, who I knew were five-, six- and seven-year-olds we called midgets, were in the front. Right behind them, a counselor sat on a folding chair reading a *Mad* magazine, separating the midgets from the juniors aged eight, nine, and ten. Behind them was another counselor on a chair, separating that group from the seniors, and eleven-, twelve- and maybe even a couple of thirteen-year-olds. Of course, there was a large space separating the boys on the right from the girls' groups on the left. Standing in the wide aisle between the boys' and girls' sections was a girl, no, a woman, wearing a day camp counselor shirt. She was spinning as she picked out the loudest kids and reprimanded them. The camper would calm down for about five seconds, get out of her range, and she'd move on to her next victim.

It wasn't just the campers who were sitting around in cliques. There were small groups of counselors, seemingly oblivious to the wild antics going on. Then suddenly I'd hear piercing shouts of "Muldoon!" or "Cottingham!" or "Cassano!" or "Burke!" from various male and female counselors.

I stood at the back of the room, not knowing where to go or who to talk to. I assumed the college guy I saw with Father O. was in charge, but I didn't want to go back up to the parking lot and bother them. The college-aged girl counselor standing between the boys and girls looked the oldest. Even older than the guy with the Beatle haircut. I couldn't tell how old she was, but her stern expression and raven-colored thin straight hair that went down to her shoulders with bangs halfway down her forehead made her look almost like a nun wearing a bonnet.. Our Sisters of Charity nuns wore black from head to toe, not even a swath of white on the bonnet like some orders of nuns had. The bonnets our nuns wore were old-fashioned bonnets, the kind you'd see the pioneer ladies wear in the Conestoga wagons like on the TV show *Wagon Train.*

I almost got poked in the eye with her pointing index finger as she whirled around to admonish two girls in sailor hats chasing a boy with a sailor hat he had just snatched from a girl. "James! Freeze!" she yelled, stopping all three dead in their tracks. He sheepishly handed the hat to one of the girls and walked away, watching the lady to see if any other admonitions would be directed his way.

"Excuse me. Uh, I'm a new junior counselor."

"What's your name?" she asked, briefly glancing at me while she scanned the room on the lookout for flagrant fouls.

"Vincent Schmidt."

"Midget boys. Check in with Gerald Fontana, the large gentleman reading the newspaper over there."

Leaning against the stage was the large gentleman, which was a nice way to say fat. His hair was black, thick, curly, and looked a little wet from his shower. He stood there reading the *New York Times,* and was chewing what looked to be a hard roll that sat on the lip of the stage next to a paper coffee cup.

I walked over and stood next to him for a few seconds, hoping he'd see me. He didn't look up from his paper. "Yeah?"

"I'm Schmidt."

"Oh shit! I mean... Oh, Schmidt!" he said, lowering the paper. He studied my face. "Just kidding, Schmidt. Call me Jerry. That guy back there who looks like Bozo the Clown, he's Jack Cavanaugh," he said, looking at a red-haired guy talking to a group of senior girls in the back. "Go in that bag there and take a couple counselor shirts. You get two for free. After that they're five bucks each. You pay me in cash. Take that list there, get the kids to sit down, and take attendance."

There was a brown shopping bag on the stage. I grabbed two white shirts, size small, and held them up. The kids wore t-shirts that said Presentation Day Camp in the center, but my white shirts had a collar with three buttons down the front. And on the left side it read Presentation Day Camp STAFF. I proudly put one on over the t-shirt I was wearing and stuffed the other one in the bag with my lunch. I picked up the list with the midget boys' names on them and began taking attendance. These kids looked like babies! I thought you had to be six years old to be in camp, and I know they let some five-year-olds in, but a couple looked like they were four. Despite their tender years, they still had mouths on them. It took about two seconds to hear remarks like, "Who the hell are you?" and "You ain't old enough to be a counselor" and "Drop dead." I just figured I better keep my own mouth shut until Jerry showed me the ropes.

"Griffith!" Jerry yelled, rattling his newspaper.

The kid who told me to drop dead got up and walked over to Jerry.

"If I hear you talking like that again, I swear to Christ I will beat your ass," Jerry said, his face contorted into overly dramatic faux rage.

Griffith looked up at Jerry, decided not to say anything back, and returned to his seat. I guessed I just had my first lesson in camp counselor discipline.

I continued taking attendance and noticed Father O. and the Beatle haircut guy had entered from the rear of the auditorium. As they walked down the center aisle towards the front, a wave a silence followed them. Kids sat in their places, counselors weaved and bobbed through clusters of campers and took their positions. Even Jerry put his newspaper down and took his breakfast off the lip of the stage. Father O. went up the side steps, lifting his cassock slightly as he did so, revealing white socks. He took center stage and without introducing himself, he said in a loud, reedy voice, "In the name of the Father and

50

of the Son and of the Holy Ghost…" making a large sign of the cross as he did so. By the time he got to the word "Ghost" the entire auditorium had stopped their idle chatter and joined with him. He said the Our Father and a Hail Mary with great authority, while the Beatle haircut guy lazily clasped his hands and was noticeably not praying along with Father O. as he stood a little behind him.

Father O. made another sign of the cross and at the end the entire auditorium said "Amen."

"I'm Father O'Shaughnesy. Welcome to another great week at Presentation Day Camp. I'm pleased to see we have many returning campers from the parish, and am even more pleased to see we have many new campers from surrounding parishes. Will all the campers from parishes outside Presentation please stand."

About a third of the campers stood up.

"Let's welcome them with a round of applause. Okay, be seated."

Father O. went on to say how wonderful it was to have them, and what a great summer it would be, and not to forget that we are wearing shirts, campers and counselors alike that identify us as not only being representatives of the parish, but as Catholics and we should always act accordingly. Griffith's hand shot up and Jerry looked like he regretted not beating his ass a few minutes earlier.

"Yes, young man?" Father O. asked.

"My father says we're not Catholic and that I'm not supposed to let you make me become one."

"Yes, well, just behave like a good camper and there won't be any problem. We have some news this morning. Charles, our camp director," Father O. said pointing to the Beatle haircut guy, "will be leaving next week to head back to college, and a new camp director will be filling in for the rest of the summer. And I will also be leaving for the rest of the summer."

A collective sigh could be heard.

"Let's hear it for Father O., everybody!" Charles said as Father O. exited the room from a side door in the front.

51

"We've got a lot of new campers and some new counselors, so I want to take this chance for everybody to take a moment, and when I say 'go,' turn around and shake hands with the person behind you. Ready, go!"

There was a short rustle as kids turned around, then a slow rumble of laughter and shouts of glee and surprise as all the kids (and a few counselors) realized it was a practical joke.

"Okay, simmer down. First thing to remember: listen to your counselors!"

Charles went on and on, telling kids not to be late, don't get lost, use the buddy system, and as he went on, there was a slow but steady roar of kids and counselors getting louder and louder as they paid little or no attention at all to what he was saying. Jerry went back to his newspaper, girl counselors began mingling, and the senior boys and senior girl groups started to mesh, until the auditorium was pretty much back to the pandemonium that existed before Father O. had entered.

"Okay, so remember, listen to your counselors!" he shouted over the noise of the crowd.

I walked over to Jerry and asked what I was supposed to do. He looked at me with a blank stare and said, "Don't lose any kids."

Without any announcement, all the kids stood up, and began moving towards the rear exit. I looked at the other counselors and noticed that as they chatted with each other, they sort of herded kids along with a few pushes and whacks of the wiffle ball bats.

In no time we were all on a bus, and just as quickly pulling out of the schoolyard with the kids even louder and more out of control than they had been in the auditorium.

I looked out the window and *uh-oh*. There was Whitey, running down the sidewalk, with his two middle fingers jammed in his mouth for his loudest whistle, then waving frantically at the convoy. He knew it was useless and just stood there watching us as we turned onto the Major Deegan Expressway, headed for points unknown.

Everything happened so quickly that I didn't even realize that they'd put the midget boys on the bus with the junior and senior girls.

I'm sure they knew that putting the senior girls with the senior boys would be trouble. And there in the middle of the bus, holding court for all the girl campers, wearing a sailor hat, baggy plaid shorts that went below her knees, and a counselor shirt several sizes too large that could not conceal her huge boobs bouncing around as she giggled with glee playing pattycake with not one but two girls, was Josephine O'Bryne. Hard to believe this was the same Josephine O'Bryne who graduated the year before I did. I hadn't seen her much around the neighborhood since she started high school. In fact, she didn't hang around much even before high school. She was one of those girls who stayed home and studied a lot. She was real quiet and you wouldn't even notice her in a crowd sometimes. But she sure looked different than I remember her in grammar school. She looked almost like a woman, despite the sailor hat. She was what my mother calls "black Irish." She had thick, wavy black hair that cascaded down past her shoulders. Her skin was so white, you'd think it could only be on an albino, which made all her striking facial features stand out even more. Those jet black eyebrows and lips so red they were almost maroon. Her eyes were greener than a rich lady's earrings on Saint Patrick's Day. I looked closely and could see tiny black hair stubble on her legs, which meant she shaved there already. And if she was doing that, you sure as hell know what's going on where those two long lovely roads come together just north of there!

The record player blasted "Do Wah Diddy" but I no longer heard the song, or giggles, or the ouches from knucks, or boys making elbow farts. All I could see and hear was Josephine O'Bryne. I stood and inched down the aisle towards her as if I was being drawn there. Whether patty-caking or playing cards, every girl on the bus, including the counselors, started singing the doo wah diddys, even though every time the bus hit a bump in the road the portable 45 record player skipped a word or two. The midget boys did not sing along. In fact, some of them were feigning epileptic seizures with their hands covering their ears.

Josephine led the girls as they did the latest dances: the swim, the hitchhiker, and other crazy twisting, herky-jerky moves. I stood there frozen, just watching her. I had never seen such a sexy dance, except for when Betty Boop did the hula topless with only the lei covering her nipples. But this was on the freaking day camp bus! Suddenly, Josephine did a double take as she saw me standing there watching her. She stopped, turned her eyes away quickly and I did an about-face and headed back to the safety of the midget boys.

"Where are we going?" I asked Jerry as he studied the cards in his hand.

"Crazy, you want to come?"

The bus driver, a plump Puerto Rican guy with forearms bigger than Popeye's and a belly bigger than Wimpy's, turned and yelled over the roar of the engine without taking his eyes off the road. "We going to visit a lady, and go under her dress and go right up into her. Oooh, gonna be a first time for you, right, kid?" He had a high pitched laugh that didn't match his low speaking voice.

"Come on. Really," I said to Jerry.

He picked up a card and said "Rummy. He's right."

The bus driver's laugh went even higher. "I don't lie. We really are!"

Griffith tugged on my shirt sleeve. I looked down at him – there was snot hanging from his nose, and his lips were purple from the Tootsie Roll pop he held in his hand. "Can I ask a question?" he said.

"Go ahead," I replied.

In a loud but very straightforward manner he asked, "Are we going to fuck a lady?"

The cards went flying; the bus drive veered half out of the lane, his laughter jumping two octaves; Bozo fell onto the floor; and Jerry laughed so hard his head hit the window. I stood there staring at Griffith who seemed perplexed at our reaction, but I couldn't get any words to form through my own guffaws.

"Well? Are we?" he asked earnestly.

Jerry, tears rolling down his face, yelled, "We're going to the Statue of Liberty!"

Griffith looked disappointed, and the laughter slowly subsided.

The bus got off the F.D.R. Drive and we wound through some side streets in lower Manhattan. We parked next to Battery Park where there were many other buses, including our two other Presentation Day Camp buses.

We got out and ate our lunches on the damp grass of Battery Park, the boys and girls separated from each other. I was assigned to hand out milk cartons to the midget boys. They were in a cooler, but the small cardboard containers with the waxy coating were merely on the verge of cool. After I watched the kids unwrap their wax-papered white bread sandwiches and wash it down with the tepid liquid, I lost my appetite. I sat on a concrete bench to read Jerry's copy of the sports section and received a tap on the shoulder. A raspy voice followed. "Hey buddy, can you spare a dime for a cup of coffee?"

I knew that phony gravelly voice immediately. "Whitey, how the hell did you get here?"

"I took the subway, whaddyuh think?"

"What happened to you?"

"You won't believe it. The super gave me some drums that somebody left in the basement after they moved out. I set them up and I was playing the freakin' drums! I wasn't bad."

"Yeah, well, you probably almost got fired on the first day."

Whitey gave me a look like, *Who made you king for a day?*

"Where's the senior boys? I have to check in."

"The guy with the Beatle haircut is the camp director, you better check in with him."

"He looks more like Moe Howard than John Lennon."

"That's him."

Whitey pushed his hair forward. "Groovy."

I was surprised Whitey was assigned to the senior boys since he would be only a year older than some of them. But I must admit he looked a lot older than they did. Maybe it was the thick black glasses, or his chunkiness. He looked a lot older since his brother got killed.

We were only on the ferry for about thirty seconds when I started to notice a couple of the midget boys getting that drained, woozy look on their faces. We practically shoved Bobby Finnegan into a garbage can on the lower deck when he started puking. Fortunately it didn't start a chain reaction. When we reached the dock of the island where the Statue of Liberty stood, the clouds seemed to open and the rays of the sun blasted us with some warmth.

It looked as though every day camp and summer school in New York City was on line to enter the statue, which from up close looked like a towering green asparagus. It seemed like every few steps we inched closer to the entrance, the temperature went up a little. By the time we were actually inside, on that narrow spiral staircase that wound and wound and wound up and up and up with the gigantic metal statue heating up like a monkey wrench sitting on a driveway in the sun, I just knew we were in for disaster.

Going up wasn't so bad, but by the time we reached the top, which wasn't even the tippy top, but just a small platform where you could peek out a porthole for two seconds before you headed back down, disaster was upon us. We were literally spiraling downward into deep doo doo. I could hear kids below and above barfing. The steps were wet with substances of assorted colors and textures that I didn't even want to imagine what orifice they came from. Girls were shrieking in terror, boys were laughing in hysterics and every few landings a uniformed security guard would tell us to keep moving.

We all reconnoitered on the lawn gasping for air, thankful to be out of the dark, stinky tower. I couldn't help think that some things are just better when viewed from afar.

Maybe it was because the kids had nothing left in them, but I didn't see anybody hurl during the ferry back to Manhattan. Once off the boat, I could see all the girl counselors rushing Charles, the director. With wagging fingers, and using girl campers with soiled clothing as props, there were shouts of many variations of "Whose stupid idea was this?" Charles played with his long hair nervously and took it all without offering much in rebuttal, as the crowd of angry females around him grew larger and louder.

Some kids sat on the bus by themselves because of the stink on them, so the other bus seats were packed with four or five campers each. Once the bus pulled out and headed for the highway, Jerry stood up with his wiffle ball bat and started banging the vinyl bench.

"Okay, campers, here we go... One, two, three... Boom! Boom!"

The entire bus, boys, girls, campers, counselors and the bus driver all knew what was coming, and all joined in the song:

Boom! Boom! Ain't it great to be cray-zee! Boom! Boom! Ain't it great to be cray-zee! Old King Cole was a merry old soul, a merry old soul was he. He tried to get to heaven on a telephone pole, his right foot slipped and his left foot fell. Instead of going to heaven he went to hell! Boom boom! Ain't it great to be crazy!

As loud as the busload of campers was already singing, they gave "hell" an extra blast of high octane volume. The midget boys especially delighted in using the curse word so openly. Jerry sat back down and tapped me with the bat, leaving the song direction to the girl counselors in back.

"What happened to your pal this morning? He's Shelley, right?"

"Yeah, Whitey Shelley. I don't know. He was late and took the subway down."

"It's a good thing he did, or his ass would have been fired. You better tell him to get on the stick if he wants to keep his job. That's too bad about his brother. Jesus."

I didn't reply. I just gazed at the giant skyscrapers that we passed as we headed back to the Bronx, and wondered what it would be like to be rich enough to actually live in one of those buildings, or important enough to work in one of them. A tap on my shoulder from Griffith brought me back to reality.

"My grandpa learned us a song. Can I teach it to everybody so we can sing it next time?"

I tapped Jerry on his shoulder.

"Griffith wants to teach the campers a song his grandfather taught him."

Jerry rolled his eyes. "Sing it to us first. Quietly."

Griffith leaned in. "The little marine he grew and grew, parley-voo. The little marine he grew and grew, parley-voo. The little marine

57

he grew and grew, and now he's screwing a woman, too! Hinkey dinkey parley-voo!"

Jerry held up his wiffle ball bat menacingly and tried to talk through his guffaws. "Griffith, don't let me ever hear you sing that again! Now get out of here!"

Griffith chuckled proudly as he went back to his seat.

"Well, now we know who he gets his sense of humor from," Jerry said, still laughing.

The singing, cheering, and chattering continued all the way through Manhattan and right into the school yard. We took our places back in the auditorium and Charles recited a quick Our Father and a Hail Mary over the unsettled group and after the Amen, dismissed us.

Whitey and I walked up the hill towards our buildings, trying to ignore the campers who were pestering us. He explained why he was late, and how his mom needed some help with some stuff around the house that morning because she was going upstate to the lake.

"I told Father O. that my mom needed some help and I lost track of the time. He was nice to me after that. In fact, he gave me two tokens out of his pocket. He asked me about my brother Alfie."

"Where is Alfie?"

"He's back at the farm upstate."

I knew it wasn't a real farm. It's the farm where people go to get off alcohol and drugs. Father O. helped get Alfie up there the first time he went, so he probably helped him again.

Chapter Five

— **Now** —

After living in Los Angeles for a while you can't help but become nostalgic for your memories of the good old days in New York riding the subway. It's like when my mom was elderly and I used to talk to her about what a selfish brat I was as a teenager; she always got that shocked look on her face and said, "You were always such a good boy. You graduated with honors from college!" Somehow, she managed to delete from her memory the fact that I was also a lazy, beer drinking, skirt chasing, pot smoking, self-centered moron who was a lot luckier than he was smart and disciplined.

I didn't think twice about taking the subway to this morning's job interview in midtown Manhattan. I took the subway to high school for four years, then college for four years after that, and every day for the few years I worked in New York before I left for the car-crazed land of Los Angeles. Just like riding a bicycle, I had my subway legs. Not to mention that I took the subway at all hours of the night back to the Bronx after crazy all-night parties, after-hours clubs, and bed-ins with girls from all five boroughs, without a second thought. I was a subway veteran.

It took exactly three stops on the number one IRT elevated train to bring back the reality of why I immediately took to the joy of riding to work in my own climate-controlled, custom CD music-filled transportation module known as a car once I moved to L.A.

Having entered the subway car at the beginning of the line at West 242nd Street and Broadway, I sat down with my morning paper, comfortable on an empty bench. By 225th Street the car was filled to capacity with sweaty bodies that reeked of cheap perfume and after-shave if you were lucky, or stank of all kinds of mysterious body odors if you weren't so fortunate. Not being a total prick, I offered my seat to an old Puerto Rican lady with a three-year-old boy in tow. So there I was, jostling back and forth with all of New York pressing and pushing against me with every turn, screeching stop, and herky-jerky acceleration. As bad as I had it, I felt sorry for the hot-looking young girls who immediately attracted some kind of pervert who made extra efforts to press up against them whether the car was in motion or not.

Having worked for each of the four major television broadcast networks during my twenty or so years in the business, I felt like working for a small local cable channel was a comedown. But a job was a job and working for *NYNow!*, a New York City-centric cable news operation, would have to do.

I thought the gentleman who met me at the reception desk was perhaps a college intern, but in fact he was the H.R. guy who would be interviewing me. Walking through the maze of cubbyhole work stations, I felt like I was in a college library, the employees looked so young.

We sat down in a room about the size of the closet in my old office, in which I stashed my golf clubs and liquor. The H.R. guy began to explain all this corporate Dilbert-esque bullshit about integrity, self-motivation, conflict of interest, transparency, six sigma, and trust, and then asked for my social security number to do a credit check. When I asked how much it paid, he looked at me as if I had asked him how many times a week he masturbated. He said they didn't discuss that on first interviews. I knew then that the salary was even less than I anticipated.

After I filled out a form the H.R. child brought me back through the workstation maze to a cubbyhole in the middle. I was introduced to the only other guy in the place who might be old enough to remember watching Johnny Carson on the *Tonight Show*. I noticed my resume sitting on his desk, next to what appeared to be an enormous manuscript. Wedged between his desk and the gray fabric of his cubicle wall was an electric guitar case.

"So you're a writer, too? The name's Mal Gurney. Call me Mal," he said, with an eager smile on his face and a hint of sausage on his breath.

He explained that he worked in television news for thirty years and for each of the major networks, and after a trying his luck as a freelance writer, merely took this job for the benefits.

"I see the name of your book is *Sewer Balls*. *Sewer Balls*? That sounds gross! Is that a medical condition?" he asked, bursting into laughter.

"Actually, sewer balls are the balls we retrieved from the sewer when we didn't enough money to buy a spaldeen..."

"Is it a novel?" he asked, interrupting me.

"Yes."

A wide self-satisfied grin stretched below his bulbous nose, which some black nose hairs protruded from. He had a large gap between his two front teeth. "Seven hundred pages. My baby," he said, patting the six-inch pile of paper. "This novel will blow the lid off the news business."

He described an epic tale of a young idealistic newsman speaking truth to power, a lone voice of sanity in a world gone mad, big corporations trying to stifle dissent. The protagonist was also a kickass lead guitar player.

"I'll look over your resume, but I'll tell you right now, the pay is probably what you made twenty years ago. But if you work here for a year, you get full benefits. I'd like to have somebody with your... experience on board. Do you have an agent? I mean for your writing, not for this job, obviously."

"I'm between agents."

"Hmm," he grunted. "Okay, not a problem."

"By the way, what exactly is the position available?"

"Assistant assignment editor on the news desk."

"Great," I said, remembering how that in fact was my first job in TV.

It was late morning when I arrived back at the West 238th Street elevated subway station after my morning interview, and on a whim decided to see who the bar patrons might be on a weekday morning.

I looked in the barred window of the Goal Post through the Guinness neon sign and saw the owner, Terrence, watching horse racing with an old man at the end of the bar.

61

They glanced at me briefly as I walked towards them and took a stool a few over from the old man.

"What'll you have?"

"Bud in a bottle. No glass. I don't know if you remember me..."

"Now I do. *Sewer Balls*," he said, cracking a rare smile. "Matt, it's the *Sewer Balls* guy."

The old man at the end of the bar turned to me. His baseball hat, which had a Yankees logo in the center with an FD on the left side of it and a PD on the right side, was pulled so low that his eyes were barely visible. I grabbed my bottle and moved two stools over, right next to him.

"I read that book. Good book. I knew your family."

I concentrated on his face, which had no color at all, except for what looked to be a bruise healing just below the rim of his hat. His skin was as white as toilet paper and looked just as thin. Then it hit me. Matthew O'Malley! He'd lived in the basement of my apartment building.

"I remember you, Matt. Nice to see you," I said, extending my hand. There was no strength at all in his handshake. His hand felt cold and bony, like a corpse.

Soon we were talking about all the guys from way back in the day, most of whom seemed to be dead, dying or living upstate somewhere. Terrence the barkeep was actually a relative newcomer, having only owned the bar for fifteen or so years. Matt, on the other hand, had been at his position under the television at the end of the bar for forty years or more.

"Are you still living in the basement apartment?"

"Yup. Our family has had that apartment for seventy years," he said with pride. "I'm the only one living there now. I heard you were out in Los Angeles."

"Yup," I said, not wanting to get into my life story.

"Hey! If you ever bump into Joe Torre out there, you tell him he owes me a jacket. Back in high school, my cousin in Brooklyn dated him and we were at a party and I lent him my Ike jacket. Remember those Ike jackets, Terrence?"

Terrence frowned as he nodded in agreement.

"We're the same age," Matt said.

"You and Eisenhower?"

"No, me and Joe Torre."

I didn't do a spit take, but I could have. Joe Torre looks like he could still play major league baseball. Poor Matt looks like he's a few boilermakers from total organ failure. He went on to explain how each of his siblings moved out of the neighborhood and how his dad passed away but his mother was living upstate by one of his sisters.

"My dad was eighty-nine when he passed," he said, taking a sip of whiskey with a beer chaser. "Good ticker he had. I guess I'm lucky I've got good genes!" He still had a charming smile, despite the fact that it revealed the poor state of his oral hygiene.

I wasn't keen on letting everybody in the neighborhood know that I was trying to track down Whitey, but there aren't many people around who have been on the block for as long as Matt has. When Terrence was at the other end of the bar, I asked Matty, "Do you remember the Shelleys?"

"Oh, yes. Tragic, it was, when Brian fell to his death."

"Ever hear what happened to his youngest brother, Whitey?"

"Whitey? Oh, didn't you know? He died years ago in a hunting accident upstate."

I didn't believe it. There were so many rumors floating around. Plus, a hunting accident? He cried when he hit a pigeon with a bottle by accident, and then he nursed it back to health. Nope. Whitey was no hunter. "I heard a lot of things about Whitey, but not that."

"He worked here for a while before Terrence bought the place. After he got back from Viet Nam he had a nice little business going. He had an old van and he'd do all the buying for the local bars and restaurants down at Hunts Point at three, four in the morning. It was a tidy little gig for him until the incident. He knew his meats and veggies, he did."

I nonchalantly took a sip from my bottle, not wanting to show my excitement upon discovering these tidbits of information. "What went down with that incident?"

Matt stuck his lower jaw out and his eyes tightened with suspicion as he took another swig of Jameson. He looked over at Terrence, who shot him a similar stare fraught with warning. "All I know is what I read in the paper," he said, making it clear that was the end of that by placing his drink down next to the Yankees coaster, and making a thud on the ancient wood bar.

They both were pleasant enough, but I could tell I was digging a little too deep for their liking. I left with polite handshakes after another beer. I shouldn't forget that there's a loyalty to people from the block that, for many, goes beyond God and country. I know from other trips back to these bars that cops hang out with Mafia-connected bookies, drug dealers, judges and priests. But if you grew up with someone, you don't rat them out. In fact, the bond that binds you isn't what you do for a living, but how you proved to your friends that you were like a brother before you were even old enough to drink.

Getting to the bottom of Whitey's incident was going to be more challenging that I thought. I had a location, Hunts Point, and a rough time period, probably the mid-seventies. A little research in the local newspapers would be my next step. Hitting some more bars for additional clues also seemed like a good idea. But after stops in four more gin mills, I didn't see anyone who I thought might have any more information on Whitey, and I was a little too drunk to drive back to my sister's.

It was five o'clock, and I was dressed like many of the men getting off the train at 238th Street. I headed back to the Goal Post and sure enough the bar was full with men just off work, and a few women, with Terrence busy and Matt still at the end of the busy bar, but alone. I dropped two twenties next to Matt and ordered myself a Jameson and whatever Matt wanted. He was all smiles again. I was buzzed. Maybe I'd have better luck this time. Our conversation jumped from sports to politics to the Dominican drug dealer standing on the corner, and Matt steadier and more articulate as I babbled like a binging college kid. I tried to focus and follow his system for the horses and blackjack, his theory that Osama bin Laden was an agent for the Mossad, and how abandoned subway stations and tunnels in New York could be turned into luxury condominiums.

I stood up, downed two fingers of whiskey and grabbed the oak lip of the bar like the safety bar in a roller coaster car. Going over the words in my head to finally ask Matt about Whitey and the "incident," I turned in his direction, only to see two blurry images of him. I gripped the bar tighter, closed my eyes and sat back down. The room wasn't spinning, which was a good sign. I opened my eyes and thank God, there was only one of Matt, drinking another tumbler of whiskey from my money pile.

"What ... happened to Whitey at Hunts Point?"

Matt put his drink down and licked his chops, deep in thought. "Like I told you before..."

I held onto the bar, concentrating, knowing full well I was bombed, but hoping I could at least comprehend and retain this one nugget of information.

"I only know what I read in the paper. A black man was murdered and a white man with glasses who drove off in a van was a suspect. Just what was in the papers, that's all."

Terrence poured him another, finishing off my pile of cash.

Matt picked up the drink and drank half. A bit of rose was finally coming into his cheeks. "We never saw him again after that day's paper."

I put a fiver on the bar and said good-bye. I somehow managed to get a cab back to Bronxville, and the first thing I did after avoiding falling down the stairs into my basement lair was write to on a piece of paper, M*urder at Hunts Point. Never seen again.* I felt proud of myself that I was able to undress, brush my teeth, and not throw up. I looked at the clock and it was just past nine. The room stopped spinning and I slept.

It took a good hour for my phone to charge the next morning, and the voicemail alert beeped as I tried to convince myself that the pounding in my head was a small price to pay for the information I'd received the night before. *NYNow!* wanted me back to fill out some forms, which meant another subway ride downtown and possibly a firm job offer. I poured my third cup of coffee, and promised myself I wouldn't take another detour to the Goal Post.

I felt like I was in a cocktail shaker all the way to Times Square, and when I passed a bum's fresh and stinky puke pile on the subway stairs and didn't barf myself, I thankfully knew I was recovered from the night before.

There was no negotiation. I would get the starter's freelance rate of $125 dollars a day, no benefits, work from three until midnight, with an unpaid hour for lunch, and I could start the next day. It wasn't merely the best offer I had received after sending scores of job applications, it was the only one. At the very least, it would give me some money, a place to go, and access to the internet. How could I say no?

"Welcome to my nightmare!" Mal sang, strumming his Stratocaster, plugged into a Pignose amp. "You'll start tomorrow?"

"Yes, sir," I said, faking my enthusiasm.

"This will be great. When you have some time, I want you to look over my manuscript. Just for general overall feelings. Not to copy edit or anything."

I gazed at the tower of paper already boxed with my name on it, and I so dreaded the very idea of it that I nearly quit on the spot. "Uh, sure. That'd be fine," I lied, hoping he would forget, or maybe the building would burn and the manuscript would be lost in a fire.

"If you're not into hard copy, I already have it on disc for you," he announced joyfully as he handed me a computer disc.

"Um, great."

"Let me show you your cubicle," Mal said, putting his guitar down.

When I first worked in a newsroom, it was like a noisy arena with a boxing match going on. There were no cubbyholes or carpeted

66

walls separating workers. It was just a big room strewn with heavy wooden desks all pointing towards the assignment desk, and the big board overhead where all the assignments for the day were written in colorful markers, with snide commentary on each story. Here there wasn't really a newsroom at all. It looked like any other office space in corporate America with its gray and wheat décor and young people sitting in front of computers wearing telephone headphones.

"Here's your space," Mal said, pointing to a tiny five-by-five patch that looked haphazardly added on to the series of other cubicles, putting me three feet from the ladies' room.

"Where's the assignment desk?"

Mal took a pen from his pocket protector and pointed at the computer screen sitting on the flimsy Ikea composite-board workstation. "You're looking at it. Everything is done from computer work stations. Assignments, scripts, research, even rolling in of segments and commercials. There's the director, right over there," he said, pointing to a young man wearing a backwards baseball hat adorned with Che Guevara, sitting in a cubicle not much larger than the one we were standing in, typing on his computer keyboard. "The assignment editor is over on the other side of the room. You can introduce yourself tomorrow. Oops, I've got to run, see you tomorrow. Don't be late!"

Mal cut his way through the maze of cubbyholes and disappeared. I walked around the large windowless room, and although I heard voices speaking, no one seemed to be talking to each other. Everyone was talking into their headsets. The ones that didn't have headsets on had earbuds plugged into iPods or iPhones. Not one person looked at me as I wandered the worn carpet that wound through the workplace. You couldn't call this a newsroom, I thought.

The main branch of the New York Public Library was a ten-minute walk away, another plus for my new job. I had a feeling that finding Whitey might involve poring through old news stories to put together some leads.

67

I stood at the bottom of the steps and looked up at the magnificent marble building which will probably stand as a majestic monument on this corner for a thousand years. But then again, I once thought that about the original Yankee Stadium.

The walnut-paneled periodical research room was filled with readers. I was amazed that they still had microfiche machines whirling away. When I asked the elderly lady behind the desk how to go about researching New York newspapers from the seventies, she politely reminded me that I would need a valid New York Public Library card and handed me an application. It suddenly hit me that I had been away from New York for twenty years, and never even got a Los Angeles library card. All my research was done from my computer.

My temporary card was issued and I started with Googling murders in the Hunts Point section of the South Bronx starting in 1970. Over five million news article hits popped up. I decided tomorrow would be a good time to start. Maybe a few more drinks on 238th Street would help loosen some more lips.

The afternoon after-work crowd was beginning to fill the bars on 238th Street. Matt wasn't at his usual place under the TV at the end of the bar. Terrence simply said he should be returning any minute. I decided to have a bourbon on the rocks and wait. On my second refill I noticed a loudmouthed guy about my age wearing a Cardinal Farley sweatshirt – my old high school. I couldn't help but hear him bitching and moaning about working in a restaurant. There was a break in the action when the patrons around him got bored and stared blankly at Judge Judy on the screen.

"You went to Farley?" I asked.

"Yeah. You?"

"Yeah."

"I don't live around here anymore. I'm out on the island. I come back every once in a while to catch up. I'm semi-retired."

We traded small talk about some guys and teachers from high school, and before I knew it, I couldn't get a word in edgewise. I had to hear about how rich his ex-wife's family was even though he didn't get a dime, and every detail about the Argentinean restaurant he semi-worked at in Massapequa.

He held his arms out wide. "I get this box from the delivery van and in huge red block letters it says *NOT FOR HUMAN CONSUMPTION*. I could tell it's filled with animal parts of some kind. I turn around and there's the owner of the restaurant standing behind me, he's a friend of mine, and he says, 'Hold the box the other way around and give it to the chef.' So I give it to the chef, and it starts dumping the whole box of who the hell knows what kind of monkey meat and horse anus into pots of boiling water. If you knew what went on in restaurant kitchens you'd never eat out again."

"So what were they making?"

"A stew. To tell you the truth, I don't give a shit what kind of meat it was, it was fucking delicious."

I sensed he felt comfortable shooting his mouth off to the old-timers in the bar, so he must have some history around here. Maybe in the restaurant business. I offered to buy him a drink. There was an empty bottle of Budweiser in front of him, but he asked for a double of Johnny Walker Black.

"Did you work in any restaurants around here, back in the day?"

"Oh, yeah. During high school, after high school, during college, after I dropped out of college."

"Do you remember a guy named Whitey Shelley?"

He put his drink down and for the first time since I saw him standing there, he became pensive.

"Whitey. Yeah. He helped me out a few times. We were buying meat for Gallagher's Steak House. Nam vet. Funny guy."

"You mean...strange?"

"Strange?" he asked incredulously. "No. Hilarious! He had me laughing my ass off. Too bad about him."

I didn't want to jump on his words too quickly. I took a few sips of bourbon and stared at Judge Judy who was scolding some sleazy dirtball, "Don't pee on my leg and complain that it's raining."

"Yeah. How did that happen?"

"How did what happen?" he asked me, like he was responding to a Judge Judy accusation.

"His...Hunts Point...incident."

"Are you like a cop or something? Internal Affairs?"

"What? No. Just an old friend."

"Well, if you were a friend, you'd know not to ask certain questions."

He downed the rest of his Johnny Walker and turned from me. After about thirty seconds he was pestering the people on the other side of the bar with his big mouth, kvetching non-stop about any annoyance he could think of.

I could see Terrence watching him out of the corner of his eye. He approached me while wiping a glass clean. "I wouldn't suggest discussing anything of a personal nature with that big-mouthed buffoon. I knew Whitey. He worked with my brother at Gallagher's. He disappeared after the incident. He had to. They tried to kill him afterwards. It was self-defense. But try to tell that to an all-black jury in the Bronx. That's all I know. That's all anyone needs to know."

He nodded and walked away. A woman who looked to be in her sixties, with bleached blonde hair and missing a front tooth, stumbled into me on the way to the ladies' room. "You're not Matty!"

"No, I'm not."

"Who are you?"

"I'm, ah, just a customer."

"Oh, go fuck yourself, asshole."

On that note, I figured maybe it was time to just shut my mouth. I walked over to the jukebox, which wasn't really a jukebox at all. It was really just a computer designed to look like a jukebox. You fed your dollars into it and it accessed virtually any song from any band from the past forty years. Terrence had the volume so low on the jukebox that you could make out Judge Judy's insults over it. More than likely that was because Terrence didn't particularly care for the musical choices his diverse clientele punched up: disco hits followed by gangster rap followed by the Irish Rovers.

70

"This fucking sucks," the sixty-something lass said as she pushed against me at the jukebox. "We used to rock in here. Now we hear all this rap shit."

She was sloppy drunk. The bright lights from the LCD computer screens lit her up her face. It was easy to see she had once been a beauty. High cheek bones and almost Asian blue eyes complemented a symmetrical classic Irish face, now ravaged by time, alcohol and cigarettes, which she had one of in her mouth as she talked despite the fact that it was illegal to smoke in bars. She sidled up closer to me and her bar-breath knocked me back a foot or two. She grabbed my arm and pulled herself right up to me.

"When your fucking buddy was in charge of the jukebox, he made this place rock!"

"Who's my buddy?"

"I heard you and fuckface yapping. Whitey, ass-wipe. He fuckin' had this place rocking. Beatles, Stones, The Who, Ramones, Allmans, Skynyrd." She threw her arms in the air and began bumping her hip into mine to the rap beat playing. "It's a fucking goddamned crime he had to split. Fuck that nigger, he deserved it." She grabbed my arm again, spilling some of my drink. As she released me, she pinched my ass, shot me a coquettish smile, winked and sashayed back to her stool. I guess I still got it.

Even though my brain was clouded by bourbon and beer, I knew this was a good time to find my way home.

Chapter Six

--Then--

There was a big announcement at camp first thing Monday morning. Charles, the director, said that Father O. was leaving his job in the parish to become a prison chaplain, but that he would continue to live in the rectory. He said a new priest was taking over Father O.'s duties, named Father Quiogue. And right on cue, a guy who looked like a college kid comes out from the wings of the stage, except he's wearing a priest's collar, so he isn't any college kid. But he had long hair that was pushed behind his ears like the Beach Boys. And he was wearing sandals with white socks. His smile was so wide he looked like the Joker. But his eyes didn't seem to smile. Then his smile disappeared.

"Hello. I'm Father Quiogue. And it's a pleasure to be here in Presentation parish and especially here in day camp. I just want you to know that we are going to keep having fun this summer! Thanks!"

And just like that he was gone. And so was Father O.

The next few days of camp were marred by lousy weather. Whitey seemed to be the last one on the bus every day, sometimes banging on the bus driver's window as it started rolling away without him. We visited pretty much every museum in New York City and a couple in Yonkers. The only good thing about our inclement weather schedule was that it allowed us to really get to know the campers as we sat in the auditorium for a couple of hours, eating our lunches early, while we waited for the museums to open. Oh yeah, we got to know the other counselors, too. I mean, the girl counselors. Especially Josephine O'Bryne.

I tried hard not to stare at Josephine. Yeah, she wore baggy plaid madras shorts that almost went below her knees, and that silly sailor hat, and the baggy counselor shirt must have been a men's extra large. But she couldn't hide the fact that those emerald eyes sparkled from one end of the bus to the other. How when she ate red licorice sticks her lips were redder than an old-fashioned World War II pin-up girl's. And no matter how big and baggy those shirts were, those glorious boobs bounced with every pothole on the Major Deegan Expressway. I couldn't wait for the sun to break through so we would finally go to the beach and I could see her in a bathing suit.

It was misting slightly, so although it wasn't a beach day, a trip to the Bronx Zoo was a welcome outdoor activity. Once again, Whitey was on another bus and I was on the same bus as Josephine. She wasn't a head counselor but she was definitely the most popular among the girl campers. She knew every pattycake hand rhyme, led all the sing-alongs, and sang the words to all the scratchy, skipping 45s playing on the portable record player. And I certainly knew why she was popular with the guys.

Our busloads were to stick together as a group when we toured the zoo, so Whitey and I were again separated for the day. Jerry, my head counselor, wasn't one for keeping up with the manic activities of the midget boys, so on those outings I was the fast-moving wrangler who had to herd them along. But this day, I had an extra strategy as I pushed them through the crowd: to merge with the senior girls' group. And Josephine.

The instant we entered the majestic building that housed the lions, everyone "peeew"ed at the strong odor of the wild animals, from the excrement and urine that had yet to be cleaned up. Josephine held her nose and scrunched her face grotesquely, so of course all the girls did the same. It appeared that whatever she did, her campers followed.

After lunch we hit the campers' favorite spot in the zoo, the chimpanzee house. The boys and girls screamed and giggled with glee with the antics of the chimps as they jumped from tires suspended on ropes, fake trees, and giant boulders. I was at the railing, just two brats away from Josephine, who was enjoying the chimp as much as the five-year-olds, her green eyes sparkling, her white teeth glistening in her open-mouthed smile. Without turning my head too much, I was soaking in as much of her as I could without being too obvious. Suddenly, her jaw snapped shut, her eyes popped wide open and her hand shot up to hold onto the top of her hat. An ear splitting cacophony of cackles, screams and laughter shot through the crowd. I looked into the chimp cage and two chimps had begun screwing right in front of us! I looked back at Josephine and for the first time in the two weeks of camp, she looked me straight in the eye and didn't turn away. Her look of shock slowly became an embarrassed smile that lasted all of two seconds before she screamed, "All girl campers follow me! Now!" and ran out backwards pulling all the girls with her.

We rendezvoused for lunch at a picnic grove under majestic trees, some familiar, others strangely exotic. The sounds of the campers blended perfectly with the nearby noises of the monkey house. I sat on the bench of the picnic table with half of our group crowded together, while Jerry sat in the folding director's chair that he'd brought along, next to the rest of the midget mob. I bit into my baloney sandwich and a large brown paper bag slammed onto the scarred table plank in front of me.

"Make room for Whitey!"

"Whitey! Squeeze in, guys! Don't you have to sit with your group?"

"Nah. They're too busy stuffing their faces."

As Whitey shifted his butt to make room on the bench, a kid fell off the other end. "Sorry, kid," Whitey lamented. He reached into his brown paper bag, pulled out an unwrapped jaw breaker, and threw it to him as an apology. It hit the dirt right next to the kid, who picked it up and popped it into his mouth.

I leaned in and whispered, "Did you hear what happened at the chimp house?"

"Yeah, I heard the zookeeper thought you escaped from the cage and he tried to put you back in," Whitey said, munching on a huge salami hero.

"You won't believe this…" I whispered even softer.

Little Griffith chimed right in, "Two chimpanzees were fucking right in front of us! It was neat!"

"Griffith, go sit at the other end!" I said, tapping him on the back of his head.

74

Whitey nearly choked to death as he laughed through the layers of salami, provolone, and crisp Italian bread stuffed in his mouth.

"And guess who was right next to me as they humped away with their chimp boobs bouncing?"

"Sister Mary Ferris Wheel? I don't know."

"Josephine."

"Holy crap! You must have flipped! What did she do?"

"All the girls were screaming like they were being raped. But Josephine..."

"Yeah, what, what?"

"She..."

"What, what?"

"Looked at me."

"Yeah? How?"

"She smiled."

Whitey shook his head, swallowed a huge mouthful of hero, and gulped down half a bottle of Nehi orange with a look of total bliss across his face. "She smiled? Wow. Maybe she likes you."

"You think?" I asked, almost trembling at the thought of such a thing.

Griffith poked his head between us. "Can we watch the polar bears fuck after lunch?"

Whitey went back to the senior boys, and our midget boys merged once again with the senior girls as we snaked through the zoo and took in the sights. I couldn't help but steal glimpses of Josephine whenever possible. Every step she took, every laugh or screech when an animal lurched, captivated me. I would position the boys so I could get a little closer to her. I didn't even know what the hell creature was in the walled area in front of us, because I was concentrating on her. I noticed that if she lifted her arms a certain way you could sort of see into her sleeve and almost see the side of her bra, but not quite. And if the sun broke through briefly and shined on her shirt, you could see the outline of her bra strap in the back. And when she knelt down to tie a girl's shoelace, her shirt lifted up and I caught a flash of flesh from behind. I noticed that her black ponytail, which was thick and reached almost to her ass, had amazing shiny highlights when the sun poked through the clouds. And she had freckles on her left calf that that would have made a star if you connected them. When she smiled the dimple on her left side was slightly higher than the one on the right.

"Do you like Josephine?" a female voice asked from behind.

I turned, expecting to see one of the girl counselors, but instead, there was a small gum-chewing blonde, a freckle-faced skinny girl wearing a sailor hat, baggy camper shirt and plaid madras shorts. In essence, a miniature blonde version of Josephine.

"We can tell you like her," she said, motioning to a nearby group of mini-Josephines of assorted ethnicities who were huddled together and giggling.

"What do you mean *like*?" I said nervously, knowing I'd been busted.

"You know," she said, blowing a small pink bubble that she popped and sucked back into her mouth. "And did you know there's somebody who likes *you*?"

"I can't talk now, I have to... take a head count of the midgets. What's your name?"

"Betty Ann."

"Maybe I like blondes."

"Unggghhh," she grunted as she walked away. "Boys!"

I didn't so much as glance at Josephine for the rest of the day. Well, except for the one time where I was hiding next to a large dumpster by the men's room. From there I could see her as she actually rode an elephant! None of the campers were allowed to ride it, but the counselors chipped in for Josephine's ride and half the camp cheered her on as she mounted the giant pachyderm. The rocking motion of Josephine on top of that monster, her embarrassed glee, her legs spread as far apart as they could go, made me hide behind there even after she finished her ride; I had to wait for the bulge in my pants to go down, which I didn't think would ever happen.

I tried to ignore her on the warm bus ride back to the auditorium for dismissal, but I had to steal a glance whenever I could. Charles took the stage for an announcement. "There's been a change in tomorrow's activities. We are not going to the transit museum. The weatherman says it's going to be hot and sunny, so the entire camp is going to Jones Beach! Bring your bathing suits! Camp dismissed!"

The room reverberated with girls' squeals and boys' cheers. I knew it would be the day Whitey and I had been waiting for. We'd get to see Josephine in a bathing suit. Somebody tugged on my shorts.

"I hope we get to see some tits," Griffith deadpanned.

Jerry hit him in the ass with the yellow wiffle ball bat, shouting, "I heard that, Griffith!" Griffith laughed maniacally and walked away, dragging his camp bag behind him.

The weatherman was right. It was probably going to be a scorcher the next day, because it was already hot that night. Whitey had bumped into Billy Fricker who said he was going to take his telescope to the roof of his building because it was so clear, and he invited us along. Having just been to the Hayden Planetarium at the Museum of Natural History, both Whitey and I considered ourselves expert astronomers.

After sunset, Whitey and I met at the side entrance to Fricker's building where there was an alleyway. It was pitch black, with broken glass and trash strewn around and the occasional rat scampering by, making it a perfect place for us to meet. We sat on two old milk crates, probably put there by teenagers years ago. Whitey pulled out a pack of Marlboros and lit one up.

"You want one?" he asked, holding the pack out for me.

"Um, no," I said, instantly recalling the time my parents caught me smoking when I was in the first grade, and took turns beating the hell out of me. "My throat's a little scratchy. Where'd you get those?"

"Where'd I get them? Snookey's. Why?"

"They sold them to you?"

"Are you kidding? I've been buying smokes there for my old man and my brothers since kindergarten."

"Where are we meeting Fricker?"

"He told me to wait for him here." Whitey took a deep drag on his cigarette, giving his face an eerie red glow. He smoked like a grown-up.

We heard footsteps coming around the back of the building towards us. I recognized the strange clicking sound immediately as the taps on Billy Fricker's shoes. Originally, local shoemakers put small metal taps on cheap heels so they wouldn't wear out so quickly. When the Beatles and the Four Seasons made Italian pointy shoes the rage, which we called "cockroach-in-the-corner crushers," all the kids wanted taps because they sounded cool. But Fricker wore taps on his wing tips. Not cool. Even in the dark you could see the white line his part made on his scalp, it was so straight and perfect. I realize he's only a couple of years older than we are, but his hair style and clothes are right out of those corny Mickey Rooney Andy Hardy movies that fill air time on Saturday mornings.

The clicking footsteps stopped right in front of us.

"Let's go," he said, holding a long cardboard box with a piece of twine tied around it.

We followed him to the heavy steel door that led into his basement. He reached into his pocket, pulled out a key ring that must have had a hundred keys on it, flipped to the proper one and unlocked the door. It was darker than a closed coffin until Fricker pulled a string hanging from the ceiling and a low-watt bulb came on. As it swung there, it created bizarre moving shadows of us on the walls. He led us down the corridor, pushed the button for the elevator and we entered.

Fricker was silent and creepy, making me feel as though he was Bella Lugosi and we were Bud and Lou in *Abbott and Costello Meet Frankenstein*. That was, until the elevator bounced to a stop on the first floor and Mrs. Stanley, a skinny old Irish lady, got on with her three yapping oversized rat dogs.

"Hello, William. How are your parents?" Mrs. Stanley said, over the threatening sounds of the trio of terror desperately trying to nip our ankles.

"Just fine, Mrs. Stanley, thank you," Fricker said, transforming from Dracula into Eddie Haskell.

The elevator squeaked and bounced to a halt on the third floor. As she left she said, "There's no smoking in the elevator!"

Fricker transformed back into Bella Lugosi and gave Whitey the Dracula hypnotizing stare. "No smoking in the elevator."

Whitey rolled his eyes, dropped the cigarette onto the floor of the elevator, snuffing it out with the tip of his sneaker just as the elevator stopped on the sixth floor.

"Quiet!" Fricker whispered, as he led us to the end of the hall and a small, dark staircase littered with cigarette butts, beer cans, and candy wrappers.

"I think this is some of our trash left over from last winter," Whitey said softly in my ear.

Fricker pulled out his key ring and unlocked the heavy door, but it was stuck. "Help me push."

We put our shoulders to the door and Fricker said, "One, two, three!"

It popped open so quickly that Whitey and I went flying through and had to stop ourselves from crashing into the waist-high wall at the edge of the roof. Whitey nervously lit another cigarette. I knew what he was thinking; his brother fell to his death one building over from here. *I don't know if this is such a good idea,* I thought.

"Are you okay up here?" I asked Whitey.

"Yeah. Why shouldn't I be? Where'd Fricker go?"

He was nowhere to be seen. We tiptoed across the tar-papered roof and around the elevator machine room whispering his name. "Billy? Earth to Billy."

I started to feel pangs of terror as we searched behind another stairway entrance. "Nobody except Fricker knows we're up here. What if he's hiding and he's going to do something to us?"

"You mean like sending his rocket to Uranus? There's two of us. Don't be a pussy, huh? Wait. Hear that?"

I could hear a *shave and a haircut, two bits,* tapping noise. We walked over to the stairwell door we'd entered from, yanked it open, and there was Fricker.

79

"I couldn't get the door open. Follow me," he said, exasperated.

He rushed past us, walked around the elevator room and placed his long box next to the waist-high wall that faced due west. It was a spectacular view. A sliver of the moon was high in the northwest sky, and millions of stars were twinkling against the clear ink-black backdrop. Since the apartment building was already on top of a hill, being six stories higher meant we towered above all the buildings below, and even above the apartments in the hills of Riverdale, a good mile away. I inched closer to the wall, and looked straight down, which gave me a queasy feeling in my stomach. "Hey, I think that's Mr. Bourne down there walking his dog!"

"Holy shit, it can't be! Mr. Bourne and his dog? Let's call the *National* fucking *Enquirer!*" Whitey said, mocking me between draws on his Marlboro.

"Keep your voices down!" Fricker barked.

"Look at this. It's freaky," I said, amazed at the dizzying height.

Whitey stood a few feet behind Fricker, who was assembling the tripod for the telescope. I thought maybe Whitey didn't want to look six straight stories down and get the queasy feeling, so I didn't push it when he ignored me.

Once Fricker finally had the tripod assembled with the telescope mounted on top, he turned around slowly and folded his arms. The ambient light of the city sky gave him a creepy soft glow. "Before we get started, there's something you must agree to."

I knew Whitey was thinking the same thing I was. Whitey took his cigarette out of his mouth.

"Will we be looking at Uranus?"

I bit the inside of my lip, trying not to burst out laughing.

"You can't see Uranus with a telescope this small! But you have to agree that no matter what we see through this telescope, it will remain a secret. I have reason to believe that this evening, we may be visited by..." he paused and moved so close to us, I could smell his hair tonic, *"them."*

"Who's 'them'?" I asked.

He walked over to the telescope and stroked it. "The aliens. UFOs. I received a communication from them last night with instructions to study coordinates in the sky for... them. I shall begin searching," he said, as he put his eye to the scope and began peering through it. "You just watch the skies carefully and tell me if you see anything."

Whitey glanced over to me as he circled his index finger around his ear.

Fricker would look at his watch, then a slip of paper, then through the scope as he panned the night sky. "I think I see something behind Jupiter!"

"Are you sure it's not Uranus?" Whitey asked earnestly. I elbowed him in the ribs.

"No, Uranus is too far. Jupiter is where they come from. It's huge. Want to see it?" he asked, turning towards us.

"Really?" I asked.

"Yeah," Billy said, as he tightened a knob on the side of the tripod.

I looked first, and in the center was what looked like a large round star with small stars around it. "Is that Jupiter in the middle?"

"Yup. It has several moons around it which look like small stars."

Whitey looked, too, cigarette still in his mouth.

"Notice how it doesn't twinkle, like a star, but it has a defined round shape?"

"Yeah," Whitey said amazed, cigarette dangling. "Cool!"

Suddenly we heard footsteps, and we jerked our heads towards the stairwell door.

"William!" A fat bald man with thick glasses in a bathrobe stood there with a baseball bat. "It's time to walk Tinker Bell!"

"Aw, shucks, I'll be right back guys." Billy followed his father, leaving us with the telescope.

Whitey immediately went over to it, loosened the knob, and lowered it significantly as he panned the landscape.

"I want to see some *real* out of this world stuff," he said, aiming it at the apartment houses nearby.

"Let me see!"

"Wait your turn, junior!"

"This is great! A lot of windows are wide open because it's warm out! Oh, yeah! Pay dirt! Oh man! Wow! Ooh la la!"

"Let me see, let me see!"

Whitey tightened the knob and jumped aside. "Look quick."

I could already feel a tingle in my pants as I focused. Ewwww! There was a gross, hairy, fat guy in boxer shorts cleaning his ears with a Q-Tip in front of his bathroom mirror. "That is disgusting!" I said, laughing.

Whitey pushed me out of the way, and commandeered it again. "Give me. I thought I saw something else over here... Hey, look at this and tell me what you see."

"Let me see. What is it this time? A dog licking his balls?" I took the position and focused. "Is that Father Q.?"

Sitting on a couch in a room were two guys smoking from a long tube.

"What is that?"

"It's a bong. You smoke hash and pot with it. It looks like Father Q. Could it be?"

"I don't know," I said pushing the telescope aside. "Now what do we do?"

"We don't do shit. Don't tell anybody. Unless we need to," Whitey said.

Billy was back and out of breath. "Did you see anything?"

"Nah," we said in unison.

Billy began searching the sky again. "You never know what you'll find out there."

"Yeah," I replied glumly. "I think I have to go home."

"Me, too," Whitey said.

"Okay," Billy said, not taking his eye from the telescope. "You'll be sorry."

"Yeah, sorry," I said, jerking the door open with both hands.

"Do you really think that was Father Q. smoking pot?" Whitey asked as we leaped down the stairs two and three at a time.

"Should we tell somebody?" I replied, holding onto the rail as I whipped around to the next staircase.

"Are you crazy? First of all, we'd have to admit we were snooping with a telescope. And who the hell is going to believe us?"

We were exhausted by the time we raced to the bottom of the six flights, which added to our bewilderment. It was the warmest night since school had ended and the sounds and smells of the neighborhood apartments were oozing out of the open windows. As we strolled past ground floor apartments, you could hear Johnny Carson blabbering and babies crying, and you could smell sauerkraut boiling. The hotter it got, the more aware you became of people who you didn't even know existed. Some younger kids we didn't recognize ran by. A chubby Puerto Rican girl about our age walked her dog past us. A guy in a cool red and white '57 Chevy with a bad muffler stopped across the street, yelled something up at a window, and then peeled out. It was clear that the later you stayed out and the hotter it got, the more you found out about what was going on right on your own block.

"Should we see who's hanging out in the park?"

Whitey lit a cigarette without stopping as we walked towards Van Cortlandt Park.   "That's where we're headed, I guess."

The park had become the only place where kids our age and a little older could go until they looked old enough to hang out in bars. In the dark stretch of sidewalk just before the entrance to Vannie, Whitey stopped to open a pack of Marlboros and lit another. I knew it wouldn't be long before Whitey was one of those underage guys who looked old enough to hang out in bars.

"Seesaws or stands?" Whitey asked, pausing at the park gate.

"Seesaws," I answered, taking the left fork in the path. The stands usually had more kids, especially older ones. In fact, lately there were college kids and guys way older than eighteen hanging out there instead of in the bars. I heard that was because there were drugs. Which was why I was nervous about going there.

Whitey and I weren't strangers to the stands. We had a few crazy times there just before graduation. Too crazy – I almost got mugged, Whitey saved a guy from getting killed by Bobby Bailey, and the cops nearly busted the whole group of us. The seesaws were kind of like having training wheels.

Most of the lights in the park were busted by the older kids who preferred hanging out in total darkness. We walked through a playground where a couple was making out dead smack in the middle of the monkey bars tower. We could see four kids hanging out at the seesaws in the next playground and in the distance to the right we could see through the trees and the wrought iron fence that there was a pretty good crowd gathering in the stands.

As we got closer we could see it was two guys and two girls at the seesaws.

"I think it's Jimmy Joe, BB, Carrie and Donna," I said, stopping just before the hole in the fence. "Should we go over there?"

Whitey threw his cigarette down and squished it out. "Shit. They don't want to hang out with us anymore. All they want to do is dry hump. Come on, let's see what's happening in the stands," Whitey said coolly, lighting yet another cigarette and leading us towards a different hole in the fence.

I followed Whitey and immediately started to worry. Did I look cool enough? Was my hair too short? Too neat? Should I act tough? Should I keep my mouth shut? Was my walk cool? Maybe I should just go home. Then it was too late.

"Hey, it's Mutt and Jeff!"

I knew that raspy voice. Bobby Bailey's voice had a deep, hoarse Louis Armstrong quality usually reserved for middle-aged cigarette smoking whiskey drinkers, not Irish kids just out of grammar school.

"Fuck you, Froggy," Whitey shot back at the group, using the nickname that Bailey reviled, which incited raucous laughter from his beer-swilling buddies. Froggy was the frog-voiced, little four-eyed brat from the worst version of the *Little Rascals* after all of the original kids were kicked off because they couldn't hide their beards or tits anymore. Seeing Froggy in an episode meant an instant channel change.

I don't know where Whitey got his balls. When I heard that Mutt and Jeff line coming from Bailey, I was ready to cut and run because I'd seen him go apeshit on guys who used the Froggy moniker on him. And since Bobby Bailey isn't a tall guy (his growth probably stunted because he started smoking Luckys in the third grade), sucker punching, eye gouging, groin kicking, and car antennae whipping are his preferred methods for street fights. But for some reason, all Bailey could muster in return was a weak "Fuck you, Shelley," followed by chugging a can of Piels.

Once our eyes got used to the darkness, I counted only five guys hanging out, including Bailey. There was a dilapidated cardboard box filled with beer and melting ice, with the water dripping down the concrete steps of the football stands.

"Take a beer," a guy I didn't recognize said.

Whitey and I walked over to the box and pulled out two cans of Piels. Several steps above us, a guy was taking a leak against the wall at the top of the steps. I noticed that the stream of piss would probably soon join with the melting ice from the box.

With Bailey were two guys I had never seen before, plus Mikey Wheeler and Patty Keenan, both three grades ahead of me and Whitey. Whitey pulled out his Marlboros and offered them smokes. Each of them took one, including Bailey. I noticed that Whitey was as tall as Wheeler and Keenan and probably outweighed them, too. I was shorter than Bailey, but probably weighed fifty pounds less than he did.

"Thanks for the beers," Whitey said coolly, sucking on his cigarette.

"Thank Spade. He stole them from the beer truck," Wheeler chortled.

We soon discovered that Spade and Finn were Bailey's friends from Inwood. Inwood was the farthest north section of Manhattan, just across the 225th Street bridge from the Bronx. Bailey worked with them at the Gristedes supermarket on Dyckman Street down there. My old man says if you want to know what our neighborhood is going to look like in ten years, just look at Inwood. I'm not sure exactly what he means, but I think it has something to do with Puerto Ricans and blacks.

I was only faking drinking my beer, but Whitey finished his quickly. There was an older group of guys farther down the stands, and Bailey warned us not to go down there because they were druggies. I was surprised there weren't more kids hanging out like there were just a few weeks ago.

"Do you know where the rest of the guys are?" I sheepishly asked Bailey.

Bailey slowly raised his cigarette in his left hand and took a leisurely drag. He then raised his right hand, holding the can of Piels high above his head. He lowered the beer gradually and took a swig and held it up again, as if he was making a toast, proclaiming in his best Froggy-throated Irish brogue, "They're in fookin' Rockaway, the lucky bastids!"

I had taken maybe two sips of beer and Whitey stopped on his second can. Bailey and his cohorts, however, were emptying the box of beer, but fast. The piss stream was making its way to the steps below us and the five of them sloppy drunk, sitting on the concrete steps and mostly staring into the distance, chain smoking, and babbling on incoherently about girls they wanted to screw and guys they wanted to beat up.

"I think I better go home," I said to the group, who ignored me.

Whitey followed me down the stairs. Nobody even said good-bye to us.

"Thanks for the beers!" Whitey said at the bottom of the stairs.

"Fuck you Shelley, you four-eyed motherfucker!" Bailey yelled, drunkenly.

"Thank you, too!" Whitey shouted back. "What an asshole," he mumbled to me as we walked across the football field. "Do you know where those guys stay in Rockaway?"

"I know where Flynn stays."

"You want to go there tomorrow? I'll bet Saturday night in Rockaway with those guys would be pretty good. Better than another night with Froggy and his gang of misfit pricks. Do you know how to get there?"

I began to hum a melody.

"What's that?"

"'Take the A Train,' by Duke Ellington."

We were almost to the gate at the park's exit when Whitey grabbed me by the arm. "Get down, quick."

We ducked into some bushes down the hill from the path as two guys walked past us.

"Holy crap," I whispered to Whitey, as Father Q. and a long-haired guy walked into the park and down the path that led to the stands. Walking past where Bobby Bailey and the guys were hanging out, they went to the end where the druggies were. "Why would they be going over there? Maybe they're going to call the cops on them?"

"Whaddyuh think? They're going to buy pot," Whitey said standing. "Let's go get some Sen-Sen."

"How could you eat that stuff?"

"It's the only thing that hides beer breath."

We walked to the corner candy store under the el on 238th Street to buy the Sen-Sen. There were three old men smoking smelly cigars by the mailbox on the corner, waiting for the night-owl edition of the *Daily News* to come in. I wondered if one day Whitey and I would be like those guys, still hanging out by the mailbox. When we were little we hung out by the mailbox because it was home base for ringolevio. I know the older teenagers hang out by the mailbox too, hiding their half-pints of liquor in brown paper bags under it, and trying to look up the skirts of the pretty secretaries walking down the stairs when they get off the train. Old guys smoke their cigars and wait for the early edition of the next day's newspaper. I guess that's just the way you grow up on the block.

The Sen-Sen burned when it hit your tongue. I guess it would have to taste this bad for it to work. Frankly, I was surprised Whitey still needed to hide his beer breath. His mother went to bed really early and got up late in the afternoon. I didn't really know what was going on with the rest of his family. He never talked about them anymore. *Whitey's really got it made,* I thought.

"Do you really want to go to Rockaway tomorrow?" I asked Whitey, just before I headed up the stairs to my building.

"Yeah! Maybe we can spend the night there, too."

"I don't know. I'm not sure I my parents would go for that."

"Aw, we'll think up some excuse for you to stay once we're down there. Bring your bathing suit. See ya," Whitey said, continuing down the block.

I tiptoed past my parents who were fast asleep on the pull-out couch in the living room. I guess I didn't need the Sen-Sen either. I got into bed and went over the lies I would tell my parents on the phone from Rockaway, and it scared me. What if I got caught? It's one thing to lie about little stuff, but sleeping over in Rockaway? And if I got my butt whooped for smoking in first grade, what kind of beating would I get if they caught me in this lie? But as I lay there staring at the ceiling, I could still hear the teenagers and older guys hanging out in front of the bar out my window down the block, cars peeling out, girls screaming, guys yelling insults and cursing at each other. That could be me and my friends in Rockaway! I knew it would be worth the risk.

Chapter Seven

—NOW—

There's a rhythm to boredom. Especially when it's lubricated nightly with beer and bourbon. Whatever idealistic optimism I had about starting a new job at *NYNow!* was knocked off my shoulder and stomped into the ground once I realized that I was nothing more than a glorified email router.

The only good thing about the job was that there were so many scripts, notes, edicts, street maps, research stories and menus to forward to assorted cameramen, reporters, crews, and bosses that it was like playing a video game all day long, which made the hours fly by. I had virtually no personal contact with any co-workers. People didn't even answer their phones. In fact, their voice mails instructed callers that they were "more likely to respond to an email with a succinct subject line."

Riding the subway to and from work was a Zen-like exercise in detachment from the physical world. I was unaware of time, space, and the assorted stink. The more crowded, delayed, and smelly the ride was, the more I narrowed my focus into my newspaper, book, or eyes-closed daydream. I never fully understood until now how successful major league pitchers in crucial situations claimed they didn't hear fifty thousand hostile fans screaming expletives at the top of their beer-drenched lungs. In fact, they didn't even see the 'roided-out six-foot-ten zero-body-fat freak waving a bat sixty-five feet six inches in front of him as he threw the ball. The great pitchers say they hear nothing and only see the catcher's glove. Narrowing my eyes on a tattered copy of *Moby Dick*, framed by the soiled crotch area of a pair of dark blue Dickies just inches behind it, I was truly beginning to understand the power of the focused mind.

My real job became training my mind to be as physically and mentally detached from my commute and the job as possible. Each morning I drove from Bronxville and parked the car near the el station at 238th Street. And each evening when I walked through the jail-like floor-to-ceiling turnstile to exit, I had to decide whether to stop in a bar before driving back to Bronxville. Soon I didn't have to decide. I just went in. It became an integral part of the rhythm of my boredom.

In a few weeks, my routine was set. At my job, I was viewed as an aloof but efficient disseminator of information. And at the bar, I guess it was the same. The assorted semi-retired alcoholics didn't bother with me much, but once in a while they did ask my opinion on crucial information, like what the original capacity of Yankee Stadium was, or who was the second man on the moon. After all, I did on occasion wear a suit jacket.

And each day after work, when I just had one, or two, or three beers or bourbons, I told myself that tomorrow I would call my son, find a better job, get my own place, start to work out, and find out the truth about Whitey. I didn't worry that many tomorrows were coming and going. My tomorrow would jump up, announce itself, and I would grab hold of it and start anew.

I actually looked forward to standing a few stools from the television where Judge Judy was holding court, and once in a while sharing a thought with Matty, who slumped and slurred a little bit more each day as he faded into the floorboards. Then Matty's tomorrow came. They found him dead in his apartment when his neighbors complained about the stench. A benefit was planned to help pay for his funeral expenses, which included corned beef and cabbage and, of course, all you could drink.

I was surprised by Matty's death but not shocked. In fact, no one was. The reactions from the regulars at the bar were merely casual observations, as though everyone knew he had a ticket for a trip and just got on the train a little sooner without telling anyone. You heard things like, *The poor bastard didn't even get to finish his Chinese takeout,* or *Too bad, he won three races at Belmont the other day and didn't get to collect on them,* or *I think I'll try to get that apartment once they get the stench out.* No shock, no sadness, no tears. At least Dr. Kevorkian's suicide contraption worked in less than an hour with a push of a button, not decades on a creaky bar stool.

Matty's spot at the bar was vacant and an empty bottle of Jameson, his favorite whiskey, was placed next to where his tumbler usually was. I wasn't sure if it was there as a reminder that Matty used to sit there, or to illustrate how he killed himself. The sight of that made me feel like not drinking anymore that night, and I decided to take a walk.

Matty lived in a basement apartment of the building I grew up in, but because he and his siblings were so much older, I never knew him or his family. I barely remember his father, who yelled at us when we were four or five years old and playing near the entrance to the basement. I heard he was found dead in a subway car at the last stop of the number one train.

The building doesn't look that much different. The basement entrance now has an iron gate with barbed wire across the top. They paved over the front courtyard side garden where we played in the grass, and what used to be stained glass windows next to the main entrance to the building have been bricked over. I could see a light on in Matty's apartment window, which was low to the ground in the courtyard, and I walked up the steps to the main entrance. The door was slightly ajar so I walked into the lobby.

I hadn't been in that lobby since I was around eighteen and we moved two blocks away to a larger apartment, which had two bedrooms instead of just one. There was graffiti on two of the large plywood squares that used to be lobby mirrors. I walked past my old apartment door, right next to the elevator. I remember there was always a large semicircle of cleanliness outside our doorway. Now it was evenly mucky everywhere.

I entered the elevator, which had a strong smell of urine, and pushed *B*. I opened the elevator door and there I was in the basement of my building where I had spent many a day hiding from rain, icy cold temperatures, and the snooping eyes of nosey grown-ups. I reflexively experienced a jolt of fear when I saw the door of the super's basement apartment. He was the enforcer of our building and he wasn't afraid to use whatever plumbing or cleaning device that was handy to swing at us in order to protect his domain. I passed what used to be the laundry room, which was now boarded up, and turned the corner where I knew the entrance to Matty's apartment was. There was a strong smell of bleach and detergent in the air, and I could hear a fan whirling. The door to the apartment was open just wide enough for the fan to fit, and there were lights on inside. I remembered Matty telling me that his family had that apartment for seventy years or so. I wondered what the building was like when they moved in. If I could remember stained glass windows and lobby mirrors, I'd imagine that this building was a pre-war luxury apartment building built just after the elevated train opened up this part of the Bronx, at the early part of the twentieth century. Matty's family, like probably all the others, were moving out of crowded lower Manhattan tenements into the wide open spaces of the Bronx, where buildings had elevators and even garbage chutes on every floor.

The fan hummed as a blast of soapy air came my way. I stood there staring at the door, wondering what to do next. An elderly stout woman wearing a flowered apron and rubber gloves appeared in the doorway. She gave me a suspicious look, pulled the fan out of the door and slammed it shut, which echoed loudly through the cave-like basement hallway. I could see the tiny door of the peephole open and I knew she was watching me. I waved slightly, with a dumb grin on my face.

"What do you want?" the voice asked from behind the dark green metal door.

"Nothing. I'm a friend of Matty's."

I heard locks being undone and the door opened, revealing the short, stout, sturdy lady now with a crowbar in her hand. "Can I help you?"

"I'm a friend of Matty's. I'm very sorry. I used to live in this building years ago."

"What's your name?" she asked, putting the crowbar on a table.

"Schmidt. Vinny Schmidt."

"I knew your family. Step in, I want to put the fan back in the door."

I walked into the foyer of the apartment and could still smell some of the stench under a cloud of Lysol and bleach. Dim, bare light bulbs hung from the ceilings of the foyer, kitchen and living room. There were at least a dozen large black garbage bags in a pile in the living room. A kettle whistled in the small kitchen. There were soapy buckets, mops, rags, and spray bottles of cleaning solutions everywhere.

"I could use a break. Have a seat. Would you like a cup of tea?"

At one time, many, many years ago, everything in the apartment must have been painted white. But now it was all a greasy shade of yellow. The kitchen table had two rickety wooden chairs and many cigarette burn marks on the edges.

"I'm surprised he didn't burn the place down," she said, placing a dainty tea cup in front of me.

"Do they know how he…"

"He fell and hit his head on the toilet. The seat was up, so he went right against the porcelain and cracked it. His head and the toilet. There's another reason you men ought to put the toilet seat down! If he had hit the wooden seat, he'd probably just have a nasty knot on his head."

She was a tough Irish lady. She didn't have a brogue, but a hard old New York accent like my dad had. She didn't pronounce toilet as *toy-let*, but said *ter-let*. Her chair creaked when she sat down.

"I'm very sorry. You're Matty's older sister, I assume."

Oh, shit. I must have said something very wrong, because she plopped her tea cup onto the table and shot me a narrow-eyed glare. I'll bet she's Matty's *younger* sister and I've insulted her.

"Sister? I'm his mother!"

It was my turn to drop the tea cup. I couldn't believe that the hardy woman sitting in front of me was older than Matty. She looked ten years younger than he did. Her hair was thick and white. Her cheeks were rosy and her teeth straight.

"His father drank himself to death, as well," she said dryly, sipping some tea. "The exact same bars. The exact same results."

There was no sadness in her voice, only grim acknowledgment of fact. Unlike my former drinking partner Matty, his mom's hands didn't tremble, her eyes didn't have trouble focusing, and she had no bruises on her face.

"Matthew could have come and lived with me upstate, but he wouldn't. He even stopped visiting at the holidays. He said it made him get 'psychological.' I have a lovely apartment just a few blocks from my daughter and grandchildren. I live alone and do everything myself. Except drive. No desire to drive an automobile. Matthew didn't drive. I was glad about that. You know, glad he wouldn't take an innocent life with him when he crashed. More tea?"

I held up my tea cup, and realized my hand was trembling slightly and hers wasn't. Maybe I had more in common with Matty than I wanted to admit.

"Your parents were good people. Are they living?"

"No."

"Not many from the old Presentation Mothers' Club are left."

"Did you know Whitey Shelley's mom?"

Her shoulders dropped, her head tilted, and a look of complete sadness overtook her.

"She passed not more than six months ago. She lived a few miles from me. Except for my family, she was my only connection to the neighborhood. I saw Whitey at the funeral."

Bingo. I'd hit pay dirt. I didn't want to appear to anxious, so I lifted my cup and sipped a little tea.

"Whitey was my best friend from Presentation. Do you know how I could get in touch with him?"

"No, I didn't talk to him much. Very sad, him not doing well and all."

Matty's mother showed me around the apartment where she raised her family. She explained what a beautiful building it had been when they moved in, and they could only afford a basement apartment. They never went in through the more direct basement alley entrance.

They always came in through the luxurious main lobby which had huge floor-to-ceiling mirrors, stained glass windows, upholstered chairs, and crystal chandeliers, and then they took the elevator down to the basement. Every piece of furniture in the apartment seemed to be a hand-me-down, except for the large portable television set sitting on an ancient massive TV/stereo console probably from the early seventies, and the microwave oven in the kitchen.

Many of the architectural elements in the apartment were identical to the ones in the apartment I grew up in on the first floor: the bathroom floor tiles, the molding, the radiators, separate hot and cold faucets, even the iron grid that hung from the kitchen ceiling where we hung our wash. But even with the obvious signs of heavy cleaning Mrs. O'Malley had been doing, it was clear that Matty had lived in a dirty bachelor's hovel. The decades-old flowered wallpaper was tattered, the rugs were soiled, the kitchen and bathroom fixtures so stained that a whole truckload of Ajax couldn't whiten them. He even had rigged ropes from several doorway arches – a device old drunken bachelors use to help themselves up from the floor after they've hit the deck.

As I was relieving myself I caught my reflection in the grimy bathroom mirror and I couldn't help but think that this could be my apartment, my life, my death.

"If you see anything you can use, just take it," Mrs. O'Malley said, dragging a large trash bag across the floor.

I looked around and on the floor, next to a half-filled trash bag, was a blue oval-shaped pocket-sized rubber change holder with a faded image of the Unisphere from the 1964/65 New York World's Fair. I picked it up and there was something inside. I opened it; there were rosary beads, crystal blue ones. I walked over to show Mrs. O'Malley.

"Can I have these?" I asked, holding up the rosary beads.

"I said take something you can use."

"I can."

"Do, then."

"Can I help you?"

"I'm done for today. But I'll start again at nine in the morning. If you're here, you're here."

"I'll be here. Oh, did you know they're having a benefit for Matt to pay some of his funeral expenses?"

Mrs. O'Malley dropped a heavy garbage bag. I heard glass break. "Oh, really," she steamed. "My Matthew's funeral expenses were paid for in full by me. The only one to benefit from that affair will be the bar owner to whom Matty probably owed a mighty sum in gambling wagers and bar tabs. So be it. Why should he bear the burden of Matty's sudden departure?"

As the words left her lips I noticed a quiver. The first crack in her tough outer shell. She shuffled backwards and I rushed to her, thinking she was going to fall, but she adroitly placed herself in the living room's upholstered chair. She removed her rubber gloves, pulled a dainty hanky out of her sleeve, and began to wipe tears from her eyes.

"My Matty. He was the smartest. Did well in school all through high school and the city college. He was a banker, downtown. A business man. I thought for sure he'd come around one day. Find a girl, settle down, raise a family. But the drink was his only love. It's that 238th Street! It sucks the life out of these men! Those goddamned bars!"

I felt uncomfortable standing there, listening to such private lamentations from Matty's own mother, in his own death chamber. I couldn't help but think of what my own parents would think of my life as it was now.

"Do right by your parents," she said, scaring me. Was she reading my mind? "Living or dead, do right by your parents." She smiled softly and waved her hanky at me. "If you're here, you're here."

Just as I was closing the door, she added, "Whitey's in Livingston Manor. He has to keep a low profile, you know. But he works somewhere in a bar or restaurant in the area. His mother was proud of him. He was a war hero, God bless him."

I shook the rosaries in the change purse that I held in my hand as I walked through the dank basement hall, through the alley and out onto the street. Nostalgia fades quickly when reality begins to reappear around you. The happy stoops of my youth where we played Chinese school and off-the-stoop with spaldeens well into the warm summer night are empty save for the occasional obvious shady drug dealer holding pit bulls on thick chains. The German deli is a Pakistani bodega and the laundromat where we huddled next to the dryers on the coldest winter days is now a bulletproof glass-enclosed check cashing store that probably launders drug money instead of the family laundry. I passed the old storefront for Vito the shoemaker's store, where the old men, and old men in the making, would sit on obsolete shoe-shining chairs and gossip the men-only gossip of the neighborhood in the safety of the store. Vito and his minions would watch the world go by and comment accordingly. From the outside you'd see Vito's friendly wave as he pounded a new heel onto a pair of shoes, with the others laughing behind him. On the inside you'd hear Vito shouting, "Hello!" and then under his breath for his peanut gallery, "you fuck!" or "Hiya, Bernadette ... oh, what a set of tits on her!" or "Hey there, Tommy Mac ... you junkie, you should die already." The storefront is now a Chinese take-out place that has the look of an establishment that may be responsible for the sudden decline of stray cats in the area.

But the neighborhood isn't in total decay. In fact, the opposite is true. Unlike when I was a kid, there are no empty storefronts. And filling the vacant lots, where we used to build forts and have our wiffle ball tournaments, brand new ten-story apartment buildings stand, complete with underground parking. And yes, there are even a few more bars.

I spent the next day, a Sunday, helping Mrs. O'Malley clean out the apartment. Garbage bags were filled with items that were part of Matty's life. The turquoise radio alarm clock on the table next to his bed must have been forty years old. There were baby cockroaches falling out of its vent holes as I tossed it into the bag. There was a corner of the living room where Mrs. O'Malley instructed me to place items that could be donated to Goodwill, but that corner stayed empty. Except for the television, which Mrs. Sullivan said she would keep, there was not one thing in the entire place that when illuminated by a

100-watt bulb was worth handing off to someone else. Everything had just been left to decompose and wither away. Like Matty, I guess.

By the end of the day, all of the black garbage bags were full and by the door, like so many body bags in a morgue. Mrs. O'Malley wasn't nearly as conversational as she had been the night before. As I left she asked me if I still had the rosaries. I took them out of my pocket to show her I did.

"I meant what I said about using them," she said quite seriously. "And if you find Whitey, be careful. God bless you."

She shut the door slowly and I could hear several locks clicking closed.

It was still afternoon, and after showering and changing at my sister's I decided perhaps it was time to keep my part of the bargain with Mrs. O'Malley. Thinking I would sit in a pew at Presentation and say the rosary, once I saw the cars in the parking lot I realized that five o'clock mass was just beginning. I hadn't been to mass in years. My ex-wife and I had tried going to churches of assorted denominations in Los Angeles, but after hearing heated admonishments from the pulpit in a Catholic church about bubble gum under the pews, and a female pastor in a "new age" church explaining how her prayers helped her get a better deal on a Lexus, we gave up searching for spiritual guidance in organized religion.

I pulled into a parking space and my car scraped bottom on the roots from the long-gone giant oak. I hadn't been in the church since my mother's funeral years ago.

The organ was playing "Ave Maria" as I entered, and I was instantly taken aback by the small crowd in attendance; perhaps the seats were only a quarter full. When I'd last attended the church on a regular basis, several decades ago, the pews were packed for every Mass, with literally standing-room only. I took a seat off to the side towards the back and as soon as my jeans hit the hard dark wood I was flush with memories: my parents' funerals, the funerals of friends and relatives young and old, baptisms, communions, confirmations, and graduations. No matter where I was living, it seemed I was always called back to this very spot for life-changing momentous events. And here I was again.

The rear sacristy door opened, and two Hispanic altar girls led the way for a crooked old priest shuffling his way along. It only took a moment for me to realize who it was: Father O.

His cassock was a little bit short, revealing his black-soled low black Converse All Stars sneakers. Father O. guided his altar girls with graceful hand gestures that belied his arthritis, and perhaps osteoporosis as well. His head and shoulders slumped forward and his gait was uncertain, but once at the altar he seemed to come to life as George Burns had in his late nineties once the spotlight hit him on a Las Vegas stage. Father O.'s reedy voice hadn't changed, and its high pitch helped it to reach the church's back corner, where I sat.

He was completely bald except for a thin ring of barely visible white hair. His trademark black-framed glasses were in stark contrast to the whiteness of his complexion and his brilliant white vestments. When the altar girls missed a cue, he gently reminded them of their duties, unlike Monsignor McNulty, who used to yell at you in a coarse stage whisper that could be heard by the first ten rows. Father O. was still famously off-key as he led the assembly in song, but did so with great enthusiasm. He went through the service, of course, like the old pro he most certainly was. He read from the Gospel, *He who eats My flesh and drinks My blood*, and I figured this would be the focus for his sermon. From grade school to high school, and through to encyclicals from the pope, this was always a deal-breaker for some. In order to be a true Catholic you had to believe that the communion wafer and wine were transformed into the body and blood of Christ. It was not a *symbol* of the body and blood; it literally *became* the body and blood. But instead, Father O. didn't include the theme of the gospel in his sermon at all. He talked about one thing: being kind. And gave example upon example for the fifty or so churchgoers: speak politely to loved ones and strangers alike; be gentle with children and animals. He even quoted Ronald Reagan saying, "A gentleman always does the kind thing."

His sermon was succinct and he breezed through the rest of the mass. I headed over to the sacristy entrance where two families stood at the open door. Father O. presented them with their altar girls with high praise and smiles all around. I waited until the families started walking away.

"Excuse me, Father O.?"

He looked at me with a quizzical expression I'm sure he had used many times before, when faces from the past appear out of the crowds at church.

"Do I know you?" he said. He extended both hands forward and shook my hand joyfully. I could feel his frailty.

"Vinny Schmidt."

"What a wonderful treat! I'm a last minute fill-in here today, because Father Garcia is ill. How are you? Do you still live in the parish?"

"No, Father. I live in Bronxville. Temporarily, I hope...."

"I read your book," he said, which stopped me cold. "I thought it was a little bit too much Good Friday and not enough Easter Sunday."

"You're right, Father. But without Jesus dying on the cross, there wouldn't be a resurrection. Do you remember what you gave me after graduation from eighth grade?"

"No. I hope it was something useful."

"A collection of stories by Flannery O'Connor. I didn't read it for twenty years. I thought it would be..."

"Lame?"

"Yes, lame. Then I read *The Violent Bear It Away.*"

"A lot of Good Friday in that, too. It's great to see you, Vincent. By the way, what was your close friend's name?"

"Whitey."

"Yes! Whitey! What a colorful personality. So full of ... life! Are you still friends with him?"

"No, Father. I haven't heard from him in years."

"Well, I hope you find him some day. I have to run. The rectory knows how to get in touch with me. Oh, how are you, ecclesiastically?"

"Um, not so good."

"Call me. God bless you," he said, doing a small sign of the cross in front of his chest.

"One more thing, Father."

"Anything."

"Whatever happened to Father Q.?"

"Father Q. served twelve years in prison for child sex abuse. I believe he passed away some years ago."

"What did he die off?"

"They said natural causes."

"Naturally."

"Satan infiltrates wherever there's an opportunity, Vinny. I hope you can see past that. Even I have trouble doing it. We do what we can. I have to say Mass at Sing Sing in an hour. Be good."

Father O. smiled, winked, waved, turned on his sneakers and seemed to float through the door as he left.

Maybe he knew something about me that I didn't know. Maybe he saw something in me when I was in eighth grade that took me decades to figure out. I thought Flannery O'Connor was a guy for years. Then when I found out she was known as a *Catholic* novelist, I put off reading her for years more. When I finally read *The Violent Bear It Away, Wise Blood,* "A Good Man is Hard to Find," and "The Artificial Nigger," I was stunned by her stark, violent, darkly symbolic prose. Yup, a *lot* of Good Friday in there.

Over the decades, as I moved from apartment to apartment and from house to house, the Flannery O'Connor book was one of the items that always moved with me, even though for years and years I never cracked open the spine. And in each new residence it sat on a shelf, signed by Father O., just waiting. Writers are secretive. I wrote the first one hundred pages of *Sewer Balls* without telling a soul, not even my wife. And, of course, no one knows the secret ratio of truth to fiction. But maybe most importantly, the relationship between planning and

101

alchemy in writing a novel is a complete mystery to me. One secret I can reveal is that it truly wasn't until I read the book signed and given to me by Father O. on eighth grade graduation day that I was able to put the seat of my pants to the seat of my chair and begin writing my first novel. I realize it wasn't a magical key that opened a door. It was more like another clue that only made sense in a series of other clues that had to be discovered in sequence, which makes the entire thing even more insanely miraculous, if there's any validity to it at all.

I drove past Matty's apartment building and all the black garbage bags were piled on the sidewalk ready to be picked up and dumped in a landfill, probably somewhere on Staten Island. There was a good chance that Matty wouldn't be far behind. Not surprisingly, Staten Island is also home to many cemeteries.

Now I know why funeral *homes* are called that. I've seen more friends and relatives at Williams Funeral Home, dead or alive, than I have in any actual home. I was quite early but thought I'd drop in for a quiet moment with Matty. The directory board listed his room as the one on the left side, which I could see was empty. On the right side of the hall was a large room filled to capacity with an usually noisy crowd for a wake. Two black-suited men sporting white carnations stood at the doorway to the room. I assumed they worked there. Suddenly I heard a woman's scream and the two men ran into the room. I stood at the door and watched several young women in black scream at each other.

"I said get the fuck out of here, bitch! You're not wanted here!"

"Fuck you! I belong here! I ain't leaving, motherfucker!"

"You better get your fat ass outta here now or you'll be in a fucking box right next to him."

"I ain't fuckin' leaving! I'm pregnant with his baby!"

"Honey, half the women in this room had his fuckin' babies! Now get the fuck outta here!"

There were more screams, a catfight ensued, and the two black-suited employees escorted the two young Hispanic women from the room and into two separate rooms down the hall.

I entered the parlor where Matty was laid out. The coffin was open and Matty looked even older than the last time I saw him. His face was too puffy and the makeup on his face didn't quite cover the black and blue bruise on his forehead where he must have hit the toilet bowl. His hands were folded in front of him and he held some rosary beads, exactly like the ones I was given by his mother. I knelt on the kneeler in front of the coffin and began to pray, with my eyes closed. Just when I re-opened my eyes and made the sign of the cross, I was tapped on the shoulder.

"I didn't realize you knew Uncle Matty," Betty Ann said, looking stunningly beautiful in a low-cut black dress.

I felt more than a little strange, being there alone with Mrs. Puggy, especially since I had been greeted by her spectacular cleavage.

"Yes, I knew Matty from hanging out in the bar," I said, trying to avoid looking at her boobs.

"Listen, I'm sorry I mouthed off at you the last time we spoke," she said, reaching out to gently shake my hand.

I nodded, and she motioned that she wanted to kneel and say a prayer. She bowed her head and prayed for a few moments.

"I came early, actually, because I have to go to a wedding. I wore this dress kind of as a double-duty thing. You know, wake and wedding, yin and yang."

I felt extremely awkward, standing here next to Matty in the box as I checked out how utterly gorgeous Betty Ann appeared in the funeral parlor's soft lighting.

"Matty's your uncle?"

"Not really, we all just called him that because he was always over the house. One of my dad's drinking buddies."

"Whose wedding?" I asked, over the continuing profanities being hurled in the hall between assorted grieving females.

"A cousin out on the Island."

Betty Ann took a step closer to me and touched my hand, which was at my side. "Actually, I was supposed to bring a date, but I RSVP'd weeks ago. I know it's short notice, but would you care to join me?"

I was already decently dressed for a funeral, but how could I just dump Matt's last respects? I glanced over at the coffin and I could swear I saw Matty wink.

"I'd love to."

She smiled broadly, lifted her shoulders like a little girl might upon hearing she was going to Disneyland, and coyly jiggled her cleavage. There's something supremely sexy about a strong attractive woman who's been around the block a few times, and is eager to keep going despite a few fender benders every now and then. I signed the guest book and followed Betty Ann to her car.

She drove a sporty car with a stick shift, and every time she changed gears her skirt seemed to hike up her thighs, revealing more freckles. I could also see the secret soft blonde hairs on her upper leg, beyond the leg-shaving line. She was a hard driver and liked to shift down when decelerating, instead of just going into neutral. I could see the white patches on her dainty pink hand as she firmly gripped the black leather ball at the top of the shifter. I must've been really horny if watching a woman drive was giving me that much of a chubby.

We were way the hell out on the Long Island. Massapequa, I think. It was one of those suburban banquet halls along a highway lodged between a Pools 'N Stuff and a BBQs Depot. It was called the Marina Beach Yacht Club, although it was easy to see there were no marinas, beaches, or yachts for miles.

I remember when I was in my twenties and friends were getting married, the wedding receptions were wild affairs filled with young singles getting drunk and partying all night long. It wasn't unusual to wake up in a strange bed and yank on what you thought was a purple satin comforter, only to discover it was actually a bridesmaid's dress. But from the looks of the function room we walked into, I was figuring it was the second or third marriage for the couple, whose sedentary guests were more interested in the dessert menu than in bagging the wedding party's matron of honor. And the only wild ones were the scores of kids running amuck and popping balloons.

I felt funny being dragged by Betty Ann to every table and being introduced to all her relatives. But I could soon tell they were used to seeing streams of suitors at family functions and didn't take our being together as anything special. In fact, she was so good at breaking the ice, before I knew it I was plied with a few cocktails and talking baseball with guys while she butterflied around laughing and bringing life to every table she landed at. The food was good, the drinks were plenty, and I knew enough about baseball to hold a conversation with most of the men. Once the drinks flow and the inhibitions are released, the male of the species begins to test his competition – thankfully, there it was in sports trivia. Back in the day, that usually meant a fistfight over girl. But some guys now, they seem to want to mix it up over politics. I'm a middle-of-the-road kind of guy who thinks evil people need to be put in jail or killed, but those are fighting words for guys who wear Crocs and have stringy ponytails bunched from whatever hair they can join from their balding domes. I spent a considerable amount of energy avoiding those guys in search of guys who understood the infield fly rule.

I was happy there were no fistfights, I wasn't forced to dance, the food was good, and I sat most of the night next to an old Italian guy from Brooklyn who had been a Brooklyn Dodgers fan and was interested in hearing about the Dodgers from a Los Angeles perspective.

Betty Ann didn't have a drink all night and drove me back to the Williams Funeral Home to pick up my car. Except for a hearse, my car was the only one left in the underground garage.

"Thanks so much for going with me to the wedding. I hate going alone to those things. Relatives ask even more questions when you show up single," she said, as I grabbed the door handle to exit her car.

"I had a nice time," I said, wondering if I should kiss her.

"Look. I like you and I'm sorry I yelled at you. But I don't want there to be any misunderstanding here. I feel stupid telling you I like you. And I do want to help you find Whitey."

"So then it's okay that I'm a private eye?"

105

"Yes, it's okay," she said leaning towards me, and planting a non-platonic brief but erotic kiss on my lips. "I have to get up early, bye."

She sped out of the garage and as the echo of her engine died down, there I was, right next to the hearse. I walked over and peeked in the back. It was dark, but once my eyes adjusted I could see the flowers I bought for Matty against the partition where his coffin would go first thing in the morning. I knew it was time to get off my ass and find Whitey once and for all.

Chapter Eight

—Then—

Whitey is always late. I stood by the mailbox under the el just like I did the night before when we decided that we'd venture to Rockaway by ourselves for the first time. Our last big subway unchaperoned adventure was when we went to the St. Patrick's parade downtown, last March. Besides almost getting the shit beat out of us, by drunken chicks as well as guys, that trip was well worth the risk. When you go to the parade on Fifth Avenue with your parents when you're little, they try their hardest to shield you from the shit-faced revelers soaked in green beer, wearing plastic green bowler hats. It scares you when you're five or six, still holding hands with your mommy. But by the time you get the picture that drinking can be loads of fun, as evidenced by assorted stewed relatives at Sunday get-togethers or weddings, you dare to wander from your parents in order to enjoy the parade sights, like teams of girls peeing in the bushes in Central Park, or drunk guys climbing way up trees right on Fifth Avenue and singing "Wild Colonial Boy" to the cheering crowds below.

I kept an eye out for Whitey, looking down 238th Street where he'd be walking from his building. It was early in the morning and I knew the longer I waited there for him, the greater the possibility that a neighbor could spot me standing there with a brown paper bag in my hand.

All of a sudden, I almost collapsed completely to the ground because some wiseass got me with the old trick where the back of your knee is pushed in just the right spot.

"Have a nice trip?" Whitey laughed. "Hey, here comes the train!" he yelled, pulling me by the shoulder, right through the traffic on Broadway. We ran up the station steps two at a time just as the train was arriving. "Here's a token. You can pay me later."

We just made it into the last car of the train and unlike on our St. Paddy's Day journey, it was completely empty. Whitey walked over

107

to the subway map and ran his finger across it to illustrate how far we would be traveling. "Can you believe we're going from here all the way to the ocean for only fifteen cents!"

"My old man says the subway is too expensive for the crappy service you get," I said, repeating one of my father's usual rants.

"And look, we're going through four of the boroughs of the city: the Bronx, Manhattan, Brooklyn and Queens. The only one we're missing is Staten Island."

"My old man says the only things Staten Island has are garbage dumps and cemeteries."

"Alright with your old man, already!"

I shut up and thought maybe Whitey didn't like me talking about my old man because he never talked about his. I wasn't even totally sure if he's dead or alive. The train didn't get very crowded. Whitey seemed pretty good at leading us off at 168th Street and following the signs to the A train which would take us all the way to Rockaway. We had to take an elevator at 168th that was scary as hell even though it had an elevator operator. That had to be one of the worst jobs on the planet. It stunk like piss and vomit, and a black bum was in there when we got on and stayed on when we got off, even though the only two stops on that elevator were where we got on and where we got off. Maybe he and the operator were friends.

When the A train arrived, I was thrilled to see it was one of the old-fashioned cars with a train conductor wearing a peaked hat riding between cars and actually hanging outside the train. Inside the car there were dim, bare light bulbs, large, slowly rotating fans suspended from the ceiling, and cushioned cane seats. It looked like the kind of train car you'd see in a W.C. Fields movie. Once we got into Harlem there were lots of blacks getting on, mostly families. I was more than a little nervous going through Harlem because there were a lot of race fights going on all over the city. There were rumors that they were going to close Palisades Amusement Park in Jersey because there were so many fights between blacks, whites, and Puerto Ricans every night. There were black and Puerto Ricans teenagers getting on, but none of them bothered us. *I think Whitey is starting to look big and tough. I wish I did.*

Once we got into Brooklyn, more and more families got on with beach umbrellas and bags filled with food and blankets. Some of the kids were already in their bathing suits. When the beachgoers got off the train at Rockaway Boulevard to switch to the Rockaway line, we followed them, and it was a good thing we did, because it was complicated. That line went across a bridge right above the water, and you went by crummy houses that were built on stilts in the bay. It was kind of like going through a slummy version of Venice, Italy, I guess. Then it was the stop we traveled almost two hours for – Rockaways' Playland! We could see the top of the roller coaster and hear the screams of the riders from the el station.

"I can't believe it! We're here! And it only took a couple hours!" I excitedly said as we bounded down the station steps. "When we drove out here last summer it took three hours because the car kept overheating. Do you know where we're going?" I asked Whitey as he led the way down the street crowded with people carrying buckets, coolers, umbrellas and chairs.

"Let's start at Playland," Whitey said, pulling out a pack of Marlboros as we hurriedly walked along the bungalow-lined street. "That's easy enough to find. Then we'll look for the guys."

"Oh, fuck!" I said, stopping dead in my tracks. "I forgot to bring Flynn's address!"

Whitey stopped and coolly used the opportunity to light his cigarette properly. After it was lit, he took a deep drag. "Eh. We'll find 'em."

I thought Whitey would be pissed off at me for forgetting and I was relieved he had such a nonchalant attitude about it. The farther we got from the train, the more freaked out I started to get. *What was I going to tell my parents? How were we going to find Flynn and the other guys? What was I going to tell Flynn's parents? Where were we going to eat? Did I have enough money? What if we got mugged? Where was I going to go to the bathroom? What if we couldn't find a*

*place to sleep? Would we take the train back home at midnight? We'd
get mugged for sure then!*

"Man, look at those chicks over there!" Whitey said, elbowing
me.

Across the street on the corner was Boggiano's Clam Bar. My
dad took us there every time we were in Rockaway. There were two
barefoot teenage girls in short shorts and bikini tops drinking sodas by
the outside clam bar.

"They're barefoot right on the filthy sidewalk!" I said, amazed
at the sight.

"They have feet? Look at the curves on those babes!" Whitey
said, standing tall and straight, shoulders back, sharply flicking his
ashes several times with his thumb. I started to get a funny feeling
standing next to him; he was a cool teenager, and I felt like a squirt. He
could probably walk over there, offer those girls a cigarette and talk to
them. I was nervous just watching them from over here across the
street.

"We'll catch them on the rebound," Whitey said, crossing the
street against the light. We followed the crowd towards the wild sounds
of Playland right down Beach Boulevard.

Whenever my parents took us to Rockaway, I could tell they
were steering us clear of certain situations. My mom usually led the
way and if we saw a group of noisy teenagers we'd take a detour to the
other side of the block. But Whitey was leading us right into all the
action. We were still on side streets a couple of blocks away from
Playland, and there were groups of teenagers hanging out by parked
cars outside ramshackle bungalows, smoking cigarettes and drinking
beer out of small brown paper bags that the cans fit snugly inside of. I
know my mom would have crossed the street, but Whitey led us right
through them. I was scared shit, but Whitey didn't break stride as we
torpedoed down the sidewalk. These guys looked like Italians from
Brooklyn with greasy hair slicked back, tight pants and pointy shoes.
They stared at us as we passed by. Whitey flicked ashes by their shoes
and we kept going.

We turned the corner onto the main drag where the entrance to the amusement park was just two blocks down. The sidewalks were jammed with baby strollers, groups of greaser guys, and girls in flip-flops and bathing suits who looked like they belonged on the cover of a Beach Boys album. There was a parade of Puerto Rican, black, Irish, and Italian families balancing candy apples, pizza, and hot dogs with stuffed animals, balloons on sticks and kewpie dolls. It looked like every storefront was either a food joint or a carnival game. Regular looking storefronts were filled with skee-ball or bust-a- balloon with dull, crooked darts, or maybe knock-over-the-lead-milk-bottles with a baseball that was about as hard as a rolled-up pair of socks. The biggest places with the brightest lights and biggest signs were for Fascination, a game where you sit on a stool and roll a spaldeen down a slightly inclined wood board into holes, trying to get five holes to light up in a row. You compete against other people and it's one of the few games in Rockaway where you actually win money and not some piece of junk made in Japan. It's always smoky in there and mostly filled with grown-ups who sit in there for hours.

There were packs of tough looking kids everywhere, but with all the families around I didn't feel too scared. And every once in a while, you'd see a chubby cop walk by with his hat crooked, shirt tail hanging out, sweating, and eating an ice cream cone or something. I have a feeling the cops liked working this beat. But still, it made me nervous when I wondered what it would be like without the families and the baby carriages, and the chunky cops, if all that was left was us and the tough looking Italians and Puerto Ricans from Brooklyn.

"Shouldn't we go look for Flynn and those guys?" I asked Whitey, tugging on his arm.

"Later. Come on! We're at Playland!" Whitey said, pushing through the crowd that was getting more dense every step we got closer to the main entrance.

And there we were: the grand entrance of Playland. The screams and the roar of the gigantic rickety wooden roller coaster were so loud, you had to yell to be heard, just as if you were standing next to the el back in the Bronx. Signs featuring a clown wearing a top hat

111

were everywhere, but he looked more like a maniacal phantom of the opera than a jolly clown. People streamed past us in both directions, bumping into us as we stood under the main archway to gaze at the excitement all around us. Suddenly we were both thumped pretty good by two shoulders. I instantly thought the next move was going to be a fistfight between us and two Brooklyn greasers. That was, until I caught a glimpse of the two perpetrators.

"Wow! It's those chicks from Boggiano's!" Whitey said, staring at the two cute teenage girls, wearing shorts so short you could see the bottom of their butt cheeks when they walked. One was a tall redhead and the other was a small brunette.

"Let's go!" I said, pushing Whitey hard in the middle of his back with both hands. "They're getting away."

We hurried through the crowd and could see them walking briskly ahead, turning back to look at us and giggling. Not wanting to be too obvious by breaking into a full tilt sprint, we moved as fast as we could past the very things I thought would be the very reasons we were there in the first place. The haunted house, the bumper cars, the BB gun shooting range, even the Atom Smasher roller coaster all went by in a blur as we tried to catch up with the two cuties wiggling away from us through the throngs. They zipped past the Davy Jones' Locker, the Fun House, and Ride the Goats, and disappeared into the Penny Arcade.

"Now what?" I breathlessly asked Whitey, as if we had cornered two wild tigers in a cave.

"Let's just hope they don't go out the rear exit," Whitey said, leading the way into the arcade. "Got any dimes?"

We stopped for a moment so our eyes could adjust as we went from the bright sunlight into the cool darkness of the arcade. We scanned the large room, which was loud with clanging bells, cackling glass-enclosed gypsy fortune tellers and banging skee-balls. I nervously jangled five dimes in my loose fist, catching Whitey's attention.

"You look like you're jerking off, jerk-off."

I shoved the dimes back into my pocket and started having extreme anxiety. Whitey lit up another Marlboro. What the heck were

112

we going to do once we found the two elusive lovelies? My stomach started to feel like I'd just swallowed a bee hive. I was secretly hoping they had run right through the arcade, exited onto the boulevard, and ran for the beach. How did we even know that their banging into us at the entrance was a come-on, anyway? Maybe they thought we were a couple of dorks and just being mean.

"There they are. Come on," Whitey said, punctuating his coolly-delivered directive with a long drag on his smoke.

I could see the backs of their red and brown heads bouncing up and down, past all the baseball, football, pinball, shooting, and horse racing arcade games that made up the many aisles of dime-driven contraptions.

"What are they doing back there?" I asked, lagging behind Whitey.

They were in the old-fashioned part of the arcade where they kept the old-style games that nobody played anymore: the bike racer where you spun an iron wheel as fast as you could to move two stupid needles on a meter; a crane where you picked up sand and dumped it in a hopper; the atomic bomber where some footage from World War II was on a tiny screen and you drop an atomic bomb. Plus insane games like the one where the entire point is to see how long you could hold onto a handle as you're zapped with high-voltage electricity.

But the girls were even beyond those games, down the end of the aisle in a small even darker room illuminated only by red light bulbs inside paper Chinese-style lanterns. I knew this was the room little kids weren't supposed to go in. I knew because one rainy day when my mom brought us into the arcade after fleeing from a storm on the beach, I wandered in there and she dragged me out, nearly pulling my arm out of its socket and not explaining why I couldn't play those games. She gave me a handful of dimes to shut me up and plopped me in front of Peppy the Clown while she tried to win a cigar ashtray by playing skee-ball. Peppy the Clown isn't a game at all. It's just this glass-enclosed box with a marionette clown suspended in it. When you drop in your dime it plays stupid songs like "The Old Gray Mare Ain't

113

What She Used to Be" and you push buttons to make it dance. What's creepy about it is that you can't tell if the puppet is a boy or girl.

But seeing the legs on those two honeys poking out from between two rusty arcade games in the forbidden room made me want to go in there more than ever.

"What should we do?" I whispered to Whitey as we stood just outside the entrance.

"We'll go in and work our way back checking out the games. I'll offer them a cigarette or something when we get close and start rapping to them," Whitey instructed me.

We took two steps towards them and I already could tell we were someplace not meant for kids. Against the wall were two life-size cutouts of a man and a sexy woman with real barrels around them like they're naked! On the man's barrel it read, *What every woman should know before and after marriage! The bare facts revealed! By Professor Kinsley.* On the woman's barrel it read, *A hammock built for two,* with a silhouette of two nude lovers on a hammock. There's a peephole to look into the barrel, for a dime.

"What do you think it is?" I asked Whitey, stopping him to study them further.

"I heard about these. They're peep shows. You know, dirty stuff."

"Man, I want to look in the girl's barrel!"

I looked around, making sure some surrogate parent wasn't going to tackle me when I put my dime in the slot and peered in. I read the writing again: *What every woman should know before and after marriage! The bare facts revealed! By Professor Kinsley.* I had often thought about married people having sex, which still kind of grossed me out. I mean, there were kids in my building with fat, smelly parents. I couldn't imagine them screwing. What if this showed something disgusting like that? I dropped in my dime and heard something whir inside the barrel. A panel moved from the peephole, and a light came on. I looked inside and I was stunned!

"Oh, shit!"

"What? Let me see, let me see!" Whitey said, pushing me away. "Ha! What a sucker you are!"

The light went off and the panel swung closed in front of the peephole.

"A freaking cookbook! What a stupid rip-off! It's just a dumb joke."

Whitey was practically on the floor, laughing his ass off. I was just about ready to kick him in the ass when we were stunned into silence. There they were. Right next to us.

"What's so funny?" the cute brunette asked, smiling.

She was wearing a yellow polka dot shirt with the top three or four buttons open, revealing a red bikini top underneath. Her hair was raven black and thick, like mattress stuffing. Her skin was as white as the cream filling in Oreos. I stood there like a moron, not knowing how to answer this Irish beauty. Luckily, Whitey chimed in.

"I don't think girls could handle what's inside that barrel," he said, straightening up and pulling a cigarette out.

"Says who?" the taller redhead asked, like she was itching for a fight. She took a cigarette from the Marlboro box Whitey held out to her, and lit it with Whitey's. She stood in front of the man's barrel and ran her finger across the words as she read aloud quickly. "'What every woman should know before and after marriage! The bare facts revealed! By Professor Kinsley.' Who's Professor Kinsley?"

"My big sister told me about him. They learned about it in college. It's something called the Kinsley or maybe Kinsey Report and it's about... you know..."

The four of us looked at each other. I caught a glimpse of the brunette's red bikini top. The redhead, whose striped shirt with the first few buttons open revealed a blue bikini top underneath, looked at the brunette. Whitey's head whipped from the two girls to me. Then the brunette said it.

"Sex."

I felt tingles shoot down from my head and up from my feet and they landed point blank right in my crotch. I couldn't believe what

I'd just heard. We'd just met these girls and we already were talking about sex!

"Here's a dime," Whitey said, holding one out to them. "Look in there if you dare."

The redhead snatched the dime, looked at her friend, who nodded, and dropped it in the slot. The machine whirred, the light came on, and the redhead looked in.

"Oh my God! How stupid!"

"What? What?" her friend squealed, pushing her out of the way.

I watched their asses as they took turns, bent over, peeking into the eye hole. I could not believe any of this. Whitey looked at me and winked.

"Let's see what's in the other barrel!" the redhead said excitedly. Again she ran her finger across the words as she read aloud, "A hammock built for two."

I held out a dime, which the brunette snatched from me, dropped into the slot and stuck her eye onto the peephole. "Ahhhhhh!" she screamed as she pulled the redhead into position, who also let out a hysterical yell.

"Let us see before it closes!" I said, wanting to get my money's worth, but it was too late.

"Is it dirty?" I asked the two giggling girls.

They looked at each other and laughed like hyenas again.

"Yes, it's definitely dirty!" the brunette said.

"I gotta see this," Whitey said, snuffing out his cigarette, putting in a dime and looking in. "Oh, yeah. That is dirty!"

I pushed him out of the way and there it was: a lady's bra draped across the inside of the barrel, dirty from hanging there for who knows how many decades.

"This is fun!" the redhead shouted. "We have dimes, too! Let's see what else there is!"

I looked at Whitey. Our exchange of silent glances meant that we knew we were onto something here, and we followed the girls down the row of naughty machines. Right in a row were three machines made to look like a brownstone you might see downtown in Manhattan. Right in the middle of the building was a round peephole, not unlike the peephole that was on the front of the barrels. Each of the three machines had signs on top: "Art Studio," "Doll House," and "Peeping Tom Headquarters." The four of us looked at the machines in silence.

"Yeah, what kind of stupid joke will these have?" I asked, reaching into my pocket for dimes. But there was something different about these machines. They weren't as goofy looking as the barrel peep shows. In fact, except for the sign that read "Peeping Tom Headquarters," I wouldn't have thought there would be anything risqué on display here.

"The Art Studio probably has a painting of Whistler's Mother or something," Whitey said, using his foot to snuff out yet another cigarette on the floor.

"Doll House probably has a Shirley Temple doll in there," the redhead said.

"Yeah, it's all stupid. Why waste your money?" the brunette said, sounding like she was trying to dissuade us from finding out what might be inside.

The brunette wasn't the only one feeling a little nervous. I decided the Art Studio would be the most likely to have another silly sight gag, so I dropped my dime in the slot. Lights appeared from behind the opaque windows and I could hear the panel slide from the peephole. I looked in, and man, was I surprised! There in full color was a huge photograph of a totally naked woman, posing with her huge breasts, gigantic erect nipples, and pubic hair showing! It was obvious to the others that I wasn't laughing.

"What is it?" Whitey said pushing me aside.   "Whoah!"

"What? What? Let us see!" the redhead said, knocking Whitey away and taking a peek. "Huuuhhh!" She gasped, then pulled away from the peephole. "Look at this!" she said to the brunette with a look of disbelief across her face.

The brunette slowly approached the peephole, but there were whirs and clicks and the lights in the windows went out before she had a chance to look inside.

"What did I miss?"

I looked at Whitey. He shrugged his shoulders and tilted his head as if to say, *I ain't saying nothing.* The redhead grabbed the brunette, cupped her hands over her mouth and began whispering frantically. The brunette's brown eyes widened and her jaw dropped.

"You guys are filthy pigs!" she said, madder than hell, and stormed away with the redhead right behind her.

Whitey and I rushed after them.

"Wait! We didn't know! I swear!" I said, touching the brunette on the shoulder from behind. She stopped in her tracks and turned around and I almost smashed into her. I couldn't believe how pretty she was. Her eyes were brown, but so dark they were almost as black as her hair. I don't think she had on any makeup, but her lips were as red as if she had been licking a cherry lollipop.

"Really?" she said softly, almost frightened.

"I swear, we didn't know!"

As I stood in front of the brunette, I noticed Whitey and the redhead were in a similar position with each other.

"Want to go on a ride or something?" I suggested meekly, knowing full well I was overwhelmed by the brunette's beauty.

She looked at the redhead, who nodded her approval.

"Let's go to the fun house!" Whitey said, pulling out his pack of Marlboros. The redhead picked one out and we headed back to the midway.

We watched their asses wiggle wildly as they zigzagged through the crowd with us in tow. They were running so fast, I was thinking that maybe they were trying to ditch us, but there they were standing at the ticket booth waiting. I handed Whitey fifty cents and he bought the tickets. The fun house would be perfect for getting to know the girls. We could help them through the tilted room by holding hands or putting our arms around their waists. But just as we rounded the corner for the entrance to the fun house, the girls stopped short, causing us to almost crash into them. They turned and extended their arms to block us from going any further.

"No! We can't go in the fun house," the redhead said, leading us quickly in the opposite direction. "In fact it's time for us to go, isn't it, Debbie?"

The brunette looked at me, giving me a subtle eyebrow tilt that I think was supposed to be a signal of some kind. Girls were always doing that, although I could never figure out what exactly they were trying to communicate until it was too late.

"Yeah, we've got to go now," Debbie agreed, almost sounding sad.

"Bye!" the redhead shouted, and they disappeared through the crowd, running.

I was crestfallen. Just like that, the two cuties were gone and I was certain we'd never see them again. Whitey lit up another.

"Come on, let's see what made them change their minds so fast," he said, walking back towards the fun house. "There's the reason right there," he said, pointing his chin towards the entrance. Taking tickets was a tough looking guy with slicked-back black hair, cigarette dangling, tight white t-shirt with a rolled-up sleeve with Lucky Strikes inserted.

"Him? He looks like he's twenty-one!"

"Yeah, well, he's the reason they ran away. He's gotta be the redhead's boyfriend."

"Maybe it's her brother?"

"Are you kidding?"

"What's the difference? We'll never see them again, anyway."

"Rockaway's like a small town. We'll find them. I'll bet Flynn and those guys know them. What street are they usually on?"

"101st, I think."

Whitey led us out of Playland and towards 101st Street. It was cooling off as the sun was setting, and more and more loud teenagers seemed to be crowding the streets. I think if I'd been alone, I'd have been scared to death. I don't know if it was the cigarettes or what, but I sensed that the tough kids were looking at Whitey and deciding to leave us alone. If I didn't know Whitey to be the goofball that I've known

119

him as my whole life, I probably would have thought he was a tough guy.

We turned right onto 101st Street and it looked just like a scene from our block back home. There were piles of kids everywhere. Little brats screaming and chasing each other. Girls in packs playing their pattycake games. Boys crowding the sidewalks with box baseball and in the middle of the street, probably the last game of stickball before it got too dark.

The street was lined with bungalow colonies, long narrow courtyards with small bungalows, each with a covered front porch. In front of every row of bungalows, grown-ups sat on porches, with more grown-ups on beach chairs in the courtyard. Barbeque grills were smoking up a tasty storm of hot dogs and hamburgers all over the place, and kids just seemed to show up, get food plopped into their grubby hands, and run off again.

As we walked down the sidewalk, the older kids were eyeing us suspiciously. I asked a fat little boy eating a hot dog if he knew Flynn, and without saying a word he pointed to the bungalows across the street. Of course! There it was, the Flynns' bungalow court. There was a white picket fence across the front, and each bungalow had two flags waving – an American flag and an Irish flag. Although the buildings were probably as old as the el train that ran just a block away, each one was freshly painted and spotless on the outside. There was a string of Christmas lights that ran the length of bungalows, but rather than being fitted with red and green bulbs, the lights were a patriotic mix of red, white and blue.

The first bungalow in the courtyard wasn't the typical single-story type, but a two-story job that looked more like a regular single family home. I heard that was the bungalow that Grandpa Flynn built first, so he could live there year 'round as he built the others with his bare hands. He was gone, but according to Flynn's father, his emphasis on bungalow colony Godliness, cleanliness, patriotism, and family togetherness was his legacy.

"This place is different from the other courts," Whitey said. We stood in awe, watching the string of lights give a magical glow to the flags and bungalows as evening was settling in.

A calico cat appeared and gave us a loud yowl.

"That's Nogard!" I said, recognizing the Flynn pet from back home.

"Nogard?" Whitey asked.

"That's dragon spelled backwards. There's Flynn!" I said, spying him on the upstairs porch of the bungalow palace.

A second later I could hear him stomping down the wooden steps.

"Hey, guys! When did you get here?" Flynn said, excitedly slapping us five.

I couldn't believe how different Flynn looked after not seeing him for only about a month. His skin was suntanned so dark, he looked like an Indian. And his hair, which was Beatles-long, had bright sun-bleached streaks. He was barefoot, bare-chested, and his ragged denim cutoffs were like short-shorts. He also appeared to be as tall as Whitey all of a sudden, which made me feel like a shrimp standing next to them.

"We took the train and got here a little while ago," I said, looking back up at the porch to see if his parents were there. "Are your parents around?"

"My mom's down the block at the Finnerans. My dad's back in the Bronx, he had to work."

I was happy to hear that. Flynn's mom is a real nice lady, and like most moms a much easier touch than dads. Flynn's dad is a good guy, but I know he can be strict at times. Flynn told me they weren't allowed to watch the Three Stooges. Now that's strict!

"Is it okay to smoke?" Whitey asked, holding his cigarette pack up.

"No. My Uncle Bobby is around somewhere."

"Well, we were wondering if there was someplace where we could spend the night," Whitey said, trying to sound nonchalant.

"I'm pretty sure you could stay with us," Flynn said. "But I have to ask my mom just to make sure."

"What do you think she'll say?" I asked nervously, because if she said no, we'd really be screwed.

"Well, I think she'll say you could stay over. My cousins aren't here this weekend and there's some extra room. How'd you get permission to come down and stay over without knowing where you were going to stay?"

"I didn't tell my parents," I admitted sheepishly.

"You better not tell my mom that or she'll be on the phone with them right away."

"We ain't saying nothing," Whitey said, cupping an unlit cigarette in his hand. "Hey, do you know a cute little brunette named Debbie who hangs out with a tall sexy redhead?"

"Debbie and Deirdre? Sure, why?"

"We almost picked them up in Playland," Whitey said, proudly.

"Deirdre goes out with one of the Lynches! He's like twenty-one and he's nuts!"

I got a sinking feeling in my stomach. What if he saw us chasing after the girls? We'd be deader than those fake cats in the Kill the Kat throwing game on the midway.

"Yeah, well, those two liked us. Screw him."

That may have sounded good from somebody as big and tough as Whitey, but from where I was standing, knowing that greaser might be after us was scarier than anything in the Haunted House.

We got a tour of the bungalow from Flynn, and it was like going through a living time capsule. Our apartment at home still had the same furniture from when my parents got married in the late forties, but the bungalows seemed to be furnished with stuff from the turn of the century. The toilet had a pull chain with a tank several feet overhead. The beds, dressers, and mirrors all looked like they were out of a silent Laurel and Hardy movie. And strangely, everything seemed much smaller. Yet every furnishing was neat and tidy, except for the bits of beach sand on the linoleum floor, which apparently is impossible to completely get rid of. They called the living room in the Flynns' big bungalow the "parlor," and it even had a potbellied stove in the corner. In the winter, that was the heater and everyone would sleep in that room instead of the bedrooms upstairs. There were ancient photographs hanging on the plain wooden slatted walls, many of them oval shaped and framed with glass. Flynn gave us a history lesson of how his ancestors came over from Ireland, and were even instrumental in unionizing the construction industry in New York City, at great peril to themselves and their families. One of his relatives was beaten to death by a bunch of cops breaking up a union protest.

"So where can we find those two babes?" Whitey finally asked, nervously fingering his unlit cigarette.

"They're usually on 98th Street by their bungalow court. Want to go there?" Flynn said, matter-of-factly.

"Hell, yeah. Let's go now. It's starting to get dark," Whitey announced eagerly.

Flynn threw on a white t-shirt, put on a pair of flip-flops and led us out onto the sidewalk.

To avoid the crowds, we walked down some side streets to 98th Street. We passed an old brick building that had a fading painted sign, an ad for Camel cigarettes from World War II, with a soldier waving and the tag line was "The Soldier's Pack."

Ninety-eighth Street was the street right next to Playland. In fact, according to Flynn, the roller coaster was literally right across the street from the bungalows where the girls were staying. The roller coaster looked like a giant honeycombed wall of white two-by-fours. When the cars came flying around the curves the entire structure seemed to shake, rattle and roll as the girls screamed bloody hell, and the steel wheels screeched and thumped across old rails and ties.

"How do you get used to that racket?" I asked.

"What racket?" Flynn asked, oblivious to the deafening noise, Tootsie Pop in his mouth.

"Never mind."

Then suddenly, there they were! Deirdre and Debbie, sitting on the steps of a front porch in front of a humongous, three-story bungalow.

"What kind of bungalow is that?" I asked.

Flynn explained how these big old places used to be mansions at one time, then were changed into boarding houses. Now they just rent rooms and the renters have to share a bathroom with others on the same floor. Entire families cram into single rooms for weeks and months of the summer. One rackety old rambling house can probably have six or seven broods of maniac kids running round.

We stood next to some bushes out of sight of the girls. After much deliberation we decided to venture in and make friends again. Whitey lit up and led the way.

"What happened to you two?" Whitey asked, holding out a pack of cigarettes.

"Put those away!" Debbie said in a desperate whisper. "My mother could be watching!"

Whitey stashed his pack and extinguished his cigarette on the slate sidewalk. Both girls began craning their necks nervously, obviously trying to see which of their nosey neighbors were watching. They quickly led, or should I say ran, with the three of us following them down a path between houses that led to the main boulevard across from the boardwalk. We dodged traffic, and Whitey and I followed as Flynn and the two girls hopped from a bench onto a concrete checkerboard table, then onto and across the boardwalk, and down the stairs onto the beach. I had almost forgotten why half of New York City comes to Rockaway – the ocean!

The lampposts on the boardwalk made dusk seem brighter, but by the time we walked to a spot far down the beach we liked, it was pitch black. The roar of the ocean drowned out the street noise and a ribbon of white waves crashing to the surf was all anyone could see. The ocean was just a black nothingness that melded into the dark horizon. The girls and Flynn immediately kicked off their flip-flops and merely left them by the stairs as we started our trek through the sand to the water's edge. Whitey and I kept our shoes on.

"You're Billy Calhoun's cousin, right?" Debbie said to Flynn, walking a little too close to him as far as I was concerned.

"I remember you when you were a little kid," Flynn said, smiling. "You've really grown up."

I didn't like the way Debbie smiled back at him.

"You were one of the big kids," Deirdre said to him, positioning herself next to Whitey as we were drawn to the surf's edge.

Deirdre and Debbie ran towards a large lifeguard chair. It was about six feet high, and the seat was wide enough for four people. Flynn and Whitey ran after them and right behind them up the ladder. I stood at the bottom, looking up at the four of them sitting there, giggling.

"How's the view up there?" I asked.

They didn't respond. Whitey began lighting four cigarettes. I thought Debbie liked me, but, like Popeye said, "You can bet your last nickel that women is fickle." I walked down to the water by myself and ambled along the shore, trying not to get my sneakers wet. I heard feet hit the sand and turned around – Debbie had jumped off the chair and she was walking right towards me. Holy crap. Now what do I do? Part of me felt like running into the water and swimming away, I was so scared, but another part of me wanted to run towards her in slow motion, like one of those corny toothpaste commercials.

"Hi," Debbie said quietly when she caught up with me.

"Hi," I responded, probably just as quietly.

We walked along the beach, leaving the other three laughing and goofing around on the lifeguard chair. I don't think we could have walked any slower. For about twenty steps, I was afraid to even look at her.

"Do you have a boyfriend?"

I couldn't believe what I had just asked her. But ever since I'd laid eyes on her that's all I could think about. It just came out.

"No, we broke up."

I wanted to run around in circles and scream in glee. But instead I just said, "Oh."

She was walking so close to me, the smell of her Prell-washed hair was beginning to overpower the smell of the salt water spray. Her bare arm brushed against mine, sending a chill up my spine. I swallowed hard, and felt my abdomen muscles tightening. I let my hand brush against hers briefly, and then I reached out for her hand for real. I couldn't believe it! She held hands with me! My head was spinning like I just sniffed a tube of airplane glue. I was afraid to look at her, but finally in twenty more steps I looked to the side and she smiled at me. I didn't hear the three of them on the lifeguard tower anymore. I didn't even hear the ocean. I think I actually could hear my own heartbeat.

"Is Deirdre your best friend?"

"Yeah. What's your name?"

"Vinny. Whitey's my best friend."

"How long are you in Rockaway for?"

We kept walking and I explained how we were on an adventure from the Bronx, and were hoping that we could sleep in a bungalow at Flynn's and we didn't tell our parents and everything was up in the air, and before I knew it we were so far down the beach I couldn't even see the lifeguard tower when I turned around.

"Look how far away we are!" I said turning her around. And as I did, I realized my arm was around her and she didn't push me away. I even thought I could hear *her* heartbeat. I leaned forward, closed my eyes, and put my lips to hers. I think my eyeballs begin spinning around and I could hear the calliope of the merry-go-round in the distance as the whole world began to spin. I pulled her closer and we began to move our heads slowly in a circle with our lips closed tightly against each other. I could smell bubble gum and Prell and cigarettes and sea salt and sand and sweat and popcorn and holy crap! *I might faint! I think I've stopped breathing!*

I pulled back and we both slowly opened our eyes. I couldn't believe this was me kissing this strange girl in Rockaway on the beach at night, without my parents in the same borough, even. I could tell by her eyes that another make-out session was eagerly anticipated, when

126

suddenly a distant high-pitched scream cut through the sound of the crashing surf.

"That's Deirdre!" Debbie said, pulling me as she ran full-speed towards the lifeguard chair.

As we got closer I heard male voices shouting too, and saw a small crowd flailing away at the base of the tower. I dropped Debbie's hand as I ran faster to the scene. I got there and two older guys were standing over Whitey, who was curled up in a fetal position in the sand. Shit! It's the guy from the Fun House. I stood there in shock, not knowing what to do. *Should I run? Should I yell something? Should I act crazy like I'm a tough guy?* He looked and sneered at Whitey, and then he kicked him hard in his midsection. Whitey grunted. Deirdre was sitting in the lifeguard chair, crying hysterically. The two guys were old. At least twenty-one. They even had sideburns. Flynn was nowhere in sight. The guys started to walk away backwards, and the one from the Fun House pointed up at Deirdre and shouted, "You fuckin' bitch! I'll take care of you tomorrow!"

They were about twenty yards away, turning their heads to watch us, when Flynn ran up to us.

"What the hell happened?" Flynn asked, out of breath, as we both helped Whitey stand up.

"Where were you?" I asked Flynn.

"I was under the boardwalk taking a leak."

Whitey wasn't wearing his glasses. His face was bloody, with blood trickling from his nose and his lower lip.

Deirdre jumped down and ran into Debbie's arms. They both cried, like they were the ones bleeding.

"How do I look?" Whitey asked, wiping blood from his mouth and then examining his hand. "Those motherfuckers!" Whitey screamed at the top of his lungs, stunning us, and even making the girls stop their wailing momentarily. "Come on, there's three of us now! Let's go get them!" he urged us.

I doubt I hid the expression on my face very well. I didn't want to chase after two big guys in the dark, on their turf, even if there were three of us. I might be okay in a fight with somebody my size, but that was probably somebody in the seventh grade, at that stage in my physical development.

"Gee, I don't know..." I mumbled.

"What? Are you kidding me?" Whitey said softly and intensely, with a look of total disbelief on his bloody face. He took a few steps, reached down and retrieved his glasses from the sand. "The heck with you guys," he said without emotion, and walked down the beach.

I stood there and just watched him disappear into the night. Debbie and Deirdre were still slobbering as they walked in the opposite direction without so much as waving goodbye.

"Want to see if it's okay to stay at my place tonight?" Flynn asked.

"Yeah," I said, feeling like a total pussy, wondering how I could ever face Whitey again.

Chapter Nine

—Now—

When we set up the funeral for my father at Williams Funeral Home a few years ago, the funeral director said there was a simple path for all people from Presentation: Presentation to Williams Funeral Home to the Gate of Heaven. He was referring to the archdiocesan cemetery, not the actual gate of Heaven. I guess that path really couldn't be simpler. It was the part that involved the actual gate of Heaven that became a bit more complicated. After all, if you're born into a Catholic family, receive all the sacraments and go to Catholic school for twelve years, you can't escape the fact that deeply embedded in your brain or your DNA or your soul is that mysterious path to Heaven. And I think it's a little more complicated than merely taking the Saw Mill River Parkway north to a cemetery in Hawthorne, New York.

Closing a casket at the funeral home is about as final as it gets. While the person is lying there with the lid open, it's still the person. There he is. People talk and carry on as if he's just taking a nap. But then the lid is closed forever.

I drove to the cemetery alone and got there just in time. There was a priest I didn't know, Matty's mom, and a younger woman I assumed was a relative, with a little girl who appeared to be about five. The young woman was dressed in an attractive black business suit ensemble and she looked around thirty years old. I stood several yards away as they conducted the short ceremony. Matty's mom and the other woman gave their farewells to Matty and the priest. Of course there were tears, but they were both composed enough to stop and say hello to me.

"This is Vinny Schmidt from the old building. This is my granddaughter, Bernadette," Mrs. O'Malley said. She wiped away a little bit of the dirt she had on her hand from when she'd tossed some into the grave.

129

"Nice to meet you," Bernadette said, shaking my hand in a firm business-like manner.

"I moved back to New York a few months ago, and I became kind of close with Matty. He was a great guy."

"They had adjoining bar stools," Mrs. O'Malley cracked.

"What does that mean?" the little girl asked.

Bernadette smiled. "Never mind. Thanks for being kind to him."

I felt like a schmuck. How kind was I to sit next to him and join in as he drank himself to death before my very eyes? And now this little girl will probably think I'm the guy who helped her Uncle Matty drink himself to death for the rest of her life. We said polite good-byes and Mrs. O'Malley told me to keep in touch with her, but I doubt she meant it.

I still had to work, so I drove back to the Bronx and took the subway downtown to the job. I expected that one of the near-acquaintances I had at work might ask why I was dressed in a suit, but no one did. I worked a full shift without talking three words to anyone.

I decided on the subway ride home I wasn't going to go any of the bars on 238th Street anymore. But by the time the train screeched to a halt at the station, my plan dissipated in the evening's humidity. My car was parked on the street next to the schoolyard. As I tossed my suit jacket and tie into the trunk, I thought of the program we used to have for Queen of the May. Mrs. Schmelzer would be pumping her spindly legs wildly on the portable pump organ as the entire school made a procession to a sacred incinerator by the rectory. That was where they burned sacred items, like old missals, vestments, or stale communion wafers. But at the Queen of the May, each student would write a secret wish on a piece of paper, and as the entire school sang hymns about the Virgin Mary, one by one we'd drop our notes into the incinerator and watch the burning smoke go to heaven. I walked over to the ivy-covered chain link fence, made a little hole through the vines and there the incinerator was, still standing. I went back to the trunk of the car and got a piece of paper. I walked through the lot to the side of the rectory where the small barrel-shaped incinerator was, and stood there staring at the blank page with my pen in hand. Maybe it was because I was next to the rectory, I felt guilty about asking for something for myself. So I wrote, *Help me find Whitey.* I pulled out a Zippo lighter, lit the piece of paper on fire and dropped it in. I watched the wisp of smoke rise to heaven.

I walked to the Goal Post and peered through the bright red neon Bud Light sign in the window. Judge Judy was on the TV and there was an old man sitting in Matty's spot. I imagined myself in a few weeks or months or years watching that guy get planted at Gate of Heaven, and wondered when it would be my turn to sit on that stool. I decided to head home.

Two weekends had come and gone and I found excuses not to drive to Livingston Manor. But that Saturday morning I had set the alarm for six and I was already on the highway heading north, munching on a buttered hard roll fried egg sandwich from the Short Stop Diner. I didn't even let the forecast of rain stop me, the way it had the previous two weekends.

Although I remember Whitey talking about Livingston Manor when we were kids, I had only passed through there. I remember him talking about a cottage on a lake but that was all I knew. I searched on the internet and found there were several mud holes in the town that could be considered a lake.

Growing up there were two kinds of families: beach families and country families. We were a beach family. The "country" was anything above Yonkers, but usually in the Catskill Mountains, the famous summer vacation spot for New York Jews. But there were also small enclaves of Catholic city folks who trekked to upstate lakes far removed from the Jewish resorts and camps. I had a cousin who lived for a couple of years in a converted chicken coop on the outskirts of a lakeside group of cottages that were primarily summer rentals. I visited him one winter, but when I got there I found out that his stoned-out girlfriend had burnt the place down trying to keep it warm with a faulty kerosene heater. During that trip over twenty years ago, the roads were poorly marked and there were not many places for gas, food or lodging. But all these years later, as I exited the highway and headed for Livingston Manor, there were the usual strip malls filled with fast food franchises and big-box stores, like every other suburb in America. It didn't look like the country any more.

I turned off the main highway in the hope that I'd find at least a section that might be a holdover from when it was a summer resort spot, and not part of exurbia. It only took a few miles of winding roads to get away from Linens 'N Things and start seeing cars on blocks in weedy front yards, so I knew I was on the right track. It amazed me how just a few minutes away there were gated communities and a Home Town Buffet, yet suddenly it was like I was driving through a forest. I drove up a sharply curving two-lane road for several miles when suddenly there was an outlook on the side of the road, marked by a faded sign with bullet holes that read "View." Seeing signs with bullet holes always means you're leaving the suburbs and entering rural America. I pulled over into a small dirt parking lot about the width of two cars. There was an ancient low stone wall at the edge, next to a dangerously steep cliff. In the distance below there was a lake surrounded by thick woods and through a clearing I could see some cottages. Down the lake I could also see what looked like a boat house or lakeside restaurant and some other old wooden structures. I hopped back in the car and meandered down the damp mountain road hoping I was getting closer to old Livingston Manor ... and hopefully, old Whitey.

What looked like a boat house from the road high above turned out to be a road house. You rarely see large wooden structures this old anymore, simply because they have all burned down. It had the familiar structure of a vintage resort restaurant, or what they used to call a casino, which was essentially a large restaurant with a stage and a dance floor. The wooden steps that led up to what I'm sure was a grand entrance at one time had weeds growing through it. The entire building was surrounded by a covered porch, which many years ago was probably chock-full of elegant diners. A couple of the floor-to-ceiling windows were boarded up and painted dark green. The amateurish hand-painted sign read "Captain Norm's Food and Drink."

I walked gingerly up the front steps, avoiding the rotten planks, and peeked in the window of the front door. It was dark, but I could see a huge bar, a few patrons, and some French doors were open in the rear, revealing a nice view of the lake.

I felt like I was back on 238th Street. A salty old bartender was watching the horse races, and two old men were drinking tumblers of booze at the bar. I sat at the end of the bar and put a twenty down.

"Coors Light," I said to the bartender who was still watching the races.

Without saying anything, he pulled a bottle out of a sink filled with ice, twisted off the cap, placed it in front of me, took my twenty, gave me change, and continued to follow the race to its conclusion.

"Goddammit," he whispered as the winners were announced.

"Is the kitchen open?"

"Not for the past two years," he said, still watching the television.

"Is there somewhere to get a bite around here?"

"There's Home Town Buffet back on 17."

"Anything closer?"

He finally turned his eyes from the television and looked at me like I had just appeared out of a genie's bottle. "Are you lost or something?"

"No, just sightseeing."

He nodded his head and tended to the other paying customers. I walked over to the French doors and looked out onto the lake. It was lovely in the misty afternoon rain. Across the lake there were bulldozers moving earth, and I could hear chainsaws at work. I would have liked to step out onto the porch, but there was a rope across the door with a sign that read *Do Not Enter*. There was a tree pushing through two planks on the porch and entire boards were rotted through.

The bartender was reading a newspaper near my bar stool when I took my seat again.

"Where are you from?" he asked, paging through a copy of the *New York Post*.

I could already tell this guy was from my gene pool.

"The city," I replied.

"Where in the city?"

"The Bronx."

"Where in the Bronx?"

"Near Van Cortlandt Park."

"Oh. What brings you here?"

I suddenly realized I was officially playing private eye and maybe he was, too. *Do I let on that I'm looking for Whitey? It's almost a certainty that if he lives around here it's because he's on the lam. But what the hell, my quest is on.*

"I'm looking for an old friend. Whitey Shelley," I said casually, then took a sip of beer.

"Shelley, huh? Hmmm. I'll have to think on that. He was a friend of yours?"

"From grammar school. We were best friends."

"How come you don't know where he is, then?"

"We just lost touch just during high school. You know how things happen."

He walked to the end of the bar to tend to the other customers. One of them looked at me and squinted. I was being checked out. I finished my beer and made it obvious I wanted another by holding it in the air for a couple of seconds. The bartender saw me, but didn't respond.

I sat there for several minutes, then returned to the open French doors to look out onto the lake. The weather was getting worse, and I could see dark storm clouds moving in. I glanced over and my empty beer bottle was still sitting there. I went to the men's room, took a leak, took my time cleaning up, and upon my return to my stool, my fresh beer was still absent.

Finally, after several commercial breaks in the horse race coverage, he came back with a fresh bottle of beer.

"Nah. I don't think I know a Shelley. Why do you think he's up here, anyway?"

"His family came up here in the summers. I thought maybe being summer and all, he might be up here."

"You knew his old man?"

"Not well. He was disabled, I think."

I was being grilled. He asked me more questions about things he already knew the answers to. He went back to his two cronies at the other end and serious discussions continued.

I finished my beer and put a fiver on the bar under the empty bottle.

"I gotta head out. Take care," I said as I was exiting.

"Thanks, pal. Nah. We don't know any Robert Shelley."

Since I never even mentioned the name Robert, which is his real name, it was obvious by the line of Joe Friday-like questioning they didn't want me to know Whitey's whereabouts. I headed down the road to the lake and looked for the cottages.

If the rumors about Whitey were even half true, then I was sure he'd keep a low profile and his close friends would be used to covering for him. I knew a guy from the neighborhood who had to hide out in a California desert town for nearly ten years because of gambling debts with some local Bronx bookies. So if Whitey was a deserter from the army and/or a murderer, he'd have to cover his tracks pretty good, even if decades had passed since all that went down.

The rain was getting heavy and the winding road slippery. Under the canopy of thick tall trees and dark skies, I wondered why the hell I was even doing that at all. Murder is serious business. Guys wanted for murder are the most dangerous because they have nothing to lose.

The faded, crooked sign for the Irish Circle Cottages wasn't illuminated and in the darkness, I almost went right by it. It was next to a dirt road that led into the woods. I pulled over on the narrow shoulder wondering if I should venture in. A speeding pickup truck swerved so close to my car it almost hit me. I decided to go down the dirt road and see what was at the other end.

There were remnants of gravel that must have been laid years earlier, but over time, the road had become mostly mud and rocks. There were a few red arrows nailed to trees so I followed them when I came to the forks in the road. Like Yogi Berra said, "If there's a fork in the road, take it." Suddenly the woods ended and there I was, about twenty yards from the lake, facing two cottages, one to my right and one to my left. There was a small dock in the middle with a small boat tied up. There were no other cars in sight. I turned off the engine and opened the window.

The raindrops made it hard to see out the windshield, and the storm clouds were so thick it was hard to tell if the sun had set yet. There were a few ducks on the lake enjoying the showers and a large fish jumped out of the water, startling me. The lake was still except for the ripples from the rain, and the movement of the ducks and fish. I was surprised that on a weekend there weren't kids running around playing, even in the rain. It was an ideal setting for a group of summer lake cottages. Yeah, it looked rundown, if not dilapidated, but for a city kid it was fantastic.

I felt something hard press against the back of my head and reached around, but before I could feel what it was, I felt it shoved hard into my head.

"Don't move," an old raspy voice outside the car said, from just behind me. I looked in my side view mirror and saw the double barrel of the shotgun held against the back of my head. I could just make out that it was a black man wearing a red and black plaid long sleeve shirt holding the gun. "Just start your engine, turn around slowly, get the hell out of here and never come back," he said calmly.

I did exactly as he said. As I drove away I could see in my rear view mirror that he was an older guy with a thick shock of white hair. He held the shotgun high as I drove up the road. Just before I turned, he started to untie the boat on the dock. I made it back to the main road and just as I made the turn I noticed on the ground a crudely painted sign that read, *DO NOT ENTER!!! PRIVATE PROPERTY!!! DANGER!!!*

Although I thought about raising the sign up so the next sucker wouldn't make the same mistake I did, I decided against it, in case the old psycho was hiding in the bushes with a bazooka.

It was getting darker and the rain had let up, so I continued driving around the lake as best I could. I was going in a general counterclockwise direction, but the roads didn't exactly parallel the shore perfectly. I hit a few dead ends. By the time I thought I might be making some headway, I saw some lights. Just my luck. I was back at Captain Norm's again. There were more cars and a few motorcycles parked in the lot, so I figured I'd try my luck there a second time.

Norm was still at the bar with the same two old-timers, but a small noisy crowd had gathered. A few middle-aged biker guys with beards, tattoos and ponytails were playing pool, some blue collar guys were at the bar, and a table of girls was yakking it up. It was Saturday night at an upstate roadhouse.

I took a seat at the bar and the bartender asked me what I wanted. After he dropped off another beer I told him about visiting the cottages, but left out the part about having a twelve-gauge shotgun shoved into my cranium. I just said a caretaker asked me to leave. His eyes narrowed and he cocked his head.

"A caretaker asked you to leave?"

"Well, he didn't exactly ask. He instructed me to leave."

"You're lucky you didn't get a belly full of buckshot," he laughed. "It wouldn't have been the first time."

A nice looking thirty-something woman in cutoffs and a jeans jacket walked up to the bar, ordered three beers, and asked the barkeep to turn on the jukebox. Suddenly, in a dark corner, a bright 1950s era vintage Seeburg jukebox whirred to life. The woman asked for four dollars in quarters and went over to the jukebox. After some studying of the playlist she dumped in some quarters, pushed some big red buttons, and next thing I knew the opening chords to the Beatles' "I Want to Hold Your Hand" was blasting through the joint. I could tell from my bar stool that the Seeburg was playing 45s! Not CDs or from some internet-downloaded mp3 iTunes whatever. This was a 45 with scratches and all! I waited until she exhausted her coin supply and walked over to get an up-close look at the old record machine. It was a beauty. The records were stored in vertical slots, clearly in view, enclosed in a fifties futuristic glass case looking something like the glass enclosure that might house a Martian's brain in an Ed Wood movie. It wasn't in mint condition, but it was obvious that someone had been maintaining it over the years. I found it fascinating that the machine made playing the records part of the visual appeal of the jukebox. I watched and listened between records as gears whirred and cranked, moving the records out of and into their slots and onto the turntable. Another yellow swirl of a Beatles single was visible briefly and as it was dropped into position, I briefly saw on the flip side of the record three small square labels: one with the number 13, one with the letter R, and the other with the letter S.

I immediately recognized those small squares. They were the standard issue labels you received when you purchased a 45 carrying case complete with dividers for organizing your collection. The letters were included so you could put your initials on the records so they wouldn't be mixed up with other people's records at parties. It seemed like a ridiculous reach, but could the *RS* have stood for Robert Shelley? I waited for "Lady Madonna" to finish and watched as it flipped around and there it was on the "Inner Light" side of the record: 13 RS.

I waited at the jukebox for another vintage Beatles song to come on, and there it was on the "You Know My Name Look Up the Number" side of "Let It Be." 27 RS. Could it be?

I went back to my bar stool and pondered the possibility that Whitey used his own record collection to stock this jukebox. Since the bartender wasn't forthcoming about Whitey's whereabouts, I thought perhaps I could get some information by focusing on the jukebox.

"That's a nice jukebox," I said the next time the bartender deposited another beer on my coaster.

"It's a beauty! A 1954 Model R," he said, dropping his rag to the bar, his face illuminated with enthusiasm. "It's a hobby of mine."

"And great tunes, too. You pick the music as well?"

"Nah, I have one of the guys do that for me. Although we haven't updated it for a while."

"Who was that?" I asked smiling, my beer bottle aloft.

His face dropped as he realized I was on to something. "I've got some business to attend to at the other end of the bar."

It was a while before he came back to my end of the bar, and when he did return, there was no time for small talk. Whitey was a buyer for the kitchens in the Bronx before he disappeared. That's probably what he would have done when he moved up here. And I'm sure he couldn't stand to be in a joint with lousy music blasting out of a gorgeous machine like that one.

The bikers were becoming louder as the beer bottles piled up on the tables next to the pool table. They looked to be about my age, which of course would mean Whitey's age, too. I took my beer and sat in a chair between them and the jukebox. I thought perhaps just sitting there would eventually give me an ice breaker into their conversation. I noticed one of them had an eagle tattoo with the word Airborne underneath, signifying the 101st Airborne; he was probably a vet. As I sat and waited for a foray into their chitchat, I realized how hard it is to start a conversation with a group of guys without arousing suspicion. That's because there must be a motive. With females, it's obvious what the motive is.

I pumped a few more quarters into the jukebox just as the biker with the 101st Airborne tattoo happened to be making a combination shot at that end of the table. He made it, winning the game.

"Nice shot," I said.

He seemed appreciative that I noticed.

"Want to hear something?" I added, nodding towards the jukebox.

"Stones," he said.

I punched up "Mother's Little Helper," "19th Nervous Breakdown," "Have You Seen Your Mother, Baby, Standing in the Shadow," and "Satisfaction." There were four bikers, ranging in age from my age to maybe ten years older. Two wore denim vests, two had black leather vests, three wore t-shirts, and the one with the eagle tattoo was bare-armed. They sang along with the Stones and banged on the

139

floor with their pool cues during Charlie Watts's famous ten drum beats after Mick's "Hey, hey, hey!" in "Satisfaction."

"Great jukebox," I said after "Satisfaction" ended.

"They keep it stocked with the best of the best!" Eagle Tattoo Guy said proudly.

"Do they update it with new 45s? I didn't know they still made them."

"The guy has a line on them down in the city. He would trek all the way down to somewhere in the Village to get them."

"Do they still make them?" I could tell I'd asked one question too many. "I mean, like today?"

"I'll ask him when I see him," he said, looking at the balls that were being racked. Then he broke them and studied them as they spread across the table.

"Can you let me know?"

He started to look annoyed as he prepared his next shot. He called out "low" and took his next shot, getting one in.

"I'll ask him," he said, moving on to his next conquest.

"Great, I'll stop in next weekend."

"Okay."

I left the bar feeling buzzed, but was higher on the fact that I'd made some headway in tracking down Whitey. Fortunately, it had stopped raining and I made it back to Route 17 where I found a diner. I finished three cups of black coffee and a full breakfast, followed by apple pie a la mode, and read the *Pennysaver.*

I was just about to ask for the check when in walked a black guy with white hair wearing a black and red plaid shirt. When he sat at the counter and ordered half-cooked bacon on buttered white bread, there was no doubt in my mind: this is the guy who put the shotgun to my head. I wondered whether he remembered my car or the back of my head. I signaled to the waitress and she brought my tab. I plopped my money on the table and exited quietly.

Besides my car, there were three other cars in the lot. Off to the side, around the corner, was a really old Dodge pickup, probably from '54 or '55. I walked past it and observed that it had a gun rack, perfect for a shotgun.

"Don't move," the familiar voice said. Something poked me in my lower back. "Get in," he said, guiding me towards the passenger side of the pickup and opening the door with his other hand.

I sat there thinking I was appearing calm, as he walked in front of the truck and got in the driver's side. He held his hand in his front pocket, like he was holding a gun in it.

"We're just going to go for a little ride and have a talk," he said as he and I headed back towards the roads that led to the lake.

I didn't feel like my life was in danger, but then thought that maybe I should. I started to panic.

"Don't panic," he said, pulling off Route 17. "Don't worry. We just need to talk."

I sat in silence for the ten minutes it took to get back onto the winding mountain road that led to the lake. We came to a fork I recognized and he took a left instead of a right. Next thing I knew, we were on a bumpy dirt road with absolutely no lights in sight.

We stopped at the edge of what looked like a swampy area and I could make out a duck blind nearby. He stopped the engine and looked straight ahead. One hand on the wheel, the other in his pocket.

"So, tell me. What gives? And don't try to bullshit a bullshitter."

"My name is Vinny Schmidt." I thought maybe if I told him where I worked it would make him less likely to bump off somebody who worked in the media. "I work for *NYNow*."

"That's the news channel, right?"

"Yes."

"Why are you looking for Whitey?"

"I grew up with Whitey and I just want to see what he's up to…"

He tapped the steering wheel with his fist three times. "Don't bullshit me."

"I swear," I said, trying not to show my panic. "We lost touch in high school. We were best friends growing up. I just want to…"

After all these weeks, no, *decades*, of wanting to find out what happened to Whitey, I realized I couldn't explain why. I had no words to describe why I should give a shit about a guy who I lost touch with all those years ago. I let him go. I never tried to reconnect then. Why now? "I don't know why. I just feel like I've got to see him."

He was doing something in his right pocket, where I'm sure the gun was. He pulled out a pen and a piece of paper. "Write down your name and your number. If Whitey wants to be in touch, somebody will call." He opened the glove box, and a light came on so I could see what I was doing. I also saw a pistol in there, possibly a nine millimeter Glock.

I wrote my name and number down and handed him the slip of paper. He stuck it in his right pocket, closed the glove box and drove back to the parking lot with both hands on the wheel. He pulled up next to my car and looked at me. The lights from the diner lit his face clearly. I could see he was once a good-looking man with strong cheekbones that now exaggerated his hollow cheeks. He was dead serious.

"If someone doesn't get in touch with you, then that's the end of this. I can find you. Capeesh?"

"Capeesh."

I got into my car, and he took off. And I did *capisce*. I felt like a moron for giving him my name and number. He could find me, no problem. All I could do now was hope that if they did get in touch, it wasn't to bury me underneath that duck blind.

Several days went by and I hadn't heard anything... then as I was exiting the subway at West 238th Street, my cell rang. I didn't recognize the number, but it was from 518, the area code for Columbia County in upstate New York. I stood at the bottom of the stairs and answered.

"Hello."

"Come to the cottages tomorrow at nine p.m. By the dock. Alone."

I recognized the voice. It was the black dude who liked to pull guns on me.

"I'll be there," I said, without thinking.

The phone went silent. He hung up.

I'd been wondering for a few decades what happened to Whitey. I'd find out pretty soon, I thought. I just hoped it wouldn't be the last thing I knew before I became the one who mysteriously disappeared.

Chapter Ten

—Then—

Flynn and I walked back towards the bungalows on 101st Street. We checked out every doorway, alley, and group of kids we say saw. We hoped we'd see Whitey and we were terrified that we'd see the guys who beat him up. Back in our neighborhood, there was a certain comfort level when you hung out or wandered in the neighborhood. But once you're off your turf anything can happen. And usually does.

It was late and there were no little kids left on the streets. Packs of grown-ups walked around, but most of them looked drunk. There were more bars around there than in our neighborhood in the Bronx, and that was saying something. Flynn suggested we take a shortcut through an empty garbage-strewn lot. We ducked through a hole in a chain link fence, and I didn't like the looks of it at all.

"Don't worry, I do this every day!" Flynn said reassuringly.

We walked over broken glass and bricks. I could see the remnants of old bungalow foundations.

Flynn gave a running commentary: *This was torn down last year, but the owners haven't done anything with it yet. We buried our cat under that big rock there. My father says the state is going to legalize gambling in Rockaway one day and we'll be rich.*

There was one crumbling bungalow that still had two walls standing next to the hole in the fence we were headed for, and just as he walked past it I heard glass crash, a man's god-awful scream, and something come flying around the corner of the demolished bungalow carrying what looked like a giant gorilla over its head.

"Arrgghhhhh!" the lunatic yelled in the dark, coming right at us.

"Shit!" Flynn yelled, picking up a short two by four.

"Fuck! Whitey, you asshole!" I said, recognizing him. He had a busted-up giant stuffed animal high over his head.

144

"This thing reeks!" Whitey said, throwing it against the ground. It made a loud thump as its soaking wet innards splattered by our feet. "You should've seen the looks on your faces!" he said laughing, poking his finger into our chests.

The three of us laughed about it as we walked down the dark street, recounting over and over how Whitey scared the bejesus out of us with his smelly gorilla. It took a while for me to realize that we didn't mention the real horror story that had just happened, when Whitey had the crap beat out of him because his two friends weren't around to help. And when we did show up we just pussied out like two French soldiers watching the Nazis march through Paris.

"What are you guys going to do for the rest of the night?" Whitey asked, still wiping the stinky gorilla stuffings off himself.

"I guess, go hang out at the bungalows until it's time to go to bed," Flynn said.

"Shit! I forgot to call my parents!" I said, stopping dead in my tracks. "I better call now. Can I use the phone at your bungalow?"

"The only phone is in my parent's bedroom. And knowing them, they're probably already asleep."

"Is there another phone?"

"There's a pay phone in the Irish Rover," Flynn said, shuffling his feet.

The Irish Rover is an old man's bar down the block from Flynn's. We walked in and the bartender didn't even notice us entering, walking through the bar, and into the back room where the phone was between the doors to the bathrooms. I could tell right away this was a crazy grown-up drinking bar, not a bar for sneaky underage drinkers, like most of the Rockaway watering holes. Everybody in there was grownup, including lots of women who were sitting at the bar and in packs at tables. The jukebox was blaring Irish music, people were dancing insanely, pounding their feet into the ground like they were trying to stomp out a fire. There were even men dancing with men. It was easy to see that everybody was bombed out of their minds.

145

"Holy crap! And I thought teenagers were crazy!" I said as we slinked through to the back room. "Where's the phone? I need some change."

Flynn pushed me along to the phone and Whitey stayed by the doorway to the main room to keep an eye out.

"What am I going to say? What about this racket?"

"Tell them my parents are having a party. You don't have to say it's a bar. Just say they gave you permission to stay over."

"What if they figure it out or something?"

"Worry about that when it happens."

The palms of my hands were clammier than raw littlenecks. I dropped in a dime that clanged on its way down, and then I got a dial tone. I dialed my home number and an operator came on and asked for forty-five more cents. I dropped in two quarters and the phone began to ring.

"Hello," my mother answered abruptly.

"Hi, Mom –"

"Where the hell are you, I've been lying here waiting up for you. What the hell is going on?"

"I'm with the Flynns in Rockaway... Don't you remember I told you I was coming out here."

"What? Put Mrs. Flynn on."

I shot my head to the left so hard I heard something crack. Flynn knew something went wrong. I held my hand over the mouthpiece.

"She wants to talk to your mother," I said to Flynn, then into the phone I said, "Hold on, I'm getting her."

Whitey rushed over. "What's going on?"

"My mother wants to talk to Mrs. Flynn!"

I could see a light bulb go on above Whitey's noggin as he pointed his index finger up in the air and smiled. "I'll be right back."

"Hold on a minute, we're getting her,"

"What's all that noise?" my mom demanded.

"They're having a party. It's... somebody's birthday."

I looked over and Whitey was walking back into the room with a lady he practically had to hold up. Her eyes were at half-mast and her hair looked she combed it with a bar broom. She slipped on something and Whitey had to grab her before she hit the deck.

"Just say, 'This is Mrs. Flynn. Everything's fine,'" Whitey said to her as he guided her towards me.

I held the mouthpiece so hard it hurt my hand. "Are you out of your freaking mind? Her? As Mrs. Flynn?"

"This is gonna work," Whitey said, pushing her right next to me. She stunk like a gym bag soaked in beer.

"Hold on, Mom, here she is," I said, my voice cracking like Alfalfa getting busted by Mrs. Crabtree.

"Hello, this is Mrs. Flynn," the stewed tomato slurred into the phone. "Everything is fiiiinnnne," she said her voice lowering into a juicy belch. "Uh-huh. Uh-huh. Uh-huh. Uh-huh. She wants to talk to you," she said giggling, as she handed me the phone.

"Mom?" I said, expecting her hand to reach through the phone and start slapping the shit out of me.

"Well, okay," she said flatly. "As long as Mrs. Flynn says it's okay. Has she been drinking?" she whispered.

"A little bit."

"Well, be home before supper tomorrow. Good night."

"Good night," I said, hanging up the phone gingerly.

I looked at Flynn, Whitey, and the drunk lady as they waited for the news. "She bought it," I said in disbelief.

All three shouted for joy and began shaking me in jubilation.

"Now, where's my drinks?" the drunk lady asked triumphantly.

"You'll have to buy them, but we're paying!" Whitey said as she hugged and kissed him on the cheek.

She led us into the main barroom and sat us at a corner booth where two other ladies were sitting. They were just as ossified as the first one, but quite a bit younger. They were probably in their late twenties, were actually kind of cute, and greeted us like we were guys who could hang out in a bar. Whitey pulled out ten bucks and told the first drunk lady to go buy six beers for the table. I kicked Flynn under the table and he looked at me with a goofy smile and shrugged his shoulders.

"If my mom says it's okay... what the hell!"

I was shocked when she returned with a Rheingold beer tray, with three tumblers of booze topped with cherries, and three mugs of beer. She sat down with the tray and we each grabbed our drinks. Whitey held his mug up high, and said, "Here's to the greatest mom in the world!"

We all clinked our glasses and lots spilled onto the table. I couldn't believe it. We were drinking in a bar with three drunk women and nobody gave a shit!

"What are you ladies drinking?" Whitey asked.

The lady with jet black hair teased up high said, "Highballs."

"Is that a drink or a medical condition?" Whitey shot back.

The three looked of them at each other puzzled, but just for a split second, and then they busted out laughing uncontrollably.

"You're cute. How old are you?" the drunkest lady (the one who'd posed as Flynn's mom) asked Whitey.

"I'm eighteen," Whitey said without hesitation.

"And how old are your little friends?" As she asked, I felt a lady's bare foot inching up my leg under the table.

"They turn eighteen tonight at midnight," Whitey said. "They're twins."

"Fraternal!" I added.

"What's that?" the drunken beehived one croaked.

"That means we've got different mothers and different fathers," Flynn interjected.

The three of them looked at each other again, paused, and then laughed hysterically.

"You're twins? And it's your eighteenth birthday at midnight? You don't look eighteen. How old are you, really?"

"We'll tell you our age if you tell us yours," I said.

"Never mind. You win," the black-haired one said.

We were joking around so much and cracking these ladies up, that next thing I knew, I had finished my mug of beer. Before long a third tray of drinks was arriving at our table and I wasn't sure I could take another sip. I realized all I had eaten all day was potato chips, a candy apple, and a fried zeppole. I reached into my pocket and discovered the grand sum of three bucks and change. I whispered to Flynn that I needed to eat and he whispered to Whitey. As they were whispering back and forth, I saw the bartender was checking out our table and talking to a guy in a blue janitor's uniform with a mop next to him. I whispered that information to Flynn and he relayed it to Whitey.

"Would you ladies like to get something to eat?" Whitey asked. I had no idea Whitey could be so grown-up with women.

"Sure!" the third lady said. She was the blonde, who also appeared the least drunk, youngest, and most attractive.

The other two looked around the bar and decided all three should go to the ladies' room. I felt exposed. The three of us were sitting in the booth against the wall, but when they left we were easily visible from the bar. Next thing I knew the guy with the mop was standing next to the table. Before he could say anything, Whitey announced, "We were just leaving." The janitor nodded and we left. We stood outside the bar sitting next a parked car by the door. "We'll wait five minutes and then go," Whitey said, lighting another cigarette and throwing the empty package under the car.

I was positive the ladies weren't coming out to be with us. I mean, come on, we're kids! But holy shit, next thing – there was the blonde! I didn't notice in there but she was wearing skin-tight pants like Dick Van Dyke's wife on his TV show. She might be old, but what an ass! She walked over to Whitey and pulled him aside. They talked by the door for a few minutes, then Whitey came over to us.

"Guys, you're gonna flip. She wants me to go with her to a party. I'll meet you back at the bungalows later," Whitey said, trying to contain his nervous energy.

"Can't we come?" I asked dejectedly.

"They said you guys look too young. Sorry. I'll see you later," he said as Blondie came over, tugged on his arm and dragged him back into the bar.

"Let's go get something to eat and some Sen-Sen," Flynn said, patting me on the back.

I don't think I was drunk, but I had a buzz. We walked to the deli, bought salami sandwiches, sodas, Sen-Sen, and walked back to Flynn's bungalow. I was worried that his mom would bust us for drinking, but he told me not to worry, that she would be fast asleep. We sat on the front porch of his bungalow for a couple of hours, and you could actually see the sky start to lighten. We talked about stupid stuff all night, like girls we liked, the Yankees, whether or not you could get high if you put aspirin in Coke, and then Whitey. Flynn and I were worried because we were both pretty short, especially me, and most people thought we were younger than we were. And there was Whitey, looking like he could hang out in a bar and go to a party with grown-up blonde who looks like she's thirty or something.

After nodding out on the beach chairs on his porch for a little bit, we headed into the bungalow to sleep. Flynn set up a cot for me next to his small bed in a tiny bedroom which also had a hot water heater in it. We both went out like lights.

The morning sun blasted through the windows so it was hard to stay asleep, but I awoke to disaster. It had happened to me before, but I always managed to throw the sheets in the washer before my mother saw what happened. I had a damn wet dream about that cute girl I made out with on the beach and there was a gooey spot under the covers. I started to panic. I looked over at Flynn and he was still fast asleep. I got up quietly and got a glass of water. I sat on the edge of the cot, took a sip, spilled the glass onto the gooey spot I'd made and whispered loudly, "Oh, shit!" But Flynn didn't wake up. I poked him. "Flynn, I spilled a glass of water on the cot."

"Don't worry about it. Go back to sleep," he groaned.

I couldn't. I put my shorts on and went out to the porch to watch the sun rise over the bungalows by the beach. A stray cat jumped onto the railing right in front of me and startled me. I scratched behind his ear and he took off, sniffing around for food, sex or a fight, I thought. Just then another stray strolled into view: Whitey. In the harsh sunlight I could see the bruises on his face from his fight the night before, yet the smile across his face was blinding. His clothes looked like they'd been buried overnight in the sand.

"Where the hell did you spend the night?"

He sat on the beach chair next to me and in his deepest black-guy voice sang the chorus of "Under the Boardwalk."

"Are you kidding me? You really spent the night under the boardwalk?"

"Just like the song says, on a blanket with my baby was where we be."

"Did you... do it?"

Whitey pressed his lips together, closing his mouth, but his smile got even bigger. He nodded his head slowly up and down and rocked back and forth. He folded his arms like an Indian chief and the muscles on his arms really bulged. For the first time, I really felt like Whitey was like a man. Maybe I'd been blocking it out, but he had sideburns coming in, smoked like a fifty-three Studebaker, and he even had stubble on his face and hair on his chest. I couldn't imagine having the nerve to have raw sex with a girl, especially a total stranger, on a blanket under the boardwalk. I just had to face the facts: Whitey was a man, and I was a kid.

"It was unbelievable. She even had a rubber in her purse!"

"A rubber? What's that?"

"A scumbag, you know."

I felt even more stupid. I never heard it called a rubber. The only time I had ever really seen one was when we saw them floating in the water. We called them "Coney Island whitefish."

"How did you... know how to use it?"

"She put it on for me."

151

I think I could hear my jaw crack as it hit the porch floorboards. I couldn't believe that a girl would actually do such a thing. It kind of embarrassed me to see a scumbag floating in the water. I can't imagine a girl having one and then putting it on for a guy.

"Is she a whore or something?"

Whitey's smile disappeared fast.

"Take that back, shit head."

For the first time in my whole life with Whitey, with all the stuff we'd been through, the arguments, the fights, the jealousies, the aftermath of his brother getting killed, I actually felt afraid of him.

"I take it back," I said softly.

Whitey looked at me like he wanted to say something mean, or sock me. He got up fast, which shot the beach chair into the wall, and he stormed off.

Flynn poked his head out the window. "What's that all about?"

"I don't know," I said, knowing full well what was going on. Whitey had grown up.

It was a scary, lonely subway ride home. I knew I was being watched by groups of blacks, Puerto Ricans, Italians, Irish kids, and in Brooklyn a few guys wearing yarmulkes were eyeing me like they wanted to jump me. I was nervous that my parents were going to grill me about staying the night in Rockaway, but they didn't even ask me one question about it. They just yelled at me, as usual, to hurry up and get ready for one o'clock mass. I had a headache all day. First I thought it was because I didn't get much sleep. Then I thought it was because of Whitey getting pissed at me, then the subway, then my parents, then the boring mass. But during afternoon dinner, I thought maybe it was because I was hung over. *Cool! Wait until I tell Whitey! Oh yeah, maybe that's the end of Whitey wanting to hang out with me.* I thought about going to knock on his door, but then I thought maybe he was still in Rockaway having sex with that girl.

I walked to Whitey's building, stood on the front stoop and looked up at his windows. I thought maybe he'd see me and wave. The wooden picket fence that his brother landed on when he fell off the roof

152

and got killed got replaced with a chain link one. You'd probably die if you landed on that one, too. They had to sandblast the concrete to get the blood stains out. They even painted the courtyard dark red, which is funny because that was the color of the blood that spread across from the stoop to the doorway. I wonder if Whitey thought of that stuff whenever he walked into his building.

There was no sign of life in Whitey's windows, so I headed down to Review Place where there were usually some kids hanging out in front of the pizza place. It wasn't until I got there that I remembered that the pizza place was closed on Sundays. It was near sundown, but it was still hot. I leaned against the brick of the building and it was warm from the sun. I knew some of the older kids played softball in the park on Sundays and sometimes they hung out until the evening drinking beers after the games. I felt nervous about going there by myself but I thought, *What the hell?* If I made it home from Rockaway alone, I could go through my own park and hang with the older guys.

Through the trees at the edge of the park, I could see that there was still a group hanging out by the softball field. Sometimes there were really old, married guys who played in the games, and I hoped those weren't the only guys who were left. I figured there would be at least somebody I knew.

I walked through the hole in the fence next to some bushes to check it out before I walked over there and *holy crap* – right in the middle of the group was the new priest, Father Q. There were six or seven guys drinking beer, and from the smell drifting my way, smoking pot. It was too weird. A priest with guys smoking pot in the park! I felt like I walked in on my parents having sex, which the mere thought of makes me want to wretch.

"Hi," I said lamely.

Nobody seemed to notice me. Father Q. wasn't wearing his priest outfit. He was in a golf shirt, khaki pants and sneakers! He had a can of Tab in his hand, whereas all the other guys had cans of Rheingold.

I felt like I was in a twilight zone between two worlds. There was Father Q. in the park, hanging out with guys who probably were smoking pot and were very much drinking beer. I knew the other guys with them, but they weren't part of my crowd. They were much older, maybe eighteen or nineteen.

"You want a beer?" a fat blond guy asked me. I thought I remembered that he used to live in Whitey's building.

"No thanks. I was just going home."

I stared at the ceiling and watched the lights from passing cars form strange shadows through the venetian blinds onto the ceiling. It seemed like I was lying there with my eyes wide open for hours. I could hear cars burning rubber, and there was an occasional ruckus in front of the bar and candy store across the street for an hour or so, but by two a.m. it was almost as quiet as being out in the country. I couldn't believe what I went through on the weekend. And the next morning at camp I was going to see Whitey and Father Q., and deal with them in a whole new way. I'm not just a dumb little kid. Whitey's not the only one who's growing up.

Chapter Eleven

—Now—

My sister has been a sweetheart. I've been living like a troll in her basement and she hasn't complained once. Probably due to the fact that I have a separate entrance, my own kitchenette and bathroom, and it seems I'm rarely there before midnight or after nine a.m. But now that her daughter Stacy moved out to live with her boyfriend, I think the time has come to settle the "borrowed" car issue. Growing up, our family was never a place for sit-down discussions or family meetings. Things seemed to happen by ultimatums and threats being shouted at times of crisis. And somehow that system worked for us. So, I was pleased to see that my sister Ann Marie left a note under my door that she wanted to discuss the car over coffee this morning in her kitchen.

After burying your parents, the relationship of siblings changes. I've seen families torn apart forever over life and death decisions and money issues when there's a death in the family. Fortunately, in our case, the bond between me, my brother and my sister has grown deeper and stronger in so many unspoken ways.

"Is this the coffee shop? I'm new here," I said, pushing open the door from the basement that opens into the upstairs kitchen.

"I think I saw more of you when you were living in California," Ann Marie said, pecking me on the cheek.

We sat at the granite kitchen counter across from each other. She knew I liked my coffee black. I knew she liked a little milk and one Splenda.

"How's Stacy?"

"Good. She's moved in with Freddy, so I'm officially an empty-nester."

"Except for me."

"Stop. You're always welcome."

"Thanks. I don't want to overstay it. Does she need her car?"

"Actually, no. Would you like to buy it?"

"Sure. How much?"

155

"A thousand?"

"She said maybe nine fifty."

"Okay. Done."

With the business of the car finished, we sat for a good half hour making small talk, catching up and enjoying each other's company. I realized it was probably the longest we'd sat down together alone in a long, long time. I wanted to tell her how good it felt and how much I appreciated everything she was doing for me, but for some reason, words like those don't come easily. And when we said goodbye, I flashed on where I was going that morning and hoped I would be back soon for more pleasant chats over coffee.

I had driven over a hundred miles on rain-soaked roads and I only had five or so miles to go before I would arrive at my destination: the dock by the lake, to meet a guy who'd introduced himself by tapping on my skull with the cold steel of a shotgun barrel. It sounded stupid to me. How could that be a good idea? I hadn't told anyone where I was going, probably because the sound of it was so preposterous. I think I didn't actually believe that I would go through with it. I passed the diner where I'd basically been held captive at gunpoint, drove down the road past the "KEEP OUT!" sign still lying in the mud, and I could see the dock next to the lake where I was supposed to show up. It seemed utterly ridiculous. Yet, there I was, as requested.

I left my car running and put it into park. Better for a quick getaway. I glanced at my phone and it was two minutes before nine, right on time. The light from my headlights lit up the dock and illuminated the mist rising off the tepid lake waters. There were ripples from the misty rain, with fish and bugs breaking the surface. It could take years for anyone to discover my catfish-eaten bones at the bottom of that mud hole.

I contemplate death often. I've flown in hundreds of planes, and each and every flight something causes me to visualize a violent, unexpected end to my journey. There have been imagined explosions, followed by scenes of me watching myself soaring through the air, still strapped into my seat and plunging eight miles to my death. Fights with

156

terrorists in cockpits, crashing on take-offs and landings, jets breaking apart in turbulence, corkscrew nose-dives into the sea, and of course crashing into skyscrapers all flash through my brain like 1970s disaster movies. Even riding the subway on a daily basis invokes illusions of cruel, untimely deaths. Every passenger, every door opening at a station, every bum walking through with a limp paper coffee cup asking for change is a potential agent of my brutal demise. So the fact that I was sitting in my car imagining a violent death while waiting for this backwoods maniac didn't seem all that unsettling.

I decided to kill my engine and wait in the eerily quiet darkness. *Why not? If I don't see him coming, maybe it'll be that much quicker if he does off me here. Or maybe he'll have a harder time getting me with a good shot in the pitch black night...*

I'm always struck by Frank Sinatra singing "My Way." Regrets? He had a few? Frank Sinatra had a few regrets? The Chairman of the Board, Ol' Blue Eyes, Frank had regrets? If Sinatra had regrets, what chance do the rest of us slobs have? If regrets were frequent flyer miles, I'd be flying to Jupiter or Mars. I've forgotten so much in my life. I can't remember one word of Italian even though I took it for three years in high school. I can't recall all the great toys I got for Christmas and birthdays. I've forgotten most of those wonderful moments of romance that led to my marriage. But I can't seem to forget every stupid, moronic, mean, thoughtless thing I've ever done to the people I love more than life itself. Why was I such a disrespectful teenaged jerk to my parents who gave me everything including life itself, yet I stood there and called them fascists because they wanted me to have lunch with them in a Howard Johnson's? Why didn't I realize I was selfish prick to my wife, Amber, and my son, Johnny, when it was more important for me to get drunk and smoke weed on the golf course at the country club with so called business associates rather than play catch in the backyard or help with housework. Why won't those memories go away? Why do all these awful things linger just below the surface of my cerebrospinal fluid ready to leap up at every family gathering, every page turn of a photo album, every alimony check written. Regrets? I've had a lot. And they keep piling up.

157

When a bright light nearly blinded me through the driver side window, I almost jumped out of my tighty-whities.

"Who's there?" a smoker's raspy voice said, on the other side of my locked door.

I knew I could start my car and blow out of there before he had a chance to fire several rounds into me, and it was unlikely he'd get a kill-shot off in the dark at a moving target. Instead I merely turned the ignition one click to the right and pushed the button to open my window.

"Vinny. Schmidt." I answered as though responding to a drill sergeant. I tried to make out who was behind the flashlight but because the light was so blinding, I couldn't see anything other than it was a human form.

"What do you want?" the voice demanded.

I still couldn't see who it was, but it didn't sound like the black guy with the gun who first introduced himself to me on this spot. "Who's there?"

"What do you want?"

I threw open the car door, accidentally knocking the flashlight to the ground. We both went for it and bumped our heads pretty good.

"Shit," I said, rubbing my bean. "Just like the Three Stooges."

He picked up the flashlight and shined it on the car, which gave us enough light to see each other. *Could it be? Is it him? Is it really Whitey?* But there was something missing. There was no response to my Three Stooges line. No "nyuk nyuk nyuk" or "why, I oughta" or "you chucklehead." *Maybe it's not Whitey?* In the haze, I thought it looked like Whitey. He didn't wear Buddy Holly black glasses, but he did have aviator glasses. He seemed the right height, but much thinner than the kid who would give you a mean noogie or Indian burn if you called him chubby, fat, or blubbery. But yeah, it looked like Whitey. I guess.

"What do you want?" he demanded again.

"It's good to see you, Whitey. I just wanted to..."

Brain freeze. I just wanted to what? After all these years, I'm finally in front of him, and I don't know why. My life was a mess: my

158

marriage had fallen apart; I got fired; my kid hated me; my sister was sick of me farting up her sofa bed; I had no idea what to do with my life; and a guy put a gun to my head warning me to "KEEP OUT" and there I was anyway.

"I just wanted to see how you're doing."

"I don't know who you are or why you're hassling me. I'm doing great, so get back in your car, and just get off my back!" he muttered through his clenched jaw. He turned away, and I swear I heard him whisper for me to get back to where I once belonged. Was Whitey was throwing in a line from a Beatles song or was I hearing things?

I turned away and got into my car. By the time I started it, put it into reverse and looked out my side window, there was no sign of him. He and his flashlight were gone in the mist.

I needed a drink but I had over a hundred miles of rainy roads to go and even though I could have easily put myself in a situation to become bottom-feeder food in a remote mud hole, I didn't want to risk wiping out a family on vacation in their minivan after a few snorts at the local gin mill. Once my stomach stopped telling me what a fool I was for this adventure, I turned on the radio, hit "scan," and after skipping through two Spanish stations, three Christian preachers and a country station, I heard the unmistakable sound of John Lennon's chugging rhythm guitar through my speakers with the intro to "Get Back." I hit the button so it wouldn't skip to another station. As I listened to the lyrics of "Get Back," for probably the ten thousandth time, it took on new meaning, as songs sometimes do after they become part of your deep subconscious mind-soul. I've always regarded the lyrics to "Get Back" as kind of silly fun. A promiscuous girl named Loretta with a sexual identity crisis and an itinerant pot-head named JoJo are the song's subjects. But isn't that really what the zeitgeist of the time was? Experimenting, merely for the sake of it? Maybe the song was saying, "Hey, wandering hippies! Smoking weed and getting laid doesn't make you cool. Get back to doing something worthwhile. Now! Go!"

I also know that deep in my subconscious, buried under lyrics to hundreds of songs that I know by heart, intertwined with scenes from favorite movies and moments at family parties and funerals, embarrassing moments with teen-aged girls, and pain from punches in the face, there are secret memories of important things aching to be resurrected to make sense of the *now*. Unexpected sounds, smells, shadows on the wall, or geometric patterns on a rain-splashed windshield seem to cause a small glow in a part of my brain where memories have been filed away. But why? Why are memories stored if not for later use? They must be stored for a reason... just like a squirrel hiding nuts all over the place during the year knows they'll be used for something worthwhile, at some time in the future. Because we don't remember everything. We don't want to remember everything. We remember things based on faith. But we don't know what we have unless we dig. Like the squirrel. If you don't dig, your nuts are gone. But you better have stored them in the first place.

I know Whitey and I fell apart. We were tighter than brothers, as many best friends are. But something happened to us. To ourselves and to our world. I'm trying to get back. I've been trying. But maybe Whitey doesn't care about old nuts.

When I started writing *Sewer Balls* more than ten years ago, it started out as a search to understand the mysteries of our youth, more than to create a literary work. And when I say our youth, I mean the collective youth of me and my friends who were thrown together on the stoops, alleys and empty lots near West 238th Street and Bailey Avenue in the Bronx. Each of us had our own peculiar families, and I do mean peculiar, because although I didn't realize it back then, every family is peculiar. There is no such thing as a *normal* family. For a while you *think* your family is normal. That lasts until you're about four years old, when you visit your relatives and realize the entire universe isn't ruled by your mommy and daddy. You visit your Uncle Dominic and realize that different rules apply. When he does a deep knee-bend and lets a fart rip with arms extended in glee, Uncle Dominic demonstrates that grown-ups may exhibit different norms of behavior . Yet saying the word "lousy" at Aunt Louise's dinner table will get you a tongue lashing and stares of contempt, as if you had let one rip like her brother Dominic might have done the week before. We were lucky to have so many aunts, uncles and cousins and we could see how different families were. Some uncles were big drinkers who balanced on a razor's edge between uninhibited joy or satanic hell-fire rage over something ridiculous. It could mean the thrill of hilarious off-color sexy or racist jokes inappropriate for the kids, or maybe physical horseplay that involved dangerous full-body-contact improvised indoor games like living room football scrimmages or intense three-on-three put-the-sock-in-the-bent-coat-hanger-loop hanging on the bedroom door. But these rollicking escapades were usually followed immediately by a scary profanity-laced neck-vein-popping tirade because somebody left their dirty handprints on a clean bathroom towel, causing extended family to make up excuses why they had to cut their visit short. After such a violent outburst at a relative's house, there was comfort in getting into your car and beginning to realize that your own parents weren't so bad after all. Yeah, maybe your father wasn't as funny as Uncle Dominic making armpit farts, but he wasn't as scary as Uncle Alfonso threatening his family with vivisection because somebody left the top off the toothpaste tube.

But the real eye-opener is when you are five or six years old and begin visiting families who you aren't related to at all. Because as different as your relatives are from your parents, there is still a strong familiar bond with your parents' brothers and sisters and their children. The smells of the food, even the brands of food are similar to your family's. And as outlandish as an uncle's behavior might be, the bond of love between your mom or dad and that uncle somehow casts a glow of loving understanding over the situation which makes you begin to realize that, yeah, we know Uncle Alfonso's acting a little nutty today, but we love him just the same. But a friend's family? That's an entirely different situation altogether.

Upon entering first grade we find that there are kids we are drawn to not because they are related to us, but because they have personality traits we like to be around. They could be good comics, or maybe they can imitate the sounds and movements that Curly (of the

161

Three Stooges) makes. Or they could be good athletes who understand the rules of basketball, or know how to place their fingers on a baseball to throw a curve ball. Or maybe there's a girl in your class you can't help looking at, from morning prayers until the final bell in the afternoon. And you don't know why, but you actually think of her on the weekends and wonder what she might be doing. And soon you aren't satisfied just being with these kids during recess or on the walk home after school. You begin to make your own choices about who to hang out with. Little did you know that *hanging out* with people you like would turn out to be the most influential activity you involve yourself in for the rest of your life.

Then your mom started asking new questions: *Who is this Whitey? Where does he live? Does he have brothers and sisters? Have you met his parents? What does his father do for a living? What's their house like? Is it clean?* In the beginning, you don't really understand these questions and just answer the best you can with the limited information you have: *He lives up the hill. His father has a job, I think. His mother is fat. Their house smells funny.* But then the questions become more specific and you realize that they're acting like Bill Friday on *Dragnet* trying get enough information out of you so they can nail you on something: *Who were you with? Where did you go? What did you do there? Did you have anything to eat? What time did you leave?*

You've learned how to cover up what you were really doing. You tell your parents that you were with Whitey and you were playing baseball in the park all day, and your pants are dirty from sliding into second base. What you don't tell them is the truth. Yeah, you were with Whitey, plus two other kids you know your mother hates because she knows that both of those kids have older brothers who hang out with your older brother and those guys gamble on the sidewalk, drink and smoke at night in the park, spend more time in the bowling alley than in high school and dress like the extras in *Blackboard Jungle*. You don't tell her that you were in the Van Cortlandt Park woods making slingshots, and that you went down to the part of the lake where it empties over a dam into a giant underground sewer tunnel, and you

162

climbed down the side of the dam, stood on a shopping cart in the water and shot the slingshots at the rats down the tunnel, where you slipped in the mud and almost fell into five feet of polluted sewer water. Afterwards you consumed enough sugar to put a grown-up into a diabetic coma, including a sixteen-ounce Coke, a package of Twinkies, a dozen Pixy Stix, a Mallo Cup and four Bazooka bubble gums. Then you watched Clooney and Lutzig shoot their slingshots at cars on the Major Deegan Expressway from about a hundred yards away, heard a cop car siren, then ran like hell out of the park to the pizza place on 238th Street, where you told the kids there what a great time you had and almost got caught by the cops. And your world is forever changed by the guys you hang out with.

After thinking my entire world consisted of my parents, my brother and sister, and a bunch of aunts, uncles and cousins, I soon found out that it's the guys on the stoop and in the park who push me, prod me, challenge me, ridicule me, inspire me, laugh at my jokes, turn me on to hits on the radio, teach me about girls, and about the rules of football, baseball, and basketball, and how to sneak on the subway, and what's in *Playboy,* and where babies come from, and how to whistle by putting two fingers in my mouth, and how to build a fort. And in this tribe of sometimes five, ten, fifteen or twenty or more, Whitey and I confided in each other more and more. I wouldn't dare ask anybody in my family if they thought a shirt was cool, but I'd ask Whitey. I wouldn't have dreamed of asking anybody but Whitey if he thought Carrie Vitelli was cute. And only I knew that the Popeye cartoon where Betty Boop was topless with only a lei covering her nipples gave Whitey a boner, too.

Digging deep into your brain requires more than just concentration. Like the strata in an archeological dig, I know that the memory of where Whitey and I lost touch isn't that far from where the original data for "Get Back" is stored in my brain. I switched off the radio when the song ended and a jingle about getting your stomach tie-wrapped the way you might fix a leaking radiator hose came on. I was still on a two-lane road with about ten more miles to go before I'd be back on the main highway. The rain was coming down harder, and oncoming headlights illuminated the greasy blobs of water that my worn wiper blades left behind, making it difficult to see whether a car was passing by safely in its lane, or barreling towards me in a fiery head-on collision. I just kept my eye on the double yellow line, my tires just inside it, and hoped the folks in the oncoming traffic were capable of doing the same.

I knew I needed to mine deeper in the layers of my gray matter to unlock the long-hidden secrets of what happened to me and Whitey. Just as every memory that remains part of your conscious mind is stored in a certain part of your brain, subconsciously, painful memories from the same time period are also locked away in the same file sector. Kind of like the rafters in the garage where you store the things you know you don't want to look at every day, but just might need *some* day, like the boxes of extra shingles the previous owner of your house left behind from the roofing job he had done twenty years before you bought the house. You don't know it, but your conscious mind hides those memories from you because even having them stored in your unconscious mind is enough to warn you in emergencies not to do certain things. You don't actually remember the pain you felt when you were three years old and touched the inside of a 450-degree oven when your mom was baking and you stood on a chair and reached inside, because the cupcakes smelled so good and you had to have one. But your subconscious mind knows and warns you every time you are near something approaching lethal temperatures. That's basically the purpose of hypnosis. Not the Las Vegas get-some-sloppy-drunk-women-in-the-audience-to-take-their-tops-off-and-shake-their-tits kind of hypnosis, but the therapeutic hypnosis that attempts to get people to uncover subconscious memories in order to improve their conscious well-being. And although I don't think hypnosis would work for me, I do believe that the nuggets I've stored – from the time I remember my mom smiling and singing "Chickery Chick" to me when I was still in the crib – are there for the mining.

Oversized balls of rain pounded the roof of my car, snapping me out of my semi-hypnotic state. I instinctively tapped my brakes to slow down, and hydroplaned ever so slightly. A tractor trailer was pulled over to the shoulder. In fact quite a few cars were pulling over to the shoulder during the thumping thundering torrential water-bucket dump. I don't like the idea of pulling over to the side of the road and would rather take my chances creeping along the highway. I've seen too many police car dash-cam videos on YouTube where a car broken down on the shoulder gets plowed into by a groggy truck driver hauling a few tons of kumquats. White knuckles or not, I prefer to continue on.

I stared at the double yellow line through the sheets of rain slamming into my windshield. My wipers were rattling and squealing like they were in pain. Everything disappeared from sight except for those two lines pulling me along the highway. Without them I'd be doomed; visibility was down to about a foot past my hood. Suddenly a blast of white light exploded like the flash from a Kodak Brownie bulb, blinding me. A horn blasted; it sounded like the Queen Mary was bearing down on me. I didn't know what was coming my way, but I was sure it wasn't small or going slow. I jerked my wheel to the right and hit my brakes hard. Bad idea. My car started hydroplaning and spinning like I was riding the Tilt-A-Whirl at Rockaways' Playland. I had no control; I helplessly squeezed the wheel so hard I thought I bent it. Three revolutions in, the ass end of my car was going down and I was going up, but not for long. I was sliding backwards down a slope and felt the driver's side of my car rise in the air higher and higher; I knew the laws of physics were taking hold and next step would be an ugly equal and opposite reaction, which it was. I covered my face as best I could as I flipped backwards and over and landed with a thud, upside down. My forehead hit the steering wheel hard. *Where's my fucking airbag?* I thought to myself, as tiny sparkly things appeared in the darkness and everything... went... black.

Shit! Water! I came to and realized water was running across my hands, which were on the ceiling of my upside-down car. *Oh yeah, I'm in a wreck!* Suddenly I heard a loud crash and little bits of glass showered all over me. Another bright light freaked me out, then the passenger side door made an awful sound as it jerked open. Gloved hands reached in, sliced my seat belt and pulled me out of the car and right onto a stretcher.

"What's your name?" a voice boomed from under a light mounted on a helmet.

"Vinny Schmidt."

"Are you hurt?"

"Just my head a little. And my pride."

"You'll be okay."

I was more embarrassed than anything, lying in the back of an ambulance with a female paramedic asking me questions and feeling me up for any hidden injuries. It's the first time a female came that close to my naked balls in ages.

My head hadn't hurt that much since I was punched out at the reunion. Figures it would come on the night that I actually did have a reunion with Whitey, which is why I went to the other reunion in the first place. I was handed off from the ambulance to the hospital emergency room staff and plopped into a bed behind a curtain. When they asked me for next of kin, I gave my sister's name and phone number, and not my ex-wife's. That really hit home. Unless blood starts suddenly streaming out of my ears, it's not serious enough to alarm my ex-wife or my son on the West Coast. Why bother them? In fact, why bother my sister? She'll see the empty sofa bed in her basement on the way to the garage and assume I'm crashing at a buddy's house after another Bronx barroom bender, like I've done on so many nights before this.

A nurse told me that since my injuries weren't severe, I'd probably have to wait at least an hour while they tended to people more seriously hurt. I couldn't read anything since my glasses were in my wrecked car, so I just lay there listening to the many voices on the other side of the six-inch opening in my privacy curtain. A female nurse with a heavy Chinese accent discussed horror movies with a man aching from kidney stones. A young woman with a bloody towel around her bare foot cried softly as her husband caressed her with one arm and read the sports pages with the other. I heard Jay Leno on the television,

"Let the buyer beware! Car for sale, Ford Exploder!" obviously doing his headlines shtick. At least I don't have to listen to Letterman.

A nurse who looked like she was barely out of high school stuck her head through the gap of my curtain. "Yeah, he's awake," she said to someone off to the side. "You can go in."

Who the hell could it be? I thought. And there he was. *Whitey.*

No longer hidden by darkness, I could see just how sickly he looked. In fact, he probably looked more like somebody who belonged in a hospital than I did.

"Hey, Vinny," he said in a voice shaped by years of Marlboros, as he poked his face into the opening. "Are you all right?"

"Whitey. Holy shit. Yeah. Come in."

The bright light of the ER waiting area illuminated Whitey's many years of a hard life. His oversized, slightly tinted aviator glasses couldn't hide the sunken eyes, dark circles, red blotchy face, and a certain sadness. Gray and white stubble from a day or two without shaving belied the color of whatever hair he had left under his John Deere baseball hat. His once chubby facial features dropped and caved to form a face a person might remember from the black-and-white Depression-era dust bowl scenes of farmers aged far beyond their years, trying to feed their families.

"After seeing your car, I'm surprised you look so good. That thing is a mess."

"You saw my car? That bad?"

"Oh, yeah. Looks like it was trampled by the giant behemoth."

Yup, this is Whitey. The Giant Behemoth was our favorite from the *Million Dollar Movie* which ran on channel nine when we were kids, over and over so many times that we could recite pages of lines from it.

His hands were deep into his dungaree pockets. I could see he had tightened the well-worn leather belt to its smallest size, with indentations marking the loss of weight. This is what a man on the run looks like.

"'The Giant Behemoth'? You remember that stupid movie?"

Whitey's head dropped slightly and I swear I could hear something crack as the corners of his mouth lifted, his eyes narrowed, and a chipped front tooth formed a giddy smile followed by a hacking chuckle.

"I don't know what the hell made me think of that. I haven't thought of that thing in decades."

Still in the curtain opening, he took a few steps and stopped a foot from my bed. There was a strong odor of cigarette smoke; his fingers were nicotine-stained. His crooked fingers appeared to be signs of arthritis, or perhaps old injuries that hadn't healed well. Hidden by the deep creases and lines on his face was a scar that started somewhere under his baseball hat and continued down the side of his neck.

"How did you find me?"

"Do you mind if I sit down?"

I shook my head, which hurt from the movement.

He got a chair from the other side of the curtain, closed the curtain behind him, and placed it by the bed facing me.

"I heard about it on my scanner. I remembered your license plate when they called in the wreck. They said they were taking you here."

My mind raced with paranoid thoughts. *Here's a guy who's been on the lam, possibly for murder, plus maybe an army deserter during wartime which George Washington used to hang guys for, and I've been stalking him. Maybe the tables have been turned and he's got me!* I looked to see where my panic button was.

"When I thought maybe..." he said softly, as rubbed his stubble and smacked his lips, "...maybe you wouldn't make it. And it's time I confronted some... things."

The nurse opened the curtain. "Everything all right in here?"

"Yes," I blurted, happy that someone was keeping an eye on me.

"The doctor will be here any minute. You're next," she said, closing the curtain.

"I oughta be going now," Whitey said, rising from the chair. "I'm glad you're okay."

I was ashamed. That wasn't a man who wished me harm. *What an asshole I am.*

"Whitey, look, I'm fine. I've got a lot of shit to do the next few days, not the least of which is figure out where my car is, how much it's going to cost me, and get my ass back to work. Give me your number and I'll call you and we can get together under better circumstances."

"I don't have a phone. Just leave a message at Captain Norm's. Here's the number," he said, scribbling it on a piece of paper towel from the dispenser on the wall.

"Oh, I guess you know I was there looking for you. Nice jukebox. I saw your initials on the 45s."

A huge smile exploded on Whitey's mug, pushing his cheeks out, and there he was, the Whitey I knew. *It's been a long and winding road, but here we are. Once again.*

"Best jukebox in the county. Nice catch! You know what? I'm glad you didn't drop dead."

"Yeah, same to you."

He smiled and ducked out through the curtain.

Then in came the doctor, who looked maybe twelve, and said, "So, you're lucky to be alive."

The x-rays were negative all around. Just bruises and a totaled car. They didn't admit me, so there I was at 3:45 in the morning standing in a deserted hospital lobby with shredded clothes, no transportation, and nobody within a hundred miles who could possibly come to rescue me. I reached into the pocket of my now-ruined jeans with tears on the legs and down my ass from the EMT guys doing their job, and pulled out the number of Captain Norm's. Would they even be open at that hour? When you run out of viable options, I guess you just start going through with the ridiculous ones. I punched in the numbers and waited.

"Hi, um, is, er, Whitey there?"

"Who's this?" a gruff voice asked.

"Vinny."

The phone wasn't hung up, so I guess I had a chance. It sounded like the receiver was being covered with his hand but I think I heard him say to someone, "Go downstairs and get Doc."

Then the phone must have been plopped down on a counter. I could hear some music in the background... sounds like... "Day Tripper." Yup. *It took so long to find out. But I found out.* The receiver bumped around, then another voice.

"Holy shit. Don't tell me. You're dead."

"I'm working on it. Listen, Whitey, I'm kind of screwed."

"I'm glad somebody's gettin' some."

"My car's upside down in a ditch, my clothes look like Freddy Krueger picked my pockets, and I think the guy who just walked through the double doors next to me is going to puke. Whoah! He just missed me by inches. I'm going to walk through this door. Okay, is there any way you could get me out of here and drop me off at a motel or something? I'd call a cab, but looking like this I don't think..."

"We'll be there in twenty minutes," Whitey said, cutting me off. "Just don't get any puke on yourself. Bye."

Could this be happening? It had been so many decades since I'd seen Whitey that the memory of him has become mixed up with other fading moments of my past, all hazy dreamlike movie images in my mind. It's like trying to separate reality from years and years of dreams where one's subconscious tries to make sense of life's most significant, yet elusive, moments. Did I really make out with Carrie Vitelli on a pile of construction debris at the bottom of the dumbwaiter shaft in the basement of my apartment building, in a fit of summer vacation passion? Did my Uncle Dominic really do the duck walk down an entire block with me and about five other cousins following him as he blasted a fart with every step? Did Flynn and Whitey and I really sneak through the hallway basement maze of Yankee Stadium after a game and stumble into the locker room of the Kansas City Athletics? Did my Uncle Nicky really stand on the precipice of my six-story apartment building one steamy hot night and threaten to jump off, only to be grabbed from behind by a pair of cops, put into a straitjacket and thrown into the back of an ambulance?

It's funny how memory-scenes of real things are stored next to old television shows and movies playing out in the brain in exactly the same manner. Just as a movie has only the angles, lighting, actors, lines, or action that are part of the movie, memories of the past consist of movie-like scenes of things that really happened and when we call on them, or they're triggered by smells (loud farts), unusual sights (construction debris in a basement), sounds (an ambulance taking off down the street) – these scenes play out in your mind as if projected on a screen from the home movie of your life. Repeating over and over in the same way, just like reruns of *My Three Sons* that pop into your brain for no apparent reason – except there *is* a good reason. Only it's up to you to figure out what that reason is.

This swirling mix of reality, dreams that somehow became real, and memories that for decades have bounced around my brain and been saturated by varying amounts of alcohol, marijuana, hormone-induced rages and euphoria, have all bubbled up to the surface of the here and now. Because I, Vinny Schmidt, put the seat of my pants to the seat of my chair and brought many of those memory ghosts back to life by putting them on the pages of *Sewer Balls*. And, of course, I didn't just drag my own past self from the deep crevasses of my mind, I also pulled out the unwitting souls connected to my ethereal self. I don't know for a fact if Whitey ever read *Sewer Balls*, but if he did, his reaction may have been exponentially more dynamic than "Tina Robustelli's" husband who sent my skull vibrating with a clenched fist like it hasn't since my high school hockey days, when punches were thrown like basketball players fake to the left. Because it's impossible to tell a story of one person without including the world of others who have shaped that person. And in the telling of that story, the influences of others *become* the person, making it impossible to differentiate where one person ends and the other begins. As was the case with Whitey and me. It wasn't as if I had a choice of what memories of our childhood past I could mine to tell the story. I used virtually every memory that remained after going through the blender of growing up. I'm a true believer that the memories which remain in your brain are there for a reason. The flotsam and jetsam have been washed away like debris that flows downstream in a winter desert wash after a storm. Sometimes, mixed with the sand, what you thought were the rocks and dirt left behind are actually gold nuggets.

Out of the stickball games, the stolen-beer parties in the stands, the kissing of bubble gum flavored lips, and the slingshot fights, emerged the bonds that allowed us to weather the storms of real life with our friends. The fact is, tragedy was all around, which is why the search for insane, crazy adventure came so easily to us. The tragedy of Whitey's brother accidentally falling to his death changed not only him and his family, it changed the whole neighborhood. When we both stood over his brother, dying in a pool of blood in the courtyard, his mangled body contorted around the remains of a wooden fence, there was a memory seared into our brains that would forever bind us, but also created an indelible pain that must be hidden. Sometimes, though, it bubbles to the surface like gasses from a decaying body deep beneath the sea; people in a boat or on the shore notice and wonder what exactly is causing those bubbles.

Chapter Twelve

—Then—

Whitey's been absent from camp for three days already. Everybody asks me where he is, as if I know. Then on Friday morning, Jason Kopel, who ratted me out for putting an I Love Ringo button on the back of Sister Fidelis's black habit, showed up with a counselor shirt and started bossing around the kids in the seniors group like he was a drill sergeant. Campers were collapsing faster than you could drop them with a machine gun, from being whacked on their bare calves with his wiffle ball bat. I was reading the sports section of the *Daily News*, checking out the latest on the now lousy Yankees, half-watching Kopel take out the senior boys.

Jerry, my head counselor, was oblivious as usual, reading his *New York Times* and munching on a buttered hard roll. I walked over to Jerry and tapped him on the shoulder.

"What's Kopel doing here?"

"He's a new senior boys counselor," he answered. "You better hope they end this fuckin' shit in 'Nam by the time you get out of high school. Christ almighty. Don't ask me what the fuck I'm gonna do when I graduate college next year."

"What about Whitey?"

"He quit," Jerry said. The rustling of the newspaper startled me as he slapped it onto his lap. "Shit, I thought you knew! Isn't he your best friend?"

"I don't know," I mumbled, and turned away.

Jerry clapped his hands and shouted as Father Q. took the stage from the side steps. "Midget boys, listen up. Prayers and announcements!"

I didn't hear a word of the announcements or the prayers, but I did notice when Father Q. took off his glasses. It looked like he had a black eye. I stood there with hands half-folded in prayer position, mulling over what I should do about Whitey. *He quit? He wasn't fired? That means he's up to something big.* I looked across the auditorium

173

and saw that Josephine's counselor shirt buttons were being tested to the limit. *I don't know if her shirts are shrinking or what. Just thinking about her makes me want to... Okay. Now I know what's up with Whitey. He got laid in Rockaway under the boardwalk. He's sick of this kiddie stuff.*

"Amen," the entire camp shouted at the end of prayers, snapping me out of my daydream. *I've got to find Whitey and find out what he's up to.*

"Let's go! Onto the bus!" Jerry shouted, before downing the last of his coffee and hard roll into his gob, and whacking the first kid he saw on the ass with his rolled-up *Times.* "Don't make me smack every one of you on the ass!"

"Jerry," I shouted, grabbing Bobby Garcia, who'd been hiding up a tree, "where are we going today?"

"Rockaway. Let's go!"

Rockaway? Holy jumpin' shit. Oh no. *What if I see those girls there? Or the guys we got in a fight with? Or should I say the guys who beat Whitey up? I mean, what if Whitey's there? He could be. Maybe that's why he quit. To be with that older girl who he had raw sex with under the boardwalk. He could be on the beach with her and his whole new gang of older kids, drinking on the beach. And there I'll be, chasing a bunch of little brats so they don't go into water over their ankles. And Whitey will be laughing at me, with his arm around that big-titted girl in an itsy bitsy teeny weeny polka dot bikini, drinking a can of Piels and smoking a White Owl. Or maybe he's working there. Like at Boggiano's Clam Bar which has a stand right where the buses would leave us off. Maybe he moved into a bungalow with a bunch of older teenagers for the summer. And every day all he does is down all the clams he can eat while he's working at the clam bar, go on all the rides in Playland, hang out on the beach, and make out with that girl.*

The milk crates, coolers, and campers were all on board and our Bronx day camp caravan bus was headed to the hinterlands of Rockaway Beach, Queens, where Whitey became a man, and I realized I'm still a kid.

174

Josephine was in the back of the bus leading the girl campers in a slew of songs, rhymes and cheers that boggled the mind. How the hell did they remember all that stuff? I can't remember a single prayer in Latin after all the years I spent as an altar boy. In fact, the only Latin I remember is the pope's phone number: *ecum spiri tu tuo*. 2-2-0. Get it?

They don't even repeat a song the whole way out to Rockaway, which takes almost an hour. The bus is buzzing as we pass the front entrance to Rockaways Playland. Everybody rushes to the right side to get a glimpse of the small amusement park teeming with fun seekers of every color, shape and form. We make a right at the corner and double park in a line of several buses, including our other two camp buses right next to the roller coaster. *We're right next to where we hung out with Debbie and Deirdre! What if they see me?*

With heads out windows, the excitement builds as the clickety-clack of a roller coaster car climbing a wooden hill of rickety wood pauses momentarily and becomes a chorus of shrieking screams, male and female, as the cars screech past us at breakneck speed and disappear around a dark corner of white wooden trestles. Girls on the bus squeal in anticipation and the boys brag how they can't wait to ride with no hands. But we're at a standstill, as I see Father Q. and the camp boss between the buses and the parked cars pointing and giving directions to the bus drivers.

The camp boss steps onto our bus, obviously for an announcement, and shushes everyone.

"There's been a change in plans. Due to a parking problem, we are going to Jacob Riis Park instead."

A collective groan of disappointment encompasses everyone on the bus. Except for me. Yeah, there's no amusement park at Riis Park. No penny arcade with nudie girl flip card machines. No clam bars or Kill the Cat booths. But there's no chance of me running into Debbie and Deirdre or Whitey.

Riis Park is part of the same long beach peninsula, a few miles down the road, but with no rides, a huge parking lot and not as crowded. The campers are more subdued as they gloomily pile out of

175

the buses and walk to the lockers like they're on the Bataan death march. Boys to the left, girls to the right. The lockers are pretty new, and actually kind of nice. I have to supervise the midget boys as they stuff their clothing into wire baskets about the size of grocery store hand-held baskets, which are checked in to an attendant who gives me an elastic band with a round number on the end for each basket checked. As we're waiting for all the baskets to be sorted and numbers to be handed out, I notice Griffith over by the toilets looking at something I can't see. I walk down there, quietly come up behind him and look down the aisle. There's a thin hairy man standing in front of a mirror. He's nude, and he's slowly applying sun tan oil to every part of his body with both hands. Holy shit, he's rubbing his dick! He's a freaking pervert! I yank Griffith by the arm and drag him away from there. He's laughing uncontrollably as we get back to the crowd of campers still checking their personal items at the counter.

"Hey, everybody! There's a guy over there giving himself a massage! On his –"

I quickly covered his mouth with my towel, shutting him up. "Never mind that, check your stuff with the attendant."

Because the girls' lockers were quite a distance from the boys', by the time we filed out of there and took up our positions on the beach, the girls were so far away from us we could barely see them. Well, we could see them, but I couldn't get a good view of Josephine in her bathing suit at all from where we laid our towels on the beach.

What a crappy day. I mean, yeah, it was perfect weather, sunny, about eighty degrees... not a cloud in the deep blue sky, the ocean not too cold, no seaweed, active waves but not too dangerous for the smaller campers, the sand white like fine, pure sugar, and the kids all pretty much having a blast in the water, playing wiffle ball on the beach, and keeping together so they were easy to watch. But here I am, unable to even see Josephine or any of the other girl counselors, no other beach chicks around, and no chance of seeing Whitey.

That's just it. I don't know if I want to see Whitey or not. I mean, I do want to see him, but I'm afraid. He's been different. I don't know why. He just is. How could he quit without even telling me? I don't even know where he is.

"Hey, Schmidt! Are you watching the kids over there or what?" Jerry yells from his towel underneath the only umbrella around.

I've been oblivious to the midgets romping in the waves, and there's Griffith with his bathing suit around his ankles bent over with kids throwing sand bombs at his ass.

"Griffith, pull up your bathing suit, you stupid ass!"

"I'm not an ass. *That* is an ass," Griffith said, pointing to his rear end.

I fake a punch to his noggin and he snaps to attention as he pulled up his bathing suit. This kid is going to either be starring in his own TV show or in jail by the time he's twelve.

"Lunch!" Jerry yells, and the kids storm to the coolers by Jerry's umbrella.

Each camper is supposed to bring their own lunch and store it in the cooler. The camp provides milk and orangeade, both of which come in waxy cardboard containers. The milk is usually sour, and the orangeade is orange in color only, tasting more like orange-Raid. Hopefully counselors have only ransacked the kids' sack lunches for Ho Hos, Twinkies and Ding Dongs, and haven't scarfed down some poor kid's peanut butter and jelly sandwich. Jerry usually keeps a slush fund of a few bucks he swipes from the camp tuition envelopes and buys a lunch or two for the lucky kid who gets a greasy hot dog from a stand instead of the wilted Wonder Bread sandwich his mom packed.

"You want anything, Schmidt? I'm grabbing a couple of dogs from the snack bar," Jerry says.

"No thanks. I'm not hungry."

"No wonder you look like a freakin' skeleton with skin. I'll be right back. Don't let anybody drown. Except maybe Griffith," Jerry says, flip-flopping away in his flip-flops towards the pavilion.

I pick up Jerry's *New York Times* and begin leafing through it. We never get the *Times* at home. My dad only reads the *New York Daily News*. Some days he gets the *New York Post* because it has an afternoon edition. He says the *Times* is too hard to read on the subway because it's oversized. I think the *Times* is just too hard to read, period. They don't seem to get to the point like the *Daily News* or the *Post* does. Especially on the front page. Like if there's a murder in a Brooklyn pizzeria, it might be on page ten of the *Times* in a little article with a headline like, "Restaurant Robbery Results in Alleged Murder." In the *Daily News*, it would be a huge front-page picture of a guy dead on the floor with the headline, "PIZZA GUY SLICED."

I've got to admit, though, there are some interesting articles in the *Times* that I don't usually see in the *News*, like this article on how they think in the future the earth might get so cold, they might have to put mirrors on the moon to reflect more sunlight on us.

I'm startled when a clump of sand falls on top of my paper, almost knocking it out of my hand. It could only be one kid. "Griffith!" I yell.

"Yes," Griffith innocently replies, munching on a Ding Dong. He's sitting in front of me a few towels away.

I whip around and my heart skips several beats as Josephine stands there with a Cheshire cat smile from ear to ear. Her camp shirt isn't buttoned, but it's tied just below her boobs where her two-piece bathing suit top is barely containing her blossoming bosom. And she's wearing short shorts.

"Do you have any extra orangeades? We ran out."

"Huh?"

I heard a voice coming from her mouth, but as I'm looking up at her from the seated position on my towel, all I see are those amazing boobs, double wrapped in a bathing suit and camp shirt, framing her beautiful smiling face. *Is she really talking to me?*

"Do you have any extra orangeades? We ran out."

I stood up. Just then I realized I'm shirtless. She's gonna see how skinny I am.

"Uh, yeah, we have some," I said, fumbling through the cooler and handing her several.

"Thanks," she said smiling. "You look cute in a bathing suit!" She ran off, kicking up sand behind her.

Did that really happen? She said I look cute? What does that mean? Oh shit. I looked down at my bathing suit and ran full speed towards the water and dove in to prevent embarrassing bulges. I could see her handing out the containers to some girls. Then she whipped off her shirt and her shorts, grabbed two girl campers by their hands and ran screaming to the waves about thirty yards down from where I was. They jumped up and down, frolicking in the water. I could see Josephine's boobs practically flopping out of her top as she led the little girls deeper into the ocean. I wished I could stay in the cold water for a little bit longer, but I could see that a sour milk fight had broken out among the midget boys. Once I'm out and pulling apart the little brats reeking of old waxy milk, no need to worry about my previous concern which had needed the cold water dousing.

The day just dragged on and on. Supervising kids in the water, out of the water, umpiring wiffle ball, building human pyramids, digging kids out of sand burials, trips to the bathroom, all just taking time away from me trying to figure out my next move with Josephine.

We got caught in traffic going back home, so when we arrived late in the parking lot there was no end-of-the-day assembly in the auditorium, just a mad rush out of the bus for everyone to get picked up by parents or run home. It all happened so fast that by the time Jerry and I got all the coolers and trash off the bus, the buses were gone, campers and counselors were gone, and the only thing left was me and two big stinky coolers we had to hose out. The first blast of water is always dangerous because the sour milk at the bottom is splashed back at you. *Shit! It went right into my mouth. Yuk!*

"Don't you know how to put your thumb on the top of the hose to direct the splash the other way?"

I turned around and there he was – Whitey. He looked different. Looking up at him, he seemed huge. His hair looked different too, with his part right down the middle, his ears half-covered.

"Where the hell have you been?" I yelled, giving a spray of water in the air, just missing his face.

179

"Very funny, schmuck!" Whitey said, ducking. "Oh, I've been upstate with my mom."

I wasn't sure what to ask next. Questions flashed through my mind about why he quit or got fired, what was he doing upstate with his mom, why his hair was parted down the middle...

"We were supposed to go Rockaway today but we went to Riis Park instead," was the best I could do. "Want to help me with these?" I asked, pointing to the coolers.

We silently carried them down the stairs into the storage room. Whitey paused in the doorway that led to the auditorium where the campers assembled every morning and at the end of every day. It's the same auditorium where we gathered in grammar school for Cub Scout meetings, school plays, assemblies, St. Patrick's Day parties, a few masses, and even an open casket wake.

Whitey gazed into the large room as if he was soaking in all those memories. He turned to me and held up his right hand. "See this bruise on my knuckle?" Whitey asked, making a fist. "That's from punching out Father Q. Let's get out of here."

Holy jumping shit. My heart was pounding as we walked quickly up the stairs and into the schoolyard between the church and the school. I mean, what if we ran into Father Q.? What would happen then? Maybe being seen with Whitey is enough to get me fired. Without speaking we headed across the street and into Van Cortlandt Park. We slowed down and intuitively headed through the hole in the fence and down the steep path to the railroad tracks towards the lake. We meandered up the tracks, sometimes balancing on one rail for a while, throwing rocks, picking up good-sized walking sticks and throwing them into the weeds.

"You punched Father Q.?"

"One shot. That was it."

We walked another five minutes or so in silence.

"Why?"

"Fucking guy's queer."

"Queer like weird? Or queer like a homo?"

180

Whitey picked up an old empty quart-sized Knickerbocker beer bottle out of the mud and smashed it against the rail.

"Homo. He tried to do something to me."

"What are you going to do?"

"I already did it."

We reached the lake and walked through another hole in the fence that led to the path where we used to go out on an old log and fish. Oh yeah, it was the log where some pervert was rubbing his dick while he was watching us from the bushes. We both sat on the log, which was a huge dead tree that fell into the lake years and years ago.

"Did he fire you?"

"Nah. I just didn't show up. When the boss called me at home, I told him I quit."

"Did he ask why?"

"Yeah, I told him I had to quit because we're moving."

"That's a good excuse."

Whitey broke a dead branch off the tree and held it over the water as if he was fishing there, like we used to.

"We are moving," he said, and chucked the branch into the water. "My mom says we ran out of money and me and her have to go live by her sister up at the lake upstate."

"What about your brother Alfie?"

Whitey snorted a chuckle.

"Yeah, what about Alfie? He's gone. Nobody knows. I think he went to Canada."

"Canada? What the hell would he go to Canada for? To play hockey for the Canadiens?"

"He's a draft dodger."

"Oh."

I knew what that was. If you went to Canada they couldn't send you to the war in Viet Nam. My dad says they're commie pinkos.

"When do you have to move?"

"I don't know."

"Let's go see if anybody's at the seesaws."

"Okay."

We walked down the dirt path back to the tracks and began our walk back towards the playground where the seesaws were. It's not that any of the kids who hung out there were riding seesaws, it was just a part of the park where we used to stay as little kids, and just never left. Whitey stopped suddenly and punched me on the shoulder.

"Listen."

"What?"

"Freight train," Whitey said.

"Do you have a penny?" I asked, going through my pockets. It was something we always did when a train was coming. You put a few pennies on the track and when the train passes over them they're flattened out to two or three times their size, with only a trace of Lincoln's smooshed face still visible. Now I could hear the slow rumble of the train. My dad told me that years ago the train carried passengers from upstate all the way downtown, and there was even a stop right near here by the golf course house.

"I have four pennies. Do you have any?"

Whitey shook his head and stepped right between the two rails, staring down the tracks in the direction of where the train was coming from. I put two pennies on one rail, and two on the other.

"Here she comes!" I said, looking south as it rounded a bend, coming towards us from downtown. "I'm going to hide in the bushes and watch." I took my position behind some tall cattails. "Come over here, Whitey. It's a good dry patch." But Whitey just stood in the middle of the rails looking towards the oncoming train. The train was just about to go through the underpass a hundred yards in front of us. We were in a patch shaded by some large trees, but when the train came through that underpass it would be in a bright sunny spot. My mind raced. *What the hell is Whitey doing, just standing there?* The locomotive went into the underpass, lumbering along like it normally does when it goes through the park, pretty slowly, but Whitey was still standing there. Just staring right at it.

"Whitey! Come on! It's almost here!" I said nervously. As the train came out of the underpass and into the bright patch of sunlight the engineer blasted the horn. The sound of the rumbling locomotive and

182

the half mile of freight cars were upon us. I jumped up and ran towards Whitey. I tugged frantically on his arm. "What the fuck are you doing? Get the fuck off the tracks, you fucking idiot!"

Whitey shoved me hard as the train was just a few yards away bearing down on us. I tumbled into the cattail weeds as the train passed, horn still blaring. I looked up and there was no sign of Whitey as the cars rumbled past me. *Shit.*

Finally the caboose went by and I jumped onto the tracks. No sign of a splattered Whitey. But as I watched the train head towards upstate and disappear around a wooded bend, there, way in the distance on the side of the train, hanging onto a ladder and leaning back, I could just make out that there was a person there. Whitey was on the train, giving me a big salute as he headed upstate, I guess. I looked down on the rail to see if my pennies were squished, but they had fallen off the rail and not gotten run over. Just like Whitey.

I didn't feel like going to the seesaws. I didn't feel like going home either. I left the tracks, went through the park, and started walking through the neighborhood. I pretended to myself I was just wandering aimlessly, but then there I was, in front of Josephine's building. *I think I'll just hang out here for a while, maybe just stand around for no reason.* Her building is a lot like my building, only it doesn't have an elevator or an incinerator chute. My mom says that's why our building is a step above those other buildings down the block that were also built in the early 1900s, have fire escapes, claustrophobic living areas, are grossly neglected by their landlords, and have roaches in the apartments and rats in the cellars. Like our building, they're filled mostly with families of three, four, or more kids to every tiny apartment, and just about every one of those kids is out in the courtyard in front, an alley in back, on the front stoop, or playing in the street as soon as they get home from school, until the very last minute before supper when kids are called home by moms yelling out windows or bratty sisters sent by parents to tug on our arms.

It's funny how your circle of friends expands when you grow up where there are lots of apartment buildings. Until you're about three and a half, you're satisfied playing with your brother or sister. But pretty soon, at about age four, you're out on your own, making friends with kids all over the building and even from down the block.

And there I sat, on the front stoop of Josephine's building, hoping she'd notice me. I couldn't deny it any longer. Boring through my brain like an earwig, she was all I could think about. I know she's a year older than I am, but physically she was like a grown woman, and I was still like a kid. I mean, I only had peach fuzz under my armpits. What the hell chance could I have with someone like her?

Down the block, in the distance (it's hard to see with the way the sunlight is behind them), I could see two people carrying bags walking towards me. *Could it be?* My heart felt like it was being pounded by a pile driver at a construction site. *What if it's her? How can I possibly explain what I'm doing here on her stoop by myself? Should I run? Hide? Climb up the fire escape? Holy shit, it is Josephine and she's with Joanie, the other counselor who lives down Bailey Avenue in that private house.* Then, out of nowhere the worst possible thing that could happen, happened

"Hi, Vinny!" Griffith yelled from a window on the second floor.

Oh, no. Griffith lives here? What kind of embarrassing foulmouthed joke will he rain down on me just as Josephine and Joanie arrive?

"Griffith. I was just leaving," I said as I stood and took a few steps away from the stoop.

"Don't leave!" Griffith yelled. "Josephine is coming down the block and she has something to tell you!"

I looked down the block, and there they were, gaining on me. It's a risk I just can't take with Griffith there. I turned, and ran the opposite direction back towards the seesaws in the park.

I stopped outside the fence and through the bushes I could see a group hanging out there, so I went through the hole in the fence. Summers were always different for hanging out because so many kids went away to Rockaway or upstate for weeks at a time or even the entire summer. And the summer after graduation is even weirder. Some of the guys who were always around are nowhere to be seen. I heard

184

that's because some of the guys are going to some of the really demanding Catholic high schools like Fordham and Manhattan Prep and they're already studying, reading their summer book list, and actually doing homework. Farley, where I'm going, isn't one of those schools. As I get closer, I see none of my old gang is there. No BB, Jimmy Joe, Flynn, Carrie or Donna. Just some kids from a couple of years behind me at Presentation, and holy shit, Father Q. is sitting there with a beer in his hand. As I get closer I can see Father Q. put the can behind him, as if he's hiding it from me. And he's wearing sunglasses even though it's getting dark out.

"Hi, Vinny," Terry said. He's one of the younger kids I know pretty well because he used to live in my building before they moved to a larger apartment on Review Place.

"Hello, Mr. Schmidt," Father Q. announced cheerfully. "Have a nice day at the beach today?"

"Yes, Father. Hi, Terry," I said guardedly. What's up with this new priest? He's drinking a beer with kids even younger than me? "Have you seen any of the guys around, like Jimmy Joe or BB?"

"BB was in the stands earlier with the older guys. I think he said he'd be around later," Terry said, looking uncomfortable.

"What's the matter, Vinny? We're not good enough for you?" Father Q. chortled, overly gregarious like someone's asshole drunk uncle. The gang of teens laughed a little too hard at his attempt at humor.

"Um, I'll see you guys around," I said, walking away. I walked through the hole in the fence and started walking towards the football field stands where the older kids hung out after dark. I turned around quickly when I heard footsteps gaining on me. It was Terry.

"Vinny. Where you headed?"

"Gonna see if anybody's at the stands yet."

We walked along the cinder track around the football field, crunching pebbles as we stepped.

"Father Q. was talking some bullshit over there," Terry said, dropping a hint like a fart at a funeral mass.

"Like what?"

185

"He was talking about how Whitey Shelley got caught stealing money from the tuition envelopes and got fired from camp, and that he was the ringleader of a counselor crime ring."

"What? Are you kidding me?" I said, stopping dead on the track. "Fucking asshole. Who ever heard of a priest talking shit like that?"

"He also said he might have to get the police involved, so if anybody sees the cops at the rectory, that's what it would be about."

"Cops at the rectory, huh?"

"I'll see you later," Terry said turning.

"Are you going back to the seesaws?"

"Not if Father Q. is still there. That guy gives me the creeps."

That was too strange. Cops at the rectory because of Whitey stealing a few bucks? Doesn't sound right. I've never known Whitey to bullshit me. He might not tell me something at first, but if I ask him he answers. Whitey said Father Q. wanted him to do "something." I think I know what that means. And I wonder if he's asked other kids to do something, too? Like maybe some seventh and eighth graders drinking beer in the park? I mean, anybody who's been to certain areas of just about any park in the city knows that you got to be careful because of perverted guys hanging around. It could be anywhere and you can easily stumble upon them. Whether in a parking lot, a certain wooded area, or even just an ordinary stairway, weird guys, usually dressed in dark colors, of every race and size slink around lurking behind cars, trees and walls. And we've seen them do all kinds of perverted stuff, from screwing tree holes, to stroking their exposed shlongs, and asking kids to spit into jars for a quarter. But a priest doing this stuff? I don't know. Wouldn't that be like a mortal sin? We've had mean priests like Monsignor McNabb who always yelled at us altar boys, but I've never heard of a priest trying to do something perverted to a kid before. Fuck, if that's possible, anything's possible. And in September when I go to high school at Farley, there are tons of priests. But I would think high school kids could pretty much protect themselves from perverts if they wanted to. Unless a priest was a devious prick, like I'm beginning to

186

think maybe Father Q. might be. I never thought of a priest as somebody you had to watch out for in that way. That's a scary thought. It's kind of like if a cop is going to rob and beat you, except it's even worse for a priest because he's supposed to be representing God himself. I would think a big school like Farley would have to look out for pervert priests and get rid of them. They would, right? They should have a class in school about how to watch out for the stuff that really could hurt you. From the time you're in first grade, nuns and priests are getting red in the face and spitting spittle across the room warning you about the evils of Satan and sin and commies, and you're sitting there trying to figure out exactly what it could be that you might be doing to have caused this much commotion. It's not until the seventh or eighth grade when the girls' blouses start expanding and the boys start pointing at bulges in their pants that the nuns and priests start talking about purity and animal urges that it dawns on you what they've been worried about all these years – sex! And now, just when all I can think about is how I want to get close to Josephine so I can touch her, smell her, taste her, and not ever let go... Just when I think that loving Josephine, and yes, someday having sex with her, is the only thing that could make me a complete human being... there's Father Q. who's turning Whitey's and my world upside down. Why didn't they warn us about that?

On the way home, I thought I'd stop by the deli on 242nd Street for one of their meat cakes. I have no idea what kind of meat it could possibly be, but on a hard roll with ketchup it's hard to beat. And much to my surprise, behind the counter is a guy I used to see in Pigeon Park where mostly Jewish guys hang out. Howie was wearing a white button down shirt, a black bow tie, and a white apron.

"Hey, Howie, you work here? Since when?"

"On and off for a couple of years. I was working early mornings and weekends, but I got a promotion. Hence, the spiffy get-up," he said, grabbing both sides of his bow tie and wiggling it up and down. "Hey, are you interested in my old job here?"

"What kind of job?"

"Well, it's officially called stock boy, but we call it shit man."

187

"Shit man? What do you have to do?"

"You start out cleaning up, mopping, pots and pans, garbage, all the shit jobs. And if you do a good job and the boss and the missus like you, you get promoted like me, from shit man to clerk."

"Wow. I always wanted to work in a nice deli. Do they let you eat for free?"

"Officially, if the owner or his wife is here, you get one free sandwich at the end of your shift."

"And unofficially?"

"If they're not here, it's like an all-day smorgasbord, and when you leave, you might get a hero with a couple of brewskies."

"They let you take beer?"

"Shhh, not so loud!"

"I'm interested. When do you have to know by?"

"The boss wants somebody to start in a day or two."

"I'll let you know tomorrow."

"The boss is a stickler for cleanliness and short hair. And the missus is a stickler for politeness, so you are forewarned."

"Thanks!"

I bounded up the block, and it wasn't until I got to my building that I realized I forgot the meat cake on a roll. Working in a deli seemed like it had real possibilities. But I'd probably have to quit my camp job, and not get to see Josephine in a bathing suit anymore. *I'll decide tomorrow. Tonight, I'll be thinking of Josephine in her bathing suit.*

Morning assembly seemed normal at first. Lots of kids, loud playing, a portable record player squawking Tommy James and the Shondells on 45s, senior girls giggling, counselors buried deep in breakfast sandwiches and sports sections, when suddenly a loud whistle blew from the stage. Standing on the stage next to Father Q. was a short, stocky man with slicked back black hair, long baggy chinos, and a black windbreaker with a coach's whistle around his neck. The boss was nowhere in sight. I looked at Jerry and even he was in the state of shock, putting his sandwich and paper down, suddenly sitting up straight in his chair.

Another piercing blast from the whistle echoed through the auditorium. "Attention everyone!" the new guy announced with drill sergeant charm. "I'm the new camp director, Mr. Santarocco. Father Q. will lead the assembly with the morning prayer, then there will be a counselor meeting on stage immediately following."

Father Q. started with the Our Father as counselors looked at each other in bewilderment and shock. What was going on?

"Amen."

"Campers will now quietly take a seat," the new guy said, as the kids could still be heard talking and laughing. Then another whistle blast. "I said quietly!" he yelled like a shrieking asshole. "Now, counselors! On! Stage!"

We all shuffled up the side steps and were led by Father Q. and the new guy backstage. We formed a semicircle around them. Father Q. was wearing sunglasses and I could see he still had a black eye.

"Listen up," the new guy barked. "I'm in charge now and things will run differently around here. Discipline starts with me, goes through you, and into each and every one of the campers. No more lax supervision. Each camper will be assigned a number and camper count-offs will be conducted every fifteen minutes. No more counselor breaks or interaction with other groups. Absolutely no counselor socializing. And tuition envelopes will be handed from the campers to me."

Father Q. didn't say a word.

"If anybody has a problem with any of this, speak up now, or get back to work and conduct your first count-off."

Everyone started towards the stairs.

"Excuse me!" I shouted, stopping everyone in their tracks. They all stared at me and the new guy approached me like a boxing opponent just before a bout began.

"What is it?"

"Um, I , er..." I was looking around wondering if I really was doing this. I think I have that deli job lined up. Fuck this guy and that

189

freak Father Q. Something smells fishy and I know who it is. "Um, I don't think I want to work here, under these conditions."

"Fine!"

Father Q. looked stunned. And pissed.

The new guy took another step towards me. I could smell his cheap Hai Karate and his garlic breath. He had a lot of nose hair, too. "Hand in your shirt."

"What?"

"Your camp shirt. Hand it over."

"Are you kidding me? I don't have an undershirt on."

"You no longer work here so you can no longer wear a staff shirt," he said, holding out his hand.

All eyes were on me.

I took the shirt off, folded it neatly, placed it in his hand, clicked my heels together, placed my first two fingers of my right hand under my nose, shot my left hand up in the air in a Hitler salute, shouted, "Sieg Heil!" turned on my heels and marched down the steps, with counselors laughing hysterically and applauding.

"Quiet! Back to your positions. Quiet!"

The door closed behind me and I could still hear short bursts of whistles and shouting. I'm in shorts and shirtless and figured it would look pretty normal for me to run home rather than walk, and within three steps I felt like I was flying. I couldn't wait to find out what was in those homemade deli meat cakes.

I got a queasy feeling getting up early and putting on my "uniform" from Presentation School (minus the tie with the PS), a white dress shirt and navy blue pants. It was all I could think of to wear for my interview at the deli and I hoped it would be the last time I'd ever have to wear it. Oddly, when I put on the shirt, I noticed the sleeves and the pants legs were about an inch short. That's strange, because they'd fit the last time I wore them on the last day of eighth grade, just a couple of months before.

Mr. Schneider, the deli owner, was a neighborhood fixture. His store in the shadow of the elevated train at 242nd and Broadway was in stark contrast to the rest of the stores on the block. The deli run by Mr. and Mrs. Alfred Schneider could have been on West 86th Street in the posh Yorktown section of upper Manhattan. The counters were well-lit and they gleamed. Shelves were neatly stocked and were often seen being tended with a feather duster. Clerks behind the counter wore white shirts, black bow ties, and full-length white aprons. There was usually a woman scurrying behind the counter with trays of freshly roasted meats, just-made salads, and still warm pastries and cakes. Although the prices at there were much higher than typical for the neighborhood, customers were always several deep for breakfast and lunch, Monday through Friday, for the top quality fare.

I was nervous as hell. It would be my first real job interview. The way I got my first job when I was in sixth grade was the owner of the dry cleaners asked me to make a delivery for him when I was picking something up for my mother. It continued on and off for two years. And the day camp job just happened because I knew Father O. since first grade. An old white-haired man behind the counter smiled and in a German accent asked if he could help me. When I said I was there for an interview, Howie's head popped up like a jack-in-the-box as he glanced at the clock on the wall.

"Good. You're five minutes early. I'll tell Alfred you're here," he said, walking towards the door that led to the kitchen. He turned back to me holding his index finger in the air, "To you, he's Mr. Schneider."

The old German giggled. "In time, you can call him Alfred. But not the missus. She'll always be the missus."

Howie poked his head out the kitchen doorway. "Come on back."

I walked behind him through the narrow hallway filled with large cans of food, bags of rice, sugar and flour, and paper bags.

Alfred was seated at an ancient butcher block table in the center of large room which obviously served as a kitchen, office, storage room, and staging area for the operation. In front of Alfred was an ornately decorated blue and white egg cup with a single egg fitting snugly on top. He had a white linen napkin tied around his neck and he was tapping the shell of the egg with the convex side of a teaspoon.

"So, you're Schmidt. Good German name," he said in a rich baritone German-accented voice.

"My dad's German and Irish," I said qualifying my heritage, as I always do, living in the Irish ghetto.

"That's a good combination in this neighborhood. Where are you going to high school? You start this fall, right?" he said, scooping egg out of the shell and onto a china plate.

"Yeah, I mean, yes. At Cardinal Farley."

"Good school. Clinton already has too many schvartzes," he said, using a derogatory Yiddish term for blacks. "Let me see your hands, come here."

I looked at Howie, who ever so slightly nodded his head in encouragement. I approached Alfred and held my hands out. He grabbed my wrists forcefully to inspect them from top to bottom, front and back.

"You can do a better job on the fingernails. Cleanliness is the number one priority. You will be punctual, honest, courteous, respectful, and work hard," he said, reminding me a little too much of the Nazi officers instructing the American POWs on the television show *Combat*. "Start tomorrow and Leonard will show you what to do. Run along."

I turned and Howie led me down the hall.

"One more thing," Alfred said loudly. "Get a haircut."

"Yes, sir," I replied trying not to reveal my disappointment. I was finally liking the length of my hair, just over my ears and barely touching the collar of my shirt in the back. I knew I would have to get a haircut before high school started because the haircut restrictions there were the strictest of all the Catholic schools around. But I was hoping to get the haircut the day before school started so I could at least look cool for the rest of the summer.

"How come your hair is longer than mine and he didn't say that to you?" I asked Howie.

"Because he likes me," Howie said proudly. "Don't fuck up, and he'll like you, too. Be here tomorrow at six."

"Six? In the morning?"

"Yes. Six in the morning. Because you have to get here before the breakfast rush so you can learn how to be a good shit man! Capeesh?"

"Capeesh."

"See you bright and early tomorrow morning," he said, wriggling his bow tie.

I couldn't believe it! I had my first real job. And I was thinking that me and Howie could become good friends. I've never had a friend who wasn't in grammar school with me at Presentation. In fact, I don't think I've had a friend who wasn't Catholic. And having a Jew for a close friend will be really cool. I don't think I'll tell my parents about everything that's been going on. At least not for a while.

Chapter Thirteen

—Now—

It's not very often you think about gravity, but when you feel like you've been for a spin in a cement mixer for a few hours, and standing erect requires every ounce of strength you can muster, it's clear that the earth wants you. In fact, you feel it pulling, and it pulls and pulls on you when you're hurting, until one day, it does actually swallow you. Then they throw dirt on you so you can't stink up the surface any more with your existential self.

No matter how bad you're hurting, waiting outside an emergency room is a good way to appreciate what you have. When you hear an ambulance with its siren wailing right up into the driveway, at least the poor guy getting dragged through the doorway has a shot, and you know you're already having a better finish to your day than he is. But when an ambulance pulls up with no siren, no flashing red lights, and the two attendants take an extra bite of their doughnut before exiting the front cab, you know the guy in the back already had the last worst day of the life he used to have.

The rain stopped and the sky was just starting to lighten at the eastern horizon. Two ambulances have come and gone and I was wondering whether the next one would have the siren blaring or not.

ahh-OOGah

I hadn't heard an ahhOOgah horn in years, and pulling into the driveway was a late forties fire engine red pickup.

"Can you sit up front or do you want me to tie you down in back?" Whitey asked through the passenger side window, engine churning like a Mack truck. Behind the wheel silently sat the gentleman who knew how to wield a shotgun to make a point.

"I can get in," I said, opening the door and slowly stepping on the running board.

"I think you already met Zipper," Whitey said, nodding to the driver. "You look like one of the Three Stooges after a stick of dynamite goes off next to them, with your tattered clothes and

194

bandages. All that's missing are angel wings and the harp as you rise into heaven."

"Yeah, well, I think mine are on backorder," I said, as Whitey shuffled over and I sat down in the nicely refurbished truck cabin. As nice as the interior of the pickup looked, I was more amazed at how much better Whitey seemed. He sounded like Whitey. In the dim light, he even looked almost well.

"Where do you want to go? Back to my place? Or grab a drink or something?"

I looked down at my pants, split up to my crotch, and I felt the bandage on my face. "I don't think I'm dressed for going out."

"Torn clothes and bandages? That's a normal Saturday night at Captain Norm's."

"I'll take a rain check."

The tires spun out on the wet driveway pavement as we hit the road. In less than a minute there were no more street lights and we were chugging along the same two-lane highway where my car was probably still lying in a watery ditch. The engine purred as Zipper changed gears, three on a tree.

"This thing is sweet. What year is it?"

"Forty-nine. It's my baby." Whitey reached over and opened the glove box, revealing a gleaming AM/FM/CD player. He pushed a couple of buttons and a country song blasted over high-quality hidden speakers.

"Who's this?"

"Hank."

"Hank?"

"Hank Williams Junior."

"Oh, the *Monday Night Football* guy."

"Former *Monday Night Football* guy. A country boy can survive."

"How's that?"

"That's the name of the song."

"This truck is nice. You do all the work on this yourself?"

"Yup. Me and Zipper. This was a barn find."

195

"What's that?"

Whitey looked at me like I'd asked him who the Beatles were. "A barn find usually means the vehicle was rusting away in some barn or garage for thirty or forty years because some old widow didn't want to touch her hubby's car and when she finally kicks the bucket the kids try to sell the rust bucket just to get rid of it."

"This was a rust bucket?"

"Yup. Weeds growing through the floorboards. A real reclamation project. Just like me."

Zipper jerked the wheel and we headed between two giant trees onto a pitch black dirt road. A line from the song came on about a guy getting murdered with a knife for forty bucks on a New York City street. We hit a pothole in the road, jolting my achy body.

Yeah, it's like we picked up where we'd left off all those years ago. The wisecracks, the looks, the references from when we most of our lives were ahead of us. But there I was, going down a dirt road in the middle of the woods with a guy who last I heard was a murderer on the lam, a deserter, a crazed Bronx boy turned redneck maniac with terminal cancer and nothing to lose. Nobody on the planet knew where I was, except for me, Whitey and a guy who'd already made it clear he'd just as soon put a shotgun shell in my sinus cavity as put three syllables together.

"What's the matter? You never drove off-road before?" Whitey said, his face eerily illuminated by the green dashboard instrument lights. His green pallor, nervous stare and bulging eyeballs reminded me of Rat Fink.

"I've been down this road before. Just not when every bump in the road makes my skin ache. By the way, where are we going?"

"Just cutting through the woods. Short cut."

I felt a drop of something wet hit the corner of my eye from under one of my bandages, and wiped it with my finger. I held my finger close to the light of the radio to see if it was indeed blood. Yes, it was.

"I reckon you're still bleedin' some?" Whitey said, and it immediately struck me that he did sound different. His Bronx accent seemed gone. He sounded like a country boy. "Right around this bend and we're there."

The *DO NOT ENTER* sign was put back up, and as we pulled up next to the darkened cabin a floodlight probably activated by our movement lit up the area. The sky was a little brighter; the sun would be up within the hour.

As soon as Zipper killed the engine and we exited the truck, the sounds of the woods were apparent. Bugs buzzing and chirping, frogs croaking, baby birds stirring. The gravel crunched under our feet and the screen door squeaked as Whitey pulled it open. We entered the cabin.

"By the way, Zipper's an old 'Nam buddy. He lives over yonder in that cabin."

That was Whitey's first reference to Viet Nam, which was close to the first level of mystery in the Whitey mythology and rumor mill started back when he disappeared from the neighborhood amidst mysterious circumstances. I'll never forget that day I tried to pull him off the railroad tracks with the train bearing down on us. When I saw him in the distance hanging off the ladder and waving to me, I had a feeling that was the end of me and Whitey and all we had been through. But it wasn't. Because when you grow up with someone and you make life's discoveries together, there is a bond that only dies when one of you dies, and I'm not so sure it even ends then.

Because after your mom and dad teach you to say "Mama" and "Dada" and to get up off your knees and start to walk, learn the alphabet and count to ten, that's pretty much it for them. Just about then you waddle out your front door and find out that what you really need to know about dealing with the real world isn't coming from the teachers in your school, or the priest hollering from the podium, the cop on the corner, or even the president. What you really need to know will come from the kids out on the street. And it's through the punches in the face, the crying after falling off fire escapes, running from cops in the dark, and egg cream and pretzel rod celebrations after a curb ball win that life's lessons are seared into your brain. And decades later when you're in meetings with suits who sound like the "wah wah wah"

197

of the schoolteacher in the Charlie Brown cartoons, you know you can handle them with ease. I mean, what are they going to do you? Make you bend over and throw spaldeens at your ass like we did to the losers in curb ball doing moons up? Dealing with an asshole boss is nothing compared to trying to talk and joke your way out of a run-in with any one of the dozen or so big fucking moron asshole bullies who got their jollies by trying to scare the shit out of skinny little wiseasses like me. Almost all those fuckhead bullies wound up dead or in jail by the time they were twenty-one, and I've seen many an asshole boss get his ass fired after HR became the new hall monitors and tattle-taled him out of a job.

No matter how many decades pass, no matter how many asshole bosses you had to put up with, how many relatives you had to bury, cities you moved to, girlfriends and wives you went through, and kids you raised, there's a place deep down in your brain, unaffected by everything that came after, where those friendships and events took place that nothing else can alter. So it doesn't matter how many of those things floated down the rushing river of time. When you once again meet one of the special people who were there for that first black eye, the stickball three-sewer shot, the look through a telescope at the naked lady, the secret subway ride downtown, and on and on and on, no matter how much hair and how many teeth have disappeared, and wrinkles, limps and lumps have appeared, it's like nothing happened between those magical times of growing up together then... and now. You just pick up where you left off, as if nothing happened in between.

"Were you drafted?"

Whitey looked at me like I was an idiot as he unlocked the front door. "You knew I enlisted, right?"

"Um, no, I didn't."

Whitey scrunched his face as if extremely puzzled and flicked on the light. We entered an enclosed porch area with a few chairs. There was another door that he proceeded to unlock. We went into a kitchen with an avocado green refrigerator, washer, and dryer straight out of a 1975 Sears catalogue. A bare, sturdy oak kitchen table and four chairs were in the center; there were no signs of frilly female touches. A large outdoor-type rubber garbage can was in the corner.

"This is it. Home sweet home. I'll show you around," Whitey said, leading the way through several rooms each with wooden tables, chairs, bookshelves, beds, couches, TV stands and paneling. "I built just about everything. Well, I mean, except the kitchen, and this bedroom. That was the original cabin."

"When you say you built, you mean you, you yourself built?"

"Well, me and Zipper. The furniture, too. I've got a shop in the garage. This was the summer cabin the folks rented when we were small. You were up here, right?

"Holy shit! Now I remember. We must've been eight or nine years old."

"Yeah, we had some good times. Who knew we were poor? You better get some rest," Whitey said, pulling down the blanket on a bed in a small, neat bedroom. He pulled down the shades. "The sun's just about up," he said closing the door behind him. "See you when you get up."

I took off my tattered clothes and got into bed in my underwear. The room wasn't very dark, and I thought I'd never be able to fall asleep. My monkey mind raced. *Where's my car? Should I tell my ex-wife and son? What if I'm bleeding internally and die in my sleep? Will Zipper come in here and slit my throat? What about my job?* And somehow, I was soon sawing wood, oblivious to it all.

The sound and smell of bacon frying was unmistakable. Although I still had aches and pains as I got out of bed, I felt like I had a good night's sleep. On the end table by the door were some neatly folded clothes, dark blue Dickey pants and a shirt. A little big, but a vast improvement.

I poked my head out the door and there was Whitey at the kitchen table reading a newspaper and smoking a cigarette. "You sleep okay?" he asked without looking up from his paper.

"Yup. I feel like forty bucks."

"Is that good or bad?"

"Forty bucks is always good."

199

"Have some breakfast."

Whitey glided around the kitchen, and almost magically, a full country breakfast was in front of the two of us.

"You didn't have to do this," I said, shoving a crispy stick of bacon into my mouth. I looked up at Whitey and he had his head bowed with his eyes closed, as if in prayer. He stayed that way for about ten seconds.

"No problem. Gotta eat, right?"

The room was bright with sunlight and full of the smells of summer by a lake in the woods. The sounds of ducks, songbirds, and crows were the only noises besides our sipping, slurping, and enjoying our meal. I was getting near the bottom of my coffee and I wiped up the last of the egg yolk with my toast. The time had come for me to talk to Whitey about all the things that had been on my mind since that day he left on the freight train. But I wasn't sure where or how to begin. Him dying of cancer? Being a deserter in Viet Nam? A murderer on the run?

"Who said that line, you've got to be honest to live outside the law?" I asked.

"Dylan."

"Are you?"

"Am I what?"

"Outside the law?"

Whitey rose from his chair and looked out the kitchen window towards the lake. "When I cash it all in, that's where I'll be. Fish and bird food. I hope they leave something for them to gnaw on when they dump my ashes there. And it could be sooner rather than later. I'm ready to go. No regrets. No worries. I ain't gonna suffer like my old man. What's the difference? You pays ya money and ya takes ya chances, right? I bet red, it came out black. I'm gonna cash in my chips and take what I got coming. That's the Lord's law." He turned to me, lit another cigarette and sat back down. "Yeah, I'm outside the law. I've lived that way for decades. It's not that hard to do. Work off the books, don't pay taxes. Change your name slightly. It's really pretty easy once you set it up."

"I've heard things, Whitey."

"I don't talk about this shit. Ever. With anybody. What's done is done. Gone. Look around. You won't see one trace of the past. That's nostalgia. Nostalgia is bullshit."

Whitey got up and walked into a bedroom. I could hear a drawer open and shut. He came back and dropped a yellowed newspaper article in front of me. It had been neatly cut out from a paper and probably stored somewhere safe and secure for many years.

The headline on the article read, "Hunts Point Murder Mayhem."

"It's about you?"

Whitey took a long drag on his smoke and dropped it into his half-empty coffee mug. His head dropped, his jaw tightened, and he began to pace the room. "I was busting my ass making a decent buck buying food and beverages wholesale and selling to the bars in the neighborhood after I got out of the army. I tell you, it was a fuckin' war zone down there. See this?" Whitey said, pointing to a scar just behind his ear that went almost to his shoulder. "A crackhead sticks you with a knife as big as a machete and you do what you gotta do. I got him good." Whitey stopped suddenly and looked me in the eye. "So yeah, I whacked him, panicked and got the fuck out of there. There was nobody around where I was at that time of the morning. Maybe I should've called the cops and pleaded self-defense, but with all the shit going down at that time I just said fuck it and got out of there. That article says it all. Fuckin' asshole blindsides me with a knife, what am I supposed to do?"

"What did you do?"

Whitey seemed to calm down, took a seat and lit up a smoke.

"I got him with a baseball bat."

"A baseball bat?"

"Yup. His blade was twisting inside me and I managed to grab my bat day special next to my seat and put the square of the barrel to the round of his skull. He missed my artery by three centimeters. I drove all the way home with my thumb in the wound. I nearly died. Says in the article he had a record from here to Sing Sing. Just another junkie on the prowl. White guy kills a black kid, I don't care if he has a knife, they're gonna put me on trial in the South Bronx and put me through the fuckin' ringer no matter what. I had to split."

Whitey got up, poured another cup of coffee in a clean mug, and looked out the kitchen window towards the lake.

"Says he didn't have a wife or any kids or anything. Thank God. So here I am," he said, sitting back down at the table. "Living 'underground.' Funny, I always thought underground shit was so cool. Underground music, movies, comics, books, all that shit. That ain't underground. This is underground. My life."

Whitey reached across the table, picked up the article and put it in his shirt pocket.

"So, I just got to watch my shit, don't talk too much to people I don't have to. Get by with odd jobs with people I know. Do some work at Captain Norm's."

"Nice job on the jukebox."

A smile so big appeared across Whitey's face, I thought his skin would crack. "Thanks. Sometimes I just peek out the kitchen door on a Saturday night and watch everybody having fun to that music. Stones. Ramones. Kinks. Hank Junior. Allmans. Young people digging the same shit we dug. We're passing it down to them. And now we gotta step aside. I know I am. I'm done. Now what the fuck happened to you?"

"Me?"

"Yeah, where have you been?"

"I feel like I've been underground. Lost my job, my wife, my kid."

"Boy or girl?"

"Boy. Sixteen years old."

"He needs you, you know."

"That's not what my ex says."

"Fuck her. He's your kid."

"They're in L.A."

"So what the fuck are you doing here?"

Whitey fuckin' Shelley of 238th Street, murderer, possible deserter, possibly dying of cancer, who has been on the lam for at least thirty years just asked me what the fuck I'm doing – *and I don't know.*

"I don't know."

"You better fuckin' know. You want to go down to Captain Norm's with me? I got shit to do."

"Um, sure. Just got to make a couple of calls."

Whitey steps out onto the porch and yells across the yard to the other cabin, "Zipper! Drop your cock and grab your socks. We're goin' to da captain's."

It didn't take long before I felt like an invisible observer sitting on the far right side of the bench seat in Whitey's fire engine red pickup. It was obvious Zipper didn't bathe much. He had that look that all guys in their sixties seem to transform into, black or white – droopy white mustache, jowls hanging, losing white hair on top, growing clumps of hair in ears and nostrils, heavy lines from each side of the nose down to the chin, and earlobes that keep growing.

"Did you pick up the payment from the Tanner sisters?" Whitey asked Zipper as we bounced hard down the dirt road.

"Nah, they gave me blowjobs instead," Zipper said smiling.

"The last time you had a blowjob, those old broads had tits above their belly button. Did you get the money?"

"I got it, all right."

"Yeah. And...?"

"And what?"

"And what. And what do you think I'm gonna do with my boot if you don't tell me where my half of three hundred dollars is?"

Zipper turned to me slowly, and I again saw that expression he had on his face when he first stuck a shotgun in my general direction. "Was he this much of an asshole when he was a kid?"

"Oh yeah," I shot back. "Assholes like him are born, not made."

"Yeah, well, you two assholes are going to have a long walk if Zipper doesn't fork over my hundred and a half."

203

"Here you go, Mr. Trump, they were short on gold bullion so they paid in tens and fives," Zipper said, sticking the bills in Whitey's top pocket.

"Were they happy with the job?"

"The blowjob they gave me? Oh, yeah!"

"No, the actual job."

"Yeah, they said the toilet is working great."

"You told them it's guaranteed, right?"

"Yup. I told them we stand behind our work. So far behind, that they'd never be able to find us." Zipper laughed hysterically at his wit.

Whitey turned to me briefly with a bemused look on his face. "You see what I have to put up with? I should have let those fuckin' rats eat you alive!"

"Aw, there he goes! I could be elected the second black president of the United States and the almighty Whitey would have to remind me that I'd be fertilizer in the Mekong Delta if it wasn't for him saving my ass. Come on, that was forty years ago! Let me have my life back!" Zipper ranted in a speech I thought he must have made hundreds of times before.

"Okay, here it comes..." Whitey said in mock exasperation.

Then they both yelled in unison, "Sometimes I think you should have let me rot in that goddamned cage in Viet Nam."

Whitey added, "You ain't in no cage but you sure as hell smell like you're rotting."

"I took a bath."

"When was that?"

"When we fixed the Tanner sisters' toilet, I had to move the bathtub to the other side of the bathroom, so technically, I took a bath," Zipper stated proudly.

"Vinny, you see what I have to put up with? See what happens when fate throws two people together? You think it's random? No! This is part of a divine design, payback for all the shit I pulled on my parents and every teacher we ever had. This is my Purgatory."

"I've gone up a few notches. I used to be a living Hell on earth," Zipper said to me in loud stage whisper.

Does anybody even know what Purgatory is anymore? Because to those of us who grew up memorizing the questions and answers in the Baltimore Catechism, Purgatory is as real as Montana. We know it's out there, we just haven't seen it yet. If there was just Hell, how could the nuns and priests keep anybody in line? If there was only Hell, then the first time you lied about attending mass on Sunday and meeting your friends at Van Cortlandt Park lake to go fishing for sunfish instead, that would be it. You'd be banished to Hell forever because you lied and skipped mass and then what was the difference? You could rob a bank every week and the punishment wouldn't get any worse. So if they added Purgatory into the mix, where they could send you for minor infractions, and you had to serve time before going to Heaven, and offered you time off for good behavior in the form of "indulgences," then they had a shot of trying to keep you somewhat honest. But Whitey talking about Purgatory? If he did kill that guy, unfortunately, Purgatory isn't an option for him. It's the express train to Hell for him.

Whitey picked up a wrapped newspaper in front of Captain Norm's door, which was locked up tight. He unlocked it and when the door opened, the smell of decades of beer, wine, and who-knows-what soaked into wooden floor boards, bar counters and carpeting wafted by in sharp contrast to the fresh lakeside air in the parking lot. Zipper and Whitey immediately went into a routine of opening doors and windows, filling buckets with hot water in a choreographed display of teamwork. Whitey reached behind the jukebox and flipped a switch or two.

"Knock yourself out with the jukebox. The paper's on the bar. Feel free to use the phone. We'll be about an hour so you can decide what you want to do by then," Whitey said, pushing a mop bucket on wheels into the kitchen.

Oh yeah. What do I want to do? No cell phone, no car, no clothes and no plans. I wondered if I still had a job.

205

It took about an hour to finally access my voicemail to find out that apparently the only person on the planet who missed me was the guy at work who wanted to know if I still had a contact at Yankee Stadium for tickets, which I don't. Luckily I wasn't fired and made arrangements to take a couple of days off without pay, because I didn't get any sick days. The insurance company was going to tow the car and if it was totaled I'd never see it again, but I'd get a check in the mail for $950, which is the book value of my clunker.

The smell of lemon scented Pine-Sol masked the overnight bar stink pretty well, and the place actually looked like it could be photographed for an ad, with the sun streaming through the patio doors and white tablecloths on the tables.

"The place looks great," I told Whitey as he washed glasses behind the bar.

"It only has to look good until it gets dark outside and the patrons get lit up on the inside. So how are you getting home?"

"Is there a bus?"

"Greyhound."

"That'll do."

"We'll be finished here in a little while," Whitey said, pushing a keg across the floor behind the bar. "Hey, Zip, I'm going to give Vinny a ride to the bus station in town. Hook up this keg, would ya?"

"Roger that. Come back and visit soon, Vinny. It's fun seeing Whitey breaking somebody else's balls for a change."

The ride to the bus station wasn't filled with overarching life-changing questions, comments and/or observations about the past or the future. Just in-the-moment small talk, like Whitey saying "Listen to this line" when a Hank Williams Junior song called "Just Enough to Get in Trouble" came on. Or me asking how I should send back the clothes he lent me. He told me to bring them back the next time I visited. But would I? Would this be another one of those I-wonder-if-this-is-the-last-time-I'll-see-Whitey-again moments. Kind of like every time you see the Rolling Stones live you wonder whether that'll be the last tour.

Whitey and I will see each other again, I thought... or should I say, I reckoned.

"Thanks for the ride, Whitey. You saved my ass," I said, closing the pickup door.

"What? For giving you a ride? Life is short. Why be a scumbag? See you soon," Whitey said, turning up the volume on Hank Junior as he pulled away.

I hadn't been on a Greyhound since college, when all the stereotypes of bus riders were in full force – low-life drifters, teenage single mothers with screaming children, and smelly hippie college kids, one of which I was back then. The bus was half full with comfortable reclining chairs, air conditioning, and fellow riders who didn't stand out as being anything other than ordinary people from all walks of life looking for an easy ride from upstate New York to midtown Manhattan. Maybe to visit a museum, go to a business meeting, visit a relative, or just go home. The scenery changed from lush woods, lakes and the magnificent expanse of the Hudson River to the beautiful, affluent suburbs, followed by the crowded suburbs, then the crappy industrial outskirts, finally to the shitty parts of the Bronx and into the bull's eye of New York City. And I'm wearing a Dickey's uniform. The bus dumps me off at Port Authority near Times Square, where I catch the number one train to the end of the line. Well, not the *end* end, but one stop short at West 238th Street. *Might as well stop in for a cold one before I catch the bus to Bronxville, back to my sister's basement and the life I decided to live because of ... things other people caused.*
Right?

No, I didn't catch a cold one at the bar. I didn't even look in the window to see who was melting away on a stool. I walked to the bus at 242nd Street, which took me almost to my sister's house. And during the mile or so walk in my Dickey's, I thought perhaps there was a reason I got in that crash. Maybe it was to spend that time with Whitey and read that article about the night that changed his life forever by sending him underground. Having worked in the news biz a bit and seeing firsthand what kind of scrutiny and fact checking actually goes into some news articles, that was one scary thought.

I returned to work the next day, and I just assumed that the reason no one said a word about my new black eye and assorted exposed bruises on my face and hands was that they were used to me showing up like that. From my cubicle computer I researched stories for reporters who looked like they'd graduated high school last week, filed reports, archived stories, constructed Excel charts for budgets and schedules, and ordered lunches without making one phone call or personally interacting with another human being for hours on end. The upside of my solitary existence was that once my tasks were completed I could use the internet for my own amusement, which usually consisted of bouncing back and forth between sports sites and stupid videos on YouTube, until it dawned on me that it could be of some interest to research the article that Whitey had showed me. Simply by the font and layout of the article I knew it wasn't from the *New York Times*, so I decided to research both the *New York Daily News* and the *New York Post*.

After about a half hour of digging deeper and deeper into the web sites of the *News* and the *Post*, having to create usernames and passwords I will never remember again, I came to discover that you can't access stories from the *News* or the *Post* from the early to mid-1970s. I assumed I'd have to access those stories the old-fashioned way, by getting off my ass and going to the library. And of course in midtown Manhattan, the library would be the main branch of the New York Public Library at 42nd Street and Fifth Avenue, one of the most truly magnificent buildings ever constructed to store knowledge.

When I was a kid in the old neighborhood in the Bronx, the local library was actually a ground floor apartment in an ancient apartment building that looked a lot like the dilapidated roach infested pre-war building we lived in. You could tell by the sink in the corner that the small office where the chubby, friendly librarian lady sat had once been a kitchen. The two small bedrooms and living room were chockablock with bookshelves and books. The tiny bathroom was still the tiny bathroom. When I was four, to get there, my mom would schlep me and my eight-year-old sister up a steep North Bronx hill to a completely different neighborhood, with strange signs on the stores, even though it was only a few blocks away. It wasn't until years later that I discovered the reason the neighborhood was different from ours was that it was a Jewish neighborhood, and the neon signs in the deli windows were in Hebrew. I was amazed that we could actually take books home for free. But as thrilled as I was about that, I was just as disappointed once I realized we had to return them.

But if the New York Public Library main branch at 42nd Street and Fifth Avenue resembled anyone's quarters, they would be named Astor, Vanderbilt, or Carnegie. Ironically, this grand palace of stone, marble and exquisite wood-paneled interior opened in 1911, about the same time my crappy apartment building was built. Fortunately the library didn't have our cheap bastard landlord as caretaker. When your parents took you there for the first time, you couldn't believe that it was a regular library and you could actually take out a book for free with the same library card you used at the converted two-bedroom apartment on Sedgwick Avenue. Of course we didn't take out a book, because that would mean another trip downtown on the subway in a week or two, when in reality we probably wouldn't make a special trip like that again for maybe the rest of the year.

Working the late afternoon shift, it was easy for me to be at the 42nd Street library when it opened to begin my search for the Whitey news article. Whether you're four years old or in your forties, standing in the library's main room is something special. The first thing that strikes you is how can a room this large, with so many people, be so quiet. The vaulted muraled ceilings must be forty feet high, paneled with intricately detailed dark wood usually seen in cathedrals. Giant chandeliers and huge arched windows visible above two tiers of high bookshelves illuminate the room, yet every long communal table filled with silent readers is equipped with the kind of cheap lamp you might see on any Bronx bedroom end table.

After finally finding a sign with an arrow marked simply with the word "Periodicals," I approached the wide oak desk occupied by a lone middle-aged bespectacled man fingering through a long wooden file card drawer. I stood there in silence until he looked up at me.

"May I help you?" he asked in a reedy voice.

"Yes, I understand the only way I can look up newspaper stories from the late sixties and early seventies is on microfilm."

"No, that is not true. *The New York Times* archives are available online at our computer kiosks over there. All you need to do is..."

"I'm sorry, I want to access the *New York Daily News* and the *Post*," I said, interrupting him meekly.

He looked at me like I said I was requesting back issues of *Jugs* magazine.

"Oh. Those papers. Yes, they are only available on microfiche or microfilm. Just fill out the form with your request, pencils are here, and bring it back to me. I'll bring you the items, show you how to operate the equipment and we'll take it from there."

"Thanks. I'll start filling these out," I said, grabbing the paper request slips.

Not having a clue where to begin, I just wrote down I that I wanted the *News* and *Post* from January 1970 to 1971. Seemed like a good place to start. And after a five-minute orientation, I was scanning the microfiche looking for the headline "Hunts Point Murder Mayhem" or anything to do with violent murders in the Bronx in the early to mid-seventies. As I zipped through the days and weeks on microfiche, and Bronx murder and mayhem seemed to be on every other page, it became evident that this might take a while.

Chapter Fourteen

—Then—

Whitey and I had lots of plans for the summer and beyond. The biggest of which was that we were going to go to the same high school. On my first day of high school, I didn't even know where Whitey was, though. All I knew was that it must've been eighty degrees at 7:20 in the morning and I was scared shitless walking past DeWitt Clinton High School on the way to the Woodlawn number four train in my blue blazer, necktie, suit-material pants, and non-rubber soled shoes, the basic dress code. Kids from all over the Bronx go to Clinton, and it's a well-known fact that kids can easily get their asses kicked simply by walking near the school. Especially little kids who look like mini-businessmen on the way to Wall Street. My oversized red and yellow Farley book bag didn't help matters. It's hard to look tough in this getup, but I was thinking I had an Elvis in *Kid Creole* sneer working for me, until a big black kid passed me and said, "Y'all better see a dentist, whitey." Funny, that he should call me Whitey, because I'd feel a lot safer if he was walking with me right now.

Since Mosholu Parkway was the second-to-last stop on the Woodlawn train, the car was almost empty. There were the usual assortment of people on their way to work, but the kids on their way to their first day of Catholic high school after summer vacation were easy to pick out. Of course the ties and jackets were the dead giveaway, but there were other telltale signs. The bad, too-short haircuts exposing white scalps that had been protected by a summer's growth of hair. The deep suntan on faces that had been outside from sunrise to sunset. But most of all, the look of abject terror on anyone who knew what was in store for them when they once again started another school year in Catholic high school, or those of us terrified simply by what we'd heard from those who went before us. I was getting knowing looks from older high school kids that seemed to say, *You poor little bastard, they are going to eat you alive.* More and more people piled on the train as we headed south. By the time we got to Fordham Road it was jam-packed

211

with sweaty people of every size, color, shape and smell. Wanting to avoid making eye contact with anyone, I cracked open a couple of the text books I had purchased at orientation a few weeks ago. I started sweating bullets when I opened the elementary algebra book. I don't think I ever got under a ninety in a subject on any grammar school report card, but even the first page in the math book looked like it was written in Greek. A peek inside my general science book sent me a few degrees closer to panic. Then I opened the booklet they handed out on orientation and read, "The Farleyman is diligent and studious. He knows that here is his training ground where he must mould himself into a useful man. The Farleyman is clean – in his speech, in his actions, in his appearance." I wondered how serious they were about this stuff.

I felt something pressing on my shoe. Looking up, I saw an acne-faced fat kid with braces and a swoop of hair hanging down, as he laughed at me while holding onto the strap above me.

"You a frosh?"

"Uh, yeah."

"You're gonna get your ass kicked."

"By who?"

"You kiddin'? Everybody. Seniors, priests, brothers, bullies. They're gonna eat you alive."

"For what?"

"For being a freshman."

"Did you get your ass kicked?"

"Sure."

"For what?"

"I dunno. For mouthing off, I guess."

"I'm not mouthing off to anyone."

"They'll still kick your ass," he said, stepping on my foot a little bit harder.

"You're stepping on my foot."

"No shit, Sherlock."

"Well, fuckin' stop it!" I said a little too loud, because the well-dressed black lady sitting next to me turned from her book and gave me a look exactly like my mom would have on her face just before she smacked mine.

"It was an accident!" he said, like a kid standing with a stickball bat across the street from a broken window.

"What year are you in?" I asked the chubby kid with the oversized Farley button on his lapel.

"Sophomore. Did you read all your summer books?"

A panic came over me. *Did I? Holy shit.* I knew I bought them all. I read *All Quiet on the Western Front* and *The Jungle,* both of which scared the hell out of me. Lots of blood and guts from humans and animals. But I only got around five pages into *Beowulf, Kon-Tiki, and Heaven Knows, Mr. Allison.*

"I didn't finish all of them yet."

"You better hope you don't get Brother Fergel. He'll quiz you on all five of them in the first class," the kid said, dripping with doom and gloom.

He got me really sweating. I think the thickest book I read in grammar school was something called *The Mudhen,* about a wiseass teenager who's kind of a cross between Dobie Gillis and Maynard G. Krebs. So to get through *Beowulf, Kon-Tiki,* and *Heaven Knows, Mr. Allison* in one week was going to be torture.

"Didn't you even get the Cliff Notes?"

"Don't you have to read the whole thing?"

"Nobody reads the whole book. Just read some of it and read all of the Cliff Notes. That's what everybody does."

The black lady gave me another dirty look and went *tsk, tsk, tsk* as she shook her head.

"Turn around quick!" the fat kid said to me. I jerked my head around to look out the window and there it was, in all its glory, Yankee Stadium! We didn't have a color television, so seeing the emerald green grass, deep blue seats, and the bright white facade around the inside of the stadium looked otherworldly in the golden morning sunlight.

Shortly after the thrill of seeing the stadium, the train took a left turn and plunged down into a deep subway tunnel. Once inside, the sound of the train became deafening. The upper windows of the train, which provided a nice breeze when we were on the elevated track, now just let all the noise, filth and soot from the tunnel come blasting into the car. It was like we were barreling down towards Hell, which perhaps was true because the next stop was 149th Street, where we would be getting off.

As dozens of us emptied out of the cars and began walking to the stairs that led up to the street, I noticed a strange transformation on the faces of the kids. The goofball smiles were disappearing and looks of worry, or rather, fear, seemed to take over as we ascended the stairs to the street level. I kept an eye on the sophomore who was breaking my balls on the ride; he also looked frightened as he kept pushing his long wisp of hair behind his ear so as not to have it hang in his face. Others were stopping to wipe their shoes on the backs of their pants legs or tightened ties right up to their Adam's apples and tucked in shirttails. A group of about fifty of us milled at the red light waiting for it to turn green so we could cross. The school in the distance looked more like a South Bronx factory than a high school. Situated right next to a railroad yard, there were no athletic fields, no stands, no campus, no benches, and worst of all, no girls.

The light turned green and as our mob crossed the street, we mysteriously began to form an almost military formation of kids three abreast. I half expected the kid at the front of the line to pull out a drum major baton to lead the way. But it was no parade. It was more like a death march. I lined up in the middle of the pack and after a few steps I saw the reason for the beads of sweat and fear smeared across the acned faces of the white, brown and black kids shuffling along the Grand Concourse. There he was: Monsignor McArdle. He'd given a short talk when we had orientation. As we sat in the auditorium, he went through all the things that wouldn't be tolerated, which included everything from chewing gum to bringing weapons to school. He'd stood there, all six foot two of him, with the scowl of a prison-yard guard in a long black cassock that reached his wing tips, and informed us, "I know *you* aren't a criminal, but I don't know about the bird sitting next to you."

And there he was, hands on hips, waiting for the next fresh batch of subway-delivered teenage boys to parade past him. I looked next to me, and the goofy sophomore from the train was licking his fingers, and trying to plaster his hair across his forehead and over behind his ear.

"What's McArdle doing there?"

"Are you kidding? He does this every morning whether it's sunny or raining piss and razor blades. He's looking at your shoes, your pants, your peach fuzz, the look on your face, and most of all, the length of your hair," he said, frantically trying to flatten his hair down.

As we got closer to McArdle, the look on his face came into focus. He had an expression like he'd just opened a wrapped Christmas present and discovered a steaming pile of dog shit inside. I looked straight ahead, afraid to make eye contact, hoping I wouldn't stand out from the pack. Out of the corner of my eye I could see him inching closer to our group as we approached him.

"Halt!" he groaned.

Everyone stopped dead in their tracks and I knocked into the guy in front of me.

Suddenly, McArdle was coming right at me. I could smell his body odor as his arm reached past me and grabbed the sophomore by the jacket collar and whisked him past me. Monsignor McArdle placed his hands on both of the fat sophomore's shoulders and gave him a slight downward shove as if he was planting him in wet cement. He stepped back, put both hands on his hips, cocked his head in an awkward position and growled, "Is this your first day of high school, bird?"

"No."

"No, *Monsignor*," McArdle corrected him.

"No, Monsignor."

"You know we have rules and regulations here, don't you, bird?"

"Yes, Monsignor."

Slipping one hand into the oversized sleeve of his cassock, reaching for something, McArdle inched towards him. Everyone in our group watched intently, although the older boys looked more amused than frightened. Then out of the sleeve a glint of shiny metal appeared and... *Holy shit! It's a fucking silver knife! Is this for real? Am I seeing what I think I'm seeing? The nuns maybe slapped kids in the face, rapped you in the knuckles with a brass ruler, or bonked you over the head with an encyclopedia, but Jesus Christ, even they didn't pull a fucking blade out on you!* He held it high in the sunlight and seemed to admire the look of it. He looked over at us to see our reaction. I couldn't understand why the older kids were trying to hold back laughter. He raised the blade high, slowly moved it to the sophomore's ear and THWAP! The sophomore's plastered-behind-the-ear hair flew outward and upward, revealing the length of his hair as it dangled across his face. The older kids giggled until McArdle gave them a nasty stare. Then he pulled a handkerchief out of his sleeve and began wiping off the knife.

"It's indefinite detention for you, Chubsy-Wubsy. I suggest you stay away from the mashed potatoes. The rest of you birds get to class!" he snarled, and we hurried towards the school door.

I turned to the older kid on the other side of me, who looked like he would have a full beard if he didn't shave every day, and said, "I can't believe he pulled a knife out."

In a deep grown man's voice the kid said, "That wasn't a knife, dipshit. That was a letter opener."

"Oh," I squeaked back, feeling like a jerk. It sure looked like a knife.

As we entered the large metal doors of the school and went from the bright light of day into the dark marble and stone hallway, I had a better idea of what was in front of me for the next four years of my life.

In grammar school I never had a single male teacher, and more than half of the kids in all my classes up through eighth grade were females. Now the only females in sight were the old ladies behind office desks and the steam tables in the cafeteria. I soon learned that with the exception of my sideburned and slightly longish-haired religion teacher, Brother Dodge, every one of my teachers, whether priest, brother, or layman, was a hard-ass laying down the law from the first minute. Each of them let it be known that this first day was the one and only day that you could be a minute late, since we all "just got out of diapers and had our butts wiped by Sister Mary Ferris Wheel," as Monsignor Brody said to much laughter. In my classes there were some other kids who looked as bewildered and borderline pre-pubescent as I did. But even in my class of freshmen, there were hulking guys who looked like they'd been shaving for several years. And in the halls and cafeteria there were students who didn't look like boys at all. They were full grown, hairy, sweaty, deep-voiced men who perhaps were masquerading as high school students, but must really be cops, Marines, and offensive linemen for the New York Giants. I, on the other hand, was still waiting for peach fuzz to turn into coarse hair, somewhere, anywhere, of consequence.

And with that fresh in mind, a new panic took root. The next day would be my first gym period and according to the instructions I was supposed to purchase a t-shirt, gym shorts and jock, and would be provided with a towel to shower after the gym class. *Shit. I'm going to have to take a group shower in a locker room with a bunch of guys.* Everybody was going to see that, well, I wasn't exactly on a par with most guys my age in that crucial area I'd managed to conceal from the rest of the world. Until now. How the hell was I going to hide the fact that I was a few secretions short in the hormone department? The first day had been a disaster. But the next day could possibly be one of the very worst days of my life.

We received a flyer with all the clubs we could join for extracurricular activities after school. The ham radio club, the poster club, bowling, ping pong, chess, drama, the weather club, the camera club. There was even a rocket club. Not to mention all the sports teams. But if I did any of those, I'd have to take the subway later in the day and I wouldn't be able to work in the deli after school. I mean, I only worked there for a half day of training so far, and I didn't want to screw that up before I even got started.

217

After day one of high school, I rushed home from the subway to an empty apartment. My mom was working at Alexander's full-time. My father wouldn't get home until later. I almost never saw my sister since she started college. My married brother was living all the way out in Jersey. My Uncle Nicky who used to live on the second floor wasn't living with his wife anymore. He's my mom's little brother and she wouldn't talk about it. I noticed she tries to avoid his wife, Aunt Doris, when she sees her on the street or in the hallway.

I couldn't get off my tie and jacket and into my t-shirt and shorts fast enough. I couldn't wait to get to the basketball courts to hear about how the other guys' first day in high school went. I flew down the stairs of my building, and ran the several blocks to the park, only to find that the kids playing basketball were a bunch of little kids! The eighth graders from Presentation. Of course I recognized a few of them from day camp. I didn't even bother going through the hole in the fence by the courts. I wondered where the guys were. I looked down to the other side of the playground, where the benches across the street from the Fieldston Bowling Alley and Pool Hall were, and there were two guys sitting there.

It cracked me up that it's called Fieldston. Fieldston is an area which is only about a half hour walk from 238th and Broadway, yet you'd think you were in some super-rich suburb in Connecticut or something. They have real mansions, with giant gates and rolling hills and brooks right on the property. I heard that a lot of the foreigners who represent their nations at the U.N. live there. I heard even some of the Kennedys had a mansion there. The Fieldston Bowling Alley and Pool Hall, sitting between the el and the subway railroad yard, ain't no mansion, though. In Fieldston the streets are lined with gigantic chestnut and oak trees and you never see kids hanging out. Whenever a group of us go up there to get chestnuts in the fall, we're the only kids around. And any grown-ups you see give you a real dirty look. The reason we go there for chestnuts is to have chestnut fights. You poke a hole in a hard chestnut, stick a shoelace through and try to break another guy's chestnut with it. But that's when we were kids. I heard that kids go to the Indian Pond Park up there to make out at night, because there's absolutely nobody in that park at night.

I walked over to the benches to see who the two guys were. It was Howie from the deli and some other guy I had seen around the park, but only in the part of football stands where the older kids who take drugs hang out.

"Hi, Howie. You're not working today?" I asked from a few feet away. When they heard me they turned towards me as if startled.

"Shit, you scared the hell out of me, man! Sit down and hang a while," Howie said, hiding something in his cupped hand.

I hadn't noticed it before, but these guys were smoking pot, right in broad daylight.

"I go in at six tonight. I'm closing, then doing some stock afterwards. Do you work today?"

"Um, um..." I stood there and stuttered because I was totally freaked out that these guys were smoking dope right there on the benches. People were driving by not thirty feet away, people were walking along the sidewalk about fifteen feet away, and people were walking all around with kids, baby carriages and old people in tow. "Um, I have off today. It was my first day of high school."

"First day of high school!" Howie's friend chortled, letting out a lung full of weed smoke. "Are you fucking kidding me?"

Howie tilted his head towards the guy. "This is Spoon. That's Vinny."

"Hi, Spoon," I said, wondering what was so unbelievable about it being my first day of high school.

"What high school?" Spoon said between drags.

"Farley."

"Farley!" Spoon screamed as if he was yelling bingo from the back of an auditorium. "Fucking Cardinal Farley! Holy shit, you poor fucking kid. How the fuck did you get roped into going to that fascist factory?"

"Um..." I paused while Spoon took a long drag on his joint. He had dark brown greasy hair, parted in the middle and curving around both sides of his long face, almost meeting under the stubble on his chain. He had thick eyebrows, and a crooked underbite that rivaled some bulldogs I've seen. "They have a good, um, they have a lot of extracurricular activities."

"Extra what?" Spoon said, an octave or two higher than before.

"Extracurricular activities," I said, wondering what the hell I was going to say next that might make sense to this pothead. "Like, um, you know, rocket club."

Spoon burst out laughing so uncontrollably that he fell to his side on the bench, then rolled onto the sidewalk. His laugh was so high-pitched he sounded like a pig getting slaughtered. He began to catch his breath and pulled himself back onto the bench.

"You mean," Spoon said through chuckles mixed with guffaws, "to tell me that they have a fucking rocket club? At Farley? Does fucking Monsignor McArdle blast off to Uranus?" he said, sending his laughs skyward.

Suddenly a giant clap of thunder, so loud it overpowered the rumble of the number one train passing by on the elevated tracks, was followed by a heavy cloudburst of rain that felt like buckets of water being dumped on our heads.

"Fuck!" Spoon yelled, as he jumped up and began darting through traffic on Broadway, heading for the entrance to the bowling alley.

"Let's go!" Howie said, leading us right behind him.

I had been to the bowling alley upstairs at Fieldston Bowling and Billiards, as it was officially known. But downstairs was the billiards part. To everybody in the neighborhood, especially parents, priests and teachers, it was simply known as "the pool hall."

We dodged cars crossing Broadway and the globs of rain falling through the el tracks onto us were brown with el crud. We shook off the water in the entryway like stray dogs.

"I can't go down there. You have to be sixteen," I said to Howie, pointing to the sign above the door leading down the steps to the pool hall.

"Don't worry about it. Just stay with me," Howie said, pulling a Lucky from a soft pack and lighting up.

The first thing that struck me was the smoke. It hung in the air, as if a fog machine from a werewolf movie was pumping the fumes out. I was surprised how many pool tables were packed with guys of every age, from teens to downright old. It was a whole new world down here, of pasty-faced guys all staring and moving around the pool tables, bobbing and weaving to get a better angle at balls on a table. I stood nervously by Howie hoping nobody would notice me. He shoved a lit cigarette in my mouth.

"You'll look older with that. Come on."

I tried frantically to suppress a coughing fit as I followed Howie through the maze of pool players desperately trying to avoid bumping into other players or pool cues slicing through the air.

Spoon was sitting on a red molded fiberglass chair that was along the wall, next to the last pool table in the corner. He had a small bottle of Coke in one hand and a cigarette in the other. The table directly in front of Spoon had some pretty unlikely characters playing each other. One was a young guy in a white tank top t-shirt, all sinew and bone, with straight hair that went just about to his shoulder. The other guy was so fat his belly hung over onto the felt when he leaned across to make a shot. He had a cigar in mouth and a crew cut, with some grey hairs poking through his nappy black hair.

"I need a light," I said. My cigarette was going out since I wasn't dragging on it.

"Shhh!" Spoon snapped at me.

The fat guy gave me a dirty look. His lower jaw jutted out and his head turned sideways as he was lining up a shot.

I sat in a chair two over from Spoon and put out my cigarette in the Cinzano ashtray. I watched the fat guy bob and weave, point his finger and his pool cue, run his fingers on the felt and slowly move his stick back and forth before tapping the cue ball perfectly so it nicked a ball, sending it into the hole. I almost yelled out a "Yeah!" but stopped myself when I saw that nobody else was uttering a sound. The skinny guy walked around the table to the fat guy, reached into his tight dungaree pocket and started peeling off a bunch of bills. The fat guy

221

had a self-satisfied smile on his face, with his cigar pointing upwards. He took the wad of cash and stuck it into loose-fitting chinos.

The skinny guy was expressionless as he placed his pool cue on the table and walked over to the other side of Spoon and sat down next to him. He pulled a Kool out of a hard pack, lit it with a Zippo, and took a drag. Then he screamed at the top of his lungs, "Motherfucker!"

That scared the living crap out of me. I looked around to see that nobody even looked up from their games. It was as if somebody sneezed.

The skinny guy reached into his tight dungaree pocket and pulled out the smallest brown manila envelope I had ever seen in my life. He handed it to Spoon who immediately slipped it into his pocket, then gave the skinny guy a roll of bills. It all happened in one smooth silent motion.

Howie tapped me on the leg and nodded for me to follow him, which I did.

"Who was that junkie-looking skinny guy?"

"That's Murph. And by the way, you didn't see nothing," he said as he went to the soda machine. You don't see those machines much anymore. It dispensed glass bottles of soda from a narrow door on the left side that contained bottles stuck straight in. After you paid, you just grabbed the top of the bottle and yanked it out. I've cut my finger many a time on the jagged bottle top.

We walked over to the counter where the oldest guy in the place stood behind the counter in deep conversation with the fat guy. The old guy was squat, bald, had a bulbous nose, a cauliflower ear and he looked like he could still kick anybody's ass in the place. Behind his good ear he balanced a thick pencil, like the ones you use to keep score while bowling. He was wearing a tight white t-shirt with a pack of Luckies rolled in the sleeve like a teenager, and the bottom part of a faded anchor tattoo was visible on his arm.

"That guy behind the counter looks familiar," I said to Howie.

"That's Slammin' Sol Ginsberg. He was a prizefighter in the forties. He once beat Rocky Graziano. When he was twelve. He still teaches boxing."

"Oh, yeah, I think I saw him in the Riverdale Press once."

Sol worked the room like the father of the bride at a wedding. And like a father at a wedding, he was collecting money everywhere he went. Behind the counter, at the pool tables, from inside the phone booth, wherever he went people of every age and color were handing him envelopes or wads of cash. I also noticed him and Murph ducking into the office. *I didn't see nothing.*

Over the next few weeks, the initial paralyzing fear I experienced on the first day of high school transformed into a kind of hyper-heightened awareness of my surroundings. Sort of like a forward infantryman on a mission in enemy territory. Most of my time was spent checking out classmates, teachers, and priests lurking in the hallways, trying to size up who was the enemy, who was harmless and who might be a potential ally. Unlike in grammar school, where me and Whitey and most of the guys were wiseasses mouthing off at will, it only took one backhanded smack across the face to the kid sitting in front of me in algebra class to realize I was better off keeping my mouth shut. That was no nun's love tap. It was a six-foot, two-hundred-fifty-pound Irishman pounding his knuckles into a pimple faced hundred-thirty-pound teenager's fresh mouth. Lesson learned!

Most of the other students seemed to have friends they already knew from grammar school or their neighborhoods. Since Whitey fell off the face of the earth, this was a solo mission for me. It's not easy to get to know guys either. There's usually only about thirty seconds of "settling in" in a class before some hard-ass whacks a blackboard with a wooden pointer signifying total silence or else. Every teacher has us sitting in alphabetical order, so I'm usually towards the rear of the class, behind the other S's and usually next to the O's or M's. Is it just me, or are the crazier guys in the class usually the ones at the end of the alphabet? The S's and T's seem to be the last of the normal letters.

Because once you get past there, the U's, V's, W's and especially the X's, Y's, and Z's are composed of the certifiably insane. Perhaps it's due to a lifetime of being relegated to the back of the class, and every other line you have to stand in from kindergarten on. In grammar school at least there was a break when you lined up for a class picture or a procession and you were in size place. If you were the tallest kid in the class and your last name started with a Z, you were doomed for life by the time you graduated eighth grade.

I didn't have one black kid in my grammar school classes, although there were several in other grades behind us. I won't lie by saying there weren't bigots in my family and among my relatives and friends. There was a lot of blaming of blacks for the upswing in crime in the neighborhood and in New York City itself. But I'll add that I've always seen my parents and relatives treat every person, black or otherwise, with courtesy and a pleasant smile no matter what the situation. I was taken aback when the guy in several of my classes who sat right in front of me was a black guy named Boone, since that's sometimes a derogatory term used for blacks by bigots. He was very outgoing and funny, too. I liked him a lot and even tried to pal around with him a little. But he obviously was already part of a clique of black, Puerto Rican and cool white guys. And I was really shocked when a fat Italian guy from the East Bronx called me a nigger lover for trying to befriend him. Fuck that guinea.

In home room we got a mimeographed flyer that listed all the clubs and extracurriculars. The one that really looked interesting to me was the school newspaper, called "The Challenger." Being in high school, I did start to think about what I wanted to be when I grow up, which was apparently something I now had to give serious consideration. In fact, you're not even supposed to use the term *when I grow up.* Now you're supposed to pick a career, and decide what you're supposed to major in college to be able to do it. Kids are already enrolling in A.P. classes, which means advanced placement, and it's supposed to put you ahead of everybody else so you can graduate higher in your class in high school, get into a better college, so you'll have a better chance of getting into a better graduate school or a better law or medical school. I can't even decide whether to join the rocket club or the school newspaper.

Although I hate writing essays that have to do with the history of Western Civilization or a book like *Beowulf*, I really liked writing a book report on *The Jungle* and I got a B+ on it. I would have gotten an A, the writing in red pencil on the top of the page informed me, if my penmanship were better. And thanks to the show *Love That Bob*, I certainly would have liked to get into photography. That show from the 1950s, which still airs in repeats, stars Bob Cummings as a playboy who takes fashion photographs of models with huge pointy breasts barely covered with open-at-the-top blouses and short shorts that barely covered their butt cheeks. That was my first exposure to the term "playboy" and I wasn't really sure what it meant. Then I saw *Playboy* magazine for the first time when my cousin Jimmy showed me one he had hidden under the cat's litter box in the bathroom, and it all became crystal clear. And the pointy breasts and butt cheeks weren't covered anymore! From then on when I watched *Love That Bob*, I knew why he was always smiling and leaving the studio with a model or two.

The school's newspaper office was down the hall from the athletic director's office in the basement near the gym. I opened the heavy oak door to a large office with a guy sitting at a desk who looked old enough to be a teacher, but the moronic senior hat and oversized Student Council button on his lapel were dead giveaways.

"What do you want?" said the senior student council member, with all the charm of a cop with hemorrhoids working the overnight desk

"I was thinking of getting involved with the school newspaper."

"Fill this out and bring it back tomorrow. Then if it's approved you'll be notified," he said, sliding a form across the desk. "This isn't the rocket club where anybody can just join up, you know. We're all selected."

"Who does the selecting?"

He looked up at me as if I'd asked him if he was retarded.

225

"The editor in chief, the senior board members, and the faculty moderator."

"Who's that?"

"Look kid, you're wasting my time. Who's who?"

"Who's the faculty moderator?"

"Father Quiogue. You don't even know him, because he's new here, so what the hell difference does it make to you?" he said, rising out of his chair.

"Um, ah, no thanks, I think I'll join the rocket club instead," I said, sliding the form back at him.

He picked it up, crumpled it and tossed it into the garbage can. I heard him mumble under his breath, "Fucking frosh."

I can't believe it. Could it be the same Father Quiogue from day camp, that Whitey gave a black eye to?

All my classes were difficult, with no-nonsense priests, brothers and lay teachers blowing through textbooks, writing illegibly on the blackboard, and making everything from the Roman Empire to the outer reaches of our solar system to the U.S. Constitution seem boring. The only two exceptions were Monsignor Guido in Italian class who at least once a week had us singing opera, with him conducting us like we were the at the Metropolitan Opera House, and Brother Dodge's religion class.

When I saw we had a period every day for religion, I thought for sure it would be an hour of purgatory daily. Religion in grammar school was always memorizing the Catechism; *Lesson 9 The Holy Ghost and Grace. Question 116. Is actual grace necessary for all who have attained the use of reason? Actual grace is necessary for all who have attained the use of reason, because without it we cannot long resist the power of temptation nor perform other actions which merit a reward in heaven.*

But Brother Dodge allowed the class to ask whatever questions you wanted. "Brother, is it a sin when my father drinks?" a kid asked.

"Does it put him in a good mood or a bad mood?"

"A good mood."

"I don't think a good mood is sinful," Brother Dodge said, smiling.

"Is smoking pot a sin?" another kid asked.

"Well, I'll answer the same way. No harm, no foul."

"Yeah, but if a cop catches you, you can go to jail."

"A lot of saints have spent time in jail, you know," Brother Dodge said, pointing a finger in the air.

Brother Dodge even had us suggesting songs that we could discuss in religion class. Any song. Then he would hand out the song lyrics on a sheet and we'd listen to the song as it played on a portable record player. One class we analyzed "The Times They Are a-Changin'." It was a far cry from Mrs. Schmelzer in grammar school tearing apart "She Loves You" for being moronic.

But despite the laughs singing "Santa Lucia" at 8:35 in the morning with Monsignor Guido, or the enlightening discussions about the meanings of Dylan songs, there was one thing we didn't have at school that weighed heavily on every student every moment of every day: no girls.

The Fall Fling was going to be the first dance of the year and my first high school dance ever. Apparently we had a "sister school" somewhere in the Bronx that would provide the girls. I'd heard rumors that the girls who show up are the ones who really want to meet boys because they know how desperate we are for females. But the thing about our school was, it's in a bad neighborhood just a few blocks from Yankee Stadium. The South Bronx is one of the highest crime areas in the Bronx and the only time there are cops around at night is if the Yankees are playing. And since the Yankees had sucked lately, there was no way they'd be playing in October that year.

In the morning you feel pretty safe on the train because the cars are filled with other students and people on their way to work. In the late afternoon, it gets a little dicier without the grown-up workers on board, and the train is mostly filled with teenagers getting out of schools all over the Bronx. Throw into the mix a steady supply of junkies, bums, muggers, and general run- of-the-mill psychos, and it all adds up to an exercise in survival of the smartest tactics: *Never sit down. Always keep your back to the door. If trouble enters the car go into the next one. Repeat if necessary. Ride between cars if violence is imminent. Wear shoes that are easy to run in but still would hurt if you kicked someone in the balls. Always keep a geometry compass in your book bag which can be just as good as an ice pick in a fight.* But riding the train at night might require even more drastic precautions.

I felt cool in my velvet collared Beatle jacket, standing without a book bag on the el platform at Mosholu Parkway after dark. For some reason, I thought it would look good to slick my hair back like a greaser and wear the tightest pants and skinniest tie I could find in the closet. I guess I thought I looked tougher. It was just me and an old guy in a windbreaker with a lunch bucket waiting on the platform. And we were the only two in our car for a couple of stops. At Fordham Road people started piling in. Groups of kids who spun around on the poles and hung from the straps dangling from the ceiling were going wild. Workers going to their night shift jobs looked pissed off. And there were couples dressed up who must have been going downtown on a date. I just stood against the door and hoped nobody would bother me.

When the train stopped at 149th Street, about five guys got off who were obviously going to the dance. I didn't recognize any of them, but walked a few feet behind them up the night-time Grand Concourse to school. It sure looked different in the dark. The post office and the luncheonette were closed and there was nobody else on the street except us. Monsignor McArdle wasn't standing guard outside the entrance and except for table inside the door, you wouldn't know there was anything going on. I handed the kid at the table my ticket, which he tore in half, leaving me with the stub.

"Proceed to the gym down the first stairway on your left," he commanded.

I followed the other guys down the stairs. At the bottom I could hear muffled rock and roll music from behind some doors. We opened the doors and I could hear Pat Boone singing "Tutti Frutti" over the same P.A. system they used to announce players at a basketball

228

game. There was a large curtain hanging underneath one of the baskets at the end of court. The entire gym was circled by wooden folding chairs and half of them occupied by guys. The other half were empty. The only two girls I saw were standing behind a table where cans of soda where being sold. Thankfully, I recognized Boone sitting with a few guys in the stands.

"Hey, Boone," I said, during a lull in their conversation.

Boone did a double take. "Schmidt? What the hell are you dressed for? The auditions for *West Side Story* aren't until next month, man."

"Um, what are you talking about?" I said, pretending not to get his jab.

"Schmidt, for a German you are one hell of a wop!" he said, cracking up the white guy, the Puerto Rican and the black guy hanging out with him.

"I'm half."

"Half what?"

"Half wop."

Boone was taken aback, and held out his hand for a "soul shake." "Hey man, I'm sorry. You can call me a nigger for that one. That was stupid."

"Okay. Nigger," I said holding out my hand for him to slap me five.

He pretended he was going to punch me, and slapped me five.

"Where's all the girls?" I asked.

"They say there's a bus coming from Mount Saint Ursula's," Boone said.

"You think those Riverdale mommies and daddies are going to let them ride the subway to the South Bronx at night? Shit, I wouldn't even do that myself," the Puerto Rican kid said.

"How'd you get here?" Boone asked.

"I walked, homey! I live three blocks from here!" the Puerto Rican kid laughed.

We sat and watched a few guys trickle in, and talked about teachers, and classes and homework as we drank cokes and ate potato chips and pretzels. The music over the P.A. seemed to get worse. Mixed in with Pat Boone, Tony Bennett and Andy Williams were Glenn Miller and Guy Lombardo.

"Who's in charge of the music?" I asked the group. They all pointed at Boone.

"Whoah! I picked the live music, not that shit!"

"There's live music?"

"Yup. That's the only reason I'm on the damn dance committee. At nine o'clock. It's my cousin's band from upstate. And they are funky as shit!"

"Really?"

"Fucking A!"

Suddenly a student stuck his head through the door and shouted, "The bus is here!"

A rumble of excitement traveled through the sporadic crowd, and groups of guys meandered towards the swinging doors where they were bound to enter at any minute.

And there they were! All five of them. I won't go into details because it wouldn't be very Christian of me, but let's just say that they weren't the cream of the crop. It's a good thing that the red and yellow crepe paper over the lights made it hard to make out anyone's facial features.

Over the next half hour, some more guys showed up and even a few more girls, and with everyone huddled on the half court in front of where the curtain was hanging, it almost looked like a crowd of people.

Suddenly the Vic Damone song that was playing on the P.A scratched to a halt, and standing in front of the curtain was Boone holding a microphone.

"Ladies and gentleman, welcome to the Cardinal Farley Fall Fling. It is now my pleasure to introduce to you, all the way from Poughkeepsie, New York, The Funky Fab Five!"

A loud crash of symbols followed by thunderous guitars, bass and organ reverberated through the half empty gym. Two priests and several volunteer dads immediately shoved fingers in their ears as the opening notes of James Brown's "I Feel Good" blasted mercilessly through their piles of amps and speakers, rendering conversation useless. The band was five guys: two black, two Puerto Rican, and one afroed white guy on drums. There were two guitars, a bass player, an organ and the drummer. The audience was dividing into those who loved the music and those who feared it. Only about ten of us stood close to the bandstand, and the rest huddled around the soda table at the other side of the gym. Nobody danced.

I walked across the dance floor to get a better look at the band as they ripped through an extended version of "What I Say." I stood all alone at the court foul shooting circle and couldn't believe my eyes. The drummer at the poorly lit rear of the stage had an afro, dark aviator sunglasses, muttonchop sideburns and a green army shirt. *But could it be?* He kind of looked like Whitey. I mean, Whitey used to fool around banging "Wipe Out" on his school desk. In fifth grade his parents got him a cheap drum set for Christmas that was in pieces by New Year's Day, so how could that be him? The guy seemed to be pounding a pretty good beat! Okay, so he wasn't doing crazy Buddy Rich type solos, but he was loud. *Nah, it couldn't be.* I wanted to ask Boone about the band, but I didn't see him by the front of the stage so I headed to the soda stand to find him. Not seeing him there, I walked down the hall to where the bathrooms were. I walked to the closest men's room and just as I was about to enter, someone grabbed my arm and jerked me away from the door.

"Can't you read? You can't go in there, moron!" a reedy voice bleated as he twisted me around.

Holy fuck. He was right under a light draped in red crepe paper and he was bathed in a satanic glow: Father Q. himself!

"Are you a girl?" Father Q. asked as he looked at me with suspicion. "The sign says 'Girls Only.' For the dance, idiot."

"Sorry, Father," I said as I pulled away and headed for the boys' locker room, hoping he didn't recognize me.

Boone was taking a leak at the urinal. I went to a spot nearby.

"That band is good!"

231

"Yeah, that's my cousin playing organ and singing," Boone said as he zipped up. "Gotta go, see ya."

I looked down to shake it one last time before zipping up and a shadow came across my dick. I looked next to me and there was Father Q. at the very next urinal with his dick out.

I froze momentarily and stared straight ahead at the tiles. *Do not look,* I told myself. But in my peripheral vision I thought I saw him shaking his thing with a little too much gusto. I quickly finished my business, zipped up so fast it almost got caught in the teeth, and ran out of there, through the hall, up the stairs and out the front of the school. I looked down the Concourse and there was the bus going northbound. If I took the bus it would take twice as long as the train, but would be a lot safer. I darted to the bus stop, got on, dropped in my subway token and sat in the almost empty bus. It gave me plenty of time to think about what happened. Could that possibly have been Whitey? And was Father Q. choking his chicken or just shaking the piss off? What a first dance!

Chapter Fifteen

—NOW—

My head was spinning like the reel of microfilm I was blowing through as I scanned the pages of the *New York Daily News* and *New York Post* starting with 1970. Yeah, today we're bombarded with politicians, pundits and parental substitutes pelting us daily with desperate cries of apocalypse, Armageddon, and global doom. But fishing through the microfiche and microfilm made it abundantly evident that we don't have to go all that far back to see a time when things seemed dangerously close to the end times on a daily basis, not just on the other side of the world, but right on your front stoop. Viet Nam was raging, it seemed like a race war was imminent, terrorists were hijacking planes left and right, the Middle East was on the verge of blowing up, nuclear war with the Soviets was palpable, protesters were marching in the millions, and violent crimes on the streets of New York were rising so fast, it seemed like the message from government and law enforcement officials was that we should just learn to deal with it, because they couldn't do anything about it. There wasn't enough space in the newspapers to report all murders, never mind the assaults, rapes, and armed robberies. Only the most horrific slaughters, massacres, accidents, explosions and fires made newspapers.

I kept scanning for the keywords *murder, mayhem, Hunts Point,* and *South Bronx*
that were mentioned in the faded article Whitey showed me. My zipping would have to come to a screeching halt every few seconds if I was going to read every story about every murder, slaying, rubout, bloodshed, hit, whack, massacre, shooting, stabbing, knifing, and carnage.

I definitely preferred the microfilm format of reading newspaper archives. It was more like a movie because you had to thread the film through a projector of sorts, kind of like a newsreel for each day of the year. Every scene, a frame on a reel zipped by in order of importance led by the biggest stories, and moving on to the lesser articles, advertisements, funnies, gossip and sports at the end. But microfiche is a single frame with many days of newspapers laid out in straight rows and columns. The slightest movement of the frame can jettison you from the front page of one day to the movie ads of another week, making it hard to keep track of the linear progression of the time line of life. Each day's newspaper is the story of that day. Huge headlines in the front, diversions in the back. Then the next day it starts all over again. It's not until New Year's Eve when the paper looks back on the year in review that you realize that 99.9% of the stuff they've been shouting about in ninety-point bold type has been just filler. All those murders and lives destroyed in fires, car wrecks, plane crashes, and sewer explosions? It turns out that except for a few family members and friends, those tragedies will be quickly forgotten and certainly not commemorated in the newspaper's year in review. Only the most sensational deaths that were either captured on film or in a photograph or involving celebrities will merit a mention on December 31st next to the mention of the winners of the Super Bowl, World Series, NBA Finals and perhaps the Stanley Cup (if the hockey team in your city won).

After two hours of microfishing, my vision is blurry and I can't focus anymore. After getting through about three months of the 1970 *New York Post*, I was afraid to walk out of the building and down into the subway due to the impression it left on my psyche. New York in the seventies was insane. But as I descended the subway steps, I don't see floor to ceiling graffiti. Muggers aren't lurking behind every column. There aren't rows of bums sleeping next to piles of excrement. Rats aren't jumping out of overflowing garbage cans. And as the subway car pulls into the station, the outside is not covered completely with spray paint and the inside with thick magic markers. How did that happen? From the time I was about ten to about the age of forty, all I saw was the slow decay of New York City. Crime and filth were the norm and the thought of it ever turning around so completely wasn't even a possibility. Sure, in hindsight I can see lots of reasons: Mayor Giuliani getting tough on crime, the economy improving, real estate values increasing. But regardless of the real reasons, the only thing that must be remembered is that no matter how fucked things are, things don't always get worse and worse throughout time, *ad infinitum.* Things sometimes do get better. Maybe not tomorrow, or next decade, but they will improve. At least that's what I keep telling myself.

Work pretty much became part of the mundane routines of daily living that you do by rote without even realizing. *Did I brush my teeth this morning? Of course I did.* You just don't remember because you brush your teeth every morning. As you get older and your brain starts to realize it's running out of storage space, your brain cells stop retaining useless information. Like when my mom was in the nursing home, she couldn't remember what year it was, but she could tell you who she was dancing with, what song it was, and what the trophy looked like on the day she won the Lindy Contest at the Club Fordham Ballroom. Yup, you remember the important stuff.

At work, I'd count down the minutes to my lunch hour, which was when I'd head back to the library to continue my search for the Whitey article. Nostalgia for those long-ago years of purple bell bottoms, white kids with afros, and Johnny Carson wearing Nehru jackets faded as quickly as one article morphed into another in a hazy blaze of scratchy microfilm and microfiche images. It was hard not to stop for irrelevant but interesting articles that caught my attention. A picture of Joe DiMaggio in plaid pants playing golf! John Lennon and Yoko Ono balls ass naked on an album cover! Yet another landing on the moon! But if I stopped at every one of those, it would take me months to find a clue about the Whitey murder story. Still concentrating on the keywords *murder mayhem Hunts Point South Bronx,* I spin the reels through time when a word catches my eye in a photo caption: Zipper. Could it be? I stop on the photo of a young black soldier pulling up a dress uniform shirt revealing a zipper scar across his abdomen, in an official-looking room displaying flags and round government seals on the wall and on a lectern. The caption under the photo read "Private Richard 'Zipper' Tully shows off his scar to Private Hector Gomez at an award ceremony for Sergeant Robert Shelley who received the Bronze Star at the Pentagon. Shelley received the award for a daring rescue of Tully and Gomez from an enemy outpost in Viet Nam. All three are Bronx natives."

Holy jumping shit. There they are. Whitey and Zipper! Whitey really is a hero. So if that was 1973, then the murder must have happened a year or two later. Maybe this Hector Gomez guy was still around. Maybe he'd want to help me save Whitey to pay him back for saving his life. Of course he would! But the odds of finding a Hector Gomez in the Bronx would be like finding Sean O'Brien in Dublin.

I wrote down the dates and the information from the official seal on the wall in the photo and decided that I needed to find Hector Gomez. Once I found him, I would have to convince him that visiting Whitey could save his life. Not having seen a doctor in decades, being forced to live underground, he might as well be in a prisoner of war cage, the way he has to live his life.

I continued blasting through the microfilm, but found it hard to concentrate with Hector Gomez on my mind, so I decided to grab a dirty dog from a street vendor and head back to work.

When I returned to my work space, I noticed that during my lunch hour they'd actually added another cubicle that connected to the side of mine. Maintenance guys were putting together a table and some drawers from an Ikea box and there was an unopened Dell computer box sitting nearby.

"What are you guys doing?" I asked a blue-uniformed kid with a tiny Allen wrench in his hand.

"We're adding on a workstation. The computer guy will be here when we're done."

I nodded, sat down, and woke my computer up from sleep mode. I had twelve emails waiting for me, including one from my boss. I opened that first. *Vincent, a new person is starting tomorrow who will be training with you. Please give her all due consideration in teaching her every aspect of your duties. We'll discuss further in the morning.* Great. I'm probably training my replacement, and something tells me I'm not getting promoted.

Whatever my reading material on the number one train, I always seem to lose interest in it when the train emerges from the underground into the bright light of day at Dyckman Street. I always ride in the first car of the train knowing that at the last stop at 242nd it puts you closest to the stairway exit. But sitting in the first car also allows you to stand at the front and gaze out the window. And by the time the tracks wind through Inwood and we arrive at the 215th Street station, the beauty of the northern end of this island called Manhattan never ceases to amaze me. From the height of the elevated tracks it's easy to see the hills of the Bronx that overlook the Harlem River in the east. To the west, the hills of northern Manhattan in Fort Tryon Park contain the only native forest that remains on the entire island. All of the other Manhattan parks were designed and trees were planted by landscape architects. Only by walking through wooded hills of Fort Tryon Park could a person appreciate the natural beauty of what Manhattan Island once was. Neighborhood legend has it that the last Indians on Manhattan Island actually lived in the wilds of this park until the el was completed in 1910.

Soon we're crossing the 225th Street Bridge, which has to be one of the highlights of all 670 miles of the New York Subway and Elevated Rail system. To the left is "the cut," the huge boulder with the enormous blue and white "C" painted on it in recognition of Columbia University, looming over the treacherous riptides where the Harlem and Hudson River currents collide. The "C" is directly across from Baker Field, Columbia's athletic fields – the same fields where Lou Gehrig played baseball and Jack Kerouac played football. The more daring kids from the neighborhood would jump off the big "C" and for more than a few, it was the last thing they would attempt in their lives. Just the other side of the bridge, where there's now the bustling neighborhood called Marble Hill, there was once a small wooden bridge that was the only connection between the island of Manhattan and the rest of the continental United States. That bridge was called "The King's Bridge" in colonial New York and the tolls, of course, went to King George III back in England. The bridge would one day allow George Washington's army to escape certain defeat by the

237

British and live another day to eventually claim victory against the most powerful empire on earth. The surrounding neighborhood is now called Kingsbridge, and just a couple of stops later I have to make a decision as I do every day on my escape from Manhattan, whether or not to utilize Kingsbridge for its present-day purpose: to stop in one of its many Irish-owned watering holes and plan my future comeback to victory. And as the doors open on 238th Street and I exit the train, the only decision that remains is, which of the half dozen or so establishments will I use to hatch my plans?

Many a plan has been hatched at the ancient bar of the Punch Bowl. Established around the time the elevated train was near completion in 1910, on the wall hangs a photograph of the original bar then called "The Buckeye," complete with western-style swinging saloon doors, wooden shutters on the exterior, and an unfinished el above. My old man told me that during Prohibition it was an ice cream parlor, but you could still buy buckets of beer in the cellar. Today the outside of the bar has a twenty-first century slapdash mix of stucco and glass, with a spray painted memorial dedicated to 9-11. Inside, not only are most of the original fixtures, mirrors, and bar still intact, but the ghosts of over a hundred years linger like the smell of beer-soaked floorboards. I can't help but think of my Uncle Alfonso as a twelve-year-old kid in knickers in 1930 buying a bucket of beer for my Grandpa Papalardo and taking a few sips on the walk back home. Or my Uncle Dominic palling with my dad watching a prizefight on the fuzzy TV screen in the late 1950s, drinking boilermakers on a hot summer evening and helping each other stumble home. Or me, sneaking in as a sixteen-year-old, drinking a thirty-five-cent glass of beer and singing "Be-Bop-A-Lu-La" and playing guitar with the two middle-aged Irish guys singing Irish songs long ago on a Saturday night, thus beginning my career as an alcohol-fueled failed rock and roll wannabe.

Thanks to satellites, these days the TV is all sports all the time. Horse races from anywhere in the world during the day, and whatever sport is in season at night, right up until the last West Coast games are finishing at around two a.m. Eastern time. Then it's time for soccer or rugby or cricket or something you can bet on, until the ponies start up again in the morning somewhere on the planet. But as I take a stool position at the corner of the bar, only the youthful bartender looks like he may have had a recent encounter with a ball of some kind in an athletic contest. There's the obese bookie with the soggy unlit cigar jammed in his yellow teeth going through his scribblings on napkins, envelopes, and bar coasters, with his phone scrunched between shoulder and ear. Two old Irishmen keep each other company, one with a magnifying glass studying the columns in the Daily Racing Form, the other staring at the end of his cigarette as he flicks more ashes into the piles of filterless butts still smoldering in the ashtrays, an idea about to fall off his tongue any minute now. A small black bus driver, still in uniform, sips from a tumbler, perhaps dreaming of a world without roads. Young Brooksie, who's about sixty going on last rites, sits at the opposite end of the bar, not to be confused with Old Brooksie, his old man who died on the same barstool twenty years earlier.

The late afternoon trains squeal to a halt above us every five minutes or so, and a minute or two later, another number one train passenger becomes a Punch Bowl patron. And before you know it, rush hour is almost over and the post-work bar rush is in full swing. The barstools are filled with everything from squat middle-aged men in subway crowd crumpled suits, to guys who look like they just came from a shoot for the "Fireman of the Month" calendar. The horses are racing at Del Mar on one screen, the Mets are playing on another, and the Yankees on yet another, but the sound is muted on all three. The bookie sits in the middle of the bar, and does glad-handing and paper exchanging like a politician at a fundraiser. The cacophony of loud conversation, laughter, and arguments are all peppered with profanities that would make a Scorsese movie sound like Teletubbies.

"Yeah, that twenty-eighth World Championship is always the fuckin' hardest," a Yankee fan screams at a Mets fan.

"Come on, the FDNY is the white man's fuckin' welfare and you know it! Show me a fireman who doesn't have a goddamn plumbing or exterminator business on the side and I'll show you a fireman out on a hundred percent disability, doin' fuckin' laps in his pool in Florida," a fit young guy wearing an NYPD Emerald Society t-shirt bleats, so the nearby fireman can hear him.

"Don't tell me Obama got Osama! Was he in Pakistan jumpin' out of a motherfuckin' helicopter in the middle of the fuckin' night with towelheads comin' at him?" one business man says to another.

The late morning/early afternoon crowd of regulars is barely visible as the bar transforms from an old man drinking bar, to a nighttime hangout bar. Small groups of pretty girls are even showing up, and placing themselves in the eye range of the young firemen and cops.

This is when the Jameson starts to flow, and the jukebox begins to rise above the conversations. It becomes easy to watch the boys and girls flirt, as you down more and more whiskey and trick yourself into thinking those girls just might be interested in you. And they would be, if you were a fit, handsome young cop or fireman who's not wearing a wedding ring.

As my twenty dwindles and I lose count of how many times my tumbler has been refilled, I call over the bartender.

"Sean, do you know anybody who works for the federal government, or the army, or anything?"

"Federal Government? Army? How about the V.A.?"

"Yeah, the V.A.!"

"Young Brooksie works at the Bronx V.A. over on Fordham."

"Oh, thanks. I'll be right back," I said as I put my glass on my pile of cash and walked to the other end of the bar.

"Hi, Brooksie. Can I buy you a drink?"

"You don't have to ask me twice," he says, staring at the TV with the horse race on it. "You mother fucker!" he yelled at the screen. "I had that bitch in my pick six and wouldn't you know it, she loses by a nose. I'll have a Stoli on the rocks."

Sean brought over the Stoli and my drink and money from down the bar.

I was a little buzzed... okay, pretty drunk, and didn't want to mess this up. I pulled out the photocopy of the article from the *Post* that showed Whitey and Hector Gomez getting their medals.

"You work at the V.A., right?"

"Thirty years and counting."

"Could you do me a favor?"

"Probably not, but shoot anyway."

"I'm trying to find a guy, from this article," I said, holding up the article.

"You think I can fuckin' see that?" He pulled out his reading glasses and began to study it. "That's that fuckin' Whitey Shelley from the neighborhood, right? I thought he was dead. He got the Bronze Star? Holy shit!"

"I'm trying to find the other guy, Hector Gomez. Think I could find him through the V.A.?"

"You're Schmidt, right?"

"Yeah."

"I went to grammar school with your older brother. How's he doing?"

"Great. He's retired. Living in North Carolina."

"North Carolina? Nice. Write down what you want to know and I'll see what I can find out."

"Can I email you with the information?"

He pulled his glasses down to the tip of his nose to take a good look at me. "I don't do email. Or twatter or whatever the fuck it's called. Just write it down with your phone number and I'll call you."

"What do you do there?"

"Mostly I jerk off, but my job title is manager of billing. Not that I give a fuck, but why do you need to find this guy? You know, in case his body winds up in Van Cortlandt lake, I want to have an alibi ready."

"An old friend is trying to find him for a Viet Nam reunion."

"Sounds like bullshit, but okay," Brooksie said, finishing off his drink.

I wrote the information I had on Hector Gomez and handed it to Brooksie, hoping he'd remember what it was when he discovered it in his pocket the next morning. The drinks continued to flow as the twenties became piles of fives and singles, until they were no more. The pretty girls were finally paired with the good looking guys and it was hard to hear anything over The Who blasting from the jukebox. The last of the West Coast baseball games were in the ninth and I was too drunk to drive back to Bronxville. I hailed a gypsy cab outside the bar and spent most of the ride trying to remember where I had parked my car earlier that morning so I could retrieve it the next day.

I paid the fare with the last of the cash I had on hand. Fumbling for my keys to the side door of my sister's garage-adjacent room so I could crash on the unmade bed, I thought about my journey to find Whitey. Yeah, I found him alive and kicking. And there I was, dead drunk.

At work the next morning, I totally forgot that I had to train a new person so they could take my job away from me, until I saw the workers completing the cubicle next to mine. I stopped in the men's room, took a leak, washed my hands, and I was stunned when I caught a glimpse of myself in the mirror. *Holy crap! I forgot to shave!* And who was that blotchy, puffy-faced, bloodshot old man staring back at me? Where did he come from? My gray whiskers caused me to flash on a photo that has haunted me ever since I saw it in the *New York Times* a few years ago. Jim Carroll, author of *The Basketball Diaries,* was a hero to anyone in New York City who fantasized about being a successful underground writer, which I know sounds like an oxymoron. He was the kid from the neighborhood, any New York neighborhood, who grew up poor but knew everything about being cool. He played competitive basketball in the park, drank and did drugs. And somehow he was hanging out with Andy Warhol, Allen Ginsberg and Patti Smith in the East Village, after his book became a bestseller. He was an international sensation. He even had a rock band and sang lead. Who was cooler than Jim Carroll? Jim Carroll died at the age of sixty, but what scared me most about seeing that photo of Jim Carroll shortly

242

before his death wasn't that he looked weak and frail or that he had a long gray beard. It was the fact that the photo was taken at his home in the same Inwood apartment building where he grew up. That was where he spent the end of his life. With everything he had accomplished, he hadn't gone anywhere. And from what I'm seeing in the mirror, that's exactly where I'm headed.

I didn't call or email my boss to ask when the person who was probably going to replace me was showing up. I just went through my silly daily assignments as I counted down the minutes to my lunch break, so I could go back to microfishing at the library.

Lunch break finally arrived and I tore out of there before my boss showed up. I decided to stop in Duane Reade to pick up a razor and some shaving cream. I figured I could take a quick anonymous shave in a bathroom at the park. The stench of stopped-up toilets and overflowing urinals put an end to that and stopped me at the doorjamb of the Central Park men's room. It would have to be the library men's room.

I stood at the urinal in the library men's room until I was relatively certain I was the only one in there, although there was a stall door still shut. I rushed to the sink and quickly slapped on some shave cream and began to shave. About three strokes in, the stall door opened and out walked what appeared to be a human being wrapped in oil-soaked rags, holding two shopping bags filled with other bags that were filled with God knows what. He shuffled to the sink next to me, dropped his bags to the floor and began searching for something in one of them. His stink was overpowering. In a high-pitched raspy voice he said, "I usually don't like to do this in public, but since you're doing it, what the hell."

I thought for sure I'd slit my throat, shaving as quickly as I could, as he began to lather up. I finished, threw my plastic razor in the trash, left the shaving cream container next to the sink, and wiped my face with the cardboard-like paper towels from the wall dispenser.

A young businessman impeccably dressed in a three-piece suit entered and paused when he saw me frantically wiping my face and the

243

poor wretch at the sink. And right on cue the bum says, "Hey, did you leave this for me?" pointing to the can of Barbasol I left there.

"Yeah, it's all yours. It's menthol. I think you'll enjoy it."

I took one last look in the mirror and noticed I had two nicks that were still bleeding. I looked at the man in the three-piece suit. "Four sinks," I said. "No waiting."

I felt much better than when I'd woken up that morning, especially after my shave. The bleeding stopped and I was ready for another research session.

Streaming words zipped by in a blur of non-stop daily urban headline horror stories. *Subway Slaughter. Mid-Town Massacre. Headless Body in Topless Bar. Grim Discovery. Remains Found. Shot. Stabbed. Decapitated. Sliced. Butchered. Blasted. Crushed. Grizzly Find. Murder. Mayhem. Hunts Point.* Whoah! That's it! The article that Whitey showed me. No byline, but at least I have an exact date. It was in the *New York Daily News,* October 8, 1974.

I searched through the file drawers for that date and the day after in the *New York Post* and *New York Times.* The *Times* had no mention of it. But in the *Post,* there was a Bronx crime roundup with listings of all the violent crimes in the borough around the eighth of October, and there were five murders in the South Bronx, ten shootings and fifteen deadly assaults. But no names, no bylines. Just human beings who became another statistic in the Bronx bloodshed of the seventies.

I made photocopies of the two articles and headed back to work. I stopped in the men's room to check on my shaving wounds, and thankfully the bleeding had stopped completely, leaving only a tiny dark spot on my dark blue collar. I turned the corner to the cubicles and saw my future speeding towards me in a head-on collision. A beautiful young redheaded female turned in her chair and rose to greet me. My replacement is drop-dead gorgeous and looked like she could still be in high school.

"Hello, Mr. Schmidt. I'm Courtney. I understand we'll be working together," she said, with a smile that exposed the tooth whiteness only possible with many hours of laser sessions, or the full bloom of youth.

"Nice to meet you. Call me Vinny," I said, shaking her hand. I motioned for her to have a seat in her cubicle chair inches from mine. *Is this person old enough to have graduated college?*

"Take your time getting settled," she said earnestly. "I can keep busy with HR stuff until you're ready. You can probably tell that I'm very excited."

"I'll be with you in a few minutes," I said, taking my computer and my brain out of sleep mode. I pretended to be reading email, when all I could think about was that in a matter of days, weeks, or if I'm really fortunate, months, I'll be out on my ass and this young beauty will be beginning her career as mine grinds to an ugly halt.

"So, are you a recent college graduate?"

"Yes, I graduated N.Y.U. in June."

"Are you from New York?"

"Yes, Chappaqua."

Chappaqua is the tony New York outer suburb where Bill and Hillary Clinton set up shop when they decided Hillary needed to have a seat in the United States Senate. Not exactly growing up killing cockroaches in the Bronx.

I took her through the paces on my computer screen, showing her all the ins and outs of what essentially is cutting and pasting emails, schedules, press releases, and take-out menus from one Excel file to another. She was attentive, enthusiastic, charming, seemed to absorb everything instantly, and was going to be bored with the job in about a week.

"I'm very excited about learning from the bottom of the business up," she said excitedly, and suddenly realized that she just told a middle-age guy with a hangover that he was working as a bottom feeder. "I'm sorry, I didn't mean it like that, what I meant was..."

"No need to apologize. I've only been here a little while. I'm between... careers."

"They're sending me around to some other areas tomorrow, so I'll be bouncing around."

"Oh, you're getting a taste of the entire operation, not just... what I do?"

"No. They want me to have an idea of everything before I start my job."

"What is that?"

"Oh, I thought you knew. I'll be anchoring the weekend news."

"Wow. That's... fantastic," I managed to utter. Glad she's not kicking me out into the street and at the same time flabbergasted that this child will be starting her career as a news anchor. "By the way, what's   your   last   name?"

"Griffith."

"Griffith. Oh, I knew a Griffith. Back in day camp in the Bronx."

"Oh, the Bronx! I've been to Yankee Stadium and the zoo."

"Yeah, I grew up there."

"That must have been... nice," she said, as she managed a smile. She headed for the elevator and waved good-bye.

I couldn't concentrate on my *New York Times* on the subway ride. I thought of Griffith, that funny little kid. I wondered how he did. Was he alive or dead? And more importantly, how did he live? And what about all the other kids from day camp? How did we all survive? Nobody was rich. All of us grew up killing cockroaches in the Bronx. But who cared? Some kids had to fight for food at the dinner table with six, seven or eight siblings. Others lived under the same roof with parents who were drunks, drug addicts, thugs, and thieves. There were kids living with parents who made them kneel together for nightly rosary and wouldn't let them watch the Three Stooges on TV. Some kids had parents who only spoke Italian or Chinese or Spanish, or who weren't right in the head and walked to the store in their robe, or maybe they tried to jump off the roof of their building. Some kids had brothers who were bullies and sisters who were the queens of their class. Some kids slept in class and got A's while other kids would have been left back every year but the nuns couldn't stand the kid another minute. But

246

in day camp, *everybody* wanted to jump in the waves at Rockaway, gaze in awe at the dinosaurs at the Museum of Natural History, or salute in attention at the Statue of Liberty, or scream in terror on a rainy afternoon watching a noisy 16-millimeter projector that broke down every ten minutes while showing *The House on Haunted Hill* on some sheets thrown up against the back wall of the stage. Who gave a fuck if the kid next to you had a violent drunken asshole for a father. He made you laugh by making soda come out of his nose. He could show you how to hold your fingers to throw a curveball. He knew where there were copies of *Playboy* hidden in the cellar of his building. He knew the words to Beatles songs. He remembered word for word the dirty jokes his uncle told. He ran up next to you with a baseball bat when Simple Symington was getting ready to kick your ass. He held your ankles when you were lowered down into the manhole to retrieve sewer balls. He was your friend. Your best friend. And there will never be another like him.

Chapter Sixteen

—Then—

As bad as freshman and sophomore years were, junior year was shaping up to be the worst year of school ever. I managed to skate through eight years of grammar school without studying, and pretty much did the absolute minimum to get by the first two years of high school. But with third-year classes like chemistry, physics, and Italian III, I knew I was screwed from the first day I received my class assignments. At the same time, my life outside of high school was really starting to take off. I was working more days and longer hours in the deli with Howie, and meeting a whole new group of kids that he hung out with up in Riverdale. And these Riverdale kids weren't anything like the Riverdale kids where Archie and Jughead in the comic book lived.

Just a ten minute walk from the deli, Riverdale had huge private homes and luxury apartment buildings with doormen and swimming pools. There were private grammar schools and high schools that looked like colleges in an Andy Hardy movie. Streets were lined with trees so massive, in the summer it was like driving through a tunnel of trees. Whereas my neighborhood might have cops, firemen, and schoolteachers living there, Riverdale had police lieutenants, fire captains, and school principals. Where my neighborhood had junkies and court officers, Riverdale had drug dealers and criminal defense lawyers. But to me and Howie the real attraction of Riverdale wasn't what kids' fathers did for a living, or how big their backyards were, or what kind of cars they drove; it was something much more important: girls! All kinds of girls. Jewish, Italian, Irish, black, Puerto Rican, Polish, Armenian, it didn't matter. And they all seemed to come from rich families with big houses or apartments that seemed to be empty every weekend. Plus they had money for the most fashionable clothes, jewelry, stereo systems, and, oh yeah, for getting high.

Riverdale wasn't loaded with bars on every block like my neighborhood was, yet it seemed like the kids up there were even more into getting high than the guys in my neighborhood, and that was saying something. Whether it was Boone's Farm apple wine, Southern Comfort, pot, pills, or stuff I wasn't even sure what it was, exactly, like speed or downers. In my neighborhood, it was more about hanging out with your friends in the park, or sneaking into bars to have laughs. But from what I've seen from the pool hall kids and guys who hang in the parks in Riverdale, those kids just wanted to get wasted.

Instead of walking up to Riverdale after work, Howie and I decided to take a detour through the park. He rolled a joint while we sat on a boulder in the protected darkness of Van Cortlandt Park at night in a thickly wooded area that might as well have been the middle of Vermont.

"You want some of this? I got it from those guys who hang out down by the river in Riverdale. They say it's some special shit," Howie said, after taking his first drag of the crackling joint.

"Nah," I said, not having smoked pot since my cousin turned me on when I was in the eighth grade.

"More for me," Howie said, then took several long hits which lit up his face in the darkness.

But then I thought about what a great time we had that night, and I figured a little pot wouldn't be as bad as getting drunk. "Yeah, I'll have a hit," I said, as though it was the hundredth time instead of my second.

Howie handed it to me, and I sucked it in slowly. I didn't feel a thing, except cool. We went back and forth with it a few times, and I still didn't notice anything.

"Do you believe in ghosts?" Howie asked, his face red from the glowing embers.

"I don't know. Why?" I asked, afraid of the answer I might hear. We began walking along a dirt trail that led up a hill towards the Van Cortlandt Vault, which was where some Van Cortlandts were buried a couple of hundred years ago.

"You know where this trail goes, right?"

249

"Up to the graveyard," I said, crunching leaves underfoot, in near total darkness. Flashes of light from the elevated train yard lit up the sky to the west like lightning. Now I felt it. *Shit. I am high.*

"Have you been inside there?" Howie asked, between long hits on the shrinking J.

He handed it to me, and I took a long drag. "No. I've only looked through the iron gate. I haven't been up here in a while," I said, trying to hide the fact that I was high as a kite and the fact that being in the woods with no lights and walking towards a graveyard was becoming more intense with every step up the trail.

"I know how to get in. There's a loose rod in the fence."

"I don't think it's legal to go in there," I said to Howie, not wanting him to think I was afraid of anything other than the legal ramifications of our stoner adventure.

"Legal? Who are you, fuckin' Barney Fife?"

I took one more hit and felt like my eyes were rolling back in my head. Howie had to grab my shoulder as I almost lost my footing and fell backwards. Howie laughed hysterically.

"How fucked up are you?" Howie giggled, finishing off the last of the joint.

"I feel like I'm about to become part of that Betty Boop cartoon where Koko the Klown becomes a ghost and sings the St. James Infirmary Blues."

"What. The. Fuck. Are. You. Talking. About?" Howie asked, lighting a match and holding it close to my face to get a better look at me.

Suddenly there was a loud squawk from some kind of animal or something, at the exact second that the match burned Howie's finger.

"Ow! Shit!" Howie said in a stage whisper, startling me as he punched me on the shoulder.

"What are you punching me for?"

"I don't know. It scared me."

We looked up the trail and could see the ancient stone wall of the Van Cortlandt Vault, where the small graveyard stood. It had three stone walls about twenty feet long, ten feet high, and an iron spiked fence with a front gate that was padlocked and chained.

"Maybe that came from the graveyard?" Howie said, without a trace of humor.

"Let's go look," I said stupidly.

We stepped quietly up the trail, trying not to make a sound, with Howie leading the way. I wanted to run back down the hill, but was terrified of being alone in the dark. The only other time I was stoned was at my cousin's party with a bunch of older teenagers who were dancing and making out in every room. An older girl even made out with me and we French kissed for the first and only time in my life. It was nothing but fun. Now I feel like I'm in one of those Edgar Allen Poe movies with the scary music playing.

"What was that?" Howie gasped.

"I didn't hear anything," I said, hoping that would mean there wasn't anything there.

"I think I heard that sound coming from inside the graveyard."

We tiptoed to the front fence and Howie went to the section where the loose rod was. He pulled it out and put it on the ground.

"Let's go," he said, placing one foot inside the graveyard.

I closed my eyes, and I swore I could still see things. It was like those stupid multi-colored wheel toys you had when you were a kid and you pushed on the bottom lever with your thumb faster and faster, and sparks actually started to fly out from behind the small plastic green, yellow, blue, and red windows on the tin disc as it flew around and around faster and faster. I opened my eyes and there was Howie motioning for me to follow him through the opening in the fence.

Once both my feet were inside, I felt like my senses were superhuman. I could taste the grass under my sneakers. The stones that comprised the wall were glowing. The tombstones started to sway. I grabbed Howie by the shirt.

"Let's get out of here! It's freaking me out!" I said quietly, urgently.

"Wait. I hear something," he said, pointing to the largest ancient tombstone.

We got as close together as we could and parked ourselves in front of the tombstone.

"Let's look together, on three," Howie whispered. "One, two, three."

We looked behind the tombstone and...

"PHHHHHHHTTTTTTTTTAAACCCHHHHHH," a strange, bizarre, giant creature screeched at us. At least I think it was giant. Although there is a chance it may have been a baby raccoon or a squirrel.

We fell over each other as we ran towards the opening in the fence and ran as fast as we could down the trail, and towards the benches in the park across from the pool hall.   As we ran across Broadway, Howie yelled to me, "What was it?"

"I don't know! A... monster?"

"Yeah, a monster!" Howie agreed, as we turned the corner.

There were only two guys sitting on those benches. One of them had a guitar and was strumming it.

I got there first, and blurted out, "Guys, you've got to come, we saw something in the park. Help us."

"Spoon!" Howie yelled. "We saw a fucking monster in the graveyard! Get some people together, quick!"

Spoon started giggling as he began strumming his guitar again.

"Come on!" I shouted frantically.

"Hey Howie, did you just smoke that shit I sold you?" Spoon said with a Cheshire cat smile on his face.

"Um, yeah," Howie said, calming down.

Spoon and the guy next to him started slapping each other five.

"Howie, I told you that was some good shit. It's dusted, man. You guys are baking."

"Baking? What's that?" I asked.

"Tripping! You're tripping on the shit! You probably saw a fucking cat or a raccoon."

"Oh, all right, then," Howie said, sheepishly.

"I think I need to come down. What do we do now?" I asked nervously.

"Just kick back and enjoy. It's not like straight acid. You'll be fine a few hours," Spoon said, with the authority of an attending physician.

"Let's go to the diner," Howie suggested.

"I'm not going through the park," I said, waving good-bye to Spoon, who was still giggling.

"Hey, don't forget the bash down by the river this Saturday," Spoon shouted from the bench.

"What's that?" I asked Howie.

"Oh man, that's the biggest party you've ever seen, in the woods down by the Hudson River. They have a live band and everything. Crazy."

"I think I've had enough with crazy."

"No, this is good crazy," Howie said as we walked down Broadway towards the Short Stop diner across the street from the park. We sat drinking tea and ordering grilled cheese, french fries, hamburgers, malteds, bagels, eggs, and whatever else we could think of until they started mopping under our table.

I sat in homeroom under a Monday morning haze and looked around at all the other kids in their short business-style hair, suit jackets, ties, non-rubber-soled leather shoes, and suit material trousers, and I felt like I was undercover. I wasn't part of this group. I was an outcast. I didn't fit in. I didn't belong. And it made me feel cool. There were some other guys like myself, and we were finding each other out daily. It wasn't obvious who the other cool guys were. They might have a bright paisley tie which they wore slightly askew. Or maybe had hair that went over the ears and touched their collar in the back, which was about as long as you could have it without getting pulled out of a line, smacked across the face, and issued a jug slip. Sometimes out of the blue, while waiting to get some mashed potatoes, or standing in line to buy a pencil outside the bookstore, a guy would just look at you, notice something, and whisper, "Are you a head?"

253

Answering "yes" meant you got high, dug Sgt. Pepper's, and more importantly, didn't go for all this regimented bullshit in school. And the guys who said they were heads came in all varieties: black, Puerto Rican, Irish, Italian, Polish, fat, skinny, pimply, it didn't matter. What did matter was that you were secretly cool, hiding your identity from the faculty and other kids who were lame. You know the lame kids. The kids who brown-nosed the teachers, ran the student organizations, populated the honor roll, starred on the football team, or sat on the student council. All those kids were buying into the system. At least that's what we told each other as we panicked during lunch period in the cafeteria while we tried to figure out from the smart kids who actually studied and did their homework what might be on that afternoon's chemistry test, because the rest of us were hanging out in parks from City Island to the Hudson River, hiding in shadows, sitting on park benches and seesaws smoking pot, drinking Gypsy Rose fortified wine and listening to Sgt. Pepper, the Stones' "Satanic Majesties Request," Procol Harum, or Buffalo Springfield – and not listening to Murray the K.

"Fuck, what the hell is Van der Waals force?" I asked Boone and anybody else at our lunch table who would listen.

"I think that's Frank Zappa's new album, right?" Boone said, leafing through his chemistry textbook.

There's a new guy sitting at our table. I don't know how he wound up here, but he's here. He's a fat guy who looks like Pugsley from the Addams Family. He's got thick black horn-rimmed glasses and he looks awfully familiar.

"I love Zappa's 'Lumpy Gravy,'" the fat kid says.

"You look like you like any kind of fuckin' gravy, Boo," Boone said, still looking for Van der Waals force.

"Hey, fuck you, Boone. Your fucking people back in Africa are still hunting fat kids like me to put in their stew," Boo stuttered back.

"Oh, by the way, this is Boo," Boone said, looking up from his book. "He just changed lunch periods, he's a friend of mine. In fact, he's from up by your neck of the woods, Schmidt."

Now I remember! This was the kid who stepped on my foot on the subway my very first day of school, and got busted for his long hair.

"You ever get out of indefinite jug?" I asked.

"Huh?"

"Don't you remember? You stepped on my foot on the train first day of class then got busted by McArdle for hair."

"That was you? Small world!"

"Where are you from, Boo?" I asked.

"Riverdale."

"I live by Vannie. Do you know about the river party this weekend?" I asked him.

"Fuck, yeah! Are you going?" Boo asked excitedly. "Boone, you coming?"

"Nope. Too many hippies in Riverdale," Boone said as he pored over the periodic table of elements.

"What's wrong with hippies?" Boo asked incredulously.

"Nothing wrong with hippies. But large groups of hippies on drugs make me nervous. It ain't always peace and love that breaks out. Sometimes there's broken heads.
Hence, my apprehension."

"Ahh, you're being paranoid," Boo said.

"Yeah, well you'd be paranoid too, if you had a fat black ass instead of a fat white ass."

We studied as much as we could in the fifteen or so minutes that remained in lunch period, but I had a sinking feeling that it was all for naught. As I looked over my notebook from chemistry class, in the margins I saw more Beatles song lyrics, poorly drawn naked women, and representations of Fred Flintstone and Barney Rubble than I did helpful tips on remembering things like the Van der Waals force. And once Boo found out I worked at the deli on 242nd Street, he was eager to hook up with me and Howie at the next available opportunity, which was tomorrow night. We planned to go to the river bash in Riverdale. He assured us it had nothing to do with getting free food.

255

By now, our co-worker at the deli, Cousin, was used to Howie and me going out after work on Saturday nights after closing, so he didn't bother going through the routine of pretending he was going to make us pay for our beer and heroes. He'd just wave at us and wink as we walked out with our brown paper bags of goodies. And since I knew Boo would be waiting for us, I packed an extra hero, some Twinkies, a bear's claw, and a knish.

As we walked out, a brand spanking new 1967 Ford Galaxie came whipping around the corner and screeched into a parking spot, barley missing an el pillar right in front of the store.

In the front passenger seat, waving from the open window, was a cute blonde with a headband and a brown leather fringed jacket. I ducked down and there was Boo, also wearing a headband, behind the wheel.

"Get in, motherfuckahs! We're goin' to a hippie river bash!" Boo said excitedly.

The girl opened her door and pulled her seat forward so Howie and I could get into the back seat, where a skinny dude with non-Catholic high school long hair was sitting behind Boo. She was wearing really short cut-offs.

"Boo, this is Howie," I announced.

Boo reached over and ran his hand up the girl's leg. "And this is Peggy!" Which caused Peggy to scream with glee. "And next to you is Ned Kelly. He's from my old neighborhood in Inwood. This is my father's car, so don't open up any sodas, beers, sandwiches, potato chips, nothing!" Boo said, laying down the law. "The only thing that you can open is... Peggy's shirt!" And he grabbed at her jacket as he pulled out of the parking spot, missing the el pillar by inches. Peggy laughed as she batted his hand away.

"Do you have any pot?" Peggy asked gleefully, fully turned around to face us.

"Peggy, I fuckin' told you I got the shit for you!" Ned Kelly said, like he was her father. The smile fell quickly from her face as she turned back around.

256

As we drove north on Broadway towards Riverdale, I tried to study Peggy, but the only time her face was lit was when we were under a street lamp. When it was dark, she appeared to have slanted Eastern European eyes and high cheekbones that formed a triangle down to her pointed chin. She didn't look like the typical Irish or Italian girls I grew up with. She was exotic. But when the light illuminated her face it revealed something that frightened me immediately.

"How old are you?"

"Seventeen!" she said in unison with Ned Kelly.

Kelly added, "And don't you forgit it, Babalooey!"

"Boo, she better not be bullshitting," I said, grabbing him by the back of the neck.

"Didn't I just fucking say she was seventeen," Ned Kelly said.

Howie and I looked at each other and gave each other a *who is this asshole* look.

"Yeah, I got some pot," Howie said, patting the front pocket of his jean jacket.

"Groovy!" Peggy said, smiling wide.

Ned Kelly gave her a dirty look.

Boo made a left onto Mosholu Avenue and within minutes, not only were there no street lights, there were no sidewalks, and we would go a couple of blocks and not see any homes, just dark woods with ornate iron gates every few hundred feet.

"We just passed the estate of the guy who owns the *New York Times*," Boo said proudly.

"How do you know?" I asked.

"My father's in insurance. He has the policy on the house."

We made a few more turns on streets that I never knew existed, down steep hills in near total darkness on roads as bumpy as you'd expect in the backwoods of upstate.

"Oh shit! I missed it!" Boo said, jamming on the breaks and practically sending us flying. He threw it into reverse, backed up about thirty feet, and went between two large trees on a dirt road.

"Are we still in New York?" Peggy asked.

257

"I think we're in Canada," Boo said matter-of-factly.

"Really?"

"Gotcha!" Boo said, running his hand up her leg.

"Stop!" Peggy laughed, pushing him away.

We went down a dirt road for about fifty yards, and a guy came from behind a tree with a flashlight and flagged us down. He looked like a college kid with long hair.

"Everybody in here over sixteen?" he said, shining the flashlight on Peggy's legs.

"Yup!" Boo said.

"Go in there, park the car, then follow this road down to the bash. It's fifty cents each."

"Each?" Boo asked incredulously.

"Come on, Pugsley, fork over or turn around," the college kid said.

"You guys can pay me later," Boo said, handing over the money.

"He called you Pugsley!" Peggy screamed. "Can I call you Pugsley?"

"You can call me anything," Boo said sexily, "as long as you call me." He put his arm around her and with his other hand he tried to cop a feel under her jacket.

"Stop!" Peggy laughed, pushing him away again.

We parked the car and started the walk down the dirt road, and were joined by kids coming from out of the woods, their cars, or from seemingly out of nowhere. We could hear music playing in the distance, and a loud party going on. We followed a few arrows this way and that and, went down a bunch of steps and turned to the right and there it was! There must have been three hundred kids in a large clearing right in the middle of the woods above the Hudson River. There were Christmas lights strung across some trees providing soft multi-colored lighting. We walked up to the crowd and just eased our way into the middle of it all.

There was a table with three guys with much shorter hair and a few years older than most of the crowd, selling beer from kegs for fifty cents a cup. They had a hard time keeping up with the demand and the line was at least five deep in front of each keg. Next to the kegs there was a generator going that powered the Christmas lights strung overhead, the stereo that was blasting the Stones, as well as orange extension cords that went to some plywood sheets laid on the ground where amplifiers, microphone stands, and a drum kit were set up.

"Ned, you're eighteen, get us some beers," Boo said, as he nudged him towards the line.

"Where's the money?" Ned asked.

"You already owe me fifty cents parking and fifty cents for gas."

"I ain't paying for Peggy and the other two," Ned said with disdain in his voice.

"Ned, you just get for yourself, I'm paying for everybody else," Howie announced, pulling a five dollar bill out of his pocket, like the hero that he was – judging by the look on Peggy's face.

Kids kept arriving from the woods above us and from the river below us to the point where the party was extending into the area where there weren't any lights. The only time I'd seen this many hippies together was on TV. You could tell there were Irish, Italian, Jewish, black, Puerto Rican, and all kinds of European-looking kids who all had one thing in common: they were getting high and having a good time.

"Here, put these on," Boo said as he handed us embroidered headbands. "You'll look cool."

Howie and I both put them on, and held up our two-finger peace sign salute.

"Peace, man," Howie and I said to each other.

Boo held up his peace sign, and said, "I want a piece, man," as he grabbed Peggy from behind and copped a feel of her tits over her leather fringed jacket, which sent Peggy into another laughing fit.

Ned Kelly looked disgusted. "I'm gonna see what kind of shit is floatin' around," he said, as he disappeared into the dark.

"What's he doing?" I asked.

"He's looking for drugs. He's into that stuff," Boo said.

259

"I'm going with him," Peggy said, running after him.

"How do you know this guy?" I asked Boo. We began to meander through the crowd of people gyrating to Hendrix's "Stone Free" exploding in the air.

"I grew up with him, but I haven't seen him since I moved to Riverdale after eighth grade. He called me out of the blue a few months ago and he's always got the wild chicks with him. And drugs."

"That guy is trouble," Howie said, pausing to look at a girl with huge tits and no bra who wore a tie-dyed tank top and was doing a crazy hippie dance. "I like a girl like that. What neighborhood was that?"

"Inwood. I went to St. Jude's but Ned went to public school. We had a private house over by Fort Tryon Park, and Ned lived in the projects. He hung out with some bad kids. I was just glad when they didn't beat me up. He still lives down there."

The beer was flowing and you could smell the pot and hash wafting over from the dark wooded areas. I had two cups of beer, and I had no idea how many Howie and Boo had downed. I couldn't believe the number of girls who went braless under skimpy blouses and dresses and were barefoot even though there was a definite fall chill in the air. You couldn't tell who was dancing with who.

"Come on! Let's dance!" Boo said, pushing us through to the center of the crowd. Once in there, he started shaking his fat ass like a regular Jackie Gleason! The hippie chicks loved it and formed a circle around him and clapped in unison as he gyrated his big belly around and around. A short fat hippie chick started doing bumps and grinds with him much to the delight of the frenzied crowd. But "Pictures of Matchstick Men" ended and one of the beer servers picked up a microphone.

"Welcome to the second annual Riverdale River Blast. Now welcome all the way from Albany, New York, the Rock 'N Soul Soldiers!"

The crowd rushed to the front of the stage, leaving me, Howie and Boo at the rear. Because the band was on ground level, we couldn't even see what they looked like with everybody standing directly in front of them.

After a minute or so of tuning up, and some *Check one, two, threes,* the cymbals crashed, the bass drum pounded, the snare slammed, and then the guitar, bass, and keyboard kicked joined in to the loudest, most ear-bleeding volume I ever heard at such close range, doing the instantly recognizable opening riff to "Wild Thing" by the Troggs. The crowd went wild as they played the riff over and over, building to a frenzy as the vocals started and the rhythmic beat repeated until the guitar solo cut through, bringing the throngs to an even higher level of pandemonium. I had to see these guys. I pushed my way through the arm waving, gyrating, spinning, jerking revelers until I could get a look at the band. It was difficult to see their faces because the only illumination was from the low wattage colored Christmas lights. It was an interracial group with a lean, tight, afroed black dude on lead guitar, a wild-haired Hispanic guy on keyboards, a long straight-haired China-Rican guy on bass, and a white drummer with a faux afro flopping in front of his face with every beat.

These guys were as good as they were loud. It was the first time I ever heard a band sound so heavy from so close. Usually the rock bands you hear at a wedding or high school dance play slow dance music you can grind to, or rock and roll oldies. But "Wild Thing" was unbelievable live! They must have played it for twenty minutes. And when that ended they went right into "Light My Fire" by the Doors. Girls were dancing so crazy I swear I saw a few nipples popping out of their loose t-shirts.

Boo and Howie squeezed in right next to me.

"I can't fucking believe this! It's better than a Beatles concert!" Boo shouted loudly directly into my ear. "Have you seen Peggy?"

"No. Why?" I yelled back at him.

"She said she needed the keys to my car to get something and I haven't seen her since."

As the band kept the relentless pace going, kicking into "White Rabbit," then the Stone's "19th Nervous Breakdown," I noticed

261

something about the drummer between songs. When his hair was pushed back, and he removed his oversized aviator-style dark glasses to wipe the sweat off, something struck me. It couldn't be. Could it? I had to get on all fours to crawl through the next couple of layers of people standing in the front and poked my head between two girls. They looked down at me like I was some kind of pervert. My heart pounded louder than the kick drum just a few yards in front of me. *It's him! It's fucking Whitey!* Pounding away like a chunky Keith Moon! I couldn't tell where he was looking behind the shades, and I was afraid to wave. I mean, why should I? *That wouldn't be cool. I'm not some groupie. If he wanted me to know he was playing in a band in Riverdale he would have let me know. Right? Why the fuck should I care whether he gets in touch with me? He thinks he's hot shit now that he's in a band. Screw him.*

Suddenly a pimply-faced redheaded teenager jumps on the stage and grabs the microphone from the black guitar player who is singing lead on the Hendrix song "Foxy Lady" and screams, "Fuck this nigger fucking bullshit!"

Simultaneously, we heard female screams, guttural shouts of anger from guys, guitar feedback, crashing cymbals, and angry words still coming over the mics.

"Get the fuck out of here, you motherfucker," the black guitarist screamed at the red-haired Irish kid, who picked up the mic stand and swung it wildly, just missing him. A second white kid with slicked back black hair jumped onto the stage holding something in his right hand, and went towards Whitey, who was bending down behind his drums.

I jumped forward and screamed as loud as I could, "Whitey, heads up!"

Whitey snapped his head up with an unsuspecting smile plastered across his face and scanned the crowed looking for a voice he seemed to recognize instantly. But the prick rushing his blind side cracked Whitey across the back of the head with either a sap or small club, felling Whitey behind his drum kit. From out of nowhere young looking greasers were punching people, yelling about fucking Jews, hippies, commies, niggers, spics, kikes, and cunts. Boo pushed me down to the ground and sat on me. I wasn't going anywhere, even though I wanted desperately to help Whitey.

"I fucking know these assholes. They're from Inwood. They're friends of Ned Kelly's," Boo said, shaking me.

From the wooded area off to the side, Ned Kelly ran around the crowd and the rest of his gang followed him through the woods. A few of the older college kids came out of the woods right behind them, looking beat up and bleeding.

"Those fucking hitters robbed us! Let's go after them!"

Howie plopped down next to us. "Those pricks started a commotion on the stage so the other guys could use that as a cover and rob the guys selling weed and the organizers of everything. Your fucking buddy was one of the ring leaders," he said, looking at Boo.

"Fuck! Peggy took the keys to my father's car. Come on!" Boo said, jumping up quicker than I thought possible for his fat ass.

I wanted to go over to Whitey and talk to him, but first I had to see what had happened with Boo's car.

We ran through the woods, the dirt path, up the hill, and there it was. Crashed into a parked car.

"Oh, no," Boo said as he took in the damage. "I am fucked. That bitch Peggy must've been using my car as the getaway and crashed it. I am so screwed," he said, collapsing against the smashed front end.

It took a while to pull the car off the other one, and we used the jack to get the metal off the tire. Boo grabbed a notepad from the glove compartment, wrote a note, stuck it on the other car's windshield, got back in, and started his car up. We jumped in and he took off.

"That was nice of you to leave a note on the other car," I told him.

Boo gave me a funny look. "Are you kidding me? My old man works in the insurance biz. He always told me, if you hit a parked car, always write a note in case somebody saw you. And on the note, write: *Dear Sir, I'm sorry I hit your car. I'm writing this note so somebody watching thinks I'm leaving my name and phone number. Sorry, signed, somebody."*

Boo stopped at a phone booth on Riverdale Avenue to call his father. He thought it would be better if we left him alone to make the call at the pay phone. "I'll have to make up a good fucking story to get through this one," he said. We got the hint and walked away into the dark night.

Howie and I walked back to the stands where we thought there would be some guys hanging out. Even two hours later, we heard police cars zooming up Broadway towards Riverdale. But nobody was around. The place was abandoned. There weren't even piles of empties or pools of piss there. Maybe the guys were in the bars, or maybe even at home studying.

Chapter Seventeen

—Now—

Betty Ann had to be in on this. I don't think there was another person from the old neighborhood who cared about Whitey as much as she and I did. I held a bouquet of roses and knocked on the door of her basement apartment. The entrance was in the driveway that separated her house from the one next door, just like all the homes on Corlear Avenue. I remembered the house as being the one she grew up in, but why would she be living in the basement apartment? That's usually where you stick the grandparents or the teenager you can't stand to have in your house anymore.

Was I positive this was the right thing to do? Nope. But if I was going to confront Whitey with the people whose lives he saved one way or another before he checked out, I wanted Betty Ann to be there, too.

"Who's there?"

"It's Vinny," I said nervously, as I squeezed the rose stems a little too hard and got pricked by a thorn through the cellophane wrapper.

The door opened, and Betty Ann looked even prettier than I remembered. She's one of those lucky women who has such natural beauty that you can't tell if she's wearing makeup or if she dyes her hair.

"Come in," she said, swinging open the door into the kitchen. "Oh, how beautiful! Let me get a vase," she said, grabbing the roses. She stopped and took a deep whiff of the red, yellow, and pink flowers. "Wonderfully fragrant," she smiled.

I sat down and she placed the flowers, now in a crystal vase, in the center of the kitchen table. The tea kettle began to whistle.

"Care for some tea?"

"Yes, thanks."

She was wearing jeans and she still had the ass of a teenager. Her hair was pulled back behind her ears, and I looked to see if there were possibly any plastic surgery scars, because she looked that good. She had one of those t-shirts that are cut for a youthful female shape, with a Hello Kitty logo on the front. Her tits weren't huge, but still were high and firm. I couldn't tell if she was wearing a bra.

"Do you take milk?"

"Um, no."

She placed two dainty china cups and saucers on the table and sat across from me.

"I was wondering if you'd come around again. At my age, I don't care to chase, and if they don't chase, I don't care."

"Isn't this the house you grew up in?"

"Yup. I turned the upstairs into two rental apartments and I live down here. I don't want to work forever."

We both took our first sips of tea and looked at each other. She smiled.

"I might even leave New York," she said, holding the tea cup in both hands right under her nose as she smelled it. "My son graduated college, and I don't think he's coming back. When we visited Pepperdine the first time, I didn't want to come back either."

"Pepperdine? Wow! That's a fantastic school. My son might be going there."

"You have a son?" Betty Ann asked, perhaps surprised this was the first time I told her. "Well, faith and begorrah! Are there any other insights into your personal life I should be aware of? Like a wife?"

"Sorry. I'm not good at talking about it. I've been divorced for a while. My wife and I didn't part good friends, like Tom Cruise and all the wives he had to pay off. I'm deathly afraid of what might happen to my son, Johnny. He's one of those kids that could easily fall through cracks. All he does lately is play those sick uber-violent video games all day in his room. And his mom isn't exactly a finalist for mother of the year. Jesus, when I heard about that school massacre in Connecticut... the missing father, the mother with an out-of-control kid, I immediately flashed on Johnny and his mother."

"Who would have thought a kid from the Bronx would get a golf scholarship to Pepperdine?" Betty Ann asked, tactfully changing the subject.

"Don't tell me he actually played golf on the Van Cortlandt Park golf course?"

"You got it."

"When we were kids we only used the golf course at night, to hang out in."

"Yeah. Remember when they had a ski slope up there on the eighteenth   hole?"

"My brother used to work there."

"So did my ex," Betty Ann said dourly. "So let's cut to the chase here. What are your intentions?"

My mind raced. *My intentions? Isn't she rushing things?*

"About...?"

"Your plan with Whitey? Is he that bad?"

"I want Whitey to know he was loved, is loved, before he leaves us."

"He's dying?"

"I don't know what he has, but he looks it. He's going to end his life. I heard him talking about how he's going to cash it all in soon. He's heavily armed, you know."

"You believe him?"

"Yeah, I hate to admit it, but that's where he's headed."

I sat back and took a deep breath. We sat at a Formica table on chrome chairs with red vinyl cushions. It had to be vintage 1960s, but it was kept in mint condition. In fact, everything in the eat-in kitchen appeared to be vintage from the sixties, yet perfectly maintained, from the black and white tiles on the floor to the chrome ceiling fan and the shiny tin napkin holder on the table. Betty Ann was a few years younger than I and had lived several blocks away from me when we were kids, which means she might as well have been living in Finland. I vaguely remember her from day camp, and we talked about some mutual friends of friends we had during that same time period back in grade school. Hanging out with the boys, I discovered that the numbers

267

of guys in our gang were dwindling because the guys who had hormones raging sooner than I did were chasing after Betty Ann and her friends down in Bailey Park, a few blocks south of 238th Street.

"I love how everything in here is vintage and kept up so beautifully," I said, taking a Stella D'oro Swiss Fudge cookie from a package.

Betty Ann took one too. "They tore down Stella D'oro just recently. I guess the cookies are made out in Ohio or something? They don't taste the same to me. Yeah, things change. I do like having nice things from the past around. But I do not want to live in the past. I have so many happy memories of my parents and grandparents, may God rest their souls, but I'll be damned if I'm going to pine away for some idea, or ideal, or guy or whatever from when I thought babies came from praying on your knees by the bed with your husband. Like the man said, 'Don't look back.'"

"The man?"

"Dylan. The songwriter. Not my son."

"Your son is named Dylan?"

"Half his graduating class was named Dylan. By the way, I appreciate the fact you called everything in here vintage. But some things aren't. They're just reproductions, or they had a little help with modern technology. Does that matter?" she asked, holding her cup of tea under her Irish smiling eyes and lips.

I paused, took another cookie and had a long sip of tea. There it is – the chick trick question. From the time you play spin the bottle at an eighth-grade party, to the time you meet a nice lady at an assisted living social, a trick question from a female and how a guy answers just may be the deciding factor in determining whether she becomes merely a friend who's a girl, or a girl friend who you want to hold hands with, make out with, and eventually get naked with.

"What's the difference if you can't tell the difference?" I said, hedging my bet.

"Every woman I know who got breast implants left her husband. Every single one."

I tried hard not to look at the Hello Kitty logo on her chest.

"It's obvious I didn't have implants. My husband got kicked out. The asshole."

"How long have you been divorced?"

"We weren't divorced. We had an annulment. We were married for six months. Just long enough for me to realize that my big bad boyfriend, the man who was feared by every badass from 225th Street to the Yonkers line was nothing but a big pussy who didn't have the fucking balls to leave his grammar school buddies in the Liffy Bar, guys who were more interested in getting a busload of shitheads to get drunk at a Giants game and betting their minimum wage jobs on it. Oh, he was more than ready, willing and able to put his fat fist into somebody's pie hole for looking at him crooked at the end of the bar, but when it came time to pay the bills and help out raising a little baby boy, he was nothing but a sniveling little wimp. Do you remember Father O.?"

I was taken aback at how quickly Betty Ann's calm tea-sipping mood had snapped into extreme attack mode. And took another calming sip of tea just as quickly.

"Of course. I knew him well."

"He helped me get the annulment. It meant a lot to my parents. It took years for it to mean something to me."

"Funny how it can take years and years to realize the importance of something. I hated everything about Farley. Especially the dress and hair regulations. And looking at kids in high school today, it's easy to see how they get compartmentalized. There's the baggy-pants thugs, crooked-baseball-hat hip-hoppers, the skinny-jeans goths, the jocks, the nerds. You instantly see who belongs to what clique. But because we all dressed the same and had short hair, we appeared to be all the same. And you didn't know who was what until you got the actually know them."

"I remember you from camp. You liked Josephine," Betty Ann said, with a quizzical look on her face. With her eyes, nose and lips scrunched together, I could see the lines and wrinkles in her face. But as soon as she dropped the exaggerated expression on her face and went to her default position of soft, pleasant smile, the years dropped away.

"She was a beauty."

"You seemed so much older than me, back then."

"Back then, a few years was a lifetime."

"Timing is everything," she said, taking her last sip of tea. "Did you two ever become a thing?"

"Well, we went out one time. I took her to a concert downtown to see the Hollies. I think I was a little too... forward on the kiss goodnight."

"What happened?"

"She slapped me and then she ignored me. Forever."

"I knew I liked her!"

Betty Ann and I started mapping out how we would contact Hector Gomez and plan an intervention on Whitey to see if we could prevent him from killing himself. Sometimes it's difficult just to decide which restaurant to take someone on a date, but with Betty Ann all the details seemed to flow like we were jazz musicians working from the same musical score. I was happy to let her take the lead part at that point in the game because I had a lot of doubt that I was doing the right thing with Whitey. But Betty Ann convinced me that in matters of life-changing events, you do what you have to do. Yeah, I thought I'd made an effort to take the bull by the horns in such matters many times, but as soon I saw the red in his eyes and smelled that funky bull breath, I pussied out. I could tell Betty Ann wasn't about to pussy out.

"Would you like to maybe continue this over dinner later tonight?" I asked Betty Ann, coyly.

She looked up from her yellow legal pad where she was writing names, numbers, addresses, and a time line of Whitey's life. "No. Not really."

My heart sank. I was never good at rejection, which is probably another reason I chickened out from the tough decisions.

"But," she continued, "if you want to take me to dinner, on a date, the answer is yes."

"What time and where would you like to go?"

"Be here at eight and I'll surprise you."

"Deal," I said, trying not to reveal my ridiculous teenager boy joy at the thought of a grown-up date and a second shot with Betty Ann.

The late afternoon crowd at the Punch Bowl is my favorite. The bookie is collecting from last night's action from most, and paying out to one or two. That's when the drinks start flowing as if some poor slob just won a half billion with Power Ball instead of three hundred bucks on a long shot at Aqueduct. It's the after-work crowd, medicating themselves after chasing turnstile jumpers or lifting a ton or so of garbage, black bag by black bag, or breathing nothing but car and diesel exhaust for eight hours while taking money from commuters at the Lincoln Tunnel, or running into burning buildings while everybody else is running out.

At the end of the bar sits Brooksie nursing a tumbler of brown liquor, reading a racing form. And if you can read a racing form, and by that I mean the *Racing Form*, and you know what every little column means and every stat and acronym and footnote and number to the decimal point, you should be reading the *Wall Street Journal* instead and reaping millions, because the Racing Form stat sheet is more complicated than the stock market report.

I never got a call back from Brooksie, so I don't know if he in fact found Hector Gomez for me. I wasn't even sure if he'd remember me, so I stood next to him and ordered a beer.

"Hey, Schmidt! Where the hell you been? I got the information for you," he said loudly and proudly as he pulled some crumpled papers from his inside jacket pocket.

"Great. I was hoping I'd find you today."

"I lost your number. Here's the information. I'm sure it's him," he said, handing me the same piece of paper I used to initially give him the information, with my phone number on there, too. "His phone number, address, is right there. I even gave you his fucking social

271

security number if you want to do a credit check on the prick. Now don't forget, you didn't get this shit from me. Because if I get busted for this and lose my job, I'll have nothing left to live for, so taking you down with me won't bother me one bit, capeesh?"

"Capeesh. I can't thank you enough..."

"You're right, you can't. But you can start by buying me some drinks."

It wasn't too long until Brooksie was tipsy and I was keeping an eye on the time. I didn't want to screw this up with Betty Ann again. I ordered coffees and water and watched the bar make the transition from guys tired from work, to the guys too hung over, too old, too sick of it, too fucked up on drugs, too smart to work for every asshole boss they ever had because they were so smart and should be running the place even though they called in sick every Friday and Monday, were late Tuesday, Wednesday, and Thursday and wouldn't work weekends. But Brooksie sat there sipping his brown liquor with half an eye on *Jeopardy* and the other on his *New York Times*.

"I remember back when *Laugh-In* was on Mondays and then *Monday Night Football* would be on right after. Those were fucking great times," he said wistfully, as though he was recalling a defining moment in his life. Maybe he was.

Even though it's been illegal to smoke in bars for a couple of decades, as I walked the several blocks back to Betty Ann's apartment I was hoping I didn't reek of cigarettes from the heavy smoke in the Punch Bowl. I was proud of myself for not joining Brooksie in reminiscing about the glory days of television-watching in the Punch Bowl and swallowing many ounces of Jameson in the process of attempting to bring them back. I did stop at a liquor store to pick up a nice bottle of wine, though.

I knocked on her door and silently asked God for strength. I didn't know what the future might hold for Betty Ann and me, but I did not want this to be yet another train wreck in my journey. Or a slap in the face.

272

The door opened and I could immediately smell something fantastic wafting in my direction. I was confused at first because I detected a delicious aroma of food cooking in the oven with perhaps a smidgen of onion or garlic, and also a light and sexy perfume swirling in the air. Betty Ann was wearing a tightly fitting black dress that a woman half her age would struggle to look good in, and she looked stunning. She gave me a welcome peck on the cheek and her fragrant perfume made me forget completely about the dish stewing in its juices in the oven across the room.

"I told you I'd surprise you. I'm making dinner," she said, taking me by the hand. "Is this wine?"

"Yeah, I didn't know what kind to get..."

"That's very sweet, but I don't drink wine. I don't drink at all. I'll leave it over here and you can take it when you leave," she said smiling. "Do you like flounder?"

"That's my favorite fish. It was impossible to get when I lived in L.A."

"I guess it's an East Coast thing. It's on auto-pilot for a few minutes. Do you want to sit in the living room or do you want to sit in here while I cook?"

"I'll just sit here at the table."

Betty Ann glided around the kitchen putting the finishing touches on a salad, some steaming veggies, and pots and pans containing assorted steaming liquids. She peeked in the oven, and she recited a monologue that detailed in minute detail every stop she made on Arthur Avenue to get the ingredients for our mini-feast.

"Do you like piss clams?" she asked, with a worried look on her face.

"That's something else I could never find on the West Coast. I love them."

"How did you survive out there?" she asked as she opened the refrigerator and took out a large bag of steamers, which she placed in a big pot of boiling water.

How did I survive out there? I wondered to myself. But just like the guys in the Punch Bowl, I was self-medicated and full of excuses and blaming everyone else for my own failures. I blamed bosses, co-workers, my wife, and yes, even my son for my not being recognized as the genius I surely am. Right? Aren't I? Wasn't I just like John Lennon screaming at the top of my lungs *I'm a fookin' genius! Genius is pain!*

"Things are the same everywhere. You forget about great pizza and find your favorite taco stand. You don't have Yankee Stadium, so being a loyal fan of American League baseball, you follow the Angels."

"Yeah, well, we don't have Yankee Stadium anymore, either. Now we have that mall with a ball field. I mean, a Hard Rock at the ballpark? Give me a break," she said, dumping a huge pile of steamed clams into a large bowl. "Appetizer's ready!"

Like a play, the meal unfolded in three acts. The first act was foods you ate with your fingers: steamed "piss" clams, and dishes of small cheeses and vegetables. Then there were things that went on large dishes like linguini with clam sauce, baked flounder, and steamed leafy vegetables. The third course, of course, was salad with pickled things like beets and artichokes.

"I thought you were Irish on both sides?" I asked, savoring the flavors that lingered in my mouth as I chewed on fresh escarole.

"I am. But you can't be from the Bronx and not know how to cook Italian. You go in the living room for a few minutes and let me clean up."

"No way! I'm helping!"

"No, no..." she said, grabbing me by the hand and pulling me towards the doorway.

"No, really!" I said, pulling back. She turned towards me and we both stopped. I thought a kiss might be coming, and I was as nervous as the time I took Carrie Vitelli by the hand during kiss-o-leario and led her to the abandoned dumbwaiter in the basement of my building where we made out, closed lips, heads circling in pre-pubescent bliss. Betty Ann and I moved closer and our lips touched ever so slightly. She pulled back and smiled as she held both of my hands.

"Okay, help me clean up."

Cleaning up the kitchen with Betty Ann scared me. Oh, I was enjoying the small talk, the kidding, and the fun of doing something that is usually drudgery but becomes enjoyable when you do it with someone you really like. It scared me because it reminded me so much of the times when my wife and I first dated and then lived together. Before I got caught up in my own stupid, self-medicated self, just like the guys in the Liffy or the Punch Bowl, and I became a pussy when it came to devoting myself to my wife and my son when they needed me most. Maybe I'm the one who hasn't changed.

"That's it!" Betty Ann said, closing the silverware drawer. "Now we can relax in the living room. Should I open the wine for you?"

I wanted the wine. But something told me it wasn't a good idea with Betty Ann not being a drinker.

"Do you mind if I do?"

"No, not at all," she said, holding the decorative wine bag.

"Nah. No, thanks. I'll save it to give to my sister. She's been great."

Betty Anne smiled in way that told me I'd answered another trick chick question with the correct answer. *Whew.*

We sat on the couch right next to each other. Her skirt rode up a little and I recalled the time she drove me to the wedding wearing a skirt and her car had a stick shift. I remembered seeing those freckles high on her leg.

"Want to watch a little TV?" she asked, picking up the remote.

"Sure."

She flipped through channel after channel of reality shows, stupid sitcoms, slasher movies and pundits screaming at each other. She zoomed past something in black and white and backed up.

"I love this movie," she said sweetly.

I'm in trouble now. She stopped on the closing scene of *Mr. Deeds Goes to Town*, one of my all-time favorite Frank Capra films. I can watch the last three minutes of almost any Frank Capra film and start weeping like an old lady at a funeral mass, as if I had just sat through the entire film. Because I've seen the movies so many times, tuning in at the very end brings to the forefront of my brain cells the entire range of emotions that the whole film put me through. But that scene at the end of this, where Jean Arthur jumps into Gary Cooper's arms and starts showering him with kisses all over his face, taps into some subconscious place in my psyche where there is this fantasy that a woman would love me that much and be unable to contain herself. And here it comes. Jean Arthur is smooching Gary Cooper and he looks befuddled, bewildered and perplexed. I'm already tearing up. I look over to Betty Ann and she's already weeping.

"Gets me every time," she said, wiping her tears with a tissue.

"Me, too," I said.

Betty Ann turned to me with a look of shock on her face. "Are you crying?"

"No, I'm not crying. Yes. I am."

"You're the first man I've seen cry at the ending since my father and I watched it when he was in the nursing home."

"Capra gets me," I said, trying to pretend I didn't cry at all.

"I love him," she said, reaching over and tenderly taking my hand. "Look. I like you a lot. And I really want to help you with this plan to help Whitey. But..."

Oh shit. Here it comes. This is why I hate getting serious with women. She's not going to jump into my arms and start showering me with kisses. Here comes the big but.

"But I don't want to rush things and screw anything up, which I used to do and refuse to do at this stage in my life. So, why don't we kiss each other goodnight here on the couch, and then you leave and when you call me again, we'll go out again. Or something."

"Can I call you tonight when I get back home?"

"That would be nice."

She leaned towards me and we made out. I didn't do anything stupid like try to feel her up, although I probably would have if I'd had that bottle of wine. Tasting the inside of her mouth was as though it was the finishing touch of the spectacular dinner she had prepared. My senses were overwhelmed as I was drenched in the fullness of the aromas, tastes and textures of her home, her kitchen, of Betty Ann herself.

"Good-bye," I said, knowing I'd better stop before I couldn't stop.

"Take care," she said.

I picked up the bottle of wine as we walked to the door, and I left.

My car was parked around the corner from the Punch Bowl, and I looked in the window; it was really packed, for a weeknight. Brooksie was still at the end of the bar. I walked right past and got in the car. I was looking forward to a good night's sleep. I savored the essence of my evening with Betty Ann, hoping it would continue in my dreams. I called her before I turned in for a sweet goodnight chat. But as I lay there trying to get a sleepy feeling, the more I tried to visualize Betty Ann, an image of Private Hector Gomez kept somehow dominating the view.

At work, I managed to keep my mind on my duties, but every time I had a few seconds I Googled Hector Gomez, his name, address, and social security number. But anything I could find out was already on the slip of paper where Brooksie had written his name, address and social security number. He lived in a part of the Bronx that was made famous by *Fort Apache: The Bronx,* the 1981 movie that centered around the 41st police precinct and the anarchy and destruction that prevailed in that area during the 1970s. Today the area is called "Little House on the Prairie." Because just as a forest will rejuvenate itself after a devastating fire, so has that part of the Bronx, where burnt-out tenements and businesses were destroyed by a perfect storm of crime, drugs and neglect, until finally it was completely demolished. There was nothing left but rubble-strewn lots. Oh, yeah, and sewer systems, paved streets, access to public transportation, schools, and in some cases, waterfront property. It was only a matter of time before total devastation gave way to a rebirth. Single-family homes were built with backyards and front porches. Lo and behold, schoolteachers, bus drivers, cops, auto shop repair workers and bodega owners moved out of their overpriced rental apartments in the north Bronx or in Yonkers and bought themselves affordable homes in this area that people once used as a symbol of the crumbling of American civilization.

It was time for my lunch break, so I figured I might as well give it a shot. I called Hector Gomez's number and waited.

"The mailbox is full. Please call back another time," a computer-generated female voice said.

At least it wasn't disconnected. I decided to grab a bite from one of the food trucks parked nearby. Why is the longest line always at the grilled cheese truck? When did grilled cheese become some sort of exotic food? Maybe it's because you have less of a chance of getting horse or cat meat than if you get a kabob or a sloppy joe.

I was sitting on the edge of a fountain with a few hundred strangers, eating my grilled cheese, when my phone rang.

"Hi, this is Hector Gomez. Did you call me?"

I almost choked on my Gouda. "Yes, I did. Thanks for returning the call –"

"Who's this?"

Shit. Here it goes.

"My name is Vinny Schmidt –"

"We don't accept phone solicitations at this number..."

"Wait, wait! This is not a telephone solicitation. I'm calling about an old army buddy of yours."

There was a long silence.

"Are you still there?"

"What is it you want?" Gomez said, not a trace of friendliness in his slight Puerto Rican accent.

"Do you remember Sergeant Shelley?"

An even longer silence.

"Look, can I call you back? I'm a little busy right now."

"Um, sure. Anytime. You have my number in your phone, right?"

"Yeah, I'll call you," he said, ending the call on his end.

Well, at least it was a start, and I knew he was alive. But it would be a surprise if he actually called back.

Three days went by and I didn't hit one bar. I talked to Betty Ann on the phone, but she was busy with friends and family and couldn't get together. I just worked and slept, and each morning I was pleased that I felt a little less gimpy as I dragged myself off the sofa bed. And three grilled cheese sandwiches later, sitting on the edge of the fountain at lunch, my cell rang. The caller ID said it was Gomez.

"Hello."

"This is Gomez. Can we meet? I'd like to talk with you."

"Sure. When and where?"

"You know Umberto's Clam House on Arthur Avenue?"

"Yeah."

"Can you meet tonight at eight?"

"Yes."

"I have a mustache, five foot eight, one sixty five, wearing a dark blue suit."

"See you then. I'll be wearing a... jean jacket."

The phone call ended and a sense of dread came over me. Umberto's Clam House downtown was where the mobster Joey Gallo got whacked. This could be a similar set-up for me at the uptown Bronx location.

I was ten minutes early and there he was, as far away from the window as possible ,with his back to the wall and in a position to see everybody who came in the front door or out of the kitchen. Just like the mafia teaches their guys. His hair, eyebrows and mustache were dyed a little too black. He looked in excellent physical condition, and he was impeccably dressed, down to his matching tie and handkerchief tucked in his jacket pocket. He stood up when he noticed my jean jacket.

"Thanks for coming."

"No, thank you," I said, sitting across from him, my back to the front door and kitchen – which is the perfect position for someone about to get a couple of bullets in the head from a .22 pistol with the serial numbers rubbed clean.

We made small talk about the Bronx, the Yankees, the weather, and ordered our food.

"I heard Doc was dead," Gomez said, grimly. "Thank God he's still alive."

The waiter placed our dishes of fried calamari in front of us. I picked up my fork and as I was deciding which juicy morsel to spear, I looked up to see Gomez with his head lowered, obviously saying a silent grace. "So, how's Doc doing?"

"You call him Doc?"

"We called every medic Doc."

"He's not doing so great. I'm going to be blunt here, Mr. Gomez."

"Hector."

"Hector. He's at the point where he wants to end his life. He's not well. And I thought it would help if people he touched over the years were to talk to him. Maybe it could help him snap out of it. Not quite *It's a Wonderful Life*, but something like it."

"I love that movie," he said, finally cracking a smile. "You tell me where to go, when, and what you want me to do, and I'll be there. I owe it to him. I owe him my life for what he did for me. I'm going to make good," he said with intensity-charged emotion.

But then the intensity dropped from his face. He began tearing up, until it became full-blown weeping, which he tried to hide behind his hairy hands and white linen napkin. "I'm sorry. I will be there for him."

He dropped a hundred dollar bill on the table and walked out, distraught. The waiter put my linguini with white clam sauce in front of me and Hector's manicotti by his setting.

"Can you make the manicotti to go, please?"

The waiter nodded and took the dish away. I figured, since I didn't get whacked, I might as well enjoy my meal and not waste his.

Betty Ann and I sat at her kitchen table to plan the whole thing out. We decided a Sunday would be best for all involved. I'd call Whitey and tell him that I wanted to give him some things from when we were kids that he'd enjoy, and we'd make a day out of it. Then we'd surprised him with Betty Ann and of course, Hector Gomez. I did an intervention on a good friend once, and it wasn't easy. It took a lot of anger and tears over several days, but eventually the threats died and the friend did go to rehab. The rehab itself didn't take, but he is still alive so I consider it a success. And he never forgets to thank me whenever I see him.

But this isn't exactly an intervention. We won't be sitting there with a professional like on the TV show, someone who's seen it a million times before and is trained to react to any eventuality, positive, negative, or whatever violent shit storm. We'd be relying on instinct and our love for Whitey to convince him that life is worth living and fighting for. Not to give up. Never to succumb to taking the easy way out.

"And why again are you living in New York, when you have a son in Los Angeles?" Betty Ann asked with perfect timing.

"My son hates me."

"No. Your ex-wife hates you and she taught your son to hate you. Don't you know what Casey Stengel said about the key to managing in baseball?"

Betty Ann never ceases to amaze me. She's part drill sergeant, part Mother Teresa, and part Joan Rivers, but much prettier than any of the above.

"No. What did he say?"

"Casey said the hardest part of managing is keeping the guys who hate him away from the ones who are undecided. She might hate you, but you've got to make sure your son doesn't hate you. So with all due respect, what the hell are you doing trying to save Whitey, when your ass is the one that needs saving?"

"Where's *your* son?"

"I know where my son is," she said, placing her hand on her heart. "He's right here. And he's right there," she said pointing to her

281

computer. "We're on Skype every day. He emails me several times a day. And we talk on the phone every day. Sometimes more than once. And every conversation ends with 'I love you.'"

"I'm sorry, I didn't mean..."

"No need to be sorry. I challenged you. You challenged me. But I won that challenge, don't you think?"

"Of course, you're right."

"My son's in California. He's living with some guys in Santa Monica."

"My son's not far from there. They live in Culver City."

"Is your ex re-married?"

"No such luck. I'm still paying through the teeth."

"Money don't mean shit," Betty Ann barked. Her green eyes were like lasers seeing right through me. "You know your son needs you."

I stood up and immediately felt dizzy; I had to hold onto the table for my balance. "I need some air."

"Are you okay?" Betty Ann said, escorting me to the door and taking me out into the driveway. There was a slight chill in the air and it felt good on my skin. I looked up and the stars were bright against the dark moonless sky.

Betty Ann placed the back of her hand against my forehead like a mom would feel for a fever on her child.

"I need to do this for Whitey. And for me."

Betty Ann looked kissed two fingers and placed them tenderly on my lips. "I'm with you."

The plan was set. Betty Ann and I would drive up to Whitey's with some old pictures, and an autograph book from grammar school graduation with those stupid sayings like, *Remember the girl in the city, remember the girl in the town, remember the girl who spoiled your book by writing upside down!* I wish I still had a sewer ball to bring him. An original from *the* manhole at 238th Street and Fort Independence across from our hangout by the stumps, where Whitey held me by the ankles as I dangled down with a bent coat hanger in my hand fishing balls out of the putrid water. I would like to see one of those real, stained and stinky-by-swill sewer balls just one last time.

I doubted we'd have a Frank Capra-type epiphany at our little powwow, but maybe it would be a step in the right direction for Whitey, and for me. All that was left was to contact Hector Gomez and clue him in. Betty Ann and I decided it would be best for him to show up about an hour after we got there. I got the impression Gomez really wanted to repay Whitey for saving his life. I just hoped Whitey felt the same way after we went through with this.

I called Whitey and was crestfallen when he told me he had plans all day Sunday and wasn't available for a visit. I was relieved when he enthusiastically changed his mind after I reluctantly (but strategically) revealed that I had intended to surprise him by bringing Betty Ann. Then he became increasingly nervous as he listed all the cleaning, organizing, shopping and grooming he would need to do before our arrival the next day. I was sure Betty Ann would be a little more comfortable since her visit wasn't a surprise anymore. She said Whitey hated surprises.

My final conversation with Hector Gomez had an air of military precision to it. Hector wanted to make sure my watch was set to atomic clock time, which my twenty dollar Casio was. He also wanted to go over the exact directions, his wardrobe, the layout of the property, house, and room where we would be "reconnoitering," plus where each of us would be standing upon his entrance. That had me a little weirded out, but there was a lot of weirdness in the air lately.

I called Betty Ann, as instructed, on Sunday at 6:15 a.m., and was told to pick her up at 8:30 so we could attend the 9 o'clock mass at Presentation before we headed to Whitey's. I hadn't been to a mass at Presentation since my mother's funeral mass more than five years ago. It was where my parents were married, too. Where my siblings, cousins, friends and I were baptized, had first communions, were confirmed, graduated from grammar school, and attended funeral masses for parents, aunts, uncles, neighbors, and friends.

Even before I was able to speak, I'd sat in those pews on my mother's lap and absorbed the sights, sounds and smells of the church. I saw the huge, multi-colored stained glass windows that illuminated churchgoers and those on the altar in deep blues, greens and reds. I watched the priest and the altar boys swing their shiny objects that released fragrant smoke that wafted over us. I heard the strange language of the priest and the altar boys, which didn't even resemble the sounds my parents or the television made. I discovered several years later that it was an ancient language called Latin, which I would be memorizing as a second grader, part of the last generation of Latin-speaking altar boys. I saw the priest climb some steps and stand behind a tall thing and begin to bark at the parishioners in a tone that resembled the sounds my parents made when they wanted me not to throw my food at the dog or put a screwdriver in my mouth. Those were the first things I had observed outside of the familiar surroundings of my crib, room, and home. And with every month and year that passed, milestones encompassing the joy of holidays and celebrations as well as the abject grief and fear of funerals and commemorative masses, such as the one they rushed us to after President Kennedy was assassinated, and the scores of memorials after 9-11, layer upon layer of memories piled up on top of each other like strata on an exposed rocky hillside, deep inside the gray matter of my brain, made me what I was on this Sunday morning.

Betty Ann looked radiant when she opened the door. The early morning was the only time of the day that a sliver of sun shined briefly in the alley and onto her front door.

"I'm ready," she said, toting a canvas gym bag and her purse. She pulled the door shut and locked the three locks.

We didn't talk on the short drive to the church. As we walked up the church's steps with several other attendants, I remembered this was where we sat when we kissed for the first time, the night of the reunion. Then my brain began to flash on all the things that had

284

happened on those steps, like hugging cousins while the hearse carrying one of my parents or an aunt or uncle idled at the curb. I had bounded euphorically down the very same steps after the final words that released us forever from grammar school, at our eighth grade graduation ceremony. We sat on those steps, sipping orangeade from a wax carton in the rain, waiting for it to stop so the day camp bus could drive us to Rockaway Beach. We walked up the steps, white-gloved hands folded, six years old, praying, *Please, I don't want to slip on the way to First Holy Communion.* Same church. Same steps. Same me.

The church wasn't packed to capacity with standing room only, as it was when I was back in grammar school. Only about a third full, the individuals and families who attended were interspersed throughout. No shoulder-to-shoulder experience of having to share hymnals. The priest looked African, not African-American, and once he began to speak my hunch was confirmed. There weren't two altar boys working in tandem, but only one altar girl.

We sat in a middle pew and stood, sat, and knelt on cue. I tried to remember the responses to the priest, but they were slightly different from when I'd attended regularly. Betty Ann knew them all, so I just followed her lead. I don't know exactly when I stopped attending mass on Sundays, but looking around at the empty pews, I could see that I wasn't alone in that regard.

The African priest's homily was far from the fire and brimstone sermons I remembered. He spoke politely about the meaning of that day's gospel and how important it was to have faith, hope and charity in our everyday lives. No spittle-spewing admonitions directed to kids putting bubble gum under the pews, no warning that anyone who was divorced or Protestant should not dare come forward for communion. And even though the church had been remodeled several times, and the priest had a Kenyan accent instead of one from County Killarney, and my parents and every aunt and uncle I ever had were now on the wrong side of dirt, I still felt those pre-spoken-word impressions deep inside my brain trying to bubble to the surface. The stained glass windows were the same, so were the stations of the cross mounted on the columns, and the life-like crucifix high on the front wall behind the altar. As the prayers and responses were spoken aloud by the handful of worshippers, and we stood, knelt and sat as if by some pre-programmed system installed at baptism, my mind swirled in daydreams, the same way as before I could talk, or when I sat with my seventh grade class and wondered which girls wore bras, or when my father was in a coffin in the aisle and I watched my mother weep. I somehow knew that all that had gone before in my life was somehow connected to this place. This parish. This church. With Betty Ann sitting next to me, singing a closing hymn, with us about to leave for Whitey's, I hoped we were doing the right thing. How could I know for sure if what we were doing was correct? I just had to have faith.

Sometimes I think it's how you feel when nothing is said for long periods of time that matters most in a relationship. Not that Betty Ann and I were in a relationship. I didn't think. Yet. Did I? We were already out of the Bronx and headed north on a highway thick with trees changing to fall colors on both sides of us. It was a stroke of genius when someone designed those parkways with beautiful rows of trees separating motorists from the suburban megalopolis just beyond the foliage. That is, unless you're forced off the road and smash into one.

I listened to Betty Ann breathing and when I had an opportunity, I'd glance at how her chest slightly expanded with each breath. I could tell she was lost in thought as she gazed at the changing landscape along the way. There would be a clearing and rolling hills, lakes and rivers would suddenly appear, and disappear again behind a forest.

"You forget that all this is so close when you live in the city," Betty Ann said as she looked out the side window. "Whenever I'm downtown, and all I see is concrete, steel and glass, I look up at the sky. It reminds me that we're on a planet. Part of nature."

"I find that when I'm in New York, downtown, the sights that overwhelm you are man-made. But in Southern California, the things that overwhelm you with beauty are nature's work. Even when you're in town, there's always the mountains, the coastline," I said, looking over at Betty Ann briefly as we drove the winding highway.

"When I was younger, I wanted all that stimulation. Now I want relaxation. Nature," she said, looking over to me. "It doesn't matter where you are. You just have to seek it out."

But as the landscape changed from manicured suburban roads and parks to raw, rural America, a sense of doom began to overtake me. Hands sweating, a nervous tic in my right eye, I did all I could to hide the fact that the onset of rustic upstate New York was anything but relaxing. I knew that when you exited the smooth highway the roads became bumpy, dangerous and sometimes impassable. And they were meant to be that way.

"If you want to know anything about Whitey, let me know," I said as I glanced at the odometer, mentally computing that we had about forty-five minutes to our exit.

"I don't think so. I don't want to be prejudiced. That's what got everybody in a tizzy in the first place. I mean, the things I've heard! He's a murderer, he's a fugitive, he's a deserter, he's dead, he's dying, he's a vegetable, he's a survivalist, he's a war criminal, he's a war hero, he's a Nazi, he's a hippie, he's insane, he's a rock star, he's a genius, who the hell knows? I want to see and hear for myself."

"Yeah, I'd like to know, too."

I'd heard all the Whitey stories, just like Betty Ann and everybody else in the neighborhood. And there's probably a little bit of everything that she mentioned in Whitey. And if I think back, there's a little bit of all that in almost everybody I grew up with, including myself. Not that being poor had anything to do with it, because back then none of us had any idea that we were poor. Everybody in your apartment building was in the same boat. We had three kids with one bedroom. So what. The Gregonios had *five* kids and one bedroom. As we got into high school and started meeting kids who came from families that really did have money, we found out their families had just as many problems as the families that had it the roughest on our block. Because it didn't matter that you lived in a tiny, roach-infested, air shaft ventilated apartment. If you had two parents who weren't drunks or junkies, and they didn't violently beat you unmercifully, and you could get your homework done, and you got a few Christmas presents, and hugs and kisses from your mom, you were way ahead of the game. Yeah, some kids had it tough. Maybe there was no dad, or a dad who everyone wished would leave. I still feel bad for those kids who had it really bad. Whether it was booze and drugs or violent beatings or psychological and sexual abuse, it didn't matter how much money was deposited into the household Dime Savings Bank account. You were fucked. And it was up to you to make it out of there. Somehow.

Roads can lead anywhere. Take a fork here or there, make a U-ey, right, left – it'll take you somewhere. If you don't know where you're going, any road will take you there. I remember that part of the trip. When you leave the main highway, every mile that you travel away from it takes you farther away from the connection to the megalopolis. When you fly at night, it's easy to see. From thirty thousand feet up, you can observe the downtown of any city, U.S.A., glistening in pink sodium vapor street lights, its arteries and veins spreading out, wider closer to the heart of the city and narrower at the extremities, just like the heart of a human body. But beyond the pink arteries, there's darkness. The bright electric stream of protons and electrons ends in the dark abyss. You may see a tiny speck of light that might be a home many miles removed from the pulse of the city, like a single distant star in deep, dark space. And just like that outlying star millions of light years away, where a world exists so different from our own, more than likely that tiny speck of light in flyover country is home to an alien world as well.

"I guess we're almost there," Betty Ann said, after a bumpy stretch of potholed asphalt.

"Actually, we have about a half hour to go after we turn onto that dirt road over yonder."

"*Yonder*? Now don't go all hillbilly on me. We have to be a team on this journey."

Betty Ann was alert, wide awake and hyper-attentive to the passing signposts. Especially the one that read *Keep Out! Patrolled by Armed Cowboys!*

288

"I shouldn't be worried. You know what you're doing. This is totally safe."

"Are those questions or declarative sentences?"

"Your choice," she said, wanting a declarative sentence for an answer.

"We're fine. We're in Whitey Land."

Betty Ann made the sign of the cross and shook her head.

I glanced at my watch and saw we were right on time, and I also knew that an hour after we arrived, atomic clock time, Hector Gomez would be arriving. I didn't remind Betty Ann of that fact. Yet.

DO NOT ENTER stared us in the face. It was straightened and re-painted since the last time I'd seen it. The bright red letters on the white background made it quite the declarative sentence. There were also little reflective dots around the letters that I'm sure made the sign shine bright once a set of headlights hit it in the dark. The tree above it had been trimmed and none of its branches hung down low enough to obstruct the sign. In fact, as I gazed down the road, it appeared that trees and growth on both sides had been trimmed back. There was even some fresh dirt piled on some of the larger potholes.

Betty Ann formed a gun with her thumb and index finger and shot at the sign.

"Are those bullet holes in the sign?"

"No. Those are reflective dots, the size of bullet holes."

"What about on the bottom of the sign on the right?" she asked, pointing her gun barrel finger at the location.

"Oh, yeah. That does look like a bullet hole. A lot of the signs have bullet holes in the country."

"Uh huh."

"Should I keep going?"

"Uh huh. Can I put my gun away?"

"Yes. I'll let you know when to pull it back out."

We drove the winding road slowly, catching glimpses of the lake through the branches of the trees, which had lost about half their leaves. The ones that remained were gorgeous reds and golds.

289

We made the final turn and descended down the last rocky downhill portion of the road, which placed us about thirty yards from Whitey's compound. There was smoke billowing out the chimneys of the two small homes and the workshop. The position of the sun in the sky illuminated the other side of the lake, but we were already in shadows due to the hill to the west.

"This is beautiful!" Betty Ann whispered as she slowly turned from side to side, like a camera panning for a slow beauty shot.

"Yeah, it does look nice. I think they painted the trim."

"Never mind the trim. Look at this perfectly bucolic setting. It's like an Edward Hopper painting. He was born in Nyack, so it's not farfetched to think that his work would reflect an upstate New York scene like this."

"Were you an art major?"

"I didn't go to college. But I can read, you know."

"I didn't mean it like..."

"Let's go," Betty Ann said, opening the car door.

The crunching gravel under our feet was the only sound we heard as we walked down the long driveway. I could tell that shrubs were cut back, junk had been hauled, and there was new wood on the woodpile. I looked at my atomic watch; we were right on time. Hector would arrive in an hour, so it was time to get this fuse lit.

We were about twenty feet from the front door when we heard a door squeaking open. We stopped. He pushed the outer door and before he was completely out, she was gone.

"Whitey!"

He didn't say a word. Or if he did, I couldn't hear him because Betty Ann was yammering like we were hard of hearing.

"Oh, my God! Is it you? How have you been? You look fantastic! I love this place! Did you build it yourself? How long have you lived here? How the hell do you get out of here in the snow? Can you skate on the lake in the winter? Do you have a boat? God, my mother loved you so much! She always said you were the nicest of all the boys who came traipsing through our living room, and believe me there was a lot of traipsing going on back then!"

290

I stood there watching, as Whitey silently straightened his glasses and Army baseball cap and Betty Ann smooshed him with hugs, tugs and kisses.

"Let's go inside!" Betty Ann said, pushing him towards the front door and waving for me to follow.

The screen door bounced shut behind them and I knew there was no turning back. I could hear Betty Ann peppering Whitey with questions and exhortations as I walked the few feet to the entrance. I grabbed the screen door handle and glanced over to the other cabin where I saw a pair of eyes peeking through two venetian blind slats. Then the slats snapped together as someone released them.

The inside of the cabin smelled like oatmeal cookies, and it was easy to see care had been taken to make the place presentable for a special guest, and there she was, bouncing around the room excitedly chatting with Whitey.

"Come on in, Vinny," Whitey said, filling the coffee maker with water. "You guys sit while I make some coffee."

I sat on the sofa next to Betty Ann and she whispered to me, "He looks good."

I knew she was lying. As neat and put together as the house looked, whatever it was that Whitey was suffering from had gotten worse. Whitey spilled some of the coffee grounds, had trouble getting water in the coffee maker, and he tried desperately to clean up his mess without us noticing.

The blotches on his face had spread, and they were redder and darker. His shirt was buttoned to the very top and seemed too tight on his neck. There were more red blotches just above his collar.

The coffee was finally poured and we sat and chatted, the kind of small talk that goes around and around the truth. Like on a first date when each person tries to figure out with talk about movies, jobs, food, and music whether the other person likes you more or less than you like them. Surprisingly, our chit-chat didn't revolve around things that happened decades ago. Perhaps we each had a fear of going down that memory lane loaded with landmines. I looked at my watch and saw that Hector Gomez was due in T minus thirty minutes.

Betty Ann couldn't contain her pride and joy when she talked about her son Dylan, and Whitey couldn't seem to get enough details about what kind of young man he had become. It sounded like Dylan was everything that I should have been in my youth: studious, disciplined, attentive to his mother's wishes, respectful, and talented.

Whitey's next question stunned me. "How's your son doing, Vinny?"

I felt the blood drain from face as I pondered the failures of my youth colliding with my failures as an adult.

"Good. Well. He's doing well. And good," I sputtered. "To tell you the truth, I don't know. I've had a news blackout with my son for a few weeks. Months. My ex has been carpet-bombing me and my reputation as a father. He's not doing well. He's having trouble at school and at home. Remember when we were kids and every day, whether it was a hundred degrees or a blizzard, there were tons of kids playing outside? Now there aren't any kids out playing. None. Zero. Zilch. They're all holed up in their rooms, alone, isolated, saturating their brains with vile, disgusting, violent video games. You'd think his mother would do something. Get him out of the house. Play basketball or off the stoop or ringolevio... before something horrible happens..."

"Sorry," Whitey sympathized.

Betty Ann took my hand and squeezed it as she looked at Whitey. *Here we go.*

Betty Ann stood up, dropped my hand, and walked slowly across the area rug to Whitey, who seemed dumbfounded. She took the coffee cup from his hand, placed it on the table, and got down on one knee as she grabbed his hand.

"Whitey, you have so much to live for. You have people who love you. Lots of people. People you don't even realize, who love you. Don't try to solve a temporary problem with a permanent solution you can never undo; don't hurt all of us who love you. We know the pain and suffering you're going through, but there are no problems – only solutions..."

"Whoah," Whitey said, standing abruptly. "I get cable, you know. What's with the intervention psycho-babble?"

I threw my hands up in a "Who me?" gesture, hoping that Betty Ann would lead the way.

"I know what's going on, Whitey. We're here to help you," Betty Ann pleaded, now standing and holding both of Whitey's hands.

"Help me what?"

"Live."

"Live? Who's not going to live?"

Betty Ann shot me a look so quickly I heard her neck crack. "Vinny told me that you were considering something awful. Something drastic. Something that could never be undone once it was done. Didn't you, Vinny?"

Whitey and Betty Ann were both staring at me like two parents who'd just caught their kid mooning the school principal.

"You kept saying you were going to cash everything in. You were going to check out. You've had enough and it was time to... end it all. Suicide, right?"

Whitey shook his head and walked to the kitchen sink. He opened the cabinet door under the sink and pulled out a large twenty pound kitty litter container. He lifted the heavy plastic bucket and placed it on the coffee table, which creaked under its weight when he did so. He lifted the top off it, and revealed an enormous stash of casino chips.

"Here's what I'm going to cash in," Whitey declared. "Vinny, you are such a jadrool," Whitey said with a crazy cackle.

"Whitey, I am so mortified," Betty Ann said, wringing her hands.

"I feel like I owe everybody an apology..."

"Ah, don't worry about it. It got us together again, right?" Whitey said reassuringly.

There was a knock on the door. I looked at my watch. Hector Gomez is punctual, if nothing else.

"Who could that be?" Whitey asked.

"I'll get it," Betty Ann said as she walked to the door. She winked at me from the side of her face Whitey couldn't see.

She opened the door slowly, and standing in the doorway was Hector Gomez and two African-American men, one a short stout middle-aged man and the other a sturdy young man, both wearing dark suits. Hector was on the left, the middle-aged black man in the middle, and the young guy on the right. I could hear a crow calling in the distance, but there wasn't a peep from a human being. I looked at Whitey, who stared straight ahead as blood filled the white spaces between the red blotches on his face and his neck. His fists clenched and he leaned forward slightly and hunched his shoulders, like a middle linebacker just before the snap. And then he snapped.

Whitey grabbed the long pole of the floor lamp next to him, let out a guttural cry, and held the four-foot cast iron pole above his shoulder like a baseball bat as he bore down full tilt towards the visitors.

Betty Ann shrieked shriller than a diva soprano in an opera, with her hands over her cheeks like the kid in the *Home Alone* ad. I didn't know whether to shit or go blind.

"Whitey, don't do it! It's Gomez!" I yelled as I grabbed the back of his belt and held on, only slowing his forward movement slightly. The three men managed to duck and push the lamp pole upward so it only hit against the door frame. The three of them manhandled Whitey, with some care, and restrained his flailing kicks, punches, and elbows.

In the middle of the ruckus, just as they were about to push Whitey back into the room, another long object entered the picture, and on the end of it was Zipper.

"That's enough. Let him go," Zipper bellowed, shoving the barrel of his shotgun between the four of them. "You three over there," he said pointing his weapon at Gomez and the two others. "And put your hands up on your heads."

"This is an outrage!" the young black man said.

"Shut up, son, and listen," the middle-aged black man said.

"Father and son, sit your asses down on that sofa. Gomez, you stand right where you are. And keep your hands on your heads," Zipper suggested strongly.

294

Obviously, they know it's Gomez, I thought to myself. And hence, the outpouring of affection for him. Betty Ann looked at me, and if looks could kill, my head would already have exploded.

"Vinny. Let's hear it," Whitey said, rubbing his shoulder.

I looked at Zipper, who had the shotgun pointed just above Gomez's head with his finger on the trigger.

"I thought if you knew how much a difference you made in people's lives, you wouldn't want to commit... suicide. You know, like in *It's a Wonderful Life.* So I got Gomez, who you saved in the war, and I guess he brought another guy you saved."

Whitey walked towards Gomez, stood next to him, and spat on the carpet right next to him. "Tell them, Gomez! Tell them how appreciative you were that I saved your sorry spic ass back in the jungle. Tell them!"

Gomez looked over at me and Betty Ann with a forlorn expression. "I set Whitey up. I was the one who set him up for the robbery and to be killed in Hunts Point. I was a drug addict. A crazed stone-cold South Bronx steal-from-your-mother and do-whatever-it-takes-to-get-drugs junkie. Whitey saved my life. And I turned on him like an animal in the jungle. Because he had money and he came to the South Bronx." Gomez turned to Whitey with a peaceful look on his face. "I've prayed for forgiveness every night since I found God thirty years ago. I hope you can grant it to me."

"And who are you? Wilson from the platoon? You don't look like Wilson," Whitey said, pointing to the older black guy.

"I'm not Wilson. My name's Davis. But you saved my life, too."

"I treated lots of guys back in the war. You were just one of many. I was just doing my job like everybody else."

"You didn't save my life in Viet Nam."

"Okay, I'll bite. Where?"

"Hunts Point."

Click CLICK

Everybody looked to the source of that sound, as Zipper pumped a cartridge into the shotgun and pointed it at the two black men sitting on the sofa.

"No! Listen to him, Whitey. Listen to his story, please, I beg you in the name of Jesus Christ, our Lord and Savior," Gomez begged.

"You might be meeting him sooner than you think," Zipper grunted.

"Red, give me the gun. I'm going to Hell anyway, so I might as well be the one to send the prick there," Whitey said, as he held his hand out for the shotgun.

The older black man stood up and lowered his hands from on top of his head. "You can shoot me if you like, but let me tell the story of how you saved my life." He looked at his son. "Shawn, I'm going to say some things that will shock you. But understand, the man who did those things all those years ago is dead. He's not here anymore." He turned back around to face Whitey and the rest of us.

Whitey now held the shotgun that was aimed at the man's heart.

"I didn't save your life. You and your dead partner in crime stole my life," Whitey said, standing his ground. "I lost my life because of you. I'm going to hell and you are, too."

"Nobody died that night. You only killed the old me. Not the re-born me. I lived. I survived."

Whitey lowered the barrel of the shotgun and his eyes locked with the man speaking, as if his life depended on it.

"That's why I'm here. Yes, I was evil. I was a thug. A street-dwelling animal who preyed on anyone that looked like they had a nickel on them. Especially if they were white. Me and Gomez, we weren't friends. We were like two drugged-out demons working in cahoots for Satan. He knew you were working Hunts Point and he told me how you had cash, lots of cash, and went in the early morning hours. My time of day. I thought it would be easy. He told me you didn't carry a gun, so I knew this was a job for me. But when I went after you with my blade, you got me good with that baseball bat. You must have, because I don't remember nothing until I woke up in that hospital bed. Then I wanted you dead even more. I put the hit out on you. I got more information from Gomez, and my boys were on your ass, excuse me, on your trail. I apologize for that, ma'am." he said, looking at Betty Ann.

"That was Vinny's Mickey Mantle Bat Day bat," Whitey said, with a half-smile to me.

"You got me good. Doctors told me I was lucky to be alive."

"From the sound it made, I can't believe you're here talking to me now. The articles in the papers said you were dead."

I pulled out a couple of the articles from my pocket. "There were five murders, ten shootings, fifteen assaults with a deadly weapon in the South Bronx that night," I reported to all in the room, as if I were in a newsroom briefing.

"As I lay in that hospital bed, I seethed with hatred for you. For what you did to me. I wanted you dead. Then something happened. An old priest poked his head in the room. He came over to me and asked if I wanted anything. I just cursed at him. He sat down and started reading from his New Testament. A good ten minutes in silence. Then he asked if I minded if he turned on the television. He did. And the news came on. And as I stand here before you, there was a miracle. Your picture was on the television screen in your army uniform saying you were a suspect in a murder. My murder. It had my picture, from an old mug shot, but an alias I used, not my real name. And the old priest, he says, 'I know that boy! It can't be him. He's no murderer. He's a good boy. He watched his brother die in front of him in a terrible accident. His daddy was a cripple and died young. He worked hard and then he dropped out of high school so he could support his mama. And when his mama died, he joined the army, and he was a medic and a hero.' And that old Irish priest he looked at me and something happened inside of me. I knew. *I knew.* And he said to me, 'Would you like to make a confession?' I told him I wasn't Catholic. He said he could take care of that. So he baptized me and I confessed every awful thing I could remember. He told me I was forgiven if I did my penance: helping others for the rest of my life. First on my list was getting me and Gomez clean. The priest even gave me the name of a plumber he knew, for when I was clean and sober. Nobody hires ex-cons. And I worked for that tough old Irish plumber. I say tough, because that's what he wanted you to think. He was an angel. My guardian angel. Just like that priest was. Just like you were, sir. And I thank you," the black man said, as he extended his hand in friendship.

Whitey put the gun down, shook his hand and looked around the room. I think I wiped the tear away before anyone noticed.

"When that plumber retired, I bought his business. I raised two sons. My son here, Shawn, he's a doctor. My other son, he runs the business now. We're number one with number two!"

"Whitey, you've got to believe us," Gomez pleaded. "Wherever our paths crossed before doesn't matter, because *now* is all that matters. Now and the hereafter."

Suddenly a huge smile beamed across Whitey's face. "You're alive! I'm not a killer! I'm not going to Hell for killing somebody!"

"And you're not a fugitive either," Betty Ann said, tenderly stroking Whitey's shoulder.

"I'll make some coffee," Zipper announced.

We sat drinking our coffee and tea and didn't mention one thing about what had just gone down in a small cabin by the lake where Whitey spent his summers growing up, far from the streets and alleys of the Bronx. And for most of his adult life, hiding from a killing that never happened in the South Bronx. There was plenty of reminiscing going on. We chatted about the old Yankee Stadium, and going to Rockaway, and the lake in Van Cortlandt Park. I wondered if I should bring up the fact that this whole episode was due to my own stupidity. But I figured that maybe sometimes, even stupidity might lead to something good, if your heart is in the right place.

The coffeepot, which had served as a kind of hour glass, emptied. Gomez and the two Davis men rose and shook hands with each of us. There wasn't much said, just guy hugs and soul handshakes all around and promises to stay in touch. Betty Ann was the only one with tears in her eyes as she saw them to the door. The younger Davis man turned to Whitey.

"Excuse me, Whitey. You know, I've never called anybody Whitey before," he joked, making everyone in the room crack up. "But can I talk to you, privately, for a moment?"

"Sure thing," Whitey said, as they walked into the yard together.

"Well," Betty Ann said, as she closed the door, "we've all had an eventful day. What kind of doctor is your son, Mr. Davis?"

"He's a skin man. Dermatologist."

"I've always been a leg man," Zipper deadpanned.

"Vinny, I want to apologize for not telling you about all this," Gomez said, looking as if he was about to cry. "I take full responsibility."

"I'm glad it worked out the way it did," I said, smiling.

Betty Ann peeked through the window and opened the front door for Whitey and Dr. Davis.

"Looks like I ain't dead yet," Whitey said cheerfully. "Thanks, doc! I'll be there," he said, holding up a business card.

Gomez, Mr. Davis and Dr. Davis gave final waves and Betty Ann closed the door behind them. We took our seats again and glanced at each other, waiting for someone to lead the conversation.

"Whitey, it's all on me," I said, cracking the ice. "I don't know," I said, having second thoughts about being totally honest, but I thought it was now or never. "I felt awful, my whole life, about how we let you down. How we hurt you."

Whitey's neck whipped around and he chuckled. "You let me down and hurt me? What the hell are you talking about?"

"When we were kids. I should have been there for you. I let you down."

"You let me down? We were best friends."

"I let you down, like that time in Rockaway when you got in that fight and me and Flynn weren't there for you."

"That night we might those two girls in Playland, and then hung out with those old broads in the Irish Rover? I don't even remember that fight. I busted my cherry that night! That's all I remember."

299

"That night at the river party, when I called your name and you got busted over the head."

"You were there that night? That was awesome! Didn't you stay until the rumble?"

"Um, no, why?"

"Oh, man, we set back up and played until the sunrise. It was unreal. Probably the best night of playing ever. Some dude from Riverdale who used to manage the Beatles and the Stones showed up with some English guitar player who jammed with us."

"That's right. Allen Klein lived by the river. He once brought John Lennon to the Fieldston Bowling Alley. Who was the guitarist?"

"I don't know. Some skinny little dark haired guy. Played a killer version of
that song... 'For Your Love.'"

"Holy shit! Was it Jeff Beck?"

"I don't know. But that dude was so high, he collapsed on stage. I had to give him CPR."

"You knew CPR?"

"I did some lifeguarding at the lake."

"And when we got the job at day camp, I got five dollars more than you per week and I didn't even tell you, because Father O. told me not to."

Whitey formed a tender smile as his head slowly rocked back and forth as if he was listening to a sweet and slow gospel song. "Father O.? He saved my family. He got the church to pay for my brother's rehab. And he gave my mom hundreds of dollars over the years when she couldn't make ends meet. Maybe thousands. The man was a saint."

Whitey walked across the room, pushed me and Betty Ann apart, and sat between us.

"Vinny, look at you. You've been chasing the past. The past is gone. Whitey and Vinny from eighth grade don't exist anymore. You can't get them back. It's history. Were you looking for me? Or yourself?"

"Hey, Zipper," Betty Ann said loudly, interrupting Whitey. "Show me around the property, would you?"

"Sure thing, sweetheart, said the spider to the fly," Zipper said, taking the hint. They went for a walk, leaving me and Whitey alone on the couch.

"I guess I do have some explaining to do," I said apologetically.

"Go ahead. Ask the questions you've been wanting to ask."

I didn't feel comfortable on the couch, or being honest. I stood up, walked to the kitchen table, and sat there, facing Whitey. "No need."

Whitey chuckled. "We've come this far, no turning back now. In fact, you don't need to ask anything. Yeah, I dropped out of Clinton after my dad died. I didn't tell anybody. We had a private ceremony up here. I worked jobs to support me and my mom. My brother Alfie was dodging the draft on some commune in Canada. It was up to me. And you know what? It was great. I worked, played the drums, got in a few bands and I got to know my mom and her sister like I never would have. She was a hell of a tough lady. Then when she passed I enlisted in the army as a medic. That was the only way I'd do it. It was insane. But I survived. Got a couple of medals, doing what I had to do. Patton once said, 'When the shells are hitting all around you and you wipe the dirt off your face and realize that instead of dirt it's the blood and guts of what was your best friend beside you, you'll know what to do.'"

Whitey got up off the couch and sat on the kitchen chair next to me. "When I saw my brother's guts that day, I knew what to do. I knew nothing in this world would ever be that awful. Because even if in the war, if I ever had my best friend's blood and guts on me, it wouldn't be as bad as seeing that. And the fact that you were there with me at the worst moment of my life when my actual brother died, that made you and me brothers. I met Zipper over there in 'Nam. We helped each other out over the years. When I was messed up, he helped me. When he goes back on the shit, I help him. We're still doing it. I've lost family, but I've always had my brothers."

I reached out to shake hands with Whitey, but he pushed my hand away, got up, pulled me out of my chair, and gave me a tight bear hug.

It was only a few seconds, but the years of wondering where Whitey and I stood with each other melted away. The door squeaked open as Betty Ann and Zipper returned.

Betty Ann walked swiftly to us, and joined in the group hug.

"Look, you two," Betty Ann said. "What's next? What do we do now?"

"Vinny, don't you have a son back in L.A.? You should be on the next flight back there to be near him. He's gonna be past history soon," Whitey said bluntly. "And Betty Ann, don't you have a son out there, too? Why don't the two of you just go out there together? See what happens."

Betty Ann held us by the arms. "Why don't the three of us go out there and see what happens? Like in *On the Road*? The book started at 242nd Street and Broadway, right in the old neighborhood. The end of the number one line."

"I'll hold down the fort, here," Zipper announced.

"We'll take my truck," Whitey said. "I just need to do a few things, like get a driver's license, get a warrant for my arrest expunged, visit the doc who says all I got is some staph infection hanging around, and I'll be good to go. Might take a little while, though. It's a plan. Let's give it a go."

The good-byes weren't teary-eyed like they could have been. In a matter of days or weeks, we'd be getting back together and beginning a new chapter in our lives. On the drive back to the city, Betty Ann and I started mapping out our trip; we sounded like newlyweds planning our honeymoon, which was weird because we weren't even really an item yet. We pulled into her driveway and I took off the miraculous medal I always wear around my neck.

"First things first," I said, putting it over her head and around her neck.

"What does this mean?"

"It means we're going steady."

302

"I thought the boy was supposed to *ask* the girl?"

Suddenly I felt the blood rush from my heart, through my neck and into my brain. I felt much the same way when I was about to ask Carrie Vitelli the exact same question next to the dumbwaiter by the trash pile in my building's cellar. I took a deep breath. "Will you go steady with me?"

"Yes," Betty Ann whispered as she placed a tender kiss on my lips.

We kissed goodnight and it wasn't until I was on the Deegan headed towards Bronxville did I realize I that I hadn't even given a thought to stopping at a bar on 238th for a nightcap.

Only three days had gone by and we already had a change in plans. Whitey would need several weeks, at least, to get his life in order. So Betty Ann and I decided to head west in a week or so, and Whitey would fly out later. But Whitey wanted us to do a reunion tour of the old neighborhood, together for one last time.

"How's it going?" I asked Whitey, pulling him into the side door at my sister's house. "You're looking good. My sister would have loved to see you, but she's upstate visiting her daughter."

"That's too bad. She was one of the nice ones. By the way, I saw the doc and he thinks I can totally beat the staph infection. He gave me some meds and so far so good. I go back next week for a follow-up. Tests and stuff. Sherman, set the Wayback Machine to 238th Street, 1964! Let's go! Zipper's still driving for me, but as soon as I get some red tape cleared up, I get my own license again. I'll be a free man!"

We stopped to get Betty Ann. She sat in the back seat of the extended cab with me. Whitey headed down Corlear and took a right by the Riverdale Diner, went under the el, and headed up 238th Street slowly. Past the deli, S & S Cheesecake, and the bars that had fueled alcohol through the area's inhabitants for more than a hundred years: the Punch Bowl, the Forge, the Goal Post, J.C. Mac's, Grecco's, Jimmy Joe's, and The Place. We passed Whitey's building. I looked at him through the corner of my eye, wondering if he'd say something about his brother dying right there. He silently made the sign of the cross, reached in his shirt, pulled out a small gold crucifix and kissed it. We went by my building, where we'd hung out on the stumps at the top of the adjacent alley.

"Zipper, pull over. Here it is," Whitey sighed. "Where it all started. Hey! What's going on over there?"

We looked across the street and there was some kind of construction project going on around the exact manhole cover that Whitey used to lower me into so we could retrieve sewer balls. We got out of the truck, crossed the street, and there was a city truck with two workers.

"Hey, guys," Whitey said with a smile in his voice. "What are you doing?"

A young Puerto Rican worker in a welder's helmet looked at us, surprised. "Oh, we're closing up this sewer. City says it's a hazard. Too much stuff going in, so we put a mesh over the opening at the curb. Then we're sealing up the manhole. It's too accessible. A hazard." His partner lifted the old manhole cover with a crowbar. The very same manhole cover Whitey used to lift with two fingers, then put it to the side, and hold me by the ankles while I fished with a bent coat hanger, looking for sewer balls.

"Are you kidding me?" Whitey asked, stepping close to the hole. "That manhole supplied us with a lifetime's worth of spaldeens!"

"How?" the young worker asked.

"That's where we got our sewer balls."

"What's a sewer ball?"

"You never heard of a sewer ball? That's what we played with. Balls we got out of the sewer."

"How'd you get them?"

"I hung him," Whitey said pointing to me, "down there by the ankles and he fished them out with a bent coat hanger."

"You guys are wack," the young worker said, as his partner placed a new manhole cover down.

"Wait! Not yet!" Whitey said frantically. "Hold on!" Whitey ran across the street to the truck, grabbed something, and hustled back carrying it in his hand.

"What do you got?" I asked.

Whitey smiled as he showed us his cupped hands, then slowly pulled them apart, revealing... an actual, fetid, water-stained, brown, black, and pink, marbleized sewer ball!

"I've been holding on to this. I even had it in 'Nam. My good luck charm. Hold open that manhole cover for a second." Whitey held the ball out to me and Betty Ann as if it were a sanctified host. We each held it briefly in our palm and gave it back to Whitey. "Is it okay if I throw it in there before you seal it up? It would mean a lot to us."

"Well, I guess it's alright," the young man said reluctantly. "If you guys got it out of there in the first place, you're just putting it back where you got it from."

We stood next to the hole, and Whitey dropped it in. We heard it splash in the water below. The other worked dropped the new and improved, kid-proof manhole cover in place and the worker started to weld it permanently closed.

"You know what that was?" I said, as we stared down while the worker sealed it closed forever. "That was the last sewer ball." We stood silently over the manhole as if a coffin just had the first shovelful of dirt thrown on it.

Whitey looked at me, forlornly. "What do you want to do now?"

"I don't know. Want to go to all our old hangouts? The alley where we played call ball? The sticker lots where we built the forts? Up in the park swamps where we hid the rowboat. The schoolyard at Presentation?"

"You know what? I thought I did. But I don't. I think I'd rather just remember them the way they were. In my head," Whitey said softly.

Betty Ann took my hand and one of Whitey's, too, and walked us back to the truck.

"I think Vinny and I will walk back to my place from here," she said to Whitey as she placed a sweet kiss on his cheek. "We'll give you updates once we head out."

"Okay, sure," Whitey said softly. He dabbed a tear from under his glasses as he got into the truck.

We waved as Whitey and Zipper drove away. Whitey stuck his head out the window and saluted, just like he did that day on the freight train.

Betty Ann and I were in Boulder, Colorado, when we got the word that Whitey was dead. He didn't have a staph infection, he'd had terminal skin cancer. I'll bet he knew it the whole time. Dr. Davis damn well would have known the difference between an infection and skin cancer. He didn't want to worry us. It was everywhere, Zipper told us. Betty Ann's son Dylan flew from California to drive Betty Ann's car with all our stuff to L.A. while we flew back for the funeral. Zipper said it would be a private affair. No wake, just a private service back where it all started – Presentation Church.

There it was: a flag-draped coffin in the aisle, in front of the altar. The same altar where Whitey and I were altar boys. The same pews where we mourned for JFK, parents, friends, and family. It was just me, Betty Ann and Zipper sitting right next to the coffin.

I held Betty Ann's hand. I had to hold onto something. Someone. A bright ray of sunlight streaked across the large crucifix hanging on the wall. Two men in Army dress uniforms walked down the aisle, one holding a bugle, the other a folded flag. Right behind them was a slender, fit looking middle-aged man with hair that was either sandy blond or white, in a black suit. Then came a crooked old bald man with a cane, dressed all in black. *A priest. Holy jumpin' shit. Could it be? Is it? Father O?*

The white-haired guy walked over to the priest and they slumped into each other's arms just behind the coffin.

"Father O? Is that you?" I whispered.

"In the flesh. Yes, it is. You're Vinny Schmidt, right? Do you know Alfie Shelley?"

306

"Alfie? Oh, my God. I haven't seen you since I was in grammar school. I thought you were... dea.. I mean, in Canada?"

"I was. I live in Salt Lake City. So good to see you, Vinny," he said, squeezing my hand with both of his. "Whitey told me everything. Thanks. I was able to see him before he passed." Alfie pulled me close to him, reached into his jacket and pulled out an envelope. "Whitey said this is for you."

"I'd like to say a few words," Father O. said. His voice was so familiar to me, it didn't seem like a lifetime had passed since the last time I'd heard it.

Father O. pulled from his inside pocket a small black book that looked like it might have been printed by Gutenberg, and began reading. "In those days, I heard a voice from heaven saying, blessed are the dead who die in the Lord henceforth. Yes, says the Spirit, let them rest from their labors, for their works follow them. Eternal rest grant unto him O Lord and let perpetual light shine upon him. May his soul and the souls of all the faithful departed, through the mercy of God, rest in peace. Amen."

"Amen," we all repeated.

Betty Ann and I were trembling as Zipper stood tall, in full salute. The two soldiers approached the coffin. The soldier snapped the bugle to his lips and began to play taps. The sound echoed through the empty church. I'll never hear taps again and think of anything other than that moment. When concluded, the second soldier marched reverently to Alfie and formally presented him with the folded flag.

God, country, family and friends 'til the end. I should have known that those years in between were just periods of transition for Whitey and me.

We drove to Gate of Heaven Cemetery. Whitey took the same path as most people from Presentation. There were a few more words said at the gravesite. Afterwards,
Alfie had a plane to catch. Father O. was rushing off to say Mass at a prison. Zipper needed to get back to feed the dogs. Betty Ann and I sat in the car and looked up at the coffin sitting by the open grave, waiting to become part of the earth.

307

"Alfie gave me this," I said, holding up the envelope. "Should I open it now?"

"Sure," she said, choking back tears.

I opened it, and found a note and another envelope.

"Dear Vinny and Betty Ann," the note said. "I know you are together somewhere. Go to the Livingston Manor U-Store It on Route 17 and open the *other* envelope there. No cheating."

"Well, let's go," Betty Ann, said starting the engine.

Once we got to Livingston Manor, the U-Store It didn't take long to find, being the only such facility in town. We pulled into a spot and Betty Ann killed the engine.

"Here we are. I just hope we don't find one of those fifty-gallon drums filled with body parts, and directions on where to dump it," Betty Ann said matter-of-factly.

I opened the second envelope and withdrew a key and a second letter from it.

"I haven't been this nervous reading something since the final numbers came in on my divorce papers. Okay, here it goes."

I unfolded the letter, and a key fell onto my lap. I pictured Whitey in the back seat. Not dead Whitey, or Whitey of the last few months, but the Whitey who was as much a part of me as my hand or my liver or my foot, or my dear departed parents. I bit my lip and read the letter.

The key is to storage locker 1503. The two of you keep what you want and throw the rest away. It's stuff from this world. The material world. I want to thank you both for saving my life. That sounds funny, since I'm dead if you're reading this, but it's true. You see, I was dead. And now I'm not. I knew I didn't have a staph infection. I was a medic, after all. I figured all along it was the big C. The doc was nice about it. Yeah, I was going to cash it all in. Kill myself. Those casino chips were worthless crap and just something I thought of at the last minute when you confronted me. It worked, too. But you see, I thought I was going to hell for that murder anyway. I had blood on my hands from killing that guy in Hunts Point, so killing

308

myself didn't matter. I was even going to kill Gomez that day, I was so
red with mad rage. But because you guys did what you did, and the
truth was revealed, I was saved. I didn't kill anybody in Hunts Point
that night. Thank God I didn't kill myself. Because now, I know I've got
a shot at everlasting life with the Lord. And thank you both for doing
what you did. I'm eternally thankful. Oh, I know I might be spending
some time in purgatory for some of the laughs we had, Vinny. But all in
all, it was worth it.

> *With love to you both, your old pal,*
> *Whitey*

P.S. Handle the records carefully, exclamation point.

I couldn't have read any more even if there had been
something else. I carefully folded the letter and with shaking hands I
placed it back in the envelope, exhausted.

Betty Ann, wiping at her tears, said, "Handle the records?
What kind of records?"

I held up the key. "I've got a feeling."

I unlocked the padlock to the storage unit and opened the door.
It was dark, so I flicked on a pocket flashlight. Its light revealed at least
fifty plastic bins, each one with a white piece of paper taped on the side
with the contents listed: *Beatles 45s, Beatles albums, Beatles stuff,
Other Rock N Roll stuff, Yankees baseball cards, Yankees stuff,
Presentation Stuff, Army stuff,* and on and on and on.

"I thought Whitey didn't want anything to do with the past,"
Betty Ann said as she gazed in awe at the boxes.

"This isn't the past," I said, putting my arm around Betty Ann.
"It's just stuff. I guess we're renting a van for the drive west."

Betty Ann put her head on my shoulder and breathed deeply.
"We'll put all this in a special place. Dylan would love going through
these boxes."

"Yeah, my son Johnny would, too."

"Why don't you call him now?"

"Whenever I call his cell, he sees my number and doesn't pick
up."

Betty Ann reached into her purse and extended her arm straight out, holding her cell phone inches from my face. I wasn't sure I wanted Johnny to answer. The last time I tried calling him, I was drunk and he knew it. Which is probably why he hasn't answered since. I dialed his number.

"Hello, Johnny. It's me... Dad..."

A soft smile appeared on Betty Ann's face.

"How are you?... It's a friend's phone... Yes, I know... A week or so... I would love that... I will... No. I won't be drinking anymore. I haven't in a while... Johnny, I... love you... Bye."

"So what did he say?"

I was overwhelmed. I felt a deep all-encompassing aching sadness. Sad for the time I had wasted. The years. Sad for my stupidity. My selfishness.

"He asked me if I was coming home. And if I was still drinking. And if I'd go with him to a father-son basketball game at school." I couldn't believe what I was telling Betty Ann. My sadness was melting away and somehow a glimmer of relief began to flow through my soul.

Betty Ann stroked my cheek with the back of her hand. "Sometimes, it's that easy. Let's go. We've got a lot of packing to do."

I closed the door to the locker and locked it. We'd be back soon to load the stuff up. I had a feeling I was finally ready to get back home.